The Theatre of Suzuki Tadashi

Suzuki is Japan's best-known director. He has been internationally acclaimed for his postmodern adaptations of classics by Nanboku, Euripides, Shakespeare, and Chekhov since the 1970s, and, equally, for his powerful actor-training system, which combines elements of Noh and Kabuki with Western realism. Inviting artists from around the world to perform at his Toga and Shizuoka International Festivals, Suzuki has fostered productive exchanges with Jean-Louis Barrault, Robert Wilson, Kanze Hisao, Ashikawa Yôko, and numerous others. This book, the first comprehensive study of any Asian theatre director in this series, traces Suzuki's rise from Little Theatre director to international festival celebrity, links his unique Surrealist dramaturgy with his intercultural training system, and gives indepth descriptions of his most acclaimed productions.

IAN CARRUTHERS has taught in the Theatre and Drama Department of La Trobe University since 1985. He is co-editor (with Minami Ryuta and John Gillies) of *Performing Shakespeare in Japan* (Cambridge: Cambridge University Press, 2001) and has contributed chapters to *Shakespeare's Books: Contemporary Cultural Politics and the Persistence of Empire* (eds. Philip Mead and Marion Campbell, Melbourne: University of Melbourne Press, 1993), *Shakespeare: World Views* (eds. Heather Kerr, Robin Eaden, and Madge Mitton, Newark: University of Delaware Press, 1996) and *Fifty Key Directors of the Twentieth Century* (eds. Shomit Mitter and Maria Schevtsova, London: Routledge, forthcoming in 2004).

TAKAHASHI YASUNARI, sadly, died in 2002. He was Professor Emeritus of English Literature at the University of Tokyo and Professor of English at Showa Women's University, Tokyo. His extensive writings reflect his wide range of interests, with special focus on Shakespeare, Lewis Carroll, Samuel Beckett, and Japanese Noh drama. Takahashi also wrote dramatic works which have been staged in Tokyo, London, and elsewhere to great acclaim. He was awarded a CBE in 1993.

What characterises modern theatre above all is continual stylistic innovation, in which theory and presentation have combined to create a wealth of new forms – naturalism, expressionism, epic theatre, and so forth – in a way that has made directors the leading figures rather than dramatists. To a greater extent than is perhaps generally realised, it has been directors who have provided dramatic models for playwrights, though of course there are many different variations in this relationship. In some cases a dramatist's themes challenge a director to create new performance conditions (Stanislavski and Chekhov), or a dramatist turns director to formulate an appropriate style for his work (Brecht); alternatively a director writes plays to correspond with his theory (Artaud), or creates communal scripts out of exploratory work with actors (Chaikin, Grotowski). Some directors are identified with a single theory (Craig), others gave definitive shape to a range of styles (Reinhardt); the work of some has an ideological basis (Stein), while others work more pragmatically (Bergman).

Generally speaking, those directors who have contributed to what is distinctly 'modern' in today's theatre stand in much the same relationship to the dramatic texts they work with, as composers do to librettists in opera. However, since theatrical performance is the most ephemeral of the arts and the only easily reproducible element is the text, critical attention has tended to focus on the playwright. This series is designed to redress the balance by providing an overview of selected directors' stage work: those who helped to formulate modern theories of drama. Their key productions have been reconstructed from promptbooks, revues, scene-designs, photographs, diaries, correspondence and – where these productions are contemporary – documented by first-hand description, interviews with the director, and so forth. Apart from its intrinsic interest, this record allows a critical perspective, testing ideas against practical problems and achievements. In each case, too, the director's work is set in context by indicating the source of his ideas and their influence, the organisation of his acting company, and his relationship to the theatrical or political establishment, so as to bring out wider issues: the way theatre both reflects and influences assumptions about the nature of man and his social role.

Christopher Innes

Figure 1 Suzuki Tadashi.

The Theatre of
Suzuki Tadashi

IAN CARRUTHERS
AND
TAKAHASHI YASUNARI

PUBLISHED BY THE PRESS SYNDICATE OF THE UNIVERSITY OF CAMBRIDGE
The Pitt Building, Trumpington Street, Cambridge, United Kingdom

CAMBRIDGE UNIVERSITY PRESS
The Edinburgh Building, Cambridge, CB2 2RU, UK
40 West 20th Street, New York, NY 10011–4211, USA
477 Williamstown Road, Port Melbourne, VIC 3207, Australia
Ruiz de Alarcón 13, 28014 Madrid, Spain
Dock House, The Waterfront, Cape Town 8001, South Africa

http://www.cambridge.org

© Ian Carruthers, Takahashi Yasunari 2004

First published 2004

Printed in the United Kingdom at the University Press, Cambridge

Typeface Palatino 10/12.5 pt.   *System* LATEX 2$_\varepsilon$ [TB]

Library of Congress Cataloging-in-Publication data
Carruthers, Ian.
The Theatre of Suzuki Tadashi / Ian Carruthers and Takahashi Yasunari.
   p. cm.   (Directors in perspective)
ISBN 0 521 59024 8
1. Suzuki, Tadashi, 1939– 2. Theatre – Production and direction – Japan.
I. Yasunari, Takahashi, 1932–2002. II. Title. III. Series.
PN2928.S87C37   2004
792.02'33'092 – dc22   2003055394

ISBN 0 521 59024 8 hardback

PN 2928
.S87 C37
2004

for Kazuko and Michi
and
in memoriam
Takahashi Yasunari
(9.2.1932–24.6.2002)

Contents

Illustrations

All photographic illustrations come from the Suzuki Company archives and attributions have been made on the best advice currently available from the Japan Performing Arts Foundation.

Acknowledgments

I would first like to pay special tribute to Takahashi Yasunari, who passed away before this book could be published. Although his long and valiant battle with cancer left him too ill to contribute substantially to the writing of it, he was nevertheless able to offer illuminating advice and direction, and very generously and patiently read, critiqued, and corrected my draft chapters as they appeared. His spirit has palpably enriched both Suzuki's work and my own. It is some small consolation that he had read the final draft and knew the end of our labor was in sight.

I would also like to thank the many other people who have helped contribute toward this book: Suzuki Tadashi for graciously granting interviews, the opportunity to take part in SCOT training, and access to his company archives in Toga, Tokyo, and Shizuoka; Saitoh Ikuko for scrupulously checking the accuracy of my Suzuki Chronology, the List of Illustrations, and all the subsequent chapters; Katoh Masaharu, Suzuki Osamu, and Iwakata Kenichirô for their patient help in locating materials and checking queries in the JPAF archives; and indeed all the members of SCOT, ACM, and SPAC, past and present, for their unfailing kindness and mesmerizing creative energies; Kawamizu Mihoko, our research assistant, for painstakingly amassing almost everything written by or about Suzuki from 1965 to 1994 in Japanese; Kazuko Eguchi, Noyuri Liddicutt, Masako Yoshida, Aya Power, Kayoko Hashimoto, Tony McGillycuddy, and Kameron Steele for their help with translation of large sections of this written record; Richard Moore, Tony Chapman, and Marianne McDonald for sharing videos of SCOT performances not available in the NHK series *Suzuki Tadashi no sekai* (The World of Suzuki Tadashi); Togawa Minoru, Katoh Masaharu (again), and Deborah Leiser-Moore for Suzuki training instruction; Suzuki Kenji, Ellen Lauren, Leon Ingulsrud, and the cast of *The Chronicle of Macbeth* for performance interviews; Carrillo Gantner for allowing me to observe the whole process of *The Chronicle of Macbeth*; Norman Price for helping to organize the 1992 Melbourne Performance Research Group Conference on Suzuki Tadashi at Melbourne University; my honors and postgraduate students for their lively and critical responses to this research: Greg Dyson, Katherine Lander, Patricia Mitchell, Kathleen Doyle, Marjorie Dean, Zhao-hui

Wang, Mary-Rose Casey, Sarah Riley, Sahar Abdul-Fattah, Laura Sheedy, and Nicola Wilks; La Trobe University for an ARC Small Grant to cover research assistance; the Japan Foundation for a Fellowship in 1993 which enabled me to travel with Suzuki's company for six months; Sir Q. C. Lee of the Hang Seng Bank for a generous grant to bring James Brandon and Minami Ryuta to the 1996 Asian Studies Association of Australasia Conference at La Trobe University; and Christopher Innes and Victoria Cooper of Cambridge University Press for their patience, expert advice, and editorial assistance. Last, but not least, heartfelt thanks to all those who have helped prepare me for this project: Michael and Maureen Carruthers, who first introduced me to Japanese culture at the age of seven; Alan Heuser and Donald Theall of the English Department at McGill University in Canada, who encouraged me to take a year abroad at ICU in Tokyo; my graduate school teachers at the Harvard-Yenching Institute, Edwin Cranston, Nagatomi Masatoshi, John Rosenfield and Benjamin Rowlands in Boston; and, in Japan, my teachers of Noh (Hirota Norikazu, Udaka Michishige, and Rebecca Teele) and Kabuki (Nakamura Matagoro, Sawamura Tanosuke, and Nakamura Matazô); finally, my partner Kazuko for her endless patience and support over many years.

Chapters Seven and Eight are significantly reworked and expanded versions of my articles on "Suzuki Tadashi's 'The Chekhov': *Three Sisters, The Cherry Orchard* and *Uncle Vania*," in *Modern Drama*, XLIII: 2 Summer 2000, 288–99; and *"The Chronicle of Macbeth:* Suzuki Method Acting in Australia, 1992," in *Performing Shakespeare in Japan*, eds. Minami Ryuta, Ian Carruthers, and John Gillies (Cambridge: Cambridge University Press, 2001), 121–32.

Takahashi Yasunari's Introduction and Chapter Nine are reprinted, with the kind permission of the publishers, from "Suzuki's work in the context of Japanese Theatre", *SCOT: Suzuki Company of Toga*, trans. Takahashi Yasunari, Matsuoka Kazuko, Frank Hoff, Leon Ingulsrud, and Jordan Sand (Tokyo, 1991); and "Tragedy with Laughter: Suzuki Tadashi's *The Tale of Lear*," in *Performing Shakespeare in Japan*, eds. Minami Ryuta, Ian Carruthers, and John Gillies (Cambridge: Cambridge University Press, 2001), 112–20.

NOTE

Japanese names in this book follow conventional Japanese usage; the surname first, followed by the given name, except when citing a source which uses the English convention or when referring to Japanese persons resident outside Japan.

A macron (ˆ) over a Japanese vowel indicates that the vowel is long. The macron is not used in the case of familiar words such as "Tokyo", or when an h is used instead, as in "Noh".

Abbreviations

SCOT: Suzuki Company of Toga, situated in Toga village, Toyama
       Prefecture

JPAC: Japan Performing Arts Center, Tokyo, run by Suzuki's
       company; now the Japan Performing Arts Foundation (JPAF)

ACM: Acting Company Mito in Mito City, Ibaraki, where Suzuki was
       artistic director from 1992 to 1996

SPAC: Shizuoka Performing Arts Center in Shizuoka City, Shizuoka
       Prefecture, where Suzuki became the artistic director after
       leaving ACM

NHK: Nihon Hôso Kyôkai, Japan Broadcasting Corporation

WFS: Waseda Free Stage (Waseda Jiyû Butai)

WLT: Waseda Little Theatre (Waseda Shôgekijô)

Chronology

1967   Directs Dazai Osamu's *Usagi to tanuki* (*Rabbit and Raccoon*) (Feb.).
Directs Dazai Osamu's *Shitakiri suzume* (*Tongueless Sparrow*) and Satoh Makoto's *Watashi no Biitoruzu* (*My Beatles*) (April).
Directs Betsuyaku's *Makushimirian hakase no bishô* (*The Smile of Dr. Maximillian*) (June).
Revives *The Little Match Girl* (Nov.).

1968   Revives *The Elephant* at Kinokuniya Hall (Jan.).
Betsuyaku wins Kishida Prize for Playwriting (Feb.).
Directs *Shite, shite, dôja – Kabuki jûhachiban* (*And Then, And Then, What Then? A Kabuki Classic*), based on the Kabuki play *Narukami* (April–June).
Directs *Donzoko ni okeru minzoku-gaku-teki bunseki* (*Folkloric Analysis of The Lower Depths*) (Nov.).
Revives *The Little Match Girl* (Dec.).
Directs Satoh Makoto's *Chikatetsu* (*Subway*) for NHK TV.

1969   Directs *Gekiteki naru mono o megutte I* (*On the Dramatic Passions I*) (April–June).
Directs *Waiting for Godot* for NHK TV (June).
Betsuyaku leaves company (Aug.).
Directs Kara Jûrô's *Shôjo kamen* (*The Virgin's Mask*) and revives *On the Dramatic Passions I* (Oct.–Nov.).

1970   Interviews Trevor Nunn of RSC with Takahashi Yasunari (Jan.).
Directs *Gekiteki naru mono o megutte II* (*On the Dramatic Passions II*) (May–June).
Directs *Natsu shibai howaito komedii* (*Summer Drama: White Comedy*) with Noh actor Kanze Hideo and Shingeki actors, including Yoshiyuki Kazuko (Aug.).
Directs *On the Dramatic Passions II and III* (Nov.–Dec.).

1971   Revives *On the Dramatic Passions I and II* at Osaka Mainichi Hall, Kyoto Miyagawa-cho Kaburenjô, and *The Little Match Girl* at Osaka Mainichi Hall (May).
Directs *Somekaete gonichi no omemie* (*Re-dyed Later Appearances*) (Nov.–Dec.).

1972   Suzuki and Shiraishi participate in Théâtre des Nations Festival workshop in Paris (April). Shiraishi wins international fame.
Writes NHK radio drama *Oni nite sôrô* (*A Demon There Was*) (July).
Directs *Don Hamlet* (Sept.–Oct.).

Develops *Shintai kunren* (*Physical Training*).

1973   Publishes *Naikaku no wa* (*The Sum of the Interior Angles*), Jiritsushobô (March).

Revives *On the Dramatic Passions II* (Feb–April) and tours it to the Nancy International Theatre Festival, France (April–May); Récamier Theatre, Paris (May); and Mickery Theatre, Amsterdam (May–June).

Grotowski visits Japan, attends Waseda Little Theatre (WLT) rehearsals, and is interviewed by Suzuki for the theatre magazine *Shingeki* (*New Drama*) (Aug.).

1974   Suzuki appointed artistic director of Iwanami Hall, first directing *Toroia no onna* (*The Trojan Women*) (Dec.–Jan.). With Shiraishi (Hecuba), Noh actor Kanze Hisao (Old Man, Menelaus), and Shingeki actress Ichihara Etsuko (Cassandra, Andromache).

1975   Tours *On the Dramatic Passions II* to Warsaw (Théâtre des Nations) and Wroclaw (June).

Directs *Yoru to tokei* (*Night and the Clock*) (Oct.–Dec.). This collage *Macbeth* wins Kinokuniya Prize for "Japanization" of Shakespeare (Dec.).

1976   Visits abandoned farmhouse in Toga village (pop. 1,300) in the Japan Alps (Feb.) and leases it. Begins intensive training.

Lease of Waseda Shôgekijô (Waseda Little Theatre) Studio in Tokyo expires (March).

James Brandon reports on Suzuki's theatre training for *The Drama Review*.

Opens his farmhouse-theatre, the Toga Sanbô (Mountain Hall), with *Utage no yoru I* (*Night and Feast I*) and performances by Kanze Hisao and Toga villagers (Aug.).

1977   Directs Takahashi Yasunari's *Kagami to kanran* (*The Looking Glass and Cabbages*) in Tokyo (March–April).

Invited by Jean-Louis Barrault to tour *The Trojan Women* to Paris (Théâtre des Nations), Rome (La Ressegna Internazionale di Teatro Popolare), Lisbon, Berlin, and Bonn (Bonn International Theatre Festival) (May–June).

Directs *Utage no yoru II* (*Night and Feast II / Salome*) in Toga (Aug.).

Publishes *Gekiteki gengo* (*On Dramatic Language*) with Nakamura Yûjirô, Hakusuisha (Feb.).

Publishes *Gekiteki naru mono o megutte: Suzuki Tadashi to sono sekai* (*On the Dramatic Passions: the World of Suzuki Tadashi*), Kôsakusha (April).

1978   Directs *Bakkosu no shinnyo* (*The Bacchae*) at Iwanami Hall (Jan.–Feb.). With Shiraishi (Pentheus, Agave) and Kanze Hisao (Dionysus). When the latter dies, the performance is terminated.
Directs *Utage no yoru III* (*Night and Feast III/Macbeth*) in Toga (Aug.). With Tsutamori Kôsuke (Macbeth 1) and Kanze Hideo (Macbeth 2).
Restages *Salome* in Tokyo (Oct.–Nov.) and Nagoya (Dec.).
Directs *Shi no kage* (*Shadow of Death*) at Festival d'Automne, Paris (Nov.–Dec.).

1979   Tours *The Trojan Women* from Nagoya to Hokkaido (April), Milwaukee, New York (May), and Nagano, Kanazawa, and Toyama (June).
Directs *Utage no yoru IV* (*Night and Feast IV*) in Toga (Aug.).
Directs *Katei no igaku* (*Home Medicine*), an adaptation of Roland Topor's *Joko's Anniversary*, in Tokyo (Nov.–Dec.).

1980   Teaches Suzuki Training at the University of Wisconsin, Milwaukee (Jan.–March).
Tours *The Trojan Women* to Ôtsu (May).
Builds new Toga Sanbô (Mountain Hall) and entrance lobby, designed by Isozaki Arata (Aug.).
Revives *Dramatic Passions II* and *The Trojan Women* in Toga (Aug.).
Opens new theatre-studio in Ikebukuro, Tokyo (Nov.).
Publishes *Engekiron: katari no chihei* (*Collected Theatre Writings: Horizons of Deception*), Hakusuisha (May).

1981   Teaches Suzuki Training at The Juilliard School in New York (Jan.), the University of Wisconsin at Milwaukee (Feb.).
Revises *The Bacchae* as a bilingual production involving actors from the University of Wisconsin in Milwaukee (Feb.–April), Toga (Aug.), and at Sogetsu Hall, Tokyo (Sept.). With Tom Hewitt (Pentheus) and Shiraishi (Dionysus, Agave).
Directs *Sweeney Todd* for Tôhô at Imperial Theatre (July–Aug.). With Matsumoto Kôshirô and Ôtori Ran.
Directs *The Trojan Women* in Fukumitsu (May), Yokohama, and Yao Seibu Hall (Nov.).

1982   Teaches Suzuki Training at The Juilliard School, the University
        of Wisconsin at Milwaukee, and the University of California at
        San Diego (March).
        Builds Greek-style amphitheatre in Toga, designed by Isozaki
        Arata.
        Forms Japan Performing Arts Center (April).
        Tours bilingual *The Bacchae* to New York and *The Trojan Women*
        to St. Louis, Chicago, and New York (May–June).
        Holds symposium on "Culture and Theatre" with Victor
        Turner, Gunji Masakatsu, Takahashi Yasunari, and others in
        Toga (Aug.).
        Holds First International Toga Theatre Festival (July–Aug.).
        With Robert Wilson, Terayama Shûji, Tadeusz Kantor,
        Meredith Monk, John Fox, and others. Suzuki redirects *The
        Trojan Women* in Toga.
        Revives *The Trojan Women* in Gifu (Nov.), Nagoya, and Tokyo
        (Dec.).
        Publishes *Suzuki Tadashi no sekai* (*The World of Suzuki Tadashi*),
        ed., Saitoh Setsurô (Tokyo: Shinpyôsha) (May).
        Publishes *Bunka no genzai: engeki o tôshite* (*Modern Culture
        Through Theatre*), Toyama-ken shokuin kenshûjo.
        Directs *Chûsankai* (*The Formal Lunch*) at theatre studio in
        Ikebukuro (Dec.–Feb.).
        Gives public lecture on "Theatre and Modern Culture" at Meiji
        University (published 1983).
1983   Directs *Ôhi Kuraitemunestora* (*Queen Clytemnestra*) at Second
        International Toga Theatre Festival (Aug.).
        Robert Wilson rehearses Tokyo section of *the CIVIL warS* with
        SCOT, Kanze Hideo, and the Butoh company Byakkosha (April).
        Launches JPAC annual Toga International Actor Training
        Program (July).
        Revives *The Trojan Women* in Shimizu, Shizuoka-ken (Sept.).
        Directs *Higeki: Atereusu ke no hôkai* (*The Tragic Fall of the House of
        Atreus*) at the Imperial Theatre, Tokyo (Dec.). With Nagashima
        Toshiyuki (Orestes), Ôtori Ran (Elektra), Shiraishi
        (Clytemnestra), and seventy other actors.
1984   Revives *The Trojan Women* at Los Angeles Olympic Arts
        Festival (June).
        Jonas Jurasas directs *Three Sisters* with WLT actors in Toga
        (Aug.).

Renames his company SCOT (Suzuki Company of Toga) in Sept.

Directs *King Lear* (with Fueda Uichirô as Lear) and *Three Sisters* in Toga (Dec.).

Publishes *Engekiron: ekkyô suru chikara* (*Collected Theatre Writings: Energy that Knows No Boundaries*), Parco (Aug.).

Publishes *Suzuki Tadashi taidanshû* (*Collected Interviews*), Riburopôto (Aug.).

1985   Tours *The Trojan Women* to San Diego, Washington D.C., London, Copenhagen, Brussels, Athens (Athens Festival), Delphi (International Meeting of Ancient Greek Drama), Thessaloniki (April–June), Frankfurt (Festival Theater der Welt), Udine (Oct.); also Toga and Osaka (July–Aug.).

Tours *Clytemnestra* to Frankfurt (Festival Theater der Welt), Venice Biennale, and Udine (Oct.); also Toga (July–Aug.).

Tours *Three Sisters* to Frankfurt (Festival Theater der Welt) and Venice Biennale (Sept.–Oct.); also Toga (July–Aug.) and Tokyo (Nov.–Dec.).

Directs *King Lear* at Toga (July–Aug.).

1986   Tours *The Trojan Women* to Geneva, Milan, Madrid (Festival de Teatro), Tenerife, and Las Palmas (Canary Islands) (Feb.–March), Chicago (International Theatre Festival) (May), Seoul (Asian Games Art Festival) (Sept.), and Hong Kong International Theatre Festival (Oct.); also Takaoka, Japan (Oct.).

Tours bilingual *Clytemnestra* to San Diego (Pacific Rings Festival) (May), Baltimore (International Theatre Festival), Delphi (International Meeting of Ancient Greek Drama), and Athens (Athens Festival) (June); also Osaka (Aug.).

Directs *The Chekhov* (*The Cherry Orchard* and *Three Sisters*) and bilingual *Clytemnestra* in Toga (July–Aug.).

J. Thomas Rimer translates *Engekiron: ekkyô suru chikara* as *The Way of Acting: the Theatre Writings of Tadashi Suzuki*, New York: Theatre Communications Group.

1987   Tours *The Cherry Orchard* and *Three Sisters* to Tokyo Seibu Hall (Jan.–Feb.).

Builds Toga Library/Studio Theatre, designed by Isozaki Arata, in cooperation with the University of California, San Diego.

Tours bilingual *Clytemnestra* to Los Angeles, Berkeley, Milwaukee, and Minneapolis (April); also Toga (Aug.).

Tours *The Trojan Women* to Paris, Grenoble, Rennes, Bordeaux, and Stuttgart (Festival Theater der Welt) (May–June); also Toga (Aug.).

Tours *The Bacchae* to Madrid (Festival de Teatro), Bilbao, Pamplona, Antwerp, and Stuttgart (Festival Theater der Welt) (May–June); also Toga (Aug.). With Nishikibe as Pentheus.

Revives *Clytemnestra* in Toga (Aug.); also Paris (Oct.).

Publishes *Kokusaika jidai no bunka* (*Culture in an Age of Internationalism*), Toyama shimin daigaku.

1988   Appointed artistic director of Mitsui Festival in Tokyo.

Directs *The Tale of Lear* (co-produced by four American regional theatres) in the United States (March–June) and Toga (July–Aug.). With Tom Hewitt (Lear).

Tours *Clytemnestra* to Yokohama and Amagasaki (March), Shimizu, and Nagasaki (Oct.); also Mito (Dec.).

Directs *Uncle Vania* and *The Cherry Orchard* in Toga (Aug.).

Tours *The Trojan Women* to Mitsui Festival, Tokyo (May–June); also Australian Bicentennial Expo '88, Sydney (June).

Publishes *Engeki to wa nani ka* (*What is Theatre?*), Iwanami shoten (July).

1989   Appointed artistic director of Acting Company Mito (ACM).

Directs bilingual *King Lear* at Tokyo Globe and Mito (April). With Tom Hewitt (Lear) and Yoshiyuki Kazuko (Nurse).

Directs *Yûjinshô: Hamlet yori* (*Ode to Playboys: after Hamlet*) in Toga (Aug.).

Directs *The Chekhov* (*Three Sisters, The Cherry Orchard, Uncle Vania*) in Toga (July–Aug.). With Ashikawa Yôko (Sonia).

Tours *The Trojan Women* to Lahti and Helsinki (ITI International Theatre Festival) (May). Shiraishi's last performance with SCOT.

Tours *The Bacchae* to Melbourne (Spoleto Festival) and Canberra (Sept.). With Jim De Vita (Dionysus) and Ashikawa Yôko (Agave).

1990   Opening of ACM Theatre, Mito, designed by Isozaki Arata, with *Dionysus – Sôshitsu no yôshiki o megutte I* (*On the Style of Loss I*) (March–April).

Revives *King Lear* in Mito and Toyama, an English version and a bilingual version at the Mitsui Festival in Tokyo (May). With Tom Hewitt (Lear).

Directs *Dionysus* in Toga amphitheatre (July–Aug.).

1991   Directs *Macbeth – Osarabakyô no ryûsei* (*Macbeth – the Rise of the Farewell Cult – Sôshitsu no yôshiki o megutte II* (*On the Style of Loss II*) in Mito with ACM and SCOT (Jan.).
Tours *The Chekhov* to Purchase, New York, and Stage West in Springfield, Mass. (Feb.).
Tours *Dionysus* to Moscow (Taganka Theatre) and the New York International Festival of the Arts (June).
Revives *King Lear* in Toga (July–Aug.). With Fueda Uichirô (Lear).
Directs *Sekai no hate kara konnichiwa I* (*Greetings from the Edge of the Earth I*) in Toga (July–Aug.). With Tsutamori as Old Man.

1992   Directs *Dionysus – Osarabakyô no tanjô* (*Dionysus – the Birth of the Farewell Cult – Sôshitsu no yôshiki o megutte III* (*On the Style of Loss III*)) and *Ivanov – Osarabakyô no michikusa* (*Ivanov – the Sidetracking of The Farewell Cult*) in Mito with SCOT and ACM. With Ellen Lauren as Agave (Jan.).
Directs *The Chronicle of Macbeth* in Australia for Playbox Theatre. Tours Adelaide Festival, Melbourne, Geelong, Hobart (Feb.–April), and Tokyo (Mitsui Festival, May). With Ellen Lauren (Lady Macbeth), Peter Curtin (Macbeth), and John Nobbs (Banquo).
Tours *King Lear* to Mito and Asaba Shuzenji onsen in Izu (May); also Toga (Aug.).
Revives *Greetings from the Edge of the Earth I (Macbeth) and II (Ivanov)* in Toga (Aug.).
Tours bilingual *Dionysus* to Vienna (Art Carnuntum) (June) and Saratoga Springs in New York State (Sept.); also Toga (Aug.).
Founds SITI (Saratoga International Theatre Institute) with Anne Bogart at Skidmore College in Saratoga Springs, N.Y.

1993   Directs *Ivanov* and *Juliet* in Mito (Jan.).
Tours *King Lear* to Fujisawa, Shimizu (Feb.), Asaba Shuzenji onsen in Izu (May); also Toga (Aug.).
Revives *Greetings from the Edge of the Earth I* in Toga (July–Aug.).
Directs *Juliet – Greetings from the Edge of the Earth III* in Toga (July–Aug.). With Ellen Lauren (Juliet), Takahashi Hiroko (Nurse), and Kameron Steele (Romeo).
Tours *Dionysus* to Santiago (Chile International Theatre Festival), Buenos Aires, and Sao Paulo (April–May).
Tours *King Lear* and *Juliet* to Saratoga Springs, N.Y. (Sept.).

Forms committee of International Theatre Olympics
organization with Yuri Lyubimov, Tony Harrison, Heiner
Müller, Robert Wilson, and others.
Publishes *Engeki to wa nani ka? (What is Theatre?)* in South
Korea (May).

1994   Recreates *Juliet* as *Shinenakatta onna Julieto – Prokofiev ni yoru*
(*The Juliet Who Couldn't Die – According to Prokofiev*) at Mito
(Jan.), Toga (July–Aug.), and Vienna (Art Carnuntum) (Sept.).
Suzuki reinterprets Ellen Lauren's role by cross-dressing
Fueda Uichirô.
Revives *King Lear* at Hamamatsu, Fuji, Shimizu (Feb.), Asaba
Shuzenji onsen (May), Saitama, and Toga Autumn Festival
(Oct.).
Directs *Kaette kita Nippon (Shrinking Japan Rises Again)* in Toga
(July–Aug.).
Revives *Dionysus* in Toga (July–Aug.), Teatro Olimpico,
Vicenza (Sept.), Shimizu, and Toga Autumn Festival (Oct.).
Opens larger Shin Sanbô (New Mountain Hall) in Toga,
designed by Isozaki Arata.
Tours *King Lear* to the RSC Barbican Center, London, for
Everybody's Shakespeare Festival (Nov.). With Fueda as Lear.
Co-founds BeSeTo (Beijing, Seoul, Tokyo) Theatre Festival as
Japan's representative, directing *King Lear* for the inaugural
festival in Seoul (Nov.).
Publishes *Enshutsuka no hassô (A Director's Starting Point)*, Ohta
shuppan (July).

1995   Directs Hasegawa Hirohisa's *Kagekiyo* at Shimoda (Jan.),
Shizuoka, and Fuji (Feb.).
Tours *Juliet* to Hong Kong International Festival (Feb.).
Revives *Ivanov* at Toga Spring Festival (April–May).
Revives *Greetings from the Edge of the Earth I* at Toga Spring
Festival (April–May) and Toga Summer Festival (Aug.).
Revives bilingual *Dionysus* in Toga (Aug.).
Directs *Elektra* in Toga (Aug.). With Miyagi Satoshi of Kunauka
as assistant-director, Mikari of Kunauka (Elektra), Takahashi
Hiroko (Clytemnestra), and Takada Midori (Percussion).
Directs *The Feudal Lord in Toga versus Pirandello* in Toga (Aug.).
Tours bilingual *Dionysus* to Athens and *Elektra* to Delphi for the
First International Theatre Olympics (Aug.); and both to Teatro
Olimpico, Vicenza (Sept.). *Dionysus* tours to Toronto (Sept.).
Tours *King Lear* to Okayama, Kudamatsu, and Kitakyûshu
(Nov.–Dec.).

Suzuki resigns as artistic director of ACM (Mito) to become artistic director of SPAC (Shizuoka Performing Arts Center).

1996 Directs *Ito to Maboroshi* (*Strings and Fantasies*), adapted from Kara Jûrô with music by Hosokawa Toshio, at Toga Spring Festival (April–May).

Directs Kara Jûrô's *John Silver* in Toga (Aug.) and Saitama (Dec.). With Takemori Yôichi (Koharu).

Revives *Elektra* in Mito (Jan.), Toga (Aug.), and Saitama (Dec.).

Directs Dazai Osamu's *Usagi to tanuki* (*Rabbit and Raccoon*) as *Kachikachiyama* (*Mountain on Fire*) in Toga (Aug.). With Shiohara Michitomo (Yakuza/Raccoon).

Revives *Greetings I* as *Hanabi no kuni kara konnichiwa* (*Greetings from the Land of Fireworks*) in Toga (Aug.).

Tours *Elektra* to Copenhagen and Stockholm (Aug.), Beijing (Third BeSeTo Festival, Oct.), and Shanghai (Nov.).

Founds Theatre InterAction to develop regional theatre in Japan and Asia (Oct.).

Directs new *King Lear* in Toga (Dec.). With Nakayama Ichirô (Lear) and Mishima Keita (Edgar) in wheelchairs.

1997 Revives *King Lear* at Toga Spring Festival (April–May) and for the opening of SPAC theatres in Shizuoka (Aug.–Sept.).

Revives bilingual *Dionysus* and *Greetings I* in Toga (Aug.); also *Dionysus* for the opening of SPAC theatres in Shizuoka (Sept.).

Directs *Lear no monogatari* (known as *Vision of Lear*), with music by Hosokawa Toshio, in Saitama (Dec.).

1998 Directs *Dionysus* for Festival Iberoamericano de teatro de Bogota (April), the International Chekhov Theatre Festival at the Moscow Art Theatre (May), and at the International Istanbul Theatre Festival (June).

Directs the opera version of *Lear no monogatari* (*Vision of Lear*), composed by Hosokawa Toshio, for the opening of the Munich Biennale (April). With German and Japanese opera singers, Katoh Masaharu, and Nîhori Kiyosumi.

Revives *Greetings from the Edge of the Earth I* in Toga (Aug.).

Revives *Kachikachiyama* in Shizuoka (Feb.–March) and Toga (Aug.).

Directs *Kagami no ie* (*The House of Mirrors*) in Toga (Aug.). With Takemori as the writer Kyôzô.

SPAC actors perform with young "P4" directors: Miyagi Satoshi (*Cinderella*) and Kanô Yukikazu (*Joan of Arc*) in Shizuoka (Aug.–Sept.).

Directs *Kanashii sake* (*Sad Sake*) in Shizuoka (Oct.).

1999   Hosts Second International Theatre Olympics in Shizuoka
(April–June), directing *Cyrano de Bergerac*, with Takemori as
Cyrano; and reviving *King Lear* and the opera *Vision of Lear*.
The latter tours to Tokyo (June).

Directs Sayonara Toga Festival and revives *Greetings from the
Edge of the Earth I* (July–Aug.).

Revives *Dionysus* (Jan., Nov.), *Kachikachiyama* (Jan., Nov.–Dec.),
Kanashii sake (Oct.), and *Cyrano de Bergerac* (Nov.–Dec.) in
Shizuoka.

Tours *King Lear* to Amagasaki (Feb.).

Republishes enlarged edition of *Gekiteki gengo* (*On Dramatic
Language*) with Nakamura, Asahi shinbunsha (Feb.).

2000   Holds SPAC International Spring Arts Festival in Shizuoka,
directing *Oedipus*, with Nîhori Kiyosumi as Oedipus, and the
Noh play *Utoh* (*Birds of Sorrow*), with Kanze Hideo; also
revives *Cyrano de Bergerac* (April–June).

Founds Japan Performing Arts Foundation and launches the
Toga Young Directors' Competition (Aug.).

Tours *Oedipus* to Delphi (July).

Directs *Cinderella, Bride of the Vampire* in Shizuoka (Nov.).

Revives *King Lear* in Shizuoka (Jan.), and *Cyrano* in Shizuoka
(Jan.), Amagasaki (Feb.), and Toga (Aug.).

Revives *Utoh* in Shizuoka (Nov.), and *Oedipus* in Toga (Aug.)
and Shizuoka (Nov.).

2001   Tours *Oedipus* to Amagasaki (March).

Revives *Elektra*, with Saitoh Yukiko; and *Oedipus* and *Cinderella*
for the SPAC Spring Arts Festival (April–June).

For the Third International Theatre Olympics in Moscow
directs the opera *Vision of Lear*, with singers of the Bolshoi
Opera and other opera houses, at the Navoya Opera House;
and *Elektra*, *Oedipus* and *Utoh* at Anatoly Vassiliev's School of
Dramatic Art Theatre (June).

Revives *Greetings from the Edge of the Earth I* for the Toga
Summer Arts program and the 8th BeSeTo Festival in Toga
(Aug.).

Revives *Dionysus*, *Oedipus* and *Elektra* in Shizuoka (Oct.). Tours
these three productions to New York, Delaware, Pittsburg,
Iowa, and San Francisco (Nov.–Dec.).

Introduction
Suzuki's work in the context
of Japanese theatre

Takahashi Yasunari

No historian of Japanese theatre will object to the view that modern Western-oriented theatre in Japan really started with the production of *Othello* and *Hamlet* in 1903 by one of the Shinpa (New School) companies, or perhaps more truly with the completely Westernized production of *Hamlet* in 1911 by a company called Bungei Kyôkai (the Literary Society) led by the famous Shakespeare scholar and critic Tsubouchi Shôyô.

It was Tsubouchi's Bungei Kyôkai and later Osanai Kaoru's Tsukiji Shôgekijô (Tsukiji Little Theatre), established in 1924, which in a real sense initiated and developed a special Western-oriented modern theatre usually known as Shingeki (meaning "New Drama"). This was a theatre form which finally succeeded in cutting itself off from the older theatre forms like Kabuki, Noh, and Kyogen as well as from more recent forms like Shinpa and Shinkokugeki (New National Theatre). Shingeki might be regarded as the culmination of long efforts in the genre of theatre which, like everything else in Japanese culture and society after the Meiji Restoration, tried to incorporate or imitate Europe.

The contemporary European drama which Shingeki made an object of devout adoration being what it was, it was only natural that all the tenets of realistic theatre were swallowed whole: the dramaturgy based on the dialectics of conflicting powers, the acting style aimed at the lifelike portrayal of individual characters, the belief in the psychological motivation of human behavior, and the underlying assumption that the ultimate standard of reality is logical explicability.

The extent to which Shingeki devoutly subscribed to the Western model might be suggested by an anecdote concerning Osanai, the great founder of the school. He went over to Russia in 1912 in order personally to watch Stanislavski direct at the Moscow Art Theatre, and, with an assiduousness which seems staggering to us today, made minute

1

notes of everything said and done by the great master. Upon his return to Japan, Osanai immediately began to rehearse the same play at his Tsukiji Shôgekijô, trying to reproduce every detail he had jotted down in Moscow.

If, to Osanai, Chekhov and Ibsen were holy texts, Senda Koreya, the earliest and most important of his disciples, turned to a more avant-garde theatre, German Expressionism, and finally came to choose Brecht as his master. Imprisoned by the military regime for his leftist persuasion during the prewar days, Senda emerged after World War II as the leader of one of the major Shingeki troupes, Haiyûza (Actors' Studio), and was greatly instrumental in bringing about the first joint production of *The Cherry Orchard* by all major Shingeki companies in 1945, which marked the promising rebirth of theatre in postwar Japan.

In fact the end of World War II was a sort of "second opening" of the country (the "first" was the Meiji Restoration) and it gave a new sanction to the rationale of progressive Westernization in all phases of Japanese culture and society. It was Shingeki above all which benefited from this general "democratizing" tendency, synchronizing as it did with the political growth of the Socialist and Communist parties. In spite of the anticommunist policy carried out by the American authorities in the early 1950s, the period of Shingeki "flowering" lasted until the late 1960s.

Seen from another angle, this "flowering" meant that Shingeki had turned itself into a form of orthodoxy and neglected to question the contradictions inherent in its structure. The first of these was the illusoriness of its politically "leftist" sympathies which became apparent in the period of high growth and economic prosperity during the 1960s. People ceased to be moved by a political appeal which sounded hollow. They had become at once more materially satiated than before and more sensitive to political hypocrisy and condescension.

These attitudes of hypocrisy and condescension which people sensed in Shingeki were certainly there, for despite its "democratic" slogans, Shingeki could never shake off a certain didactic posture, the air of being intellectually elitist and preaching from above. It failed to reach down to the real grassroots of popular sensibility and culture, as is patent in its complete negation of the traditional and popular forms of theatre (Noh, Kabuki, etc.) and entertainment (vaudeville arts such as Manzai and Rakugo).

Last but not least Shingeki failed to establish its own theatrical esthetics about the ontological identity of the actor. It never questioned the priority of the written text provided by the playwright, taking for granted the idea that all that is required of the actors and director is to bring forward the meaning which has been authoritatively built into the text by the author. Shingeki naively relied on the simplistic mimetic doctrine of realism that the actor had only to try to imitate and reproduce the lifelike and lifesize reality of the ordinary world.

It was against this status quo of Shingeki that the violent Little Theatre movement burst out in the late 1960s. It coincided with a global upsurge of student revolt, and was part of the larger wave of radical critique of the assumptions which underlie modern rationalistic, technological, democratic culture. Among the prominent theatre groups involved in this revolutionary movement were the Jôkyô Gekijô, led by Kara Jûrô and nicknamed *Aka tento* (Red Tent) because of the color of the tent which they pitched for their performance, the Center 68/69 led by Satoh Makoto and nicknamed *Kuro tento* (Black Tent) also because of the color of their tent, and Terayama Shûji's Tenjô Sajiki.

But perhaps the most austere, rigorous, and systematic troupe of all was the Waseda Shôgekijô (later SCOT) led by Suzuki Tadashi. Suzuki ruthlessly exposed the political and moral hypocrisy which was subconsciously built into Shingeki as a social institution. And he did this not only through his polemical discourses but also through the very form of his theatrical activities. His was typical Poor Theatre of which Grotowski would have approved.

Suzuki also drew much of his nourishment from the traditional and popular theatre forms of Japan. No other director has learned and stolen so much from Noh and Kabuki, and certainly none has utilized so effectively the popular folk songs (*enka*) which have entered the unconscious mechanism of the psyche of the nonelitist Japanese populace.

But one of Suzuki's greatest subversive achievements was to undermine the privileged priority of the written text provided by the playwright at the top of the pyramidal structure of the theatre world. He triumphantly succeeded in transferring the priority from the text to the actor.

All of these critical-creative achievements by Suzuki were nowhere more powerfully apparent than in *Gekiteki naru mono o megutte* (literally *"In search of whatever is dramatic,"* usually translated as *"On the Dramatic Passions"*), which many critics consider one of the milestones in the history of postwar Japanese theatre. In this the heroine is a madwoman confined by her family who enacts in her fantasies several roles from classic Kabuki and Shinpa. Although structured as a collage of disconnected scenes, the play centers on the unrequited passions and savage resentments of an archetypal Japanese woman who, as played by the actress Shiraishi Kayoko, overwhelmed the audience with the all-powerful sense of her physical presence and metamorphosis.

Suzuki was fortunate enough to find in Shiraishi an actress who could perfectly embody his theories about the depths of the Japanese psyche and physique which had heretofore been left sadly unexplored by Shingeki. Shiraishi struck the audience as an incredibly atavistic reincarnation of the actress-founder of Kabuki in the seventeenth century, Okuni, with all her pristine magical power.

Suzuki and Shiraishi were able to incarnate a unique theatrical image between them. By creating an intricate spatio-temporal experience both in the actress and the audience, Suzuki could unleash a dramatic energy in a way which was totally out of the reach of Shingeki.

In doing this Suzuki was not only criticizing the Western-oriented realism of Shingeki and its shallow avant-garde modernism, but also revitalizing the tradition-bound possibilities of Noh and Kabuki. The riches of these traditional theatres have become so built into the unconscious memories of actors' bodies and theatrical conventions that Suzuki's searching eye was necessary to bring them out into the light of critical examination.

Number II in the series *On the Dramatic Passions* made it abundantly clear how much Suzuki had stolen from the "myth" and "method" of Japanese traditional theatre. But he did not remain content with the success. In 1974 he ventured on an experiment of fusing Greek material with Japanese theatrical form. He recast Euripides' *The Trojan Women* in such a way that the wailing speeches of the defeated Trojan queen and princesses were made to recur in the fantasies of an old Japanese beggar woman who, helplessly cast out of the ruined city of Tokyo immediately after World War II, bemoaned her fate and that of her country.

One may be reminded of Kurosawa's film *Throne of Blood* (an adaptation of *Macbeth*), in which he attempted to deal with Macbeth's story transposed into medieval Japan with samurai and witches. Suzuki in his *The Trojan Women*, however, seems to me to have gone deeper in search of common mythical layers of human (especially female) passion and suffering. Perhaps the difference is in the media used by the two directors. The theatre is obviously at a great disadvantage in that it cannot use the technical apparatus at the disposal of film. But in the hands of a shrewd theatre director that very disadvantage can turn into infinite advantage, for after all there is nothing like the real presence of actors on the stage with their power of gripping our imagination. I should add in passing that, in the first performance of the play in Tokyo, Suzuki used a famous Noh actor (Kanze Hisao), a no less famous Shingeki actress (Ichihara Etsuko), and Shiraishi Kayoko. It is impossible to describe how deeply exciting it was to watch the clashing of these three actors brought up in different theatrical traditions. One realized how skillfully Suzuki managed to visualize his critique of the whole gamut of Japanese theatrical tradition.

It is therefore no wonder that Suzuki proceeded further with this experiment to use both Japanese and American actors in his bilingual production of *The Bacchae*. It was a logical and necessary step in his insatiable quest for answers to the fundamental question: What makes it possible for histrionic acts and theatrical events to exist at all? And how can they be justified? Suzuki seems to believe that such a quest is ineluctable if one wishes to go beyond the apathies which numb the rootless Shingeki as well as the tradition-bound Noh and Kabuki. And he knows that the way forward is also the way back, the way up the way down; that an international communion is possible only through delving into one's own body. That he is neither an anachronistic chauvinist exploiting a "samurai exoticism" nor a superficial cosmopolitan smoothing over undeniable differences will, I hope, be amply proved by our ensuing presentation of Suzuki's major productions in relation to his training method. Through his rigorous and continuous negotiation of the many dislocations between traditional Japanese theatre and Western-imported realism, he, more than any other living Japanese theatre artist, has contributed substantially to the modernization and postmodernization of Japanese theatre.

1 Rethinking Japanese theatre: cracking the codes

Ian Carruthers

In America the theatre for the most part is naturalistic. People want to be comfortable. They want to identify immediately with the situation. They want everything finished, put in a box and wrapped up with a bow. But I believe, ideally, you want to leave the theatre still thinking about it, still questioning it. What I find exciting about Suzuki's work is that we come into the theatre and we have a surprise. We have to think about what we have seen and we leave the theatre thinking about it.

I believe that in a sense my work is similar to what Suzuki is doing in his work. Theatre that you have to rethink. It poses more questions than answers.

Robert Wilson, "Theatre That You Have to Rethink"[1]

When I first visited Toga as a guest of Suzuki Tadashi to witness the two-month process of putting on an international festival in a remote mountain village in the Japan Alps, I had come fresh from six months of observing him engage with actors and audiences in Australia. His adaptation of *Macbeth* had been hugely controversial here, widely reported in the press and on television, its process made the subject of an SBS documentary and the performance screened on national television.[2] It had even become the subject of a specially convened conference by the Melbourne Performance Research Group at Melbourne University.[3] By the standards of the great experimental Russian director Vsevelod Meyerhold, the controversy generated would rate it a *succès de scandale*.

Detractors of the show – and there were many, though not nearly as many as its enthusiastic supporters – had loudly decried Suzuki's impertinence in attempting to teach Australians a new approach to Shakespeare performance.[4] Aware (from my own experiences teaching traditional Japanese theatre training) of the difficulties facing actors attempting to relocate their work in a wider cultural framework, I arrived in Toga eager to see how his *Macbeth* would be received "at home."

The version I witnessed in 1993 (*Greetings from the Edge of the Earth I*) was much freer and more creatively intertextual than *The Chronicle of Macbeth* had been in Australia in 1992. In fact so free was *Greetings* that I came away, night after night, not only amazed by the superior invention and technical skill of SCOT (Suzuki Company of Toga), but irritated by my inability to grasp the production's obviously complex meaning structures. It was all the more frustrating because Japanese audiences of different ages and from all walks of life were so vocally appreciative. I left Toga armed with a copy of the performance text, believing that translation would provide most of the answers. Three months later a rough draft had certainly produced answers – but also raised an entirely new set of questions. The truth of Robert Wilson's observation about Suzuki's work was becoming alarmingly evident.

Not only has Robert Wilson been astute in identifying the fascination of Suzuki's directorial work, he has also appreciated his colleague's significance as a festival organizer who continues to help shape cultural policy at national and international levels:

André Malraux said, just after the war, that what he would like to see as a cultural policy for France is a balance of interest in four areas. He said we want to create a balance of interest between protecting the art of our nation, and art of all nations. On the other side of the coin, we want to protect the art of the past along with the art of our time, the art of the future. We must maintain a balance in these four areas, the art of our homeland, the art of all nations, the art of the past, and [new] creation. What is happening in Toga in many ways represents the ideals of movements like the American regional theatre. It is artistic activity based upon principles very similar to those of André Malraux's cultural policy. It is really quite extraordinary.[5]

Wilson's reference to Malraux is apposite, for the latter's cultural policies became familiar to the young Suzuki in 1972 through his involvement in Jean-Louis Barrault's Théâtre des Nations Festival in Paris. Inspired by his experiences there, Suzuki returned to Japan determined to emulate what he saw Barrault, Grotowski, and Brook achieving in Europe. This would eventually lead him to set up the International Toga Festival in 1982, become a founding member of the International Theatre Olympics organization in 1993, and host the Second International Theatre Olympics in Shizuoka in 1999. Suzuki's beginnings were more humble.

BEGINNINGS (1939–67)

He was born on June 20, 1939, the third child of a timber merchant in the small port of Shimizu, situated under Mount Fuji in Shizuoka Prefecture. He was old enough to remember seeing the bombing of shipping in the harbor at the end of World War II, and the terror on his mother's face as she pulled him away. But his most vivid memories were of the difficulties of communal existence in an old-style Japanese house. Family members were only a sliding paper-screen away when his maternal grandfather chanted *gidaiyû*, his father intoned Zen sutras, his brother listened to Beethoven on a wind-up gramophone, and his sister read aloud with friends from the democratic literary journal *Sekai* (*The World*). According to Gotoh Yukihiro, he would jokingly refer to such extended-family living as a condition of "cultural schizophrenia."[6] The young Suzuki, like all Japanese caught in what Takahashi Yasunari has called a "second opening" of the country, was daily faced with the gap between traditional and modern (Western) values. One of his lifelong concerns as an artist has been not so much to resolve this dilemma as consciously to make theatre out of its tensions, contradictions, and ironies.[7]

In 1954 Suzuki transferred to a junior high school in Tokyo to increase his chances of getting into a top university. However, while happy about this opportunity to "cut off blood ties" (his father used to burn him with moxa, a Chinese medicine used in child-rearing in premodern Japan, as a punishment) the young fifteen-year-old found boarding-house life in the big city desperately lonely. He would drink alcohol to excess in cheap bars with lodging-house "friends" much older than he, sing *enka*, play mah jong into the early hours to socialize, and cut classes to sleep in and read.[8] Paradoxically, on winning a place at Waseda University to study political science and economics, he never again had as much time to study the likes of Dostoyevski and Chekhov. The drama society he joined to avoid isolation discussed only Marx and Engels. To them Chekhov was not an artist but a harbinger of revolution.[9]

As Gotoh describes it, "In the late 1950s the WFS [Waseda Free Stage] was the most prominent student theatre group in Japan, having some 150 members and attracting 5,000 spectators a year."[10] Many of its graduates went on to careers in the theatre after graduation. But when Suzuki joined, the group was involved in violent mass protests against renewal of Japan's Mutual Security Pact with the USA (AMPO), an agreement which gave the US military a nuclear presence in Japan. The failure of this mass student movement to achieve tangible results – the treaty was renewed in 1960 – led to widespread disillusionment as young radicals were faced with the hard choice of either joining the ranks of the "salarymen" or "dropping out" of society.[11]

When Suzuki joined the Waseda Free Stage, the Marxist "Old Left" were producing Hauptmann's *The Weavers*. He was given a walk-on part to tell striking comrades that their leader Dreissiger had disappeared; however, as he recalls, he was criticized for failing to convey the look of a starving man. The approach to performance taken in the society was highly ideological and this was formative for Suzuki in both positive and negative ways. For Gorki's *The Lower Depths*, he was asked to research the social and historical background, while a colleague was assigned to study how Stanislavski directed the play; and "[e]verybody had to submit reports once or twice a week. Actors had to write about their role's personality, social background, age, personal history, family tree, everything. They even had to sketch a portrait of their character in costume, and always they kept on debating. I like debate now, because of this experience."[12]

While theatre activities soon brought the reclusive literature student out of his shell, they also nurtured his growing awareness of the inadequacies of socialist realism. He noticed that when putting on *The Weavers*, his colleagues "felt they had to smear-on dirt, wear baggy trousers, and carry work-tools in their hands; but, because they were so self-conscious, they didn't present their roles very well . . . Although they tried very hard with their realism to attract people to the revolution, their lack of skill showed because they had no adequate training system. It was unbearable just to be in the rehearsal room watching them."[13]

Believing himself to be "a total failure" as an actor yet sensing what was wrong with WFS performances, he decided to try directing. His first production, Chekhov's one-act farce *The Anniversary*, seems to have offered Suzuki the opportunity for a nonideological approach. As he was aware, "When drama is produced under the banner of revolutionary ideals, so much else goes missing, like kindness and consideration."[14]

In early 1960 Suzuki was surprisingly elected president of the WFS. This was due to a power shift in the club from the "Old Left" to the "New Left" as AMPO street battles with the riot police intensified. In the faction-fighting between the Yoyogi (Marxist) and Zengakuren (Trotskyite) groups within the society, Suzuki rose to prominence as an articulate moderate and mediator, able to introduce a new system of balloting which avoided gridlock. As president he was expected to be at the head of demonstrations, but he would sensibly warn younger members that discretion was the better part of valor.[15]

Suzuki's second directing assignment after his election involved two plays by a young radical student called Betsuyaku Minoru, later to achieve fame as Japan's first Absurdist. The plays were *Kashima ari* (*A Vacancy*) and *Hokuro sôsêji* (*Hokuro Sausages*). The latter was about a butcher who kills his wife to make sausages for his shop; as Suzuki tells it:

one of the boarders in his tenement realizes this, and launches a campaign to boycott the butcher. Ironically, the Zengakuren (United Japanese Student Unions) demonstrate against the boycott, insisting the butcher is being made a scapegoat and the action is an infringement of human rights – in short, insisting that the butcher is being victimized. Then a tenant mentions that the butcher's wife used to have a beauty spot from which hair grew. So the tenants cut open all the remaining sausages, find the beauty spot, and prove the butcher to be a criminal.

Suzuki wryly observes that "[s]uch a cynical play was troublesome to direct."[16] One of the obvious problems was that it provided no apparent psychological motivation for character or action; in his words, "The play was too much for my actors who only knew acting techniques and rehearsal methods based on the Stanislavski system."[17]

Suzuki's third directing assignment, Arthur Miller's *Death of a Salesman*, was another indirect critique of current trends at the WFS; its choice demonstrated Suzuki's sensitivity to the changing mood in the country after the failure of AMPO. For him it was:

a play about American consumer society. With the revolution in mind, I felt there was no point in selecting a play about Russia before the revolution. Because it was us seeking to make our own [failed] revolution, I thought we should produce a play about the kind of social structure in which we were enmeshed at that time . . . When I read *Death of a Salesman*, I found it very interesting, for it could be Japan too. It's a tragedy about urban consumer society in an era of high economic growth – the world of the salaryman.[18]

One particular technique of Miller was to make a significant impact on Suzuki's later approach to playmaking. As he noted in discussion with Betsuyaku, "The gap between [Willy Loman's] illusions and reality . . . , the technique of transforming the space suddenly through a 'mental flashback' . . . surpasses anything previously seen in realism."[19] Just as significantly, all the actors in this production – including Ono Hiroshi, who played Willy Loman, and Takeuchi Hiroko, Suzuki's future wife – were to join Suzuki and Betsuyaku in forming their own Little Theatre company in December 1961.

However at the start of that year, when Suzuki put forward the idea of directing Chekhov's *Three Sisters* to the WFS repertory committee, its members, including Betsuyaku, were involved in demonstrations against American nuclear presence on Niijima Island, off the Izu peninsula. Suzuki was asked to create "a clear connection between Chekhov and Niijima" in his production, and when he refused to do so a group of eighteen put forward a no-confidence motion. It was defeated by a margin of fifty-two votes, but Suzuki was labeled "an art-for-art's-sake neo-fascist" by the eighteen ideologues, who went off to join more extremist interventions by Ôshima Nagisa in his film *Nihon no yoru to kiri* (*Japanese Night and Fog*) and by Saeki Takayuki with his Tokyo University production of *Saboten o sude de tsukame* (*Grab the Cactus with Both Hands*).[20]

After this Suzuki and Betsuyaku resolved to set up their own company, also called the Waseda Jiyû Butai (Waseda Free Stage). Too poor to use the subway or trains, they conceived the idea on a long walk from Waseda University to the cinema complexes in Yûrakuchô, not far from Tokyo station. At that time only three major Shingeki companies offered aspiring artists a guaranteed salary,[21] and having rejected these options on artistic grounds, the pair were faced with the prospect of starting up on their own. In Suzuki's words, it felt "just like jumping off a cliff."[22] However, the nervous excitement generated by their decision triggered a burst of short-run professional productions in rented spaces: Betsuyaku's *A to B to hitori no onna* (*A and B and a Certain Woman*) at Sabô Hall in November 1961, Sartre's *Les Mouches* (*The Flies*) at the Kôseinenkin Hall that December, and Betsuyaku's *Zô* (*The Elephant*) at the prestigious Haiyûza in April 1962.

A and B and a Certain Woman is significant for Suzuki because the favorable reception of the play among students "motivated us to found the Waseda Little Theatre." According to Gotoh, it concerned the nonsensical conversations of two men whose relationship of dominance and submission resembled that of Pozzo and Lucky in *Waiting for Godot*. His production of Sartre's *The Flies*, itself a free adaptation of *Elektra*, was not considered particularly significant by Suzuki, although Sartre's existential philosophy certainly did exert a formative influence on his life.[23] It seems he had to take over direction at a late stage from a second-year student in the WFS.[24]

Performance of *The Elephant* at the Haiyûza for six nights was expensive and poorly received, the drama critic Fujita Hiroshi even suggesting that "[t]hey should have selected a better play."[25] In 1968, ironically, Betsuyaku would win the prestigious Kishida Prize for Playwriting, but in 1962 Andô Shinya's translation of *Waiting for Godot* had only recently been published, and Beckett's play would not be performed in a major production[26] until 1969; hence Fujita's inability to appreciate *The Elephant* is understandable. Even Tsuno Kaitarô, who was present in 1962, would write of his disorientation at the shock of the new:

> At the time *The Elephant* did not strike me as a particularly easy play. I remember that Suzuki Tadashi, who directed the performance, stressed in the program the newness of the "language" Betsuyaku had used, but, to be perfectly frank, I was not able to get a firm grasp on the essence of that newness at first . . . Now, as I go back and reread the play [ten years later], I find it almost impossible to imagine why this succinct and lucid work was once so difficult for me to comprehend.[27]

The play is now firmly acknowledged as the first and possibly finest example of the Theatre of the Absurd in Japan, David Goodman calling it "one of the first of Japan's postmodern theater."[28] It centers on the opposition between two survivors of Hiroshima, the Man and his uncle, the Invalid. One is seeking to die quietly and unnoticed in hospital, the other is prepared to make street-theatre out of his suffering in order to force an apathetic public to acknowledge his miserable existence. Betsuyaku's saturnine vision, set in a hospital where even the nurses are dying of radiation sickness, is densely poetic, reminiscent of the central image in the fourth section of T. S. Eliot's *East Coker* (ably translated by Nishiwaki Junzaburô): "The whole earth is our hospital/Endowed by the ruined millionaire,/Wherein, if we do well, we shall/Die of the absolute paternal care/That will not leave us, but prevents us everywhere." The existential symbolism of the image has since worn a deep groove in Suzuki's theatrical vision.[29]

While working as stage manager on Suzuki's *Death of a Salesman*, Betsuyaku had been inspired by Ono Hiroshi's performance as Willy Loman and decided to write the part of the Invalid specifically for him. As Betsuyaku explains, "Ono hesitates just before he carries out an action, so when someone tries to hurry him, he gets more nervous and hesitates even more. When he does this, a new relationship is born between actor and text, like a line suddenly and mysteriously drawn in the empty sands of a desert . . . in this way the stage . . . becomes an abstract space."[30] Anyone reading even the first page of *The Elephant* in David Goodman's translation can readily appreciate how these nervous rhythms of Ono's have affected Betsuyaku's writing. For Suzuki "[t]he text of *The Elephant* belongs to Betsuyaku, but the performance realization of it is Ono's . . . It's as if they were tied together in creation."[31]

Following the failure of *The Elephant* at the Haiyûza, Betsuyaku stopped writing for four years, during which time Suzuki was forced to put on revivals of past productions to hold the company together. However, the play was successfully performed by the Seinen Geijutsu Gekijyô (Youth Art Theatre) in 1965, and this finally spurred Betsuyaku and Suzuki to "make a fresh start"[32] with *Mon* (*The Temple Gate*), an adaptation of Natsume Sôseki's translation of Kafka's *At the Door of the Law*. Its production was to prove a lesson in Shingeki marketing. The venue chosen was the Art Theatre Shinjuku Bunka, a cinema in which Kuzui Kinshirô was putting on alternative theatre after the movies had finished. In Suzuki's words, "Kuzui and I decided to boost Betsuyaku by producing *Mon* as the first production of the Waseda Little Theatre as we now called ourselves. This experience was truly amazing. Kuzui told me it was not enough to advertise him as a member of the WLT, we would also need to involve a famous star."[33] After a fruitless round of pleading with well-known actors, none of whom would commit themselves to working with an unknown group, Kuzui also advised the young hopefuls to resort to advertising gimmicks in order to gain the attention of the newspapers. "Because there was a scene in our play where someone gets their shoes polished, he thought it would make a good story if we polished shoes . . . before the performance started."[34]

Such were the prevailing patterns of expectation in Shingeki production, but because they had been students used to doing everything for themselves, Suzuki and company were disgusted by these ingratiating activities. When discouraged, they would repair to their hang-out, the Mon Cheri coffee shop next door to Waseda University. Since few of them had any money, everything was shared – accommodation, food, even jobs. Most had been disowned by their parents, as Suzuki was, and lived in squalid conditions. As Suzuki remembers it, "Somebody might have had only a bowl of noodles all day, but still distributed leaflets and did shoe-shine duty . . . When I got up in the morning I sometimes found myself sleeping with 5 or 6 other people."[35]

Their luck finally changed when the owner of the Mon Cheri, Takubo Yoshio, offered to build a studio theatre over his coffee shop on condition that they pay for the construction costs. According to Suzuki, Takubo wanted 2,140,000 yen,[36] so each of the fourteen or fifteen members of the company was given a separate target figure between 30,000 and 300,000 yen and asked to raise it over the next six months. Even today part-time work (*arubaito*, from the German *Arbeit*) is still the usual way for most young Japanese theatre companies to raise money for shows.[37] Luckily Japan was just entering a period of high economic growth and they were able to raise the money quickly.

The extraordinary generosity of Takubo, considering Tokyo land prices, also extended to a very low rent of 15,000 yen a month for a three-and-a-half-year period. This apparently raised problems with the Tax Office, which was suspicious because the rental cost was less than the interest charges (Takubo had also borrowed money from the bank for part of the building costs). At the end of that period, which happily coincided with the company's first smash hit, *On the Dramatic Passions II*, rental costs went up to 100,000 yen a month. In Takubo's words, "I liked the large-hearted personality of 'Chû san' [Suzuki's nickname][38] and I trusted him too, so we decided on an oral contract . . . I explained to the Tax Office that these students didn't have any money, that I too was a Waseda graduate, and that I was happy to do one or two good turns for charity. Finally they were convinced."[39]

Having a theatre space of their own in central Tokyo released an extraordinary amount of energy in the group. On the one hand it freed them from the humiliating dependencies they had experienced with Kuzui and others; on the other it allowed unlimited access to very cheap rehearsal space. The benefits were almost immediately obvious in Betsuyaku's next play. *The Little Match Girl* (*Matchi-uri no shôjo*), based on Hans Christian Andersen's story, presents the invasion of a middle-class couple's privacy by a young man and woman who claim to be their abandoned children. At first audience sympathy is likely to be with the middle-aged couple whose ordered routines are so rudely upset. However, uncertainty sets in as the young man describes how, to survive after World War II, his sister would sell matches on street corners: "When a match was struck, she would lift her shabby skirt for display until the match went out."[40] No matter how we interpret the hearsay on both sides, Betsuyaku's intention, according to Robert Rolf, was to show how "[t]he affluent veneer that Japan had acquired by the 1960s could not erase the stark images of the 1940s."[41] The show premiered in November 1966 to mark the official opening of the Waseda Shôgekijô (Waseda Little Theatre) studio, and, in the opinion of the critic Dômoto Masaki, was the company's first real success.[42] This probably had a lot to do with being able to control every aspect of the performance – a lesson not lost on Suzuki. The Waseda Shôgekijô Studio was what Gotoh has called "a typical 'poor theatre' in the Grotowskian sense," a rectangular space 30' × 40' with a 14' × 25' stage and a flexible tatami-mat

Figure 2 Suzuki giving notes during a rehearsal at the Waseda
Shôgekijô Studio in 1973. Shiraishi Kayoko faces him in the front row.

seating capacity that ranged between a comfortable seventy and a very
uncomfortable 120.[43] [Figure 2]

Paradoxically, acquisition of the Mon Cheri Studio and success with
The Little Match Girl (which won Betsuyaku the Kishida Prize for Playwriting in 1968) led to a parting of the ways between director and
playwright. Betsuyaku was starting to get commissions from other
companies, writing *Kangaroo* for the Bungakuza in 1967, and cared to
work only with Ono Hiroshi. Suzuki, on the other hand, was becoming
more interested in the possibilities of ensemble physical acting:

The theatre's small performance space, where the audience could easily sense
the actor's breath and sweat, invalidated all the elements of the Shingeki stage . . .
It was a great discovery for me that the energy of the actor alone enabled the
cultural activity called theatre to be accessible to so many people . . . Although I
had no choice but to use the small theatre, the experiences I gained from it have,
to a large degree, set my theatrical direction ever since.[44]

It led him to ponder how he could open up the potential he saw in
the group's spontaneous physical expression. "I didn't mean simply to
cultivate the potentialities of my actors, I also tried to think what sort
of scripts could emerge from and would resonate in that group. How

could I put all these things together to open up a different dimension? In pondering this, I began to realize that the expressive territories of writer and director overlapped."[45]

For the next three years, until Betsuyaku left the company in August 1969, Suzuki tried to operate what he called "a bi-polar system." He would direct new Betsuyaku plays, such as *Shitakiri suzume (Tongueless Sparrow)*, an adaptation of a Dazai Osamu folk tale, and *Makushimirian hakase no bishô (The Smile of Dr. Maximillian)*, but would also develop an actor-devised approach. This prompted him "to think of experimenting with Kabuki scripts, which leave a relatively large margin free for the actor to exercise choice."[46] In 1968 his *Shite, shite, dôja – Kabuki jûhachiban (And Then, And Then, What Then? A Kabuki Classic)* won audiences with its successful adaptation of scenes from *Narukami*. His use of Elvis and *enka* (popular song) in a rearranged mambo style both updated and parodied this erotic play about an imperial princess sent to seduce a priest whose ascetic power to prevent rainfall threatens the nation. Suzuki's aim was to satirize Shingeki's exclusive reliance on Stanislavski's methods by suggesting realism's inappropriateness for Kabuki production. In Gotoh's words, "Each of the play's three scenes had a 'thesis' title displayed on the stage so as to inform the audience what the scene was about. For instance, the second scene, in which Taema's seduction destroys Narukami's magical power, bears the title, 'The Actor trained in the *sutakora* System'. Here, the Japanese word *sutakora* (helter-skelter) is a pun on the name Stanislavski, implying that his acting system causes a lot of confusion."[47] The show ran for six weeks with Fukao Yoshimi playing the hesitant priest and Saitoh Ikuko the seductive princess, initiating a "Kabuki phase" in Suzuki's work from 1968 to 1971; during this time he mixed Kabuki texts with more modern texts in a "collage drama" format to answer Artaud's call for a Theatre of Cruelty. [Figure 3]

BREAKTHROUGH: KABUKI "COLLAGE DRAMA" (1968–71)

His next adaptation, *Donzoko ni okeru minzoku-gaku-teki bunseki (Folkloric Analysis of The Lower Depths)* is regarded by Suzuki as a forerunner of *On the Dramatic Passions II*, the work that would bring him his first major success two years later.[48] His actors were allowed to use whatever they wanted as improvisation exercises – poems, melodramas, even Tanizaki Junichirô's realist play *Okuni and Gohei* were brought in – and Suzuki provided the logic for their use by turning Gorki's doss-house into an asylum where the patients/actors amuse themselves with found texts.[49]

Figure 3 Princess Taema (Saitoh Ikuko) seduces the mountain-ascetic Narukami (Fukao Yoshimi). "The route to the mountain!" *Shite, shite, dôja* (*And Then, And Then, What Then?*) at the Waseda Shôgekijô Studio, 1968.

Possibly Suzuki found his rationale for this maneuver in the framing device used by Peter Weiss for *Marat/Sade*, a production widely reported in 1967–68.[50] However, Suzuki's adaptation remains distinctively his own. In Senda Akihiko's terms:

There's always something similar about the situation of the people Suzuki depicts on his stage. The miserable social outcasts who live in slum housing reminiscent of *The Lower Depths* are seeking for a way out of that reality but subconsciously know it can never happen. That's why they put as much of their unsatisfied passions into the dramatic fiction as they can, struggling night and day to realize their dreams, if only for a moment. These fictitious mind-games have much more weight and substance than real life through a kind of reverse energy – an energy that gives an unusual heat and shine to the stage.[51]

This was a fictitious mind-game in which Suzuki, his actors, and their restless, young, intellectual audience were all complicit. It was about the realities of the WLT, the realities of a generation experiencing "life after AMPO," and as attuned to the times as the lyrics of Bob Dylan and the Beatles on the other side of the world. It is also worth recalling that Suzuki had commissioned and directed the premier of Satoh Makoto's *My Beatles* the previous year, mixing memory and desire in a critique of imported pop culture and homegrown racial and sexual discrimination against a Korean schoolgirl in Tokyo.[52]

While the critic Asô Tadashi was generally favorable toward *The Lower Depths*, he made two telling criticisms of the production which Suzuki would acknowledge and work to rectify: "first, that the adapted materials were arranged randomly without a cohesive element to tie them together; and, second, that due to the actors' limited abilities, the scenes staged freely according to each actor's own style failed to achieve dramatic excitement."[53] By the time he produced *Gekiteki naru mono o megutte I – Miiko no engeki kyôshitsu* (*On the Dramatic Passions I: Theatre Lessons for Miiko*)[54] in April 1969, Suzuki had found a rationale in Surrealist *dépaysement* (dislocation or disorientation), fusing it with Zeami's ideas on acting and *honkadori* (intertextuality), and with Merleau-Ponty's theory of the phenomenology of the body.[55] And Shiraishi Kayoko, whose poor showing as the middle-class housewife of Betsuyaku's *The Little Match Girl* had drawn comment,[56] suddenly started to produce incandescent performances using these techniques.

On the Dramatic Passions I included scenes adapted from Iizawa Tadasu's neo-Kyogen *Hahaki* (*A Broom*), Ozaki Kôyô's Shinpa melodrama *Konjiki yasha* (*Golden Demon*), Betsuyaku's *Zô* (*The Elephant*), Kikuchi Kan's Shin-Kabuki *Tôjûrô no koi* (*Tôjûrô's Love*), Rostand's *Cyrano de Bergerac*, and the Kabuki classic *Kanadehon Chûshingura* (*The Treasury of Loyal Retainers*). These were framed as dramatic exercises set by an acting teacher (Tsutamori Kôsuke) for a young female student (Takahashi Michiko). Shiraishi was given roles in scenes from *Cyrano* and *Golden Demon*, and while she "was not terribly successful" as Roxanne, "turned around completely [as Omiya] in *Golden Demon*."[57] Her performance won her the appellation of "the mad actress of the Waseda Shôgekijô" (Waseda Little Theatre) for her portrayal of a woman driven to insanity by a loveless marriage. In Ôzasa Yoshio's words:

It's rare to see a scene which has such a distinctive sense of actual existence, although we're currently in a theatrical boom. Its vivid physical sense of condensation – as if the space itself is sweating – always makes the audience feel suffocated. In the epilepsy-twisted, agonized and yet humorous physical body of the crazy woman played by Shiraishi Kayoko, we experienced the dark forces of an irreplaceable existence . . . Her eyes were wide open yet crossed [in Kabuki fashion], her mouth cracked open in a leer, her cheeks twitching with extreme tension, and all of her fingers fluttering and trembling a little as if trying to clutch at empty space – in fact I was scared to watch.[58]

Senda Akihiko, in a lucid analysis of the development of Suzuki's theory and practice, which I quote below, concludes with a description of one more remarkable scene from this production:

It's rather easy to be radical and carried away by ideas, and Suzuki knows very well that this is often achieved when the lower body is forgotten. Against the "floating" quality of ideas, Suzuki and his company set "miserableness" as a sign of the lower body. This feeling is a consistent thread running throughout the drama he produces . . .

This "miserableness," in the form of theatrical expression, opens a fissure at many different levels of human existence. On Suzuki's stage, the upper and lower halves of the body – the conceptual and the physical, the conscious and the unconscious, dream and reality, script and body language – always have a big gap between them, though they are also entwined and in a state of tension and struggle . . .

Also important is Suzuki's unique method of creating a collage text. This method of construction – although he hardly includes anything of his own – makes Suzuki a new and unique type of theatrical creator. This aspect should be particularly foregrounded alongside his theory of acting . . . We can say that the dramatic and theatrical are twisted together intricately to produce a text with four levels of entry. These levels are also non-contiguous, and refract and critique each other in a pluralistic way to complete Suzuki's unique "theatre of the feet."[59]

Senda describes the first text as verbal (the "quoted" acting script); the second is the choreographed movements of the actor speaking that script; third is the layer of consciousness of the dramatic characters who speak and move. All three are harshly and deliberately dislocated from each other – and out of this "fissuring" the fourth text of dramatic criticism appears. Senda's description of the scene from *Tôjûrô's Love* in *Dramatic Passions I* illustrates how it works:

. . . there's a scary but stimulating scene I can never forget. The verbal text is taken from the scene at the climax of Kikuchi Kan's novel in which [the famous Kabuki actor] Tôjûrô makes advances to a married woman [in order to learn how to play an adulterous love scene in a new play], but the performance text is quite different – abnormally so.

In the adaptation, a retarded and possibly incarcerated adult brother and sister (played by Ono Hiroshi and Miura Kiyoe) were forced to act out *Tôjûrô's Love* for the entertainment of their female keeper and her guests. The two had collars round their necks and were chained. Obviously they desire each other strongly, but only during the time they act out *Tôjûrô's Love* can they come together. For this reason, the words of the play are spoken in whispers, vacantly, in a business-like but fragmentary manner that enables them to be close to each other for as long as possible.

However, the subtext of the words they spoke seemed to convey their sibling situation. Ono Hiroshi crawled on the floor like a chained dog, and stared longingly at his sister while he spoke in an expressionless, distracted, monotone whisper. It sounded weird: "As I recall – it was so long ago – it was in the autumn of your sixteenth year, when I was twenty; we danced that entire sequence of dances for the Gion Matsuri (Gion Festival) in that hut by the river."[60] When he started to whisper these famous lines, so strangely interjected into this incestuous relationship, a very vivid multi-layered chasm of possibilities opened up at the audience's feet.

The great distance between these beautiful and famous words (the first text) and the situation and posturing of the retarded brother and sister who recited them (the second text), contrasted with the very different subtext of passion that burned fiercely in the bowels of those two animals who spoke the words quite consciously but mechanically . . . This complex human scene – a scene between those who can't express their painfully vehement passions without playing-through such a miserable drama and those who can't find satisfaction without forcing others to play such games – emerged with critical sharpness from the complex chain of those unrelated elements to produce the fourth text.[61]

Suzuki's critical imagination is particularly keen, for Kikuchi Kan's portrayal of the famous Genroku Kabuki actor as an art-for-art's-sake realist was, ironically, part of an attempt in the 1920s to psychologize Kabuki in line with Western practice.[62] Suzuki himself describes his approach to the scene in this way:

In *Tôjûrô no koi*, even if I gave the script to the actors now, they would give it a psychological reading . . . They would kill it. That was why I tried in *Dramatic Passions I* to separate the lines from the concrete physical self-consciousness on stage. I was trying to cancel out their significance, and create a state of meaning in which there was no "correct approach" to lean on . . . I don't do a reading of the script . . . it's enough for the actors to remember the lines as a game . . . So the details emerge over time, gradually and in sudden spurts . . . One actor will have a different awareness from others, grounded in that actor's life history . . . The best action is to create a whirlpool of new material creation out of the old.[63]

This last sentence sounds as though Suzuki the economics student were remembering the famous adage about "gales of creative destruction" from Schumpeter's classic study of business cycles.[64] It was to remain another key feature of his developing artistic method.

After Betsuyaku had left the company in August 1969, Suzuki decided to commission a new play, *Shôjô kamen* (*The Virgin's Mask*), from Kara Jurô, a popular comrade-in-arms in the Little Theatre movement. Kara's interest in fantasy seemed to sanction the approach Suzuki's company had been taking with *Dramatic Passions I*, for his plays, like Suzuki's, might well be considered "*kabuki* brought up to date."[65] Kara had obviously attended performances of the Waseda Little Theatre (WLT) above the Mon Cheri coffee shop, for he sets his fantasy "in a subterranean coffeehouse called 'The Body,' which is owned by Kasugano Yachiyo, a former heart-throb of the Takarazuka all-female review." Unfortunately the aging process and a life of dissipation have separated the actress from her body (this is enacted by a Ventriloquist and Dummy) and when she meets Midorigaoka Kai, "a young virgin . . . eager for a life on the stage," the two can consummate their passion for each other only in an imaginary staging of *Wuthering Heights*. In this Shiraishi as Kasugano plays Heathcliff to an already famous guest-artist, Yoshiyuki Kazuko as Kai/Catherine. [Figure 4]

The overwhelming dramatic effectiveness of this central metaphor of a coffee shop called The Body run by actors is best appreciated physiologically, through James Brandon's description of WLT training in that space:

Knees flexed deeply, the actors circle the stage, stamping in time to the music [*Shinnai bayashi*, a popularized Kabuki melody]. Flat feet strike directly under the center of the body. There is fierce concentration. Every part of the body is held motionless except pile-driver legs and feet. The sound is deafening. We are on the second floor of this tiny building and with each rhythmic foot stamp, the whole structure bounces. (I think of the story of the bridge collapsing when a column of soldiers marches in step across it. I hope it's apocryphal.)[66]

The image of Shiraishi's superheated body dilated to the mythic proportions of the body/shop of a Takarazuka "goddess" is a Kara masterstroke. At least one reviewer at the time characterized the work as "like seeing the universe from the thighs," and, while pointing out how "Shiraishi Kayoko and most of his actors inhabit Suzuki's theory of acting very effectively," also observed that "much of the success of *The Virgin's Mask* was due to Kara Jûrô's script itself."[67] Indeed *The Virgin's Mask* won the Kishida Prize for Playwriting that year. Suzuki was successfully learning to calculate all the angles of his art.

His next project was *On the Dramatic Passions II* in 1970. This he subtitled *The Shiraishi Kayoko Show*, seemingly to answer Asô Tadashi's two criticisms of *The Lower Depths*, and probably to recall the

Figure 4 Love scene between the Takarazuka *otokoyaku* (male impersonator) Kasugano (Shiraishi Kayoko) and Midorigaoka (Yoshiyuki Kazuko). *The Virgin's Mask*, 1969.

shamanic/Takarazuka star nexus of Shiraishi's performance in *The Virgin's Mask*. In hindsight the magnitude of his overnight success with this production seems almost a foregone conclusion. It had been carefully and painstakingly prepared for by calculating what Suzuki, in his first collection of essays, *Naikaku no wa* (1973), would term "the sum of the internal angles." For him the objective application of training to performance was what made the difference:

The actor must be conscious of *kata* [the fixed exercise forms of training] as a reference line ... *Kata* exist as indispensable aids for an actor to use in objectifying his own body, but precisely because that is the case, their function is necessarily a negative, fictitious one. The relation of *kata* to the actor's true work is similar to the technique in geometry where, in order to prove that the sum of the interior angles of a triangle equal two right angles, one draws a reference line from the apex of one angle perpendicular to the opposite side. The *kata* form that reference line that assists each actor in his individual confrontation with technique, aiding him as he strives to attain a special awareness of himself as a performer. In a sense, the *kata* perform the function of a director in the world of Kabuki, where traditionally there is no such individual, for like the *kata*, the director's first purpose is to actualize the "drama" that the body of an actor holds as potential and to give that drama a specific form in relation to a given script and audience. Only through the mediation of a director or of the *kata* can an actor develop his own unique meaning. But in performance, the less the director or the *kata* are in evidence the better.[68] [Figure 5]

The show was a "smash hit" that drew high critical praise and ran intermittently for six years. Opening in May, the production was restaged with a "sequel" (*Dramatic Passions III*) in November–December, then toured with *Dramatic Passions I* to Osaka and Kyoto in May 1971. Its national success led Watanabe Moriaki to invite Suzuki and Shiraishi to attend the 1972 Théâtre des Nations Festival in Paris. Watanabe, a professor of French literature at Tokyo University, had been invited by Jean-Louis Barrault to put together a presentation of Japanese acting techniques with the famous Noh actor Kanze Hisao, the Kyogen actor Nomura Mansaku, and an unnamed Kabuki star. When the latter had to drop out because of other commitments, Suzuki and Shiraishi were asked to step in and represent modern theatre's reengagement with Kabuki. Their phenomenal success in Paris as Kabuki-style exponents of a new Theatre of Cruelty led to a full production at the Nancy International Theatre Festival in April 1973. It also inspired Grotowski to visit Japan that August.

This famous production will be considered in depth in Chapter Four. Suffice it to say here that being catapulted into international prominence

Figure 5 Actors dance off the stage and down the *hanamichi* (exit ramp) through their packed audience. *On the Dramatic Passions I.* Waseda Shôgekijô Studio, 1969.

provoked a crisis in the company, the issue being whether the success of the company was due to Shiraishi and Suzuki or to its ensemble approach. The question was kept squarely in the public eye by Sekiguchi Ei and ten other WLT actors who left the company on December 19, after the close of the fourth run of *Dramatic Passions II*. Calling themselves The Abandoning Group of the Waseda Little Theatre, they published a joint statement in *Shingeki*, a leading theatre journal: "No one should remain in a group when he realizes that the group is no longer sharing its original goal and solidarity . . . To us, artists with brilliant talents are not of the greatest importance. What is most important are the conditions and directions which germinate these artists . . . Until *Dramatic Passions II* the troupe belonged to everyone's hand [sic]. Now the more we recognize this fact, the more powerless we feel."[69] Forming a new company called Sôkû (The Running Dogs) they produced a Sekiguchi play the following year. Lack of success would cause them to disband five years later; however, the WLT had also sustained a setback and Suzuki was forced to suspend artistic activities for almost a year in order to regroup.[70]

Luckily a new cycle of "creative destruction" proved to be under way, firstly when Suzuki, Shiraishi, and Saitoh Ikuko traveled to Paris for the Théâtre des Nations festival and secondly when a group of young actors joined the WLT, inspired by *Dramatic Passions*.

SYNERGIES: FROM PARIS TO TOGA VILLAGE (1971–76)

The former event was a major turning point in Suzuki's career, bringing him into the international spotlight in a "workshop" attended by a host of theatre practitioners, including Peter Brook and Jerzy Grotowski. The organizer was Jean-Louis Barrault, now at the height of his fame, and this, too, had important ramifications. Although Suzuki's work with Shiraishi was one of the main talking points among practitioners and academics at the festival, the groundwork for their success had been prepared by a convergence of forces within European and Japanese theatre over the better part of a century; this was boosted by an intense interaction between two great actors, Barrault and Kanze Hisao.

Popular Euro-American awareness of Japanese theatre culture begins with the International Expositions held annually around the world.[71] One of the earliest, the Paris Exposition of 1867, had led to the formation of "La société japonaise" by the Goncourt brothers, Sarah Bernhardt, Emile Zola, and others, touching off a craze for *japonisme*. The cultural interaction between Japan and Europe has been highly productive over time, ranging from Camille Saint-Saëns's operetta *La princesse jaune* (1872); Katsu Genzô's Kabuki-style adaptation of Shakespeare, *It's a World where Money Counts for Everything* (*The Merchant of Venice*) (1885); Gilbert and Sullivan's *The Mikado* (1885); Kawakami Otojirô's adaptation of Henry Irving's *The Merchant of Venice* (1903); Puccini's *Madame Butterfly* (1904); Osanai Kaoru's production of *John Gabriel Borkman* (1909); Tsubouchi Shôyô's production of *A Doll's House* with Matsui Sumako in the role of Nora (1911); and André Antoine's *L'honneur japonais* (based on *Chûshingura*) at the Théâtre de France (1912) – to name but a few of the earliest. Its most fascinating theatrical manifestation may well be the acclaim given in Europe and America to two actresses, Sada Yakko and Hanako, who were both promoted by the American dancer Loie Fuller between 1899 and 1908. W. B. Yeats's adaptations of Noh in *Four Plays for Dancers*, and the production of *At the Hawk's Well* with Itoh Michio in 1916, are better known. So, too, are the *Lehrstücke* of Bertolt Brecht (1929–30) and the plays of Paul Claudel (French ambassador to Japan,

1922–26) which adapt elements of Noh to serve very different forms of nonrealist Western drama.

The history of this exchange of ideas and techniques is yet to be fully documented; however, one of the most fruitful must surely be Barrault's engagements with Kanze Hisao and, later, Suzuki Tadashi. The first extensive encounter was in 1960, when Jean-Louis Barrault's Compagnie de France toured Japan for a month with *Hamlet* and Claudel's *Le livre de Christoph Colomb*. Barrault's fascination with Asian forms of theatre largely came through Artaud, whose belief in the actor as an *athlète affectif* ("all physical activity has an analogous basis in the movements of the passions") had led Barrault to seek out traditional Japanese theatre forms at first hand: "In Tokyo our happiness was complete. What with the Noh schools, . . . our competing improvisations, . . . our close friendship with the Kabuki actors, and so on, I began to feel I was becoming Japanese, I must have been one in some other life. I made friends with a *shite* of the dynasty of the Kanze [Kanze Hisao]. I would gladly have gone through a course at the Noh school."[72]

Although he did not have time for lessons, he certainly did attend a demonstration of *Hajitomi* given for him on the Tessenkai stage by Kanze Hisao.[73] In discussion afterward, when Hisao had apologized for the undramatic nature of this contemplative, poetic play, Barrault had defended it, citing Greek tragedy to the effect that drama is a solution to the conflict between Man and Fate. Barrault's encouragement was deeply felt. In Hisao's words, "What he said was influential on us Noh players; we and the scholars became aware of the value of Noh in the modern world."[74]

Because of Claudel's long involvement with Noh, and his own deepening understanding of its principles, Barrault's production of *Christoph Colomb* was a stunning success in Japan. He had read and absorbed René Sieffert's *La tradition secrète du Nô*, an annotated translation of Zeami's theoretical treatises, and could appreciate how "[t]he style of our acting, completely Western though it is, is strongly related to theirs."[75] Knowing of the rupture between traditional Japanese theatre and Shingeki (Western realism), Barrault even went so far as to suggest that "[t]hrough our *Christoph Colomb*, they could . . . glimpse a possibility of joining up the two periods, which had been separated by a no-man's-land of more than a century . . . According to them, our style of acting gave them encouragement and hope."[76]

One of Barrault's interlocutors was certainly Kanze Hisao. Born into the oldest and most revered acting dynasty in the Japanese theatrical world, he was a descendant of Zeami,[77] the great fourteenth-century actor, playwright, and theorist, and had been active in a reform movement called "Renaissance in Noh" since 1950. This aimed to create a living Noh for the modern age. So great was the cultural cringe toward Western drama from the turn of the century that, despite initial attempts to modernize after 1868, Kabuki had suffered a failure of nerve and retreated to the safe ground of being a purveyor of traditional values for the middle class.[78] Noh had got into similar difficulties at the Meiji revolution because of its long-standing ties to the discredited Tokugawa shogunate. The efforts of Umewaka Rôkuro and state visits by the then Duke of Edinburgh, Prince Alfred, and President Ulysses S. Grant may have saved it from extinction when the new government, casting around for suitable official entertainment, decided Noh was the Japanese equivalent of Western opera.[79] However, Noh's reduction to museum status was deeply dissatisfying to a young artist wishing to extend his tradition. Barrault's visit in 1960 and performance of Claudel's *Christoph Colomb* were thus timely, provocative, and cross-culturally sensitive.

Weight was added to Barrault's opinions regarding Noh at the 1963 International Theatre Institute conference in Tokyo. Upon seeing him perform *ranbyôshi*,[80] Eugène Ionesco informed Kanze Hisao that "[t]he Noh . . . is an avant-garde play, and its production has permanence." The manager of England's National Theatre is also reported to have been similarly impressed.[81] In that same year Kanze Hisao won a French government scholarship to study with Barrault for six months in Paris, and performed at the prestigious Théâtre de France. The results of this collaboration soon became evident. Made aware of Barrault's "Brazilian" *Oresteia*, into which Pierre Boulez had integrated Noh music in 1955, Kanze Hisao organized in 1965 the first program of Noh ever given at the Herod Atticus amphitheatre in Athens. Then, between 1967 and 1971, he attempted to overcome the ghettoization of the Japanese theatre arts by engaging in a series of progressively more radical productions of W. B. Yeats's *At the Hawk's Well*.

At first it was enough to translate the work as *Taka no ido* (*The Well of the Hawk*) back into a performable Noh format (music, chant, and dance are integral parts of Noh). Then, dissatisfied with the mediocre results, Kanze Hisao and his Noh colleagues decided to try to stretch Noh in the direction of Yeats, now calling the play *Takahime* (*Hawk Princess*). Since Noh knows no director, this would require bringing in a Shingeki actor with a sensitivity to Noh structures (Hisao's brother Hideo). It also called for a mixed cast of Noh, Kyogen, and Shingeki actors. Because of the physical and vocal difficulties of integrating highly specialized performance styles, such a thing had never been tried before; however, it proved to be the most interesting – if not necessarily the most polished – version. The relative success of this venture encouraged the Kanze and Nomura brothers to set up the Mei no Kai (Society of Darkness) in order to engage in further experiments involving theatre artists from the different disciplines of Noh, Kyogen, Kabuki, and Shingeki. Their next productions were *Oedipus* (1971), *Agamemnon* (1972), *Waiting for Godot* (1973), and *Medea* (1975).

It is a sign of the cultural synergies of the time that, during the *Takahime* experiment, Kanze Hideo (who had been forced to abandon Noh when he started performing Shingeki) should also have been acting with Suzuki Tadashi on *Summer Drama: White Comedy* (1970), a collage of three Kabuki plays by Tsuruya Nanboku. Although Suzuki was too busy touring *Dramatic Passions* to take part, he probably saw the Mei no Kai *Oedipus* and took heed of the convergence between ancient Greek and traditional Japanese theatre. In Hisao's words, "The reason we picked a Greek play is possibly because of Jean-Louis Barrault. Noh and Greek drama have common ground between them, because their original theatrical characteristic is the confrontation between Man and Fate."[82]

In April 1972, not long after this laboratory production, the fruits of Suzuki's, Kanze Hisao's, and Barrault's intra- and intercultural experiments finally came together in Paris to sensational and far-reaching effect. For Suzuki both Barrault and Kanze Hisao would open up new ways of thinking about theatre. Barrault's Récamier Theatre was an old converted townhouse, "sober and simple, and what is more, the performing space had been constructed in a surprising way . . . In the middle of this space an unusual stage had been built, with steps leading up to an elevated platform on all four sides."[83] What particularly impressed Suzuki was the way in which the informal, intimate space worked to create a sense of collective experience, as if "all of the participants . . . had been part of a dramatic happening." The second surprise was the way in which Barrault's choice of space enabled, rather than hindered, Kanze Hisao's performance. Suzuki's description vividly evokes the excitement generated:

As Japanese people, we have the image in our minds that the *nô* is to be performed on a properly designed *nô* stage. The nature of that stage is fixed: it has four pillars, a bridge, a wooden back wall with the traditional pine tree design, and musicians seated in front. The word *nô* immediately suggests such a fixed scene. As presented in Paris, however, *nô* gave an altogether different impression. When Kanze Hisao and his brother put on *Dôjôji*, the crowd swelled around the stage, more and more people pouring in until they had crowded right up to the raised stage itself, so that the playing space was narrowed considerably.

As presented in this fashion, *nô* revealed a strength it never exhibits in Japan, and I remember how deeply moved I was by what I saw. Surrounded by spectators, Hisao, in his mask and costume, performed the final scene with all his might, to thunderous applause. In the midst of his huge audience, sitting, crouching, sprawling, witnessed by Frenchmen, Chinese, and Indians, this *nô* actor matched his voice to the rhythms of the music as he played on through the voices thundering their appreciation. I became conscious all over again of both the mystery and the force of the *nô*.

What I saw gave me enormous motivation . . . When a tradition can be successfully broken, the profundities of the *nô* can become all the more apparent . . . My experiences in France were very powerful ones, and upon returning to Japan, I harboured the dream of building a theatre similar to Barrault's . . . "Wouldn't this be", I thought, "the right environment for a truly contemporary theatre?"[84]

However, Suzuki had to wait four years to find exactly what he was looking for in the mountains of Toyama Prefecture. In the meantime he would continue to work closely with the Kanze brothers and Nomura Mansaku to realize their collective dream of a theatre *sans frontières*. Half of his time during these years was spent riding the wave of international success that exposure in Paris had brought him. In 1973 *Dramatic Passions II* was revived for a spring tour to Europe, and in August Grotowski visited the company to watch training. This had intensified in seriousness, partly as a result of international scrutiny, partly out of a newfound confidence, and partly from the need to train a new generation of actors, including Toyokawa Jun, Oda Yutaka, Shin Kenjirô, and Tominaga Yumi, who replaced defectors to The Abandoning Group of the Waseda Little Theatre. The matter was particularly urgent because of Grotowski's invitation to travel to Poland.

The other half of Suzuki's time was given over to new productions. He was increasingly being told that he could not go beyond what he had achieved with *Dramatic Passions II*. "However, I couldn't just leave it at that. Ever since, I've been thinking of ways to build up the logic of a group process which can reach that level again, even if only temporarily."[85] On return to Japan from Paris in 1972, Suzuki began rehearsals of *Don Hamlet*, an adaptation of Shakespeare in which a Don Quixote of the Tokyo slums mistakes everyone he meets for Hamlet or Ophelia.

Critical reponse was poor. Many inexperienced new members such as Oda Yutaka and Tominaga Yumi were involved, and the acting was generally considered weak.[86] Kanze Hisao, on the other hand, had began work with Mei no Kai on *Agamemnon*, which was performed at the end of that year. The general interest that this stimulated in exploring relationships between ancient Greek and traditional Japanese theatre led to the Greek National Theatre being invited to Tokyo in April 1974. Its largely realistic productions of *Agamemnon*, *Oedipus Rex*, and *Orestes* were coolly received. To the Japanese the Greeks seemed to have lost touch with their own theatre traditions. However, this served Suzuki well in December 1974, when, after more than a year of intensive training and script work, his adaptation of *Toroia no onna* (*The Trojan Women*) was presented at the prestigious Iwanami Hall. Kanze Hisao played the Old Man to Shiraishi's Hecuba, and Shingeki star Ichihara Etsuko played Andromache and Cassandra. Something of the theatrical sense of occasion is implied in Shiraishi's sense of awe for those with whom she was working: "I've been going to the theatre since I was young. I've never seen the Bungakuza [Literary Theatre] and Mingeiza [People's Art] theatre companies, but I did see Ichihara Etsuko. Whenever I watch her onstage, I get very excited. My blood boils. It's something to do with vital power – that's what I think."[87] And it was her own vital powers she was learning to harness by working alongside the best actors of the Noh and Shingeki worlds.

The Trojan Women is discussed in detail in Chapter Five. Here it is enough to say that it was undoubtedly the longest-running success of Suzuki's career, creating a new kind of audience for a physical approach to ancient Greek theatre which crossed sectarian lines, both at home and abroad. Takano Etsuko, the manager of Iwanami Hall, evaluated the success of this first production: "Fortunately, all seats for *Trojan Women* were booked out for the entire second half of the season. This allowed us to continue the run for an extra month. After a while audience numbers topped 10,000[88] and we refused group bookings." Takano gave three reasons for the production's success: first, that the press gave very full accounts of the performance, making it a subject of broad social interest; second, that it attracted the fans of very different segments of the theatre-going public who came to see Ichihara Etsuko (Shingeki), Kanze Hisao (Noh), and Shiraishi Kayoko (Little Theatre); and, third, that the whole cast, with Suzuki at its center, worked together to produce an inspiring and powerful staging. This, she felt, was partly to do with the production's long gestation (a year for development, three months for rehearsal). She recalls many invited guests at the preview questioning whether the actors could sustain their high-energy performances. Suzuki's response to the worried query was simple: "We've been practicing every day at this level of energy for three months, so it's not going to be a problem to sustain." Takano adds, "He had certainly calculated all the angles on these sorts of issues, training the actors to be at their peak by 7 o'clock when the performance commenced, and giving them just one day off a week. From the beginning he had decided not to have matinees, and not to perform twice a day. In this way the energy onstage built up daily over a two month run, and nobody collapsed from fatigue."[89]

The huge success of the production (from December 10 1974 to January 31 1975) was not something Suzuki could immediately exploit, for he was to take *Dramatic Passions II* to Poland in June 1975. Iwanami Hall was booked out for the following year, and the lease of the Waseda Little Theatre Studio – a hopeless venue anyway for a large-scale production like *The Trojan Women* – would expire in March 1976. The only answer was to travel, and again Jean-Louis Barrault came to the rescue by inviting the company to Paris in May 1977. Engagements in Rome, Berlin, and Bonn soon followed for June. At this time Kanze Hisao and Ichihara Etsuko were otherwise engaged. In many other companies this would have been a disaster, but Suzuki turned negatives into positives by having Shiraishi play both the Old Woman and Cassandra, as well as Hecuba. Her brilliant differentiation of the three characters and rapid onstage transformation between them did more than anything else to establish her in the eyes of the world as a great actress. Once again it led to a split in the company, however, as the young actors who had joined in 1971 left. After considerable Tokyo successes in Suzuki's *Yoru to tokei*, (*Night and the Clock*, 1975) and *Kagami to kanran* (*The Looking Glass and Cabbages*, 1977),[90] they had bonded with each other rather than with the older members of the company and were impatient to chance their luck as Shinkûkan (Thermionic Tube), a company dedicated to performance of Samuel Beckett's work.

However, this was not to be the end of Suzuki's association with the Kanze brothers, for they participated in the inauguration of his first Toga Sanbô (Toga Mountain Hall) theatre in 1976. Kanze Hisao would play Dionysus in Suzuki's premier of *Bakkosu no shinnyo* (*The Bacchae*) at the Iwanami Hall in January 1978 (tragically dying during the run), and Kanze Hideo would play Macbeth's double in *Night and Feast III* at Toga that August. And much later, for Suzuki's Second International Theatre Olympics at Shizuoka in 1999, Kanze Hideo would perform one of the greatest of all Noh plays, *Sotoba Komachi*.

The second major creative chain-reaction experienced by Suzuki in the 1970s was the decision by Iwanami Shoten, the publisher which owned Iwanami Hall, to set up a "think-tank" for artists and intellectuals. Encouraged by public interest in *The Trojan Women*, its aim was to coordinate a new wave of modern Japanese culture by bringing together prominent young artists and scholars to create Rei no Kai (The "Blank" Society). The resultant discussions and exchanges over a decade of monthly meetings were finally published in ten volumes by Iwanami as *Bunka no genzai* (*Culture Now*) in the 1980s. As Suzuki and Kanze Hisao successfully sought to open a working dialogue among theatre artists from different schools, so Rei no Kai sought to encourage a wider, more coordinated networking between arts and letters. A list of members, kindly provided by Takahashi Yasunari, reads like a Who's Who of Japanese avant-garde culture in the 1970s. In the group were the composers Takemitsu Tôru and Ichiyanagi Toshi, the novelists Ôe Kenzaburô and Inoue Hisashi (also a playwright), the poet Ôoka Makoto, the theatre director Suzuki Tadashi, the architects Isozaki Arata and Hara Hiroshi, the philosopher Nakamura Yûjirô, the anthropologist Yamaguchi Masao, the French literature specialists Watanabe Moriaki and Shimizu Tôru, and the English literature and drama specialist Takahashi Yasunari.

Ôoka Makoto had written original sections for Suzuki's *The Trojan Women* in 1974, Watanabe Moriaki was the Claudel specialist organizing Shiraishi's and Kanze Hisao's performances for Jean-Louis Barrault at the Récamier, Nakamura Yûjirô would co-author *Gekiteki gengo* (*On Dramatic Language*) with Suzuki in 1977, Isozaki would design nearly all of Suzuki's theatre spaces: the Toga Sanbô (Mountain Hall) and foyer (1980), the Toga amphitheatre (1982), the Toga Library/Studio (1987), the Mito theatre (1990), the new Toga Sanbô (Mountain Hall) (1995) and two mountain and two downtown theatres in Shizuoka (1996–97). Takahashi Yasunari was to act as dramaturg for Suzuki on a number of occasions, notably on his tour to Poland in 1975, and, in turn, Suzuki would stage Takahashi's *The Looking Glass and Cabbages* in 1977. Yamaguchi Masao was responsible for inviting Victor Turner to a theatre anthropology colloquium during the 1979 tour of *The Trojan Women* to Brooklyn College, New York, and to a 1981 symposium on "Theatre and Culture" at the Sôgetsu Hall in Tokyo during the run of Suzuki's Japanese-American production of *The Bacchae*. (The symposium included Yamaguchi, Takahashi, and Nakamura, as well as the Kabuki scholar Gunji Masakatsu.) And all of the above, with the inclusion of Ôe Kenzaburô, Inoue Hisashi, and Shimizu Tôru, would contribute significant newspaper, journal, and book articles on Suzuki's work in the coming years.

However, in 1976, when Suzuki took the momentous step of moving *away* from the center of Japanese cultural, political, and intellectual life in Tokyo to settle in the remote mountain village of Toga, his association with this artistic and intellectual support network was, for the most part, only just beginning.[91]

Inaugurating an age of decentralization

Ian Carruthers

GETTING OUT OF TOKYO (1976)

Suzuki has ironically referred to his move from Tokyo to Toga as "a long march," a strategic retreat "like Moses'or Mao's" into the wilderness of the provinces. It amazed many people at the time that, having achieved such success with *The Trojan Women*, he could apparently walk away. Suzuki certainly gives the impression that success was getting hard to handle. In his memoirs he writes:

> because of things like Ono Hiroshi's death [1974], I thought I would stagnate if I stayed where I was. I had already been accepted in Europe. And the same thing had happened to me as an artistic director at Iwanami . . . And then company members started falling into mannerisms as a result of being a group. My consciousness also became unfocused as I got more and more involved in social relationships . . . When things were going like this, I didn't feel like flowing with the stream. So I thought of getting out. Another reason, as I've said before, was that I wanted to work in the space of a mountain farmhouse (*gasshôzukuri*).[1]

The search for a festive space as efficacious as the Récamier theatre was one motivation. The other was the desire to achieve Malraux's dream of a center for artistic exchange which could produce new fusions between the traditional and the modern, Japanese theatre and world theatre forms. Most importantly, he had realized the impossibility of achieving these goals in Tokyo.

His dissatisfaction with Tokyo theatre is evident in this description:

> The audience and actors are conditioned to experiencing only the unusual in such a space, not to sharing the common feelings of their everyday lives. They get into a lift, and sit in mass-produced seats that can't be moved, and although they meet other people, they don't talk or eat together, and after the curtain falls, they just go home in a hurry without speaking. Theatrical community is only experienced in the time between the raising and lowering of the stage-curtain.

In other words, one might as well say that the experience of theatre has become that of private reading.[2]

Elsewhere he exposes the causes for the isolation he feels in Tokyo theatre-going:

If a discussion with an audience were to be planned after a play in Tokyo today, the promoters would have to hire the hall for the extra time required. This would involve a large sum of money and so pose economic difficulties. As for the spectators, if they missed their trains they would be forced to go home by taxi, and, since most of them live in the ever-expanding suburbs, the price would be prohibitive. In practical terms then, for reasons of economic efficiency, theatre can be performed only on a small scale and in as brief a time as possible . . . The luxury of leisure must be purchased.[3]

What Suzuki refers to here is the "donut phenomenon." Tokyo theatres are built on some of the most expensive real estate in the world, in the heart of the city. Their logic is centrist. However, disillusionment with pollution and housing costs has driven many residents to satellite cities from which they commute – often for an hour or more – to jobs or entertainment in the inner city. Thus the population density of central Tokyo, which comprises only those who sleep there at night, is comparable to sparsely populated areas of northern Japan, whereas the suburbs have the highest population densities in the country.[4]

Suzuki would later expose the capitalist logic which produces this state of affairs by ironically suggesting that Toga should become a National Theatre because "[l]and is cheap there." But he concluded that such an obvious solution would never occur to the bureaucratic mind. "If a National Theatre is in question, the familiar pattern of thought runs like this: in a truly national theatre, performances should be played next to the Supreme Court, facing the Imperial Palace and the Emperor." But, he argues, "such a centralization of administrative power isn't healthy. I think it would be better to inaugurate an age of decentralization."[5] Hence his attempt to "relativize Tokyo" by creating high-quality theatre in a marginalized part of the country.[6] Such spaces, he argues, can never be created in Tokyo. Because a relaxing, multilayered environment is so important, "a place must be chosen in the middle of nature, where people can feel free."[7] Basically what he was seeking was an environment conducive to greater audience interactivity in which spectators would spread theatrical time across the whole program: "The time of 'performance' lasts from the moment they leave home until the time they return back to their daily lives. If there is no play, there is no stimulus to action, but the play itself isn't the whole thing. More than half the total experience [of the Toga Festival] is left up to the audience to construct in their own way, and once it's finished, it can all be considered theatrical time."[8]

The relentless logic of high rentals for Tokyo theatre space means the cost of running a two-month international festival in multiple venues is prohibitive there.[9] Thus, according to Suzuki, "no plan for a festival in a large urban area in Japan has ever succeeded."[10] Obviously an old, disused farmhouse in a remote, depopulated part of the country would be much cheaper than the Waseda Little Theatre Studio let alone the Iwanami Hall, but who would want to go there? It took all Suzuki's debating skills to persuade his company that it was worth considering, and when they did agree to a trial period of five years, for most it was largely because their lease from Mon Cheri was expiring within the month and they had nowhere else to go.[11] Again it looked as though Suzuki were walking off a cliff – and yet he was remarkably in tune with economic logic and a major change in national sensibility which would eventually be reinforced by an advantageous demographic shift.

Japan's industrial revolution, part of a conscious program of "catching up with the West," had led to massive population shifts from rural areas to cities. In 1888 only 7.3% lived in cities of 50,000 or more. By 1980 this had climbed to 80%. The worst-hit areas were villages in remote mountain areas, the so-called "Snow Country." In 1940 the ratio of villages to cities was 9,614 to 178 respectively. In 1976, at the time Suzuki was moving to Toga, it was 635 to 644. In this context his move looks rash. However, by 1960, migration to the greater metropolitan area of Tokyo had begun to slow, and then, from 1962, it actually declined as those dissatisfied with the quality and costs of life in the big cities began to return to their hometown areas. The LDP government, which drew much of its political support from farmers through rice subsidy, was growing increasingly alarmed as the farming population dropped from 48.5% to 13.9% of the total population between 1950 and 1975.[12] Huge subsidies were given to depopulated villages in order to improve infrastructure in the hope that this would stem the tide of internal emigration, and, in 1970, a massive advertising campaign, promoted as "Discover Japan," was undertaken by Dentsû for Japan Railway to encourage tourism to remote, scenic areas. The program was so successful that in 1984 it was renewed as "Exotic Japan."[13]

Thus not only were there heritage buildings left abandoned in a growing state of disrepair, there were also tax concessions at state, prefectural, and village levels for those offering to occupy them. As Suzuki remarked of Toga in 1983, "The yearly budget of the village is over [US]$7 million, of which ninety-five percent is supplied by the central government."[14] Since Suzuki's ultimate goal was to set up an International Festival (a dream realized in 1982), he was able to attract large subsidies not only from the Japan Foundation, a national funding body for the arts, but also Toyama Prefecture and Toga village. All involved appreciated that an influx of initially 600 (and eventually upward of 10,000) cultural tourists once (and eventually twice) a year into a village of 1,200 inhabitants would boost incomes and increase business opportunities for young people wishing to stay or return.[15] So successful did the venture prove that a government film was made in 1985 holding up Suzuki's activities in Toga as a model for others, "Toga: Village for Theatre".[16] Of course all of this was premised on Suzuki's actually being able to attract a theatre-going audience out of Tokyo on a five-hour train ride and a one-hour bus journey which would necessitate at least one overnight stay before return.

Paradoxically the audaciousness of the move, at a time when Suzuki was in demand by the press, helped to generate "cheap advertising" and he was intensively reported "precisely because I went somewhere difficult to cover."[17]

At the time, however, Suzuki was reacting intuitively[18] and the risks were great. He describes how he heard about five *gasshôzukuri* farmhouses for rent in Toga and visited the village for the first time on February 12 1976 in the midst of record snowfalls:

In the snowfield, which was white as far as you could see, the tops of steep, black-beamed, straw-thatched roofs could just be seen above the snowline in falling snow. *Gasshôzukuri*, which means "hands together in prayer," is the perfect name for them. It looked like they had surrendered to nature's overwhelming power, holding their "hands" up to the sky in prayer. I stumbled over the snow on my hands and knees, as if I were swimming, and got into [one] house through the upstairs window. Inside were solid ranks of blackened, sooty pillars in sharp contrast to the white world outside. Those pillars were also very different from the newer ones in the village on the flat. They were thick and tall, and their natural sinuous lines were preserved. They looked rough but forceful . . . and I was impressed by a Japanese house for the first time . . . On the spot I made up my mind to turn that old *gasshôzukuri* into a theatre.[19]

The impression made on him was evidently as emotionally powerful as seeing Kanze Hisao dance *Dôjôji* at the Récamier – and it needed to be in order to sustain the effort required to survive there.

The inaugural performance took place on August 28 1976 on an improvised stage in a corner of the house to a packed audience. In Suzuki's words, "One can't imagine doing Noh, a folk dance, and modern theatre together [in Tokyo] . . . There's just too much institutionalized discrimination . . . However, in our first year we had Toga village *shishimai* [a lion dance], and Noh by Kanze Hisao with a full complement of musicians [*Tsunemasa*]. They performed in our theatre while we did a 'dirty beggar' play [*Night and Feast I*]. But no-one in the audience saw this as unnatural, though it had never happened before in modern theatre history."[20] Suzuki's own play was a collage of scenes from *The Three Sisters, Godot, The Trojan Women, The Bacchae,* and Oka Kiyoshi's absurdly right-wing *The Soul of the Japanese,* the extracts "remagnetized" as the memories and fantasies of three marginalized characters: an Old Woman, a Transvestite Clown, and a Military Officer. At the end of the play, the latter's irrelevance is underlined as, dressed in nothing but peaked cap and loincloth, he climbs up into the rafters while the music of Carl Orff's *Carmina Burana* blares and two beggars below monotonously play out a scene reminiscent of *Godot.* For Senda Akihiko the play examines social isolation in modern Japan and forces the audience to create their own dramas mentally.[21]

The audience came to the opening with the air of punters placing a bet, animated by apprehension at the possibility of getting soaked (it was the rainy season and their lodgings were half an hour away on foot)[22] and yet determined not to miss a thing. Suzuki had managed to reduce his risks by inviting Kanze Hisao;[23] he also cannily instituted a membership system which netted him "five years' entrance fees in advance from about 500 subscribers . . . At that time membership cost 15,000 yen with 3,000 yen for postage; so altogether it cost 18,000 yen." This all went on building repairs in the first year, however.[24] Many of the subscribers were close friends and fans: Iwanami Yûjirô (president of Iwanami Shoten), Ôkôchi Takeshi (manager of the Imperial Theatre), Kanze Hisao, Nakajima Kenzô, Kinugasa Teinosuke (the film director), Nakamura Yûjirô, Ôoka Makoto, Isozaki Arata, and Matsuoka Seigô.[25]

The time of year was also an important consideration. To gain maximum participation performances were scheduled at the height of the holiday season (July–August) when crops ripen, schools are out, and families flee the humid heat and smog of the big cities for the relative cool of the Japan Alps. At this time, aided by JR's "Discover Japan" advertising and the "hometown boom" (*furusato bûmu*) created by an urban Japanese "return to roots," the long journey to Toga could achieve the status of a secular pilgrimage, in which passionate theatre-goers might trek to Toyama to catch a glimpse, paradoxically, of an international, outside world unavailable in Tokyo. Not unlike Kanze Hisao with Mei

Figure 6 Above the lakeside amphitheatre designed by Isozaki Arata are, from left to right, the current Toga Sanbô, Isozaki's foyer, and the old Sanbô.

no Kai and Hijikata Tatsumi with Butoh, Suzuki was "aiming at a revival of darkness" in his *gasshôzukuri* theatre. For him, "Darkness, because it makes you feel the depths of nothingness, gives you the premonition that something ominous is about to happen . . . This pre-dramatic mood is the very ground of drama."[26]

With this in mind he asked the postmodern architect Isozaki Arata to help him relativize Tokyo and Toga by designing a modern entrance lobby to the renovated theatre-farmhouse. As Isozaki puts it, "Because audiences enter different spaces consciously to start with . . . I thought of contrasting the stage space with the lobby space."[27] Still later on, below this lobby overlooking a lake, Isozaki would build a ferro-concrete Greek-style amphitheatre. Its style and construction materials would again be different, but the tension and visual play set up between the two theatres and the lobby is thoroughly postmodern. And this is as appropriate to the great variety of international theatre forms that play here during the Toga Festival as it is to Suzuki's own collage style. [Figure 6]

However, in 1976 the renovation of the new Toga Sanbô (Mountain Hall) was four years away, and Suzuki was making do with what is now the costume storehouse, a corner of which he had converted, in a traditional way that required no structural changes, as a reverse Noh stage. As he describes it:

What's impressive about Japanese houses is that one can't help being sensitive to their atmosphere. Imagine that there's somebody behind just one *shôji* (sliding screen). You can sense it from the slightest movement of air or the sound of clothing chafing. If you get rid of *shôji* and *fusuma* (sliding doors) all the small rooms become one large one. People often remove these partitions to turn their houses into banqueting halls for public meetings and suchlike [as they do annually for Kurokawa Noh]. The point is that there are no permanently individual rooms, except for the bathroom, toilet, and maybe a closet.[28]

In conscious recognition of this custom, Suzuki's annual Toga productions from 1976 until 1980 were called *Utage no yoru* (*Night and Feast*) *I, II, III and IV*. The title helped to signal, in Japanese terms, his ideal of theatre as a community event. It was not dissimilar to what Welfare State were putting into practice in England – and indeed John Fox and his company would perform a festive, ecologically oriented adaptation of *King Lear* for the inaugural International Toga Festival in 1982.

Matsuoka Seigô was one of the first to recognize what the *Night and Feast* series was about. In an article describing forms of social gathering and entertainment in the Middle Ages, he lists *Ohban furumai* (a big feast), and goes on to add:

Someone who has been invited even once to a "night feast" at Togamura's thatched cottages in Toyama prefecture will understand what I mean without explanation. Suzuki directs banquets very carefully and stands up to his full height like one of the two Deva Kings, which makes him look as though he is putting more energy into directing a banquet than into theatre. If it were theatre, the audience could be relaxed because they are not onstage, but because it's a banquet, they are the focus of attention, the guests of honour, so it's harder for them.[29]

They, too, are engaged in performance. However, I can confirm myself that the initial formality breaks down quickly after performance with the onstage broaching of a vat of sake from which all are invited to imbibe.

FROM *ALICE* TO *SWEENEY TODD* (1977–81)

In his first five years at Toga, Suzuki did not sever all his connections with the outside world, but rather used them as a way of drawing national and international attention *to* his mountain base. Initially Toga was where he took his company to train and try out new productions which then transferred to the capital. All of the *Night and Feast* series were transferred to Tokyo in this way – first to the old WLT Studio (now called the Dramakan) and then, from 1980, to the new Ikebukuro Atelier.

In 1977 Suzuki presented Takahashi Yasunari's *Kagami to kanran* (*The Looking Glass and Cabbages*) at the Dramakan from March 22 to April 20. Takahashi had edited a special issue on Lewis Carroll for *Gendai shichô* (*Poetry Today*) in 1972, and this had touched off a Carroll craze, which led Suzuki to approach him for a play. Takahashi had agreed, but, with two books to complete for publication,[30] procrastinated until finally "kidnapped" and confined to a hotel room to write. In the author's words, "I worked away, as if spell-bound, and emerged after five days with a finished manuscript."[31]

Takahashi's idea was to combine the figure of the White Knight from *Alice* with Don Quixote. However, Suzuki changed his original title, "The Knight in Looking Glass Land," to "The Looking Glass and Cabbages," presumably to suggest not only the reversibility of illusion and reality (the looking glass) but also the impossibility of arriving at a "core" (cabbage). The consequence of this change, as Takahashi recalls, was that "[e]very morning someone had to go to the green-grocery to purchase twenty fresh cabbages for the show: four for the four actors to consume by the end of the play, and the rest to be sliced and poured down from above onto the stage just before the curtain. The peculiar smell of those nightmarish cabbages still seems to hang with me."

Professor Takahashi describes how, on the dimly lit stage, four shabby-looking men sat at a long table, chopping cabbages as they ate and talked. In the nonsensical, overheated conversation which followed, it transpired that everyone was called Alice. In his own words:

The thin, scary, bearded "Man A" (Toyokawa Jun) turns into the Duchess suddenly, and begins to moralize. After a few moments the conversation is switched over to the reminiscences of "the school under the sea" exchanged between Mock-Turtle and Griphon. This does not last long either, and the Mad Hatter's Tea Party takes over. Accompanied by the banal tune of a popular song, who should descend on a rope but a small fat man, who introduces himself as "Alice" (Oda Yutaka) . . . Man A, by this time possessed by Don Quixote, calls the little fat man "Sancho" and what follows is a dialogue between the Spanish knight and his servant Sancho Panza. But they soon dissolve themselves into the White Knight and Alice . . . Eventually a hole opens in a corner of the table, and the "real" Alice (Sugiura Chizuko) appears from the trap . . . However, she must run the gauntlet of "linguistic abuse" thrown at her by Tweedle-Dee and Dum, The Mad Hatter, and others. The men around her sing in chorus a ghastly variation of "Twinkle, Twinkle, Little . . ." It all fades into darkness. Alice is alone on the stage with a copy of *Alice* in her hands and begins to read the first paragraphs. Once again the lights are on, and we hear the drama's first scene (between Humpty Dumpty and Alice) repeated again. The audience is just about to imagine that the whole drama is going to repeat itself, when a patch of Spanish music bursts out, and a huge shower of cabbages falls from the flies instead of the curtain.[32]

Performances were packed to overflowing and the show had to be extended beyond its one-month run. The run ended on a slightly sour note when Fukao Yoshimi, Toyokawa Jun, Oda Yutaka, and six other members left the WLT a month later.

By 1978 Suzuki's program was becoming hectic. In January he was invited back to the Iwanami Hall to direct *The Bacchae*; for this he cast Kanze Hisao as Dionysus against Shiraishi's Pentheus and Agave (see Chapter Six). Then, at Toga in August, he produced an adaptation of *Macbeth* as *Night and Feast III* with Kanze Hideo playing opposite Tsutamori Kôsuke as "two halves" of a schizophrenic Macbeth (see Chapter Eight). After touring *Salome* (as *Night and Feast II* was now called) to Tokyo and Nagoya from October through December, he spent February and March preparing *The Trojan Women* for a three-month tour of the United States (Milwaukee, New York, Seattle, Austin) and Europe (London, Amsterdam). On return to Japan that June, the company took a short break before beginning month-long rehearsals of *Night and Feast IV* for the annual Toga performance in August. It too would transfer to the Dramakan in Tokyo from November 15 to December 22.

Some idea of Suzuki's growing dramaturgical assurance can be gained from a description of *Night and Feast IV*. This was an adaptation of Roland Topor's novel *Joko tanjôbi o iwau* (*Joko's Anniversary*), retitled *Katei no igaku* (*Home Medicine*).[33] Shiraishi was absent from the company for this production, hospitalized in Tokyo for suspected liver disease.[34] And so the young Togawa Minoru took center stage for the first time as Minoru, a psychotic young man tortured to death in his room by mysterious and violent intruders who look suspiciously like his alter egos. The play is unusual for its psychological realism; there are no scene breaks, no juxtapositions of jarringly different materials with different associational histories, written in different styles or genres. The prose is ordinary everyday speech and, unsurprisingly, concentrates on bodily functions, desires, and repressions. The setting is claustrophobically fixed and yet subtly unstable; it could be Minoru's room or his mind into which other people or figments of his imagination enter and from which they vanish mysteriously.

As in a Pinter play, little details gradually make us aware that beneath the air of normality in this Japanese house something is not quite right – for instance, the way Minoru's mother comes in with a cup of tea for him, but ignores his five guests. In fact the whole household seems both familiar and yet a little odd: the invalid father with his pot of glue and newspaper clippings, the mother obsessed with her silverware and her daughters' marriages, and the son who has a job as an insurance salesman but prefers to stay in his room and listen to music. Like many urban dwellers they have features that can easily be appreciated, such as their desire to win enough money on the lottery to leave "the newly built factories around here" for "somewhere warm in the south." As with Pinter, or *American Beauty*, the banal realities need to be firmly anchored in order to heighten the shocking violence and obscenity to come.

The mask of normality starts to come off as one of Minoru's five guests, the Woman (Sugiura), makes use of a portable toilet onstage. As Man 2 (Nikuma Eiji) hands her toilet paper, their scatological exchange is the stuff of masturbation fantasy; indeed, when they start to engage in erotic foreplay, the stage directions state that "Minoru stiffens. He moves his hand restlessly as if brushing off the surrounding Voices from his body. The movement also looks like masturbation." Into one ear Man 4 (Tsutamori) yells, "If you let out a scream, then Mother will rush in. And we shall all be in trouble." Into the other ear the Woman cries, "Stop! If you don't love me, stop! Stop kissing! Leave me alone. You are a bad man. I know it. But when I see you, I can't say no." This sounds like the territory of *Portnoy's Complaint*, with an anxious mother hammering on the door because her young son is taking too long in the toilet, but it has a more jagged edge; we are both inside and outside the fantasy, unsure of what is real and what is not, and therefore unsure how to respond morally and emotionally. The action becomes still darker and more frantic when Minoru and Man 1 get stuck together; "Professor Furuido" (Man 4) is called in, and Minoru, resisting wildly, is gang-stripped to his underwear. Hearing all the commotion, the Mother knocks on the door – and Minoru freezes. The released demons are temporarily bottled again.

Minoru returns to normality by putting an SP (45) song on his wind-up gramophone, "Kitaguni no haru" ("Spring in the North Country").

It seems to invite reflection on the past as Man 4 interrogates Minoru regarding his high-school worries about sexuality and anal retentiveness. Although Minoru takes himself very seriously, his five visitors are luridly unrepressed and *manga*-like, their manic energies alternately childish and thuggish. Their costumes also proclaim them to be stereotypical fantasy figures: whore, *yakuza*, playboy, colonialist in topee, and "Uncle Sam" in top hat, waistcoat, and comically short trousers. As Minoru screams, "Ah, it really hurts!," Professor Furuido pushes a huge syringe into his stomach and remarks, "It's a good sign. We have to awaken your ego, which is asleep in your body, and force it to create an antibody!" By this point Minoru is in a feverish state, dripping with sweat, and his psychosis takes an Oedipal turn; the four men and the woman tie a rope round his father's neck, hang him, and thrust his dead mother's body between his legs. Then, as Minoru mouths the words, they give voice to his thoughts about killing himself, and haggle with him about possessing his body in turn on a four-hourly basis. As the unendurably tormented Minoru screams, "I want to die! I want to die!," the patient professor tries to persuade him that he doesn't know himself, that "they" are only figments of his imagination and desire, and that his parents are not really dead. Minoru refuses to believe it, however, and after the professor's departure with his colleagues we are left with a final image of his mother's ghost rising from the floor to accuse the by now catatonic Minoru of murder. Behind her his nightgowned father swings from a rafter. [Figure 7]

What is disturbing about the play is that its unrelentingly violent and emotionally explosive physicality has forced the audience enclosed in this intimate space into physiologically experiencing what the world looks like from the point of view of a psychotic. Suzuki's achievement, like Meyerhold's with *The Magnanimous Cuckold* and *The Government Inspector*, is to have penetrated psychology by a purely physical route;[35] he makes the invisible world rise up, visible and terrible from the dark recesses of the mind/stage. In a chapter entitled "Aiming at a revival of darkness," Suzuki describes the way his *gasshôzukuri* space works to enhance this effect:

The new Toga Sanbô foyer consists of a hall that can be considered a modern western building and, from another point of view, a *gasshôzukuri* style of traditional Japanese house. Constructed of concrete, glass and plain wood, it lets in the light of the sky. When you pass through this space and progress along a little corridor, you enter the Sanbô theatre, in which the old farmhouse is constructed of massive black beams of wood and the stage floor of black anodized aluminum. The surface of this floor has an effect like lacquer. It collects subtle

Figure 7 The Doctor (Tsutamori Kôsuke) yells at Minoru, "I'll give you a shot with this syringe." *Night and Feast IV*. Toga Sanbô 1979.

lights, and sometimes magnifies objects like a mirror. The sharp and flat surfaces [of pillars and sliding doors] tighten the [rhythms of the] space, and I have the feeling that it can give birth to an atmosphere in which *kami* (gods) can manifest themselves in its dark recesses.[36]

Suzuki is speaking metaphorically here, for he adds, "Of course I do not advocate that the gods be called back again into the contemporary theatre."[37] As he has said often enough, the gods of the modern theatre are the audience, and in his plays "the audience is forced to create its own drama mentally."[38] In Anne Bogart's words, "Theatre takes place in the minds of the audience." [Figure 8]

By 1980 Suzuki had developed his actor training and refined his dramaturgical style in four experimental "Night Feasts." All of these explorations of unusually heightened states of mind would now culminate in a powerful bilingual revival of *The Bacchae* (aborted after Kanze Hisao's untimely death during the production's first run in 1978). In interview with William O. Beeman in 1981, Suzuki would now declare that, "As Merleau-Ponty pointed out, the word is an act of the body . . . In Japan the director and the writer serve the actor. The director is also

Figure 8 Frontal view of Isozaki Arata's Toga Sanbô with anodized
aluminum stagefloor. The *shôji* (sliding screens) have been removed
from the width of the playing space to reveal the backstage
passageway. Toga, 1980.

responsible for bringing out the latent power that resides below the
surface in an actor – something that the actor himself may not even be
aware of. In the Kabuki of Nanboku's time, the actors were in a very real
sense *shamans* . . . In order to restore this kind of mystical shamanistic
sense to the acting process, I have devised numerous physical exercises which help to restore magical power to the actor."[39] Emphasis was
shifting from raw importation of the theories of Merleau-Ponty, Artaud,
Grotowski, and Brook to the strategic value-added export of Kabuki-
style "shamanic" training[40] to meet the growing demands of an
American avant-garde.

Suzuki's *The Trojan Women* had moved and impressed international
audiences wherever it toured in 1977 and 1979; and training institutions
in three of the four American cities toured would invite Suzuki to initiate
actor-training programs. Initially, from January to March 1980 he gave
a semester-long workshop at the University of Wisconsin, Milwaukee.
The response from young actors such as Tom Hewitt was enthusiastic,
word spread, and from January to February of 1981 further workshops
in "Suzuki Method" were given at the Juilliard School and the University
of Wisconsin; and in 1982, also at the University of California, San Diego.

Beginning in 1988, month-long international training sessions were held every summer in Toga, organized by the Japan Performing Arts Center.

Part of the snowballing success of these workshops was due to Suzuki's readiness to mount a bilingual production of *The Bacchae* in 1981. This involved his actors working alongside twelve young American actors from the University of Wisconsin to give performances in Milwaukee (February to March), Toga (August 27, 29–30), and Tokyo at the Sôgetsu Hall (September 10–18). In between he accepted an invitation from the Imperial Theatre to direct the Prince/Sondheim musical *Sweeney Todd* for Tôhô from July 3 to August 30. Suzuki's casting of a star Kabuki actor, Matsumoto Kôshirô, created a buzz of excitement in different theatrical constituencies when it was learned that he would be played against Ôtori Ran, a former star male impersonator (*otokoyaku*) of the Takarazuka all-female theatre company. The object was to make money to help to fund the First International Toga Festival in the coming year. But it did more than make money; it publicized and popularized his avant-garde endeavors. In Senda Akihiko's words, "the show is very close in spirit to the works of the great Kabuki playwright Tsuruya Nanboku IV (1755–1829) . . . and Suzuki's direction is dynamic and intense," creating effects "close to the powerful atmosphere of the Brecht/Weill *Threepenny Opera* . . . The methods by which Suzuki has placed his production in the context of the oppressed people are extremely effective, and, in that sense, *Sweeney Todd* represents a natural extension of the Japanese director's own vision."[41] As Senda's examples indicate, Suzuki's approach was culturally bifocal, suggestive of both Nanboku and Brecht, and yet distinctively different from both. In May 1982 Suzuki was back in the United States, touring his bilingual *Bacchae* to New York, and *The Trojan Women* to St. Louis and Chicago as well as New York. By a process of gaining recognition at home through success abroad (*gyaku yunyû*), he was building a new national and international audience for Toga in the run-up to the opening of the International Toga Festival (July 24 to August 7).

THE FIRST INTERNATIONAL TOGA FESTIVAL AND ROBERT WILSON'S the CIVIL wars (1982–83)

Suzuki's "Night Feasts," which had been held every summer since 1976, were small affairs limited to one or two try-outs before the show went on to Tokyo for a six-week run in November. With Isozaki Arata's completion of a postmodern amphitheatre beneath the new Sanbô theatre in 1982, however, Suzuki could accommodate 900 spectators in two venues, and thus inaugurate a Festival. In Uchino Tadashi's words:

Historically speaking, the year 1982, when the first Toga International Arts Festival was held, was an important point of departure for theatre culture. As the festival was a rare occasion for postwar avantgarde theatre artists both from the East and the West to present their work . . . [a]udiences, including myself, were very excited about the sumptuous display of diverse and provocative visions, and were led to imagine theatre arts in the future tense. For critics like me, at least, the festival signaled the coming of an age of truly intercultural theatre . . . It was the first international festival in which mostly avantgarde theatrical works were presented to Japanese audiences.[42]

The inaugural Festival set the benchmark for all subsequent Toga Festivals and best indicates the range of Suzuki's interests. The foreign avant-garde were represented by Robert Wilson (Overture to Act 4 of *Deafman Glance*), Tadeusz Kantor (*The Dead Class*), Meredith Monk (*Education of the Girl Child*), and JoAnne Akalaitis (lecture/demonstration). The Japanese avant-garde included Terayama Shûji (*Directions for Servants*), Ôta Shôgo (*Komachi fûden*), and Suzuki (*The Trojan Women*). Festive community theatre was juxtaposed with John Fox's Welfare State International (*The Wasteland and the Wagtail*) and the Toga village Lion dancers. Traditional Asian theatre was represented by Dasho Sithey and the Royal Mask Dancers of Bhutan, Suresh Awasthi, K. N. Panikkar, and Noh and Kyogen artists from the Kanze and Nomura families. Into this exacting arena Suzuki would bring his JPAC training program for international inspection. Among the sixteen participants that first year were Robyn Hunt and Steven Pearson (instructors at San Diego), Jewel Walker (instructor at Wisconsin), and Eric Hill (Milwaukee Repertory Theatre). Suzuki was ably assisted by Suzuki Kenji.

Over the next eighteen years, the changing themes of the festival would allow Suzuki and his actors to work closely with kindred spirits they had met on their travels abroad. Although the festival was to "provide a theatrical window on the world"[43] for Japanese audiences, and a window on contemporary avant-garde theatre in Japan for foreigners, it was also intended to be a laboratory for actors. This is one reason why so many of Suzuki's company stayed with him for so long, despite the spartan living conditions and regime. Of those who joined the WLT during its seven-year "long march," only Sugiura Chizuko (1975–83) and Suzuki Kenji (1975–85) would leave within three years of the Festival's inauguration, the former to get married, the latter to start his own company, Theatre Group TAO.

The rest of his company would become his "old guard." They include Nakajima Akihiko (1974–94), Togawa Minoru (1975–94), Fueda Uichirô (1977–95), Takahashi Hiroko (1982–96), Nishikibe Takahisa (1983–96), Sakato Toshihiro (1983–98), Katoh Masaharu (1979–present), Takemori Yôichi (1978–present), and Shiohara Michitomo (1981–present). Alongside these were the veterans who had been there from the beginning: Shiraishi Kayoko (1966–89), Tsutamori Kôsuke (1966–present), and Saitoh Ikuko (1966–present; company manager from 1971). Their names – and those of two American guest-artists who remain "on call," Tom Hewitt (from 1981) and Ellen Lauren (from 1991) – will forever be identified with SCOT, the company which won worldwide acclaim from 1984 to 1995. These were undoubtedly the most creative years of the company, when, already confident of their internationally recognized skills as tragedians, Suzuki's actors would extend themselves to embrace the comic-grotesque as well.

Into this laboratory of the actor would come many avant-garde little theatre groups. Suzuki's interest in Indian theatre and dance was particularly strong between 1982 and 1984 and again in 1987 and 1994, when Suresh Awasthi and K. N. Panikkar, Sanjukta Panigrahi, the Chau dancers of Seraikera and of Purulia, H. Kanhailal, and Ratan Thiyam participated. Butoh and modern dance were on the agenda in 1988 with "Invisible Languages," an intercultural collaboration by Maro Akaji of Dairakudakan, Ruby Shang, and Bill T. Jones; and again in 1989 with performances by Ashikawa Yôko, Maro Akaji, and Teshigawara Saburô, the latter a truly exciting combination for dance enthusiasts (Ashikawa also performed in Suzuki's *Uncle Vania* and *The Bacchae* that year). Regional interest in China, Hong Kong, and Korea was a constant, their representatives seen six times between 1985 and 1994 before the BeSeTo (Beijing-Seoul-Tokyo) Festival was set up with Suzuki's participation to foster further cultural exchange between China, South Korea, and Japan. Companies from Brazil and Argentina were also invited six times, and from Australia seven times between 1988 and 2000. France, Poland, Russia, and the UK were also of special interest, although the lion's share of attention went to the United States, represented in thirteen of seventeen festivals.[44]

The collaboration between Suzuki and Robert Wilson, which also dates from the First International Toga Festival, has been profoundly significant for both men. Arguably Suzuki's example has edged Wilson toward adapting literary classics and working with actors who can allow themselves to be shaped like Edward Gordon Craig's *über-marionette* and yet maintain a strong magnetic presence. Wilson's visual esthetic

Figure 9 The Man (Robert Wilson) and The Woman (Sugiura
Chizuko) prepare to feed/kill their children, two of whom read
manga comics on stools while two sleep under futons. *The Prologue to
Deafman Glance*. Toga Sanbô. First International Toga Festival,
1982.

has likewise inspired Suzuki to direct with a cleaner sense of space and
greater attention to lighting and costume design.

Because of the shoestring budget on which the First Toga Festival
operated,[45] Wilson himself performed in *Deafman Glance* alongside Sugiura Chizuko from Suzuki's company. In the intimate space of the Sanbô
theatre, Wilson decided to multiply the postmodern tensions between
traditional Japanese space and anodized aluminum floor, by restaging
his play as an American and Japanese couple's double murder. Instead
of having Sheryl Sutton hand a glass of milk to her child and then calmly
kill him with a kitchen knife – the basic action of this 45-minute piece –
a father (Wilson) and mother (Sugiura) each despatch one of their children. The collaboration quickly suggested another. [Figure 9]

According to Janny Donker, Wilson had been approached by Robert
Fitzpatrick in 1981 to bring *Einstein on the Beach* to the 1984 Los Angeles
Olympic Arts Festival. However, knowing that Suzuki would be taking
The Trojan Women there, he had decided on a grander intercultural ex-
change. Donker confirms that at the end of the Toga Festival in August
1982, Wilson invited Suzuki to take part in his Los Angeles project. "As a

sequel to this, sponsors were persuaded to participate in the realization of *the CIVIL warS*."[46] Wilson's plan was for a twelve-hour "intercultural" performance of segments developed independently by him around the world in six cities: Rotterdam, Cologne, Tokyo, Marseilles, Rome, and Minneapolis.

The story of the project's failure is, as Arthur Holmberg suggests, a dismal chapter in American theatre history.[47] Funding had already been committed from Dutch, German, Italian, French, and Japanese sponsors when the project was canceled at the last minute on March 30 1984 in Los Angeles. This despite the fact that, by the end of 1983, the Rotterdam section had received its premier, the Cologne section (put together with Heiner Müller) had been given in January 1984, and the Rome section in March 1984. Only Marseilles and Minneapolis, set for April, lacked time to make presentations to their sponsors.[48] In Tokyo a five-week workshop had been held as early as April 1983 "in order to prepare a first draft version of the Japanese segment." In addition, a ten-day development rehearsal took place before this section was shown to its sponsors.[49]

Suzuki was instrumental in this process, both in finding the performers and in arranging sponsorship. Donker records that "*Nô* and Kabuki were [to be] represented by a single actor each, and there were two modern groups, Tadashi Suzuki's ensemble and the *Byakko-Sha* [Butoh] dancers."[50] Unsurprisingly, the Noh actor chosen was Kanze Hideo, a Suzuki comrade-in-arms in the struggle for a new Japanese theatre incorporating elements of old and new, East and West. As Donker rightly observes:

In Tokyo Wilson did not have to go through the laborious process of vocal training and posturing with his actors as he had been obliged to do in Rotterdam and Cologne. Apart from this, *Nô*'s unhurried, circumspect style of acting accords well with Wilson's theatre of slowly developing visual and acoustic understatement. Similarly, Kabuki with its spacious stage sets, sumptuous costumes and acrobatics is bound to appeal to the "nineteenth century" Wilson, who loves to stage panoramic scenes with a lot of people in them and does not shun a bit of artifice.

When Donker interviewed Kanze Hideo, he would quote Zeami to the effect that "[i]t doesn't do you any good to act on the basis of how you feel; you've got to act on the basis of how you look," a remark of which Wilson would surely have approved.[51]

Donker's account of the three scenes of the performance describes the surprise visit to Japan of a *marebito*, the overseas guest Hercules, mythical founder of the Olympic Games. He crosses upstage at speed as a tortoise crawls across downstage; then the Noh actor (Kanze Hideo) crosses in the role of an old man, followed by several young SCOT actors. Tiger Woman (Shiraishi Kayoko) sits motionless midstage while a child plays round her; then forty giraffes (made by Matsuno Jun) appear on long poles "in the fashion of Bunraku puppets." Finally Tiger Woman dies symbolically and her place is taken by Tiger Girl (Sugiura Chizuko) – perhaps suggesting the transmission of performance knowledge across generations, a major Suzuki concern derived from Zeami.

In the second part the civil-war theme is represented by contrasted scenes depicting the conflict between the Hunt brothers in nineteenth-century America and the Minamoto brothers Yoshitsune and Yoritomo in twelfth-century Japan. Abraham Lincoln watches the performance of a section of a genuine Noh about Yoshitsune (*Funabenkei*), danced by Kanze Hideo.[52] And the scene concludes with the arrival of Commodore Perry. In Scene 3 Kanze Hideo plays General Lee and Shiraishi is one of four actors to play Madame Curie.

Donker was fascinated to watch Kanze Hideo as General Lee and Shiraishi Kayoko as Madame Curie, remarking, "I was simply very much impressed by their acting."[53] It is hard to draw conclusions about the artistic effectiveness of an unfinished project such as this, but what is beyond question is the efficient way in which Suzuki, Kanze Hideo, and Robert Wilson worked to realize the Malraux/Barrault dream of practical avant-garde exchange across cultures. (The Butoh group took instruction from no one, and eventually decamped.)[54]

Over the next six months, with a brief break in September to perform *The Trojan Women* in his hometown of Shimizu, Suzuki would work on a spectacular version of *Clytemnestra*, retitled *Higeki: Atereusu ke no hôkai* (*The Tragic Fall of the House of Atreus*). It was premiered at the 1,900-seat Imperial Theatre in Tokyo from December 2 to December 26, and included the movie star Nagashima Toshiyuki as Orestes, ex-Takarazuka star Ôtori Ran as Elektra, Shiraishi as Clytemnestra, and a cast of seventy. The galaxy of talents drew 45,000 spectators, and this assured Suzuki of paying off his building-program debts, but this time the show was a critical flop. The space was so vast that, even with chest microphones, actors were often inaudible to audiences.[55]

SCOT: FROM THE LOS ANGELES OLYMPICS TO SHIRAISHI'S
DEPARTURE (1984–89)

The Trojan Women received a much better response at the Los Angeles Olympic Arts Festival in June 1984. So great was the publicity generated by the event and the critical acclaim given that Suzuki was once again in demand on the international festival circuit, spending much of the next five years touring the production to the United States, Denmark, Belgium, Greece, West Germany, Italy, Switzerland, Spain, South Korea, Hong Kong, France, Portugal, Holland, and Australia. For publicity purposes the company name was changed in September 1984 to the Suzuki Company of Toga (SCOT). With morale high after the Olympics, Suzuki was now able to hone the skills of a talented group of actors who would form the backbone of his company into the mid-1990s. As he comments, "When a group's unity is getting stronger, it sometimes happens that people start to develop a similar way of feeling and thinking . . . The reason is that, in order to create a group . . . they must first make a set of company rules. But when you see their performance, I am sure you will be able to see subtle but clear differences within their similar performance styles."[56] These differences would affect Suzuki's choice of productions.

The company was also developing international links. Of the many places they toured in these years, it was significant that San Diego, Athens, and Delphi would develop long-term associations. At the University of California in San Diego, Steven Pearson and Robyn Hunt helped to facilitate the building of the 100-seat Toga Studio Theatre in 1987 and, in return, would be granted free use of a well-preserved but disused high-school building in upper Toga. Here they could run a five-year Toga international summer-school program which centered on Suzuki Training but also gave students home-stay experience in the village and a range of other activities, including visits to the Festival.

The company's extraordinary physical approach to ancient Greek theatre was what ensured its lasting appeal in Greece. Athens would host *The Trojan Women* at the Herod Atticus amphitheatre in 1985 and 1986, *Dionysus* in 1995, and *Oedipus* in 2000. And for Delphi's International Meeting on Ancient Greek Drama, Suzuki would stage *The Trojan Women* in 1985, *Clytemnestra* in 1986, and *Elektra* in 1995. SCOT's link with Delphi, the home of sibylline prophecy, is evident from road signs which declare Delphi to be a sister city of Toga. The linkage has proved beneficial to both villages, dependent as they are on tourism, and Delphi's international conferences on ancient Greek drama have provided Suzuki with an important intellectual forum for his work.

Four other sets of events were remarkable in the period between 1984 and 1989. The first had to do with Suzuki's renewed interest in Shakespeare and Chekhov. After successfully performing Jizô in *The Trojan Women* in Los Angeles, Fueda Uichirô took the unusual step of asking to be allowed to play King Lear. When Suzuki agreed, an abbreviated but otherwise straightforward version of *King Lear* was produced for the Toga Festival in August (see Chapter Nine), alongside Jonas Jurasas's direction of Suzuki's company in *Three Sisters*. These productions mark the start of a new stretching of sinews for the company.

While touring the Greeks abroad, SCOT concentrated on Chekhov at home, Suzuki premiering *Three Sisters* in 1986, *The Cherry Orchard* in 1986, and *Uncle Vania* in 1988 to produce a cycle called *The Chekhov* (see Chapter Seven). *Lear*, however, which had no part for Shiraishi, was held in reserve until five years of summer-school training in Suzuki Method had produced American actors strong and mature enough to play it in 1988 as *The Tale of Lear*. This production was co-produced by four American regional theatre companies,[57] and toured the United States before going to the Toga Festival. Arthur Holmberg's review draws attention to the cross-casting, recognizing that "Tadashi Suzuki and Lee Breuer by a sexual sleight of hand are each shaking up the world's greatest play and forcing us to look at it with new eyes . . . Charles Lamb claimed that King Lear could not be acted . . . But Suzuki and Breuer have shown that it can be performed, and performed brilliantly."[58] After this American production and Shiraishi's 1989 departure, *Lear* would replace *The Trojan Women* in the SCOT repertory as the showcase for a now largely male company. Already by 1992 the ensemble work was so finetuned that, when I saw *Lear* revived in Toga for that year's festival, Suzuki stopped rehearsal after only ten minutes, declaring it "performance ready;" it was next run the night before the festival opening.

The second important event was Suzuki's appointment in 1988 as artistic director of the Mitsui Festival in Tokyo. Mitsui had helped to sponsor and organize the Japanese cultural festival in London to which *The Trojan Women* had been invited in 1985, and its president was impressed both by Suzuki's reception in England and his ability to run an international festival in Toga. Increasingly Suzuki was becoming recognized as an international director of standing and the leading exponent of a regional theatre movement in Japan. He was next invited to take on directorship of ACM (Acting Company Mito) in Mito City, in 1989; and then SPAC, the Shizuoka Performing Arts Center of Shizuoka Prefecture, in 1995, stepping up from village to city to prefectural level in the scale of his endeavors. Mito was a prosperous city an hour's express ride north of Tokyo which wanted to attract commuters with young families to a better lifestyle outside the metropolis. An hour south of the capital by bullet train, Shizuoka was Suzuki's home, but, more importantly, the fifth-richest prefecture in the country. It could thus offer Suzuki the kind of budget he needed to stage the Second International

Theatre Olympics in 1999; this was a major strategic objective in his battle to challenge the hegemony of Tokyo and restore the circulation of theatre culture throughout the Japanese archipelago.

The third significant set of events in these years was his publication of two major books: *Engeki ronshû: ekkyô suru chikara* (1984) and *Engeki to wa nani ka* (1988). The first, *Engeki ronshû: ekkyô suru chikara* (*Collected Theatre Writings: Energy that Knows No Boundaries*) (Tokyo: Parco 1984) would be selectively translated by J. Thomas Rimer and published as *The Way of Acting: the Theatre Writings of Tadashi Suzuki* (New York: Theatre Communications Group, 1986).

If *Energy that Knows No Boundaries* sums up a particular phase of activity between 1977 and 1984 when Suzuki was trying to relativize Tokyo's place in Japanese cultural life, then his next phase of activity, necessarily overlapping the other from 1980 to 1996, was increasingly international in focus, involving collaboration with foreign actors. Consequently, in the second volume of his theatrical writings from this period, *Engeki to wa nani ka* (*What is Theatre?*), Suzuki pares away many of his Japanese references in order to search for broader principles which could be shared with foreign actors taking Suzuki masterclasses in Toga and, increasingly from 1988, taking part in Festival productions. Often asked at this time whether he didn't think his Method might be *only* applicable to Japanese actors, he would wryly remark that he hadn't heard of Western critics loudly complaining that Stanislavski's was a peculiarly Russian system! It is unfortunate that the translation of *What is Theatre?* on which Suzuki and others worked in 1993 still remains unpublished, for it is a clearer introduction to Suzuki's work for foreigners than *The Way of Acting*.

The fourth significant event was Shiraishi Kayoko's retirement. The Toga premier of *The Cherry Orchard* in 1986, in which she played Ranyevskaia as an aging star wracked with regret for the loss of her childhood, was thus also her SCOT swansong. It was not quite her last performance, for *The Trojan Women* played around the world until 1989, but it was her last new work with SCOT.[59]

It was a testing time for Suzuki, too. He had already begun to operate another bipolar system, touring the Greeks while exploring Chekhov, and had even begun to add the latter to SCOT's international repertoire, touring *Three Sisters* with *Clytemnestra* to the Frankfurt Festival Theater der Welt and the Venice Biennale in 1985. But with Shiraishi's intentions known in 1986, the Chekhov trilogy planned for 1987 could not be realized until the following year when the great Butoh dancer Ashikawa Yôko was invited to play Sonia in *Uncle Vania*. As a guest artist Ashikawa was an invaluable drawing card, for Butoh, like Suzuki Training, was an international buzzword in the 1980s.[60]

One of Shiraishi's last public appearances in *The Trojan Women* was at the 1988 Australian Bicentennial in Sydney. The production was so well received that Carrillo Gantner of Australia's Playbox Theatre Company would invite Suzuki to Melbourne. With Shiraishi no longer available, Ashikawa's interest made it possible to tour *The Bacchae* to Melbourne and Canberra in October 1989 with Jim De Vita as Dionysus to Ashikawa's Agave.[61] This led to Suzuki being invited back to match his American production of *The Tale of Lear* (1988) with an Australian production of *The Chronicle of Macbeth* (1992). Thus, at the end of 1989, with a highly disciplined group of ten veterans still in SCOT, with a new company of young Japanese actors to train at ACM, and with many young American and Australian trainees graduating from JPAC, Suzuki did more than survive Shiraishi's departure. But the remaining question was whether his Method could produce another Shiraishi.

FROM MITO TO THE FIRST INTERNATIONAL THEATRE OLYMPICS (1990–95)

Suzuki took over the artistic directorship of ACM (Acting Company Mito) deeply affected by Shiraishi's loss, but determined to repeat his international successes. By changing the title of *The Bacchae* to *Dionysus – Sôshitsu no yôshiki o megutte I* (*Dionysus – On the Style of Loss I*) he reshaped the play as a sign of intention to move on. First he tried out a sultry film star, Natsuki Mari, as Agave for the opening of the ACM theatre (March 23 1990). Then he tried the SCOT veteran Takahashi Hiroko at Toga (July–August). But it was not until the ACM New Year performance in 1992 that he finally found what he was looking for in the performance of a young JPAC trainee, Ellen Lauren. For now Suzuki was making a fresh start with both a strong group of veterans and a young company in a brand-new space. As he put it in *What is Theatre?*, "We either have to create a new self not affected by our past, or we have to create a new situation where we can capture ourselves from a different angle and feel fresh beings again."[62]

Isozaki Arata's new performing arts complex for Suzuki in Mito was a stunning piece of postmodern collage, complete with a triple-helix tower of stacked tetrahedrons and a whimsical decentered fountain which flushed over a massive riverbed boulder suspended in mid-air by steel rods. The space also comprised a piazza, reception hall, restaurant, bookshop, modern art gallery, concert hall, and theatre – the latter a

Figure 10 The intimate Globe-style ACM Theatre, Mito, 1990.
Designed by Isozaki Arata.

very intimate space inspired by Elizabethan theatres. Isozaki had also
been a consultant for the Tokyo Globe in Shin-Okubo, the main site of
international Shakespeare performance in the capital, but, according to
Takahashi Yasunari, he was dissatisfied with that result and wished to
improve the intimacy of the actor-audience dynamic at Mito. As designer of the Toga Sanbô, Isozaki was aware of Suzuki's desire "to bring
the audience and stage into extremely close contact with each other, allowing the audience almost to feel the actors' bodies, so to speak." He
decided to attempt "to reestablish the relationship with the audience –
in the form of dramatic space – that had existed in the era that produced
both the Noh stage and the style of theatre represented by Shakespeare's
Globe Theatre."[63] The result was a beautifully elegant three-tier theatre-
in-the-round with a flexible thrust stage. [Figure 10]

The space certainly precipitated a renewed interest in Shakespeare for
Suzuki. After trying out his bilingual *King Lear* with Tom Hewitt and
SCOT at the Tokyo Globe in April 1989, he brought the production to
Mito in May 1990, thus allowing aficionados to savor the differences
between the two spaces before returning to the Mitsui Festival in Tokyo

the following week. Then, at Mito in January 1991, he directed *Macbeth – the Rise of the Farewell Cult*, in which the audience was invited to join in a lavish onstage banquet with both SCOT and ACM. Again in Mito the following month, he directed the young actors of ACM in *A Midsummer Night's Dream*, taking note of Isozaki's comment that "the textured wall surface, somber colors and lighting initiate the audience for a woken [sic] dream."

Isozaki's "waking dream" space would also inspire the two other parts of Suzuki's ambitious *Osarabakyô no ryûsei* (*The Rise of the Farewell Cult*) trilogy. In it he uses three great classics of Western theatre: *The Bacchae*, *Macbeth*, and *Ivanov*. For him these represented the rise to power, the overreaching, and the decline of an AUM Shinrikyô-style "New Age" cult. Since Suzuki devotes two sections of *What is Theatre?* to analysis of the different production styles needed for Greek tragedy, Chekhov, and Beckett,[64] I think the series can be seen formally as an experiment along these lines: "My concept of acting struggles with the problem of how to weave an experimental combination of the plethora of physicalities which are visible in modern everyday reality with those that engendered theatre like Noh or Kabuki, and questions whether or not this will enable me to make a whole new form of expression which can guarantee the endurance of such a combination."[65] At a public level "The style of Loss" was also part of an experiment in prerealist styles. For SCOT and ACM actors it was a test of their ability to shift gears from the high-energy, frontal approach of ancient Greek and traditional Japanese theatres to the fantasy-driven conversational style of Chekhov and Beckettian interior monologues (preserved as a fourth option in this trilogy by a *Cascando*-like liturgy used as the Farewell Cult's opening and closing article of faith).

One last expression of Suzuki's sense of loss and willingness to strike out in a new direction after Shiraishi's departure can be seen in *Sekai no hate kara konnichiwa* (*Grand Review – Greetings from the Edge of the Earth I*), first staged in 1991 (see Chapter Eight). This was a collage of scenes from many earlier Suzuki productions which together created a retrospective Japanese meditation on the dark legacy of World War II via *Macbeth*. Lady Macbeth is absent partly because V.iii and V.v are the only scenes quoted ("*Japan, my lord, is dead*"). However, a tape-recording of Shiraishi's performance of the role in *Night and Feast III* gives ghostly expression to these lines: "Wash your hands very clean. No, no, don't pull that face. Those people have all been buried. Don't you know they can't come out of the grave?"

In 1992, in the midst of a range of projects aimed at self-reinvention, Suzuki and Anne Bogart set up SITI (the Saratoga International Theatre Institute) at Skidmore College in Saratoga Springs, N.Y.[66] The agreement was that Bogart would direct an annual production at the Toga Festival in August, and Suzuki would transfer his Toga productions to SITI each September, with workshops in Suzuki Training and Viewpoints to be given in both places. Suzuki's *Dionysus* (with Ellen Lauren as Agave) and Bogart's *The Medium* (also including Lauren) were transferred this way. When Suzuki and Bogart became SITI's artistic directors, they agreed that the former would serve in that position for the first three years, and the latter for the next three. After three years Suzuki withdrew from being a co-director, but exchange/collaboration between the two companies endures, with SITI productions still being invited to the Toga Festivel and Suzuki still being invited to give open rehearsals in the United States by Bogart. SITI continues today as a highly productive base for Bogart's company.[67]

From 1993 to 1994, as part of his programatic exploration of the style of loss, Suzuki staged three remarkable productions of *Shinenakatta onna Julieto* (*The Juliet Who Couldn't Die*). The first opened at Mito in January and featured Ellen Lauren as an old woman remembering young love (*Romeo and Juliet*) while facing death in an *Endgame*-type situation. The second was a revised version at *Toga* in August, again centering on Lauren as a dying woman recalling young love *and* a failed marriage (as Masha in *Three Sisters*). For the Mito New Year performance in 1994, however, because Lauren was still on tour with Bogart's *The Medium* in the United States, a replacement had to be found. Suzuki's choices were either Takahashi Hiroko, who had played Masha in Suzuki's *Three Sisters*, or Fueda Uichirô as an aging transvestite "Juliet." That year Fueda was playing King Lear at Hamamatsu, Toga, and Saitama in the run-up to performance at the RSC's Barbican Center in November. Suzuki's decision to cast him as Juliet was a daring choice which made a startling but utterly absorbing contrast with the interpretation created by Lauren, and which aimed to stretch Fueda's artistic sinews to their limits.[68] In recognition of the darker erotic appeal he brought to the production (he had previously played a transvestite maenad in Suzuki's 1978 *The Bacchae*), the title was altered from *Juliet* to *Waiting for Romeo*. [Figures 11 and 12]

Suzuki's program from 1994 to 1995 was as frenetic as it had been in 1984 at the time of the Los Angeles Olympics. The central-heated 400-seat New Sanbô (Mountain Hall) now extended playing time in Toga beyond the summer months to allow Spring and Autumn Festivals. The

Figure 11 A male cross-dresser (Fueda Uichirô) fantasizes being
Juliet with a chorus of lovers. In his imagination he decks out the
wheelchair-bound male inmates of his hospital ward with red high
heels, revealing mini-kimono in bridal white, black bonnets, and
white umbrellas. *Waiting for Romeo*. Mito, 1994.

first Toga Autumn Festival in October 1994 was primarily a musical one.
It featured *King Lear* before its tour to the Barbican, but a longer-range
plan was already in motion for turning the SCOT *Lear* into an opera. This
had been proposed by the composer Hosokawa Toshio, who was invited
to see the stage play and a variety of possible musical partners. The
well-known concert violinist Urushihara Asako, who would work on
the project, gave an impressive recital, joined by the American soprano
Lucy Shelton, the vocal ensemble Vox Nova from France, and Ex Voco:
Fonetika Teatra from Germany.

The Spring Festival of 1995 was also special in that it saw Suzuki
nurturing the talents of four promising young Tokyo directors by providing them with festival space for the months of April and May. The
so-called "P4" group of companies were Kanô Yukikazu's Hanagumi
Shibai (Flower Group Players), an all-male cross-dressing group which
would tour a neo-Kabuki *The Tempest* to the United States later that year;
Yasuda Masahiro's Yamanote Jijôsha (Uptown Gossip); Miyagi Satoshi's
Kunauka (Not Yet A Science), a group fusing traditional and modern
theatre concepts; and Hirata Oriza's Seinendan (The Youth Group), a

Figure 12 "First sight of 'Romeo.'" An aging actress (Ellen Lauren) fantasizes being Juliet with a chorus of lovers. In her imagination she decks out the wheelchair-bound male inmates of her hospital ward with red high heels, revealing mini-kimono, black bonnets, and white umbrellas. *Waiting for Romeo*. Toga amphitheatre, 1993.

neo-realist company creating a new trend in "quiet theatre". Other young companies invited by P4 were Suzuki's ACM group, who produced an adaptation of Kara Jûrô's *John Silver* by one of their members, Hasegawa Hirohisa; and Shimizu Nobuomi's Gekidan Kaitaisha (Theatre of Deconstruction). The move created a fresh wave of interest in Toga, especially among the young.

It also gave Suzuki further collaborative opportunities. After seeing Miyagi's production of *Salome* at the 1993 Toga Festival, he had invited him to produce *Elektra* for the 1995 Spring Festival in May, and then to take part in a joint production of the play with SCOT for the Toga Summer Festival. The venture would culminate in performance at Delphi as part of the First International Theatre Olympics later that August (with Suzuki directing and Miyagi assisting). Kunauka's sensational dancer Mikari would play Elektra while another guest-artist, Takada Midori, would provide onstage percussion. For Suzuki much was at stake in this collaboration, for he would be hosting the Second Theatre Olympics in Shizuoka in 1999.

In August 1995 *Dionysus* opened the First International Theatre Olympics before an audience of more than 5,000 at the Herod Atticus amphitheatre in Athens; this was followed by Theodoros Terzopoulos's *Antigone* at Epidavros. Then, in Delphi, from 22 to 27 August, to coincide with the Eighth International Meeting on Ancient Greek Drama, performances were given of Heiner Müller's *Liberation of Prometheus*, Tony Harrison's *Labourers of Herakles*, Aeschylus' *Prometheus Bound* directed by Terzopoulos, Aristophanes' *Birds* directed by Yuri Lyubimov, Suzuki's *Elektra*, and Robert Wilson's *Persephone*. From Greece the company toured to Italy where they performed both *Dionysus* and *Elektra* at the Teatro Olimpico in Vicenza, again to enthusiastic reviews (see Chapter Six). But on return to Japan, Fueda announced he was leaving to start his own company, and a majority of ACM actors, faced with the choice of staying in Mito or transferring with Suzuki to Shizuoka, decided to remain in Mito.

THE SHIZUOKA THEATRE OLYMPICS AND BEYOND
(1996–2001)

The choice of most young ACM actors to remain in Mito rather than shuttle with Suzuki and SCOT between Toga and Shizuoka suggests to me a failure to bond with the older generation of SCOT actors, despite all Suzuki's provision of opportunities through mixed casting, in Mito, Toga, and on tour. Put the other way, the SCOT old guard was a tightly knit group with a strong *esprit de corps* which could be intimidating. What the company was experiencing, I feel, was a rift between generations that ran deep, not just through the company, but through the whole of Japanese society at this time.

SCOT values were formed in the early 1970s, whereas ACM's were those of the late 1980s. The former's members had grown up in the aftermath of World War II, experiencing political turmoil, privation, and hardship as well as the rewards of hard work. The young actors of the 1990s knew only the Japan of the Economic Miracle and the Bubble Economy years; without being particularly aware of it, they were weaned on the "throwaway" culture of conspicuous consumption. In some respects this parallels the American experience, in which, as Warren Susman argues, "the 'modal' personality type has changed from one of 'character', stressing order and discipline, to one of 'personality', emphasizing the idiosyncratic self." Self-discipline, deferred gratification and restraint are rejected in favor of "quick, glamorous money." The value-shift is from "impulse control" to "self expression."[69] Toga had generated its own spartan mind-set through communal dormitory living, rostered chores, struggle to maintain playing spaces against the harsh elements, and the art of "making do" with little; these were the very things the city-dwelling ACM actors came to resent as an intrusion on their privacy and self-expression. They voted with their feet for a freer, easier lifestyle in Mito City where they could spend their salaries on private apartments, and a variety of entertainment and leisure activities in between working hours.

In taking on artistic directorship of the Shizuoka Performing Arts Center (SPAC) from 1996, Suzuki was moving on from this experience. He was careful to train and perform in both Toga and Shizuoka in order to allow his young actors to appreciate the differences between rural and urban Japan. But he was also careful *not* to allow his old guard to maintain their exclusivity, indicating that they were there primarily to train the young. However, although training was as rigorous as ever, it must have been quite clear to the remaining SCOT veterans that, in the beautiful, well-appointed facilities of the Shizuoka "mountain base" at Nihondaira, with its tea gardens and breathtaking views of Mount Fuji, they could no longer be quite the same avant-garde company the Toga wilderness had tempered. [Figures 13 and 14] They were now training young actors who saw acting as a career rather than a vocation.

The First International Toga Festival had been Little Theatre-oriented in its programs run over two weeks. Now, seventeen years on, the Second International Theatre Olympics in Shizuoka, spread between

Figure 13 Aerial view of the Atelier Theatre (shaped like the cone of Mount Fuji, top left) and the Open-air Theatre (with its backdrop of trees, center), flanked by guest accommodation, the rehearsal halls, and the SPAC administration building (lower center). The Shizuoka Performing Arts Park, 1998.

Figure 14 Aerial view of the Toga Art Park of Toyama Prefecture, showing the SCOT facilities above the Momose River. From left to right along the riverbank are two dormitories, three guest chalets (for six visiting directors), the octagonal Studio theatre, The Volcano restaurant, and the lake which forms a backdrop to the Amphitheatre. Two very long *hanamichi* (entrance ramps) project out from the stage into the lake, left and right. Above this open-air theatre are, from right to left, the First Mountain Hall, Isozaki's foyer, the Second Mountain Hall, the administration building and rest house, the Third (centrally heated) Mountain Hall, and, top left, the guest house and company refectory/reception hall.

two "mountain" theatres at Nihondaira and two downtown venues in Granship,[70] was intercultural on a grand scale. It took place over three months, from April to June 1999, and was lavishly funded by the Prefectural government on a scale to rival Tokyo. According to one SPAC brochure, "the initial prefectural allocation as foundation money to SPAC was 500 million yen; by the end of 1998 [just before the Shizuoka Olympics], the annual target was 2,000 million yen." The Theatre Olympics was in danger of becoming the celebration of an older generation whose very success as avant-gardists had made them mainstream priests of high art: Olympians rather than young athletes. This can be seen by looking at the program list of participants.[71]

The paucity of opportunities for young artists has led Suzuki to set up the Toga Young Directors' Competition at the Toga Summer Festival in 2000. A number of classic texts from world drama are offered annually, ranging from Kishida Kunio's *Kamifûsen* (*Paper Balloon*) to Tennessee Williams's *The Glass Menagerie*. Entrants must present a complete production of one of a number of texts listed. Winners and runners-up, adjudicated by an international jury, are given the means to undertake full productions in Shizuoka which are then toured to Tokyo and elsewhere in Japan. In 2000 the winning presentation was of *Paper Balloon*, by a German entrant, Peter Gessner.

The period between the First and Second International Theatre Olympics (1995–99) was another watershed for Suzuki and his company in two particular ways. The success of *Dionysus* and *Elektra* at the first had been important for Suzuki as host of the second in Shizuoka. But Nishikibe's and Fueda's departures had precipitated the retirement of more SCOT veterans. Takahashi Hiroko left in 1996, and at about the same time Sakato moved over to administration before departing in 1998 . Only Katoh, Shiohara, Takemori, and Tsutamori would remain active in central roles.

The rapid thinning-out among SCOT veterans meant new opportunities for those who had crossed over from ACM to SPAC, principally Nakayama Ichirô, Kuboniwa Naoko, Tateno Momoyo, Nîhori Kiyosumi, Mishima Keita, and Kijima Tsuyoshi. When Fueda left, Nakayama was moved up from playing Regan to the title role, and *King Lear* was now entirely reworked as a double-fantasy. Mishima (who had played Cordelia in 1994) took over Katoh's role as Edgar and played it in a wheelchair, as Nakayama did Lear, to create a more grotesquely modern approach to the play. Nîhori, who took over as Regan, would work his way up through a succession of supporting roles to a leading one as Oedipus in 2000. Kuboniwa would create the role of Jocasta in *Oedipus*, take over Takahashi's role in *Greetings I*, and, with Tateno, another powerful female performer, produce a successful series of "sister acts" – as Street Girls in *John Silver* and Country Geisha in *Kachikachiyama* (*Mountain on Fire*).

Increasingly the most talented of the young SPAC actors were women and this was reflected in Suzuki's creation of many minor female roles for *John Silver*, as well as his choice of *Kagami no ie* (*House of Mirrors*) for 1998. This incorporated strong individual female roles to match the intelligence and skills of Kuboniwa Naoko, Fukami Keiko, Aiba Chisako, Takizawa Emi, Naruse Mihoko, and Matsunaga Miho. *House of Mirrors* was a collage of scenes from *Three Sisters*, *The Cherry Orchard*, *Ivanov*, and *A Doll's House*, and critiques an aging Chekhovian writer's confusion of his love-life and fiction. *Cinderella, Bride of the Vampire* continued this trend in 2001. It is difficult at this stage to predict whether the new SPAC company will be able to match the successes of the WLT and SCOT abroad, but Suzuki's commitment to the next generation of theatre artists is certain.

Another Suzuki project of national significance is the Regional Theatre movement he is currently developing through Theatre InterAction. This harks back to André Malraux's vision for the theatre (cited at the beginning of Chapter One). Founded on October 20 1996 with Suzuki as its first president and with theatre critics Mori Hideo and Kan Takayuki and scenic designer Takada Ichirô as executive committee members, Theatre InterAction has five main areas of endeavor:

(1) To facilitate a network for theatrical exchange between different localities, to organize such things as theatre festivals, and to promote events based in regional areas. (Regional Division)
(2) To promote theatrical exchange of productions and personnel internationally, especially through the formation of an Asian theatre network and theatre festivals on the basis of international understanding. (International Division)
(3) To establish a permanent rural infrastructure of public theatre management, led by theatre professionals, and to establish links with theatres already managed by theatre workers in many areas. (Theatre Division)
(4) To organize and manage independent theatre courses for the education of theatre professionals who will carry on such training activities. And to establish theatre schools in universities. These must be headed by prominent theatre specialists of proven experience. (Education Division)
(5) To ensure the proper functioning and accessibility of information necessary for the activities mentioned above; and magazine publication, or promotion of publications, which aim to disseminate theatre- or theatre-arts-related information in society, develop theatre theory, or promote theatre education. (Information Division)[72]

The organization has been successful in galvanizing the Japanese theatre community, especially its younger members. Prominent among its division heads are the young directors of P4, with Hirata Oriza heading the International Division, Miyagi Satoshi the Information Division, and Kanô Yukikazu the Executive Committee.

Points (1) and (3) above recognize the strategic importance of the direction Suzuki has taken in developing regional theatre programs independent of Tokyo. According to Takahagi Hiroshi (manager of the Tokyo Globe in 1994–5) the problem is that, despite the plethora of regional theatres built in the "bubble economy" 1980s, local governments still face indifference from theatre professionals who prefer to remain "at the center" in Tokyo rather than go "into exile" in the regions. Takahagi believes that two solutions are needed. One involves sending capable young regional staff abroad to train as arts administrators, the other is an interim "company in residence" program whereby local governments contract Tokyo companies to work in Fukuoka, Nagoya, or elsewhere for a number of years. But the staff of Theatre InterAction know that these can be only short-term solutions. There are already talented artists in the regions whom the Tokyo-fixated media still do not adequately report. Supporting local talent through the Toga Young Directors' Competition is thus a vital priority. So, too, in the eyes of the Theatre InterAction management, "the most urgent issue in the Japanese regional theatre scene is the need to find its own way creatively rather than learning from abroad."

Point (2) recognizes a general national policy shift, in which Japanese cultural exchanges with Europe and North America are still respected and encouraged but in which more focus than ever before is being given to exchanges within ASEAN countries. The BeSeTo Festival, set up between China, South Korea, and Japan, reflects a burgeoning regional interest that aims, according to the Festival program, to encourage "Asian theatre people to get to know each other's cultures, work together for deeper understanding, and help overcome a general decline in human communication in the world today."

Point (4) underscores the stark fact that, until recently, Waseda University was one of only a handful of Japanese universities offering a full program of courses on Japanese theatre leading to a BA. The implementation of Theatre InterAction policies has meant that more universities are now hiring prominent theatre specialists, such as Ninagawa Yukio and Senda Akihiko, as teachers.[73]

Now that he has become an elder statesman of Japanese theatre, invited as a Visiting Fellow to give the 2002 Donald Keene Memorial

Lecture at Columbia University in New York (April 30), Suzuki recognizes, above all, the need for professional training as well as recognition of Theatre Studies as an educational subject. For him, "The real problem, practically speaking, is that today's actor does not have a system of training."[74] Too much of youth theatre is about bonding with audiences of the same generation through a socializing process. "The relationship is one in which the actors express themselves to confirm their position within the homogenous group, and the audience see them as self-affirming."[75] Thus they lack the self-awareness that comes through exposure to the gaze of people with quite different natures or cultures.

Suzuki reflects back on the situation of Noh and Kabuki artists in order to link intracultural national experience to the positive aspects of modern intercultural exchange. "Noh and Kabuki," he asserts, "were quite the opposite [of 1990s Japanese groups such as Noda Hideki's]. For them [in the fifteenth century] the audience were people with very different natures, and from different classes.[76] In other words, for them the audience was not a means by which they verified their homogeneity, they were being presented with feed-back by socially unrelated people of a quite different nature . . . Thus the conscious power of self-objectification becomes stronger in this environment."[77]

For Suzuki self-objectification and theatre training work together to build artistic individuality. It will be of more than usual interest to see what comes of his collaboration with the Moscow Art Theatre on *King Lear* in 2004.

3   Suzuki Training: the sum of the interior angles

Ian Carruthers

Since 1972, when Suzuki first began to develop a system of physical training, two journal articles, a book chapter, and two thesis chapters have attempted to describe it.

The earliest and in some ways still the most interesting is James Brandon's account of fifteen days of training at the Waseda Shôgekijô (Waseda Little Theatre) Studio in 1976.[1] The best known is certainly Suzuki's own "The Grammar of the Feet," first published in *Engeki ronshû: ekkyô suru chikara* (1984) and translated by J. Thomas Rimer in *The Way of Acting* (1986). Surely the most comprehensive treatment, however, is Gotoh Yukihiro's, based on the Toga International Training Class he took in 1985.[2] Paul Allain's and Kevin Saari's accounts from the 1990s are also valuable as personal responses to Suzuki Method at one remove or two from Suzuki himself. Allain took a twelve-day workshop run by Ellen Lauren at Vicenza in 1995 during Suzuki's tour of *Dionysus* to the Teatro Olimpico.[3] Saari gained his workshop experience with SITI instructors at Saratoga Springs, N.Y., in 1997.[4] Like Brandon I came to Suzuki from a background in Noh and Kabuki training (1986–93), but have been fortunate enough to observe Suzuki's training and rehearsal process integrated, with Australian actors in *The Chronicle of Macbeth* (1991–92) and SCOT actors in *Waiting for Romeo* (1993). My own training was with Deborah Leiser-Moore in 1992 and with SCOT in 1993.[5]

From all of these accounts, a reasonably clear picture can be presented of the development of Suzuki Training from the mid-1970s to the late 1990s – almost the whole span of his activities. I shall first consider some principles of Suzuki Training in relation to the above accounts, and then go on to a detailed description of a selection of disciplines to illustrate further principles.

70

FIRST PRINCIPLES

Brandon was the first to recognize that "[h]ere was a serious, concerted and carefully thought out attempt to bridge the awful gap between traditional and modern theatre that is the despair of so many performers" (30). However, his enthusiasm for noting the Kabuki and Noh elements that Suzuki recycles has led some later commentators to gloss over what is original in the training. Brandon has rightly noted that "the WLT is following attitudes toward learning a 'way' (dô) and the strict master-pupil relationship that are typical of traditional arts of all kinds in Japan" (31). But this is only half the story.

Suzuki was at pains to point out to Brandon in 1976 that his knowledge of Noh and Kabuki came from reading and performance observation only: "We don't copy the forms (kata) just as they are. We aren't learning to perform Kabuki. It's the feeling of the particular form that I try to teach, so the actor can revitalize that marvellous physicality that comes from Noh and from Kabuki" (32). He was also concerned to emphasize that he calls his training exercises "disciplines" (kunren) because "[a]nytime an actor thinks he is merely exercising or training his muscles, he is cheating himself. These are *acting* disciplines. Every instant of every discipline, the actor must be expressing the emotion of some situation, according to his own bodily interpretation" (36). He clarifies this in "The Grammar of the Feet" by insisting that "the actor composes . . . on the basis of . . . sense of contact with the ground."[6] Since, as we shall see, the disciplines all relate to the possible ways in which the feet can make contact with the ground, what they give the actor is a heightened physical awareness of the way foot positions can generate sensibility. In a now famous passage, Suzuki asserts:

the way in which the feet are used is the basis of a stage performance. Even the movements of the arms and hands can only augment the feeling inherent in the body positions established by the feet. There are many cases in which the position of the feet determines even the strength and nuance of the actor's voice.[7]

This, of course, is against the logic of realist acting (although not of dance theatre anywhere in the world); a typical taxonomy of the realist view can be found in Julian Hilton's *Performance*:

We may divide the concept of movement as a function of character into three main parts: expression (which involves facial movement), gesture (involving head, torso and hands), and locomotion (the legs). These categories are in descending order of significance . . . The legs are naturally the least expressive part of the body.[8]

Naturally, from a Eurocentric, realist point of view, but Hilton's thinking is dangerously "universalist" in its narrow assumptions. To name but a few forms, it would exclude Noh, Kabuki, Butoh, Beijing Opera, Kathakali, Balinese Topeng, commedia dell'arte, the theatre of Meyerhold, and a host of other non-European and even prerealist European ones such as melodrama.

Suzuki was also at pains to guard against formalistic closure (the very thing restricting the continued growth of Noh and Kabuki). When Brandon asked whether "your disciplines have 'correct' forms (*kata*)", he pointed out, "It's not whether the outer form is right or wrong. [But does] the outer form express the emotion or feeling? And does it do so fully, with power?" And when Brandon countered, "You often tell an actor he isn't doing a discipline properly," Suzuki laughed and admitted, "I do. When it is wrong for *that* actor. Actors' bodies are all different and the motion one person finds in a discipline will be different from the emotion another finds. So you can't say one form is correct . . . That's what the disciplines are for, to give him [the actor] strength and control he can use *as he wants*" (37, my italics). Beauty is not a conscious aim for Suzuki; he is equally happy working with the grotesque (as we shall see in his treatment of Nanboku and Chekhov). Nor is relaxation the royal road to artistic expressivity. Brandon's query about the "great tension" found in Suzuki's disciplines provoked this response:

Well, it may seem like that. Suppression [*tame*] is fundamental to traditional Japanese theatre. What do I mean? Expression in Japanese theatre isn't natural or real. There is nothing natural about a *mie* [squint-eyed pose] or the leaping *roppô* [flying in six directions] exit in Kabuki . . . So there is this almost unbearable tension in the actor . . . using unnatural movements and voice to express natural emotions . . . The Kabuki actor engulfs the spectator in his overwhelmingly dynamic stage image. *The secret of this kind of acting is instantaneous release of suppressed action, then suppression . . . and so on . . .* I suppose you call it tension, but it is not muscular tension, it is psychological tension. (40, my italics)

Anne Bogart, whose SITI company has learned much from Suzuki, clarifies the above "secret" in her chapter on "Resistance": "Compression makes expression possible . . . The Japanese word *tameru* in Noh drama defines the action of holding back, of retaining. *When you feel ten in your heart, express seven* (Zeami)."[9] In practical terms, Bogart explains, "It is actually more challenging to find the necessary resistance for an 'easy' task . . . Sitting in a chair, for example, might be considered easy. How do you create resistance, or something physical, unbeknownst to the audience, to push against while sitting in a chair?" (143–44). (Bogart had seen Suzuki's solution to "doing the energized act of sitting" in Toga, and the reader will find it described by Peter Curtin in Chapter Eight.)

While Bogart and other practitioners such as Yoshi Oida and Eugenio Barba have firmly grasped the principle of *tame* and been able to apply it successfully to their own creative work in non-Japanese contexts, exoticism has proved a stumbling block for some. J. Thomas Rimer's translation of Suzuki's *Ekkyô suru chikara* (*Energy that Knows No Boundaries*) as *The Way of Acting* has tended to obscure what Suzuki's original title aimed to clarify. As Suzuki has said of the training in 1995:

You can do it either the Japanese or the American way, both of which we have cultivated. Americans still think Japan is exotic. So, first of all, I show Americans that we're not exotic but ordinary. We explain that our style is a little bit different, but that it can supplement their own practices and possibly create a new fusion.[10]

This bifocal approach can be seen in a number of places in "The Grammar of the Feet." Carefully balancing the ideas of Gerhard Zacharias's *Ballet* (1964) with – but not against – those of Origuchi Shinobu, he works in an inclusive "both/and" mode rather than exclusively "either/or," affirming yet again that "[a] Japanese actor has no special claim to success . . . , any more than anyone else."[11] And the success of his work with American actors such as Tom Hewitt and Ellen Lauren – not to mention Anne Bogart's successful "fusion" of his training with "Viewpoints" in the United States – would seem to bear him out. But Suzuki, like Stanislavski before him, is aware that use of a training method does not guarantee success; ultimately the individual's imaginative application and talent are decisive.

In showing his awareness that powerful foot stamping was "originally used to magically ward off evil," as Origuchi Shinobu claims, Suzuki is equally aware that, in the contemporary world, its usage is simply to "eradicate the ordinary, everyday sense of the body" (11) in order to build a powerfully expressive stage presence. The legend of the goddess Ama no Uzume's release of the Sun Goddess from the heavenly rock cave by exorcistic stamping on an upturned tub (interpreted by Origuchi as a summoning of spirit-energy in a *tamafuri* rite) suggests to Suzuki, as it has to others such as Carmen Blacker, that shamanic techniques have greatly influenced the development of Noh. In Suzuki's words, Noh's special stage "includes empty jars implanted underneath the floor . . . to help in the calling forth of the spiritual energy [*tama*] of the place, a summoning of the ancestral spirits to come and possess the body of the performer in a kind of hallucination" (14). But Suzuki is not atavistic; for him, "the [actor's] self must answer to the desires that other people place upon them . . . The actor's role can be compared to the role of a 'shaman' in this respect."[12] He knows that the strongest contemporary "possession" is likely to be consumerist. This he ironically signals by arming Chekhov's three sisters with department store shopping bags when they pine for Moscow, and by placing large cylindrical red-and-white Marlboro ash-cans on the stage of his *The Bacchae*. As Heiner Müller puts it pithily in *HamletMachine*, "Heil Coca-Cola."

Hence Suzuki's postmodern training and acting style need a performance space that is both ancient and modern, or neither ancient nor modern. Isozaki Arata's renovated farmhouse, the Sanbô theatre, with its high-tech anodized aluminum dance floor, is reminiscent of but significantly *different* from a Noh space. The latter has its one point of stage entry and exit along the *hashigakari* (raised walkway); however, Suzuki's Toga Sanbô ingeniously and economically "consists of two walkways which themselves serve as the playing space. In between the forward and rear walkways, a flexible partition-like structure (*shôji*) is installed" (23). Any of these shutters, whether paper, wood, or reflecting/opaque glass can become an exit or entry point. His playing space aims to optimize continuous flows of movement (elsewhere he has referred to the director as "a traffic conductor"[13]): "It is my view . . . that a modern man, who has no place to call his own and whose gods have departed, lives best on the kind of stage I have constructed. All of us, at all times, everywhere now seem to live a life of composed passages" (24).

Such a flexible playing space, in which architectural structures frame and accentuate actor rhythms and proxemics, is well suited to Suzuki's postmodern style of performance.

Nevertheless, despite Suzuki's evident bifocality, commentators such as Allain and Saari have too often assumed monofocal "either/or" positions. The confusions of Allain (who is unaware of Gotoh) are particularly evident in two apparently contradictory claims: the first, that "[Ellen] Lauren has recontextualized and thus reinvented the Suzuki Method. It has developed a long way from what Brandon described as a 'training system that is especially Japanese'" (86–87); the second, that "[t]here may be 20 years between the two accounts [his and Brandon's] . . . but there is surprisingly little difference between them" (77). Had he read Gotoh's account, these discrepancies might have been avoided; certainly Lauren herself would never claim to have "reinvented the Suzuki Method," although Saari's record of her alleged remark that "Anne Bogart uses Viewpoints to build a show and Suzuki to maintain it" may have compounded Allain's difficulties. For Bogart's creative use of Viewpoints and Suzuki Training is uniquely her own, although SITI's success has shown it to be a combination highly compatible with American needs.

However, what no Western commentator has yet satisfactorily explained is why Suzuki's company did not need and does not need Viewpoints in order to create efficaciously. The question was first raised in print, and tentatively "answered" by Saari's dissertation supervisor, Professor Andrew Tsubaki (who had attended Toga training in 1983):

While watching Kevin Saari's workshop on Viewpoints, a thought hit me to illuminate the reason why SITI needed Viewpoints training while SCOT [did] not . . .

The answer is rather simple. Most Japanese who work in Suzuki's system are quite familiar with traditional training systems in many performance, martial arts, or other art forms in which physical exercises or even some mental functions are directed by the pattern [kata] set up by the discipline being engaged in. You seldom question why you are doing this or that; you know it is good for your work and will help you in what you need to do. They can concentrate on the assignment given to them and work on it diligently to acquire that discipline as fully as possible. That will keep them busy and satisfied.

On the other hand, the Western actors training in the SITI environment will not be as satisfied as their Japanese counterparts if whys and what-fors are not clearly explained. Even after they understand the reasons why they are doing the Suzuki system, they [may] feel some emptiness in their minds after a while due to the repetitive nature of the Suzuki system . . . bound by one-directional control forced by the leader . . . This will seldom happen to Japanese actors in SCOT due to their lifestyle.[14]

Put another way, working within the improvisational frameworks provided by Viewpoints, the actors are free to create their own choreography; this Bogart will shape with Suzuki's energy- and concentration-raising disciplines. Since the actors have created it themselves in the Viewpoints phase, they are more committed to it, more willing to stay with the shaping process, through all its rigorously repetitive refining. However, this answer is *too* simple. The irony is that Suzuki *also* works like this – as SITI members Akiko Aizawa, Will Bond, Leon Ingulsrud, Ellen Lauren, Kelly Maurer, and Tom Nelis can attest, for all of them have performed with Suzuki (two as full-time members of SCOT) before joining SITI. In brief, Suzuki demands that his actors creatively develop their *own* work in the initial stages of rehearsing a new play – but not, of course, when they're taking over an established role. (SCOT's repertory system requires that other roles be as little disturbed as possible for reasons of economy.) From Suzuki's point of view the matter boils down to a question of professionalism. In the words of Katoh Masaharu and Leon Ingulsrud, "People often ask what the difference is between Australian and Japanese actors. On an artistic level, such a question is a nonsense! Those who are good are those who have overcome the same sorts of problems. The bad are bad anywhere."[15]

Saari, too, gets into difficulties with his claim that the Suzuki technique "is not improvisational: it relies on mastering essential, immutable forms . . . These are only rarely created by the actor" (179–80). It needs to be pointed out that the training *does* balance mechanical and improvisational disciplines, as I aim to show, and that the forms are not immutable – some have been discarded, others added. Moreover, the *forms* of the training disciplines (*kunren*), which are intended to put the actor in touch with the body's expressive possibilities, should not be confused with rehearsal creativity (*keiko*). The forms provide a "grammar" of the feet – but not a "vocabulary." Saari has clearly never seen Suzuki in rehearsal giving actors "homework" for presentation the following day. For example, the Sleepwalking Scene described in *The Chronicle of Macbeth* (Chapter Eight) was initially choreographed by its three actors "after hours," but finetuned in rehearsal by Suzuki.

Gotoh is more accurate in noting Suzuki's strategic shift from description of his disciplines as tapping "the Japanese actor's . . . deeply buried . . . racial consciousness of the body" (227) to an "'operational hypothesis' allowing actors [in general] to feel fully 'fictional' on stage" (230). This shift was obviously needed as Suzuki Training began to draw interest abroad and Suzuki's productions of *The Bacchae*, *Clytemnestra*, and *The Tale of Lear* accommodated increasing numbers of American actors. But while presentation of his disciplines has been culturally modified to satisfy the Western demand for technical explanation rather than personal discovery, and while certain disciplines have been phased out or new ones included, the principles informing them have remained constant. Between the times when Brandon and Gotoh took training (1976–85), disciplines such as "Ladder," "Impro walk," "Squatting," "Kneeling" and "One-legged squat," were dropped and "Arm," "Sitting positions," "Statues," "Slow-motion walks," and *"Echigojishi"* ("Lion dance of Echigo") added. Moreover, Brandon's "Five Walks" had become Gotoh's "Nine Walks." However, between Gotoh and Allain (1985–95), little more than "Arm" and *"Echigojishi"* appear to have been dropped and a new "Pivot/Slice" added. This would seem to suggest that Suzuki had sufficiently articulated the training for his own purposes by about 1990.

The development of Suzuki Training

BRANDON 1976	SUZUKI 1984	GOTOH 1985	CARRUTHERS 1991–98	ALLAIN 1995
Disciplines marked with an asterisk involve voice work:				
Basic stance		Yes	Yes	—
*Ashi o hôru**		Yes	Yes	Yes
—		*Fumikae*	Yes	Yes
—		—	*Kunjitsu*	Yes
5 Walks:		*9 Walks:*	*11 Walks:*	*10 Walks:*
Ashibumi	(Yes)	Yes	Yes	Yes
Uchimata	Yes	Yes	Yes	Yes
Waniashi	Yes	Yes	Yes	Yes
Sotomata	Yes	Yes	Yes	Yes
Tsumasaki	Yes (photo)	Yes	Yes	Yes
Impro walk	—	—	—	—
—	Yes	*Yokoaruki 1*	Yes	Yes
—		*Yokoaruki 2*	Yes	Yes
—		—	Side stamp	Yes
—	Yes (photo)	*Suriashi*	Yes	Yes
Shikko	Yes	Yes	Yes	Yes
—	—	—	Backward	—
One leg	—	—	—	Yes
Metal ladder		—	—	—
Backbend		*Agura**	Yes	—
—	—	Fast arms	—	—
—	—	3 Sitting positions*	Yes	Yes
—	—	Statues (Sitting)*	Yes	Yes
—	*Bacchae*	Statues (Standing)*	Yes	Yes
—	*Bacchae*	Slow-motion walk	Yes	Yes
Stamp and *Shakuhachi*	Yes	Yes	Yes	Yes
Kanjinchô	Yes	Yes	Yes	—
—	—	*Echigojishi 1–5*	Yes	—
Recombined:				
Squatting*	—	(part of *Ashi o hôru*)		
Kneeling*		(part of *Agura*)		
—	Crouching	—	—	—
—	Crawling	—	—	—
—	Leaping	—	—	—
—	Tumbling	—	—	—
—	—	—	Pivot/Slice	Yes

If we need any reminder that "the Suzuki training method and the Suzuki style of presentation are different,"[16] a glance above will show that Suzuki has no disciplines for "Crouching," "Crawling," "Leaping," and "Tumbling" – although he has referred to all these forms of movement in "The Grammar of the Feet" and we find these forms given magnificent artistic expression in *The Trojan Women*, particularly in the scene following the Greek rape of Andromache (discussed in Chapter Five). Suzuki Kenji's animalistic leaping and tumbling and his colleague's dim-witted crawling and crouching perfectly delineate their characters; however, since these stage actions are ungrounded, they are unsuitable for training purposes.

THE DISCIPLINES

The amount of time devoted to training annually has varied considerably over the life of the company. Brandon noted that the WLT gathers "four nights a week, after working at their [day] jobs . . . [for] an hour,"[17] and that was still about the length of time allotted to training during rehearsals in the 1990s when I was visiting SCOT; however, it was not continuous throughout the year. Because of the many jobs demanding company attention in the lead-up to the Toga Festival, for example – from box-office duties and bump-in of guest-artists' shows, to restaurant roster, to props, wardrobe, and lighting duties – training is an individual matter in the first weeks. Once the initial mundane tasks of cleaning, repairing, and mowing have been carried out, and rehearsals started, a two-week period of group training helps to focus the company before the pace of general preparation becomes too severe in the immediate run-up to the Festival. Suzuki likes to call his training "a blood test" because each actor must use it to diagnose his or her quotidian state. All of the company take part, unless unavoidably assigned to other duties, and all train in groups, in order of seniority for "The Walks," male and female veterans first, followed by male and female inductees and foreign guests.

Training during rehearsals often starts with "Stamp and *Shakuhachi*," but, as Brandon has noted, not all the disciplines are performed every session. I will describe them in the order presented at the Melbourne training-audition for *The Chronicle of Macbeth* in September 1991 (adding "Basic stance" at the beginning and "*Kanjinchô*" at the end because of their historical importance):

1. The Three Basics for Center of Gravity:
    i) *Ashi o hôru* (Side stamp) – with Voice
    ii) *Kunjitsu* stamp – with Voice
    iii) *Fumikae* – with Voice

2. Slow-motion walk (*Tenteketen*)
    ii) Slow-motion *Tenteketen* with Statues
3. Stamp and *Shakuhachi*
4. The Three Sitting positions
    i) Sitting positions – with Voice
    ii) Sitting statues
    iii) Sitting statues – with Voice
5. Standing statues
    ii) Standing statues – with Voice
6. Walks:
    i) *Ashibumi* (Stamping)
    ii) *Uchimata* (Inward walk)
    iii) *Waniashi* (Pedaling)
    iv) *Sotomata* (Outward walk)
    v) *Tsumasaki* (Tiptoe)
    vi) *Yokoaruki 1* (Side slide)
    vii) *Yokoaruki 2* (Side cross step)
    viii) *Ashi o hôru – ichi ni* (Side stamping)
    ix) *Suriashi* (Sliding walk)
    x) *Shikko* (Squat walk)
    xi) All the above backward
7. *Kanjinchô*

When training complete beginners, before going into the "Three Basics for Center of Gravity," instructors often explain the "Basic stance" position. This is Brandon's Discipline 4.

Basic stance

The upper body is held relaxed but straight, with eyes fixed straight ahead in a soft but intense focus which allows use of peripheral vision without turning the head.[18] Arms hang relaxed by the sides, fingers closed lightly into fists as if holding poles parallel to the floor. The center of gravity is slightly lowered as knees are flexed, heels centered under hips.

    This represents what was described in the Melbourne training workshop for *Macbeth* auditionees in 1991. Brandon does not mention any of the above but records Suzuki as teaching two basic postures: *koshi o dasu*, in which the pelvis is "thrust out behind," which lifts the chest and tucks the chin (Noh posture); and *koshi o ireru*, in which the pelvis is "tucked forward," which straightens the spine and centers the upper body over the hips (Kabuki posture). By 1985, when Gotoh attended training, Suzuki seems to have dropped the Noh posture.

Between the hips (*koshi*) lies the *hara* (the psycho-physical center) just below the bellybutton. To create a sense of "presence," the actor needs at all times an artificial sense of "resistance" in the *hara*. It is the home of the breath, the platform on which we place our torso, the center of gravity. The fundamental importance of this center, used for centuries by Buddhist and Shinto priests and exorcists, samurai, and itinerant performers is evident in 1976 from the fact that Suzuki lectured the WLT "several times a week" on it. Today, however, it gets much less individual attention, although all discussion on subsequent disciplines relates back to it. "Basic stance", although physically relaxed in the upper body, is not a flabby stillness. Suzuki describes the actor in this state as like a racing car at the starting line (or a Boeing 747 on the runway just before take-off): engines are revving at high speed but the brakes are on. The actor's stillness is really a state of highly energized "restrained motion." Two equal energies – one driving forward, one restraining – are balancing out. In this sort of theatre, any series of movements is a balancing act between a force which drives forward and a force which holds back. Nowhere on stage is this tension completely relaxed. As Kanze Hideo has said, "Energy . . . is the consequence of tension between opposing forces."[19] In Japanese performance tradition this state is called *hippari-ai* ("to pull something or someone towards oneself while the other person or thing is trying to do the same").[20]

One of the mental images given to help the trainee find the necessary resistance-energy in the *hara* is that of the actor as a puppet (*pace* Edward Gordon Craig): one string pulls upward from the crown of the head, another pulls down from the pelvis, a third draws forward from the bellybutton, and a fourth restrains from the small of the back. All these imagined lines of force help to build resistance in the center. With practice the actor can get into this charged state instantly just by going into the "Basic stance" (the "ready" position), but the trainee needs further disciplines to help to build deeper awareness of this sensibility.

As Barba notes, this *hippari-ai* can be found, on the one hand, between the upper and lower halves of the body and, on the other, between the front and the back. In relation to the former, one of Zeami's *dicta* is "[v]iolent body movement, gentle foot movement; violent foot movement, gentle body movement."[21] The image of a swan or duck is used to convey this idea to actors; under water its feet may be paddling furiously, but above water it appears to glide effortlessly (the opposite effect of "active mind/still body" is achieved in the Noh *iguse*). The tension between front and back is based on Zeami's *mokuzen shingo* aphorism, "the eyes look ahead and the spirit looks behind."[22] There is also, Barba notes, *hippari-ai* between actors and musicians as to who "leads" and who "follows" (Suzuki tells his actors not to "follow" the electronic music but give the effect of "producing" it). Still another form of *hippari-ai* occurs between actor and audience (addressed by Ellen Lauren in Chapter Eight). Lest the above be thought of as only of interest to the Japanese performer, it is worth emphasizing that Eugenio Barba's and Nicola Savarese's *A Dictionary of Theatre Anthropology: The Secret Art of the Performer* shows how "this principle . . . is also part of the Occidental performer's experience" (12). To see how, of course, the actor must be able, in Suzuki's and Bogart's words, "to light a fire under the stereotype."[23]

Since body and mind are a psycho-physical unity (the word *kokoro* includes mind, heart, and spirit), their play of oppositions structures both meaning and feeling. Suzuki's "stop" is as profoundly attractive as the Noh *iguse* (a state in which the dancer's body stops dancing while the mind continues the dance). Herein lies the fascination of W. B. Yeats's poem "Long legged Fly":

> That civilisation may not sink . . .
> Our master Caesar is in his tent . . .
> His eyes fixed upon nothing . . .
> Like a long legged fly upon the stream
> His mind moves upon silence.[24]

And behind Yeats, of course, stands Zeami:

Sometimes spectators of the Noh say that the moments of "no action" [*iguse*] are the most enjoyable. This is one of the actor's secret arts. Dancing and singing, movements on the stage, and the different types of miming are all acts performed by the body. Moments of "no action" occur in between. When we examine why such moments without action are enjoyable, we find that it is due to the underlying spiritual strength of the actor, which unremittingly holds the attention. He does not relax the tension when the dancing or singing comes to an end or at intervals between the dialogue and the different types of miming, but maintains an unwavering inner strength. This feeling of inner strength will faintly reveal itself and bring enjoyment. However, it is undesirable for the actor to permit this inner strength to become obvious to the audience. If it is obvious, it becomes an act, and is no longer "no action." The actions before and after an interval of "no action" must be linked by entering the state of mindlessness in which the actor conceals even from himself his own intent. The ability to move audiences depends, thus, on linking all the artistic powers with one mind.

"Life and death, past and present–
Marionettes on a toy stage.
When the strings are broken,
Behold the broken pieces!"

This is a metaphor describing human life as it transmigrates between life and death. Marionettes on a stage appear to move in various ways, but in fact it is not they who really move – they are manipulated by strings. When these strings are broken, the marionettes fall and are dashed to pieces. In the art of the Noh too, the different types of miming are artificial things. What holds the parts together is the mind. This mind must not be disclosed to the audience. If it is seen, it is just as if a marionette's strings were visible. The mind must be made the strings which hold together all the powers of the art. If this is done the actor's talent will endure.[25]

For this reason Suzuki does not disclose his secrets, preferring to test Brandon by suggesting that the "tension" in the disciplines is not so much physical as psychological.

In Australia the basic (*kihon*) disciplines which enable beginners to find the center of gravity were treated first in training. "*Ashi o hôru*," "*Fumikae*" and "*Kunjitsu* stamp" are also known as Basic Nos. 1, 2, and 3.[26]

Basic No. 1: Ashi o hôru (Throwing the feet)

Actors stand in line with heels together and toes turned out (in the "box" position). On the count of "*Ichi!*" ("One!"), the right leg is cocked upward and stamped out to the right. The center of gravity is now over the right heel and the left leg is straight (the lower-body movement for a *mie* pose in Kabuki). On the command "*Ni!*" ("Two!") left heel is pulled in to right heel to restore the original "box" position. On "*San!*" ("Three!"), to a fast or slow count of anywhere from one to ten, actors flex knees and slowly lower their center of gravity until buttocks rest on raised heels. With the back straight, the weight of the body is now balanced on the toes. On "*Shi!*" ("Four!") actors slowly and evenly rise to the original "boxed" standing position. The sequence is then repeated to the left. [Figure 15]

At a more advanced level, voice can be added to this exercise. Brandon sang the *enka* "Nagasaki Blues" at full volume while doing "Three" and "Four." In Melbourne, because the actors were being tried out for *The Chronicle of Macbeth*, Macbeth's "Tomorrow, and tomorrow, and tomorrow" speech was used.

Figure 15 Training on the stage of the First Toga Sanbô, Toga, 1976.
The actors are chanting text while slowly raising and lowering the
center of gravity in what is now called Basic No. 1.

The side stamp sends an emphatic shockwave back up the body which
needs to be stopped in the center so that no jarring is evident in the upper
body. It is not so much a stamp as a "throwing out of the leg" (*ashi o
hôru*) to establish a new center of gravity to the side. The stamp is only
the effect of catching the body at the point of falling. Speed, precision,
and energy are important in (1) and (2) while extreme (and extremely
painful) restraint is necessary in the slow-motion movements of (3) and
(4). Slow movement provides another obstacle to overcome in voice-
production, another artificial way of "raising the stakes" to challenge
control of the center. It also teaches proper segmentation of the body
for expressive purposes; while the center is absorbing the stress caused
by slowly raising and lowering the center of gravity (while singing) the
upper body must be free of tension – the swan on the surface of the
water. Finally it is important to stress that the first step of this exercise is
remotely akin to the lower-leg movement of the Genroku *mie* pose. But
in Kabuki the more painfully close the actor can bring his center to the
floor in an extreme stretch position, the more arrestingly beautiful the
effect and the more shouts of appreciation (*kakegoe*) from the audience.
This is of no consequence in Suzuki's *"ashi o hôru."*

Basic No. 2: Fumikae *(Stamp and change)*

This starts with the center of gravity slightly "dropped," knees flexed, and toes turned out in the "box" position. On "One!" actors kick the right leg forward and up to waist height to show the sole of the foot. This is held for varying, unpredictable lengths of time. Then, on "Two!," they stamp down hard with the right foot slightly ahead of the supporting left foot. The same action is then repeated with the left foot. After these segmented moves have been assimilated, both are combined: on "One!" the right foot is raised and stamped; on "Two!" the left is raised and stamped, and so on, allowing the actor to progress slowly forward.

To create a more complicated basic training sequence, *"Fumikae"* has been combined with elements of March No. 5 of *"Echigojishi."* After the completion of *"Fumikae* Two!" above, the new exercise requires the right leg to slide forward across the floor on "Three!" until the hips and the center of gravity are over the right heel (this is right for the individual when the back leg can be lifted without falling over). On "Four!" actors rise on toes, lifting the center straight up. On "Five!" they sink heels to the floor again. What is being cultivated is the ability to control the center of gravity by creating situations that challenge it (*ekkyô suru chikara*). The simple test mentioned above allows instructors to ensure the center is precisely returned over the right heel. If the weight is truly on the right leg, they will be able to lift the left without falling. "Dueling" is a more advanced exercise still, in which actors carry out these movements in facing pairs to work off each other's energy.

Basic No. 3: Kunjitsu *stamp*

Actors start in the "box" position, but with the heel of the right foot slightly ahead of (and pressed into the instep of) the left foot in a "Y" formation, toes turned out. On "One!" the left leg is swept diagonally out to the side, and pulled up and back in to the center. On "Two!" it is stamped down hard fractionally ahead of the instep of the right foot; and the same set of actions is then repeated with the other foot to produce an incremental but highly energized forward stamping movement. The forward shift of the center of gravity is challenged in this discipline by diagonal rather than sideways or forward "leg throwing."

Slow-motion walk (Tenteketen)

This discipline is not mentioned by Brandon because it was first devised to aid choreographic work on *The Bacchae.* It uses the music of Perez

Prado's *Voodoo Suite* at half speed. Again the exercise is about moving the center of gravity through space, maintaining the same speed and height so that, if an electric torch were to be attached to the hip and the walk performed in darkness, its light would make a continuous, unbroken line across stage.

Actors stand in two lines facing each other on opposite sides of the stage, keeping a strong focus on a point on the wall directly in front of them. They are required to approach their point of focus in a slow walk across stage, through the line of the other group.

Although the task looks simple, it is hard in practice, for obeying the rules of the discipline challenges physics, in particular the tendency to "bob" slightly as the center of gravity shifts from one hip to the other. Effort is also required to keep an even flow of movement, the actor having to "push through" the shifts of weight. And when walking too slowly, toppling over becomes a danger. No specific form of walking (*kata*) is prescribed, for the discipline is partly about finding one's own way to move the center economically. Certainly the sliding walk (*suriashi*) of Noh and Kabuki is discouraged, for it is used elsewhere as one of the Ten Walks. The discipline also aims to enable the actor to develop a sense of *ma*, a sensitivity to shifting temporal and spatial relationships.[27]

After the rules of the exercise are described, the music is played over so that participants have a subjective sense of how long the walk to the other side must take. If they misjudge the *ma* and arrive too early, they are to freeze at the wall with their upstage foot forward in anticipation of return. As the saxophones and trumpet come in, they are to swivel-turn downstage toward the audience and travel back the way they came. Other constraints added in to the discipline, once beginners have tried basics, are the need for each group to maintain their line in the walk (using peripheral vision only), and the necessity of maintaining a balanced relationship to the other group in time-space. Ideally the two groups should meet center-stage and reach opposite walls at the same time. The first part of this requirement is not difficult, for the groups can see each other approach; but, once they have passed, they must use their senses to judge the other group's position behind them relative to their own in the space. This is one practical application of Zeami's *mokuzen shingo* ("the eyes in front, the heart behind") principle.[28]

The principle of *hippari-ai* is also being applied, for beginners are often told to imagine they have two "ropes tied to their middle," one pulling them forward and the other back. Having to maintain an even line, right and left, within the group heightens awareness of another major directional forcefield. Furthermore, the image of the light on the hip creates awareness of the body's need to restrain the "swing up" and "step down" mechanics of the walk – as if two taut threads above and below simultaneously balanced each other out on the vertical plane.

Sometimes, in order to give trainees a lively sense of the imaginary "weight" which needs to be given to the slow walk, real weight is applied and a chair is carried overhead across the space. The exercise seems to be a later, less severe adaptation of Brandon's "Metal ladder," albeit without the one-legged stand in between steps.[29] Once trainees have a sense of how this feels in the center, they are asked to repeat the slow walk without the chair and artificially create the necessary "weight" through inner tension. An even stronger sense of resistance is created by having trainees of similar heights and weights take turns at piggybacking each other across the space, and then repeat the move with only the memory of the partner's weight.

At an advanced level a more creative component is added. After the initial crossing of the space, actors are to use the musical change to imagine a great weight pressing down on one part of the body as they swivel. This distorts body shape further in the slow, center-lowering screw-turn, producing a new "accidental" asymmetric form which they must try to carry back across stage using all their resources. Sometimes the shape created will be too hard to maintain without shaking or collapsing, but the struggle to pit will against physics is always fascinating for the spectator. This advanced level of the exercise involves what Suzuki calls *asobi* (play) in his interview with Brandon (42). From the above it should be clear, *contra* Saari, that improvisation, playing within the rules of the discipline, is indeed encouraged as the next step along the road after the development of strength and concentration. Most exercises contain this movement from "restricted" or "neutral" to "free" artistic expressivity.

Finally, at the most advanced stage, the "Statues" exercise is added to "Walks"; the artistic transformation of this discipline is evident in the cross-walks of maenads, doll women, and priests in *Greetings from the Edge of the Earth I* (see Chapter Eight).

Stamp and *Shakuhachi*

This exercise, so called because of the use of a bamboo flute in its second improvised half, is also known as the dreaded "Three-minute stamp." It often begins Suzuki training because it so well reminds participants and spectators of the extra-daily nature of this approach to theatre. In Brandon's day actors used to move in a circle but these days they move freely and independently of each other.

First, to the pounding beat of the first part, they must stamp continuously and vigorously as they move at random about the space for three minutes. Then, on the last beat of the section, they must drop to the ground in a line upstage, lie still without losing focus, and, as the Zen flute of the second part floods over them, stand in their own time while maintaining centeredness, like "Atlas lifting the earth."[30] They then approach the audience downstage, using any free-form movement their inner sensibilities suggest. This they must do in such a way as to reach the front of the stage exactly on the last note of the music, while striving to maintain audience attention throughout (no easy feat in a group of from four to eight).

The purpose of the exercise is to raise a very high level of energy (through stamping), control it (by stopping energy in the hips to ensure that vibration does not travel up the torso to produce tension in arms, shoulders, or neck), and focus it (through a peripheral-vision stare) on a point straight ahead of the body. Ideally the knees are to be raised to a point level with the hips, but the main thing is to gauge a level of raise and an energy of stamp which are challenging, yet can be maintained at the same level for a full three minutes. This is more easily said than done, for muscles run out of stored energy after about one and a half minutes of stamping, and it then becomes a personal fight for survival. For the last minute and a half, participants must depend on a combination of willpower, concentration, and faith in the body's ability to cope with stress in this deliberately simulated emergency. Of course constant practice builds strength, stamina, and sensory knowledge of how to cope individually – and this has forced Suzuki to create new obstacles for his increasingly adept veterans.

The exercise also involves careful attention; intuitively calculating when to start and when to stop as a group is the most obvious skill (*ma*). When participants collapse to the ground at the end of the fast stamping section, they are supposed to do so on the same beat, suddenly, as if the strings of so many puppets had been cut. But once in contact with the floor, they must lie completely still, as blood pounds wildly through the body, without giving way to the temptation to relax (they are still onstage, "doing the act of being seen"). In the second half of the exercise, which must start within a few seconds of the flute's entrance, they are to summon all this heightened energy and awareness of the center for expressive purposes as they approach their audience (usually the other half of the training group).

In *The Trojan Women* (see Chapter Five), Cassandra's long visionary speech uses the same basic "grammar" as the second part of

"Three-minute stamp," although it is a much more advanced, creative form of it (for Suzuki, "Speech is an act of the Body"). Thus, when Shiraishi collapses to the floor, the Chorus chant of "Water flowing, Bone flowing" is, on one level at least, an internal description of Cassandra's/Shiraishi's heightened physical state at this moment. The "*Shakuhachi*" exercise, in other words, provides an artificial means to acquaint the trainee actor with the experience of what Victor Turner would call a liminal heightened state, in which "the invisible world is made visible." For the novice this is not yet artistically creative, but daily training over long periods of time will gradually, in combination with other physical and physical/vocal exercises, enable him or her to explore the possibilities of the instrument which assays to bridge this gap. Most members of the Suzuki company take a year or two before they are ready for minor roles in public performance. Graduating to a major role, on the other hand, may take many years more, depending on the unique talents and level of application of the individual, Suzuki's program schedule, and the rate of attrition among veterans.

Three Sitting positions

First introduced sometime after Brandon and before Gotoh, these begin from a "foetal" sitting position in which actors curl up into a ball, hugging knees against chest with head lowered. On "One!" the body is tilted back to balance on the coccyx, taking the soles of the feet off the ground. Eyes are fixed straight ahead (to help to maintain balance through concentration on a focal point) and the feet flexed upward, exposing the soles. At another signal the body returns to relaxed, stable sitting. On "Two!" the legs shoot forward together while the torso tilts backward to a point of balance, arms relaxed by the side with fists resting on hips, eyes focused ahead over the upwardly flexed toes. After a variable length of time, on another signal, the body returns to neutral sitting, head on knees. On "Three!" legs shoot out again, wide open at an angle of 45 degrees, while the torso again tilts back to find a counteracting point of balance. The time before the next signal is again varied – to prevent anticipation and to test concentration and balance. When it comes, the actors return instantly to neutral.

The trainee must make sure that the toes are turned up in all three positions, the torso is as straight as possible, and the feet far enough off the ground to balance the body on the base of the spine. Raising the heels is intended to provide a barrier to stability which the actor has to fight against to maintain equilibrium.

When they have practiced getting quickly to a stable point of balance, learned to breathe through a taut solar plexus and to ignore aching thighs, Voice can be added to positions 1–3 on the commands "Speak!" or "Sing!" Suzuki's ideas about keeping the upper body relaxed and about using compression of the *hara* (center) for expressive purposes are drawn from traditional Japanese theatre practice. Nevertheless they find interesting support from Cicely Berry, Voice director of the RSC in the 1980s: "relaxation of itself is not a virtue, for we have to come to terms with the fact that there is a tension which we acquire in acting which is a positive and a good one . . . Too much relaxation can be dulling. What is important is to find where our energy lies, and that is always with the breath."[31] Suzuki's disciplines, both physical and vocal, are all about "finding where our energy lies" and learning to focus it for different creative purposes.

Any choral passage or song the group needs to work on can be performed in rehearsal training, but for new trainees it is usually Menelaus' testing monologue from *The Trojan Women*:

> O splendour of sunburst breaking forth this day
> Whereon I lay my hands once more on Helen my wife;
> And yet it is not so much for the woman's sake I came to Troy,
> But against that guest proved treacherous who like a robber carried
>   the woman from my house.

Minor breath pauses are allowed only at the ends of these four lines, the last of which is especially long and difficult. Because of the tendency for the voice to grow weaker as it runs out of breath, the actor must consciously *build* intensity in the last phrase of each line. This Noh technique is the vocal equivalent of what willpower must do to maintain energy in the last minute and a half of the stamp in "Stamp and *Shakuhachi*."

Precisely because positions 2–3 are highly strenuous, they give the novice a very vivid sense of how to find the center. Sound must issue from here, and actors are asked not to get too caught up in the sense of the words but to think of them initially as a form of energy released by the center. As Cicely Berry has rightly pointed out, "words are themselves a movement" and "we have to find the precise energy for that movement." Actors need to "get closer to the sense that a character can be possessed by the words . . . driven by them . . . how the character breathes is how the character thinks."[32] Ellen Lauren is clearly aware of this in her anecdote about Shiraishi's ability to change instantly from one character to another by shifting her center of energy and breath-pattern (see Chapter Eight).

In basic training, however, the advice is more technical. In the words of Katoh and Ingulsrud:

> If you think about trying to produce a strong voice, it'll come up into your chest. Just do all the physical things you're asked, and that will allow it to happen. If your shoulders are not relaxed, breathing will start to rise into the chest. Looking up as soon as you start to speak will produce the same result. You need to be more aggressive with your own bodies. As the position gets more exhausting and painful, the tendency is to "let go." You have to *increase* the concentration.[33]

Another refinement on this exercise is to combine it with "Sitting statues" in which the actor can take any position while balancing on the coccyx to deliver a speech or song – so long as both feet and hands are off the ground. Again an element of experimental play is built in at an advanced stage to test the actors' ability to create freely within the constraints of the discipline.

Statues

"Sitting statues" are as described above. In "Standing statues" the actors go from a neutral standing position into free-form poses reminiscent of Greco-Roman statues, moving the center of gravity between "High" and "Low" positions. On the command "High!" they strain upward on their toes to assume any position they feel confident of being able to maintain. After a certain amount of time taken to test stability and concentration, another signal returns them to a relaxed squat, feet flat on the floor, chest on knees, head down and arms held loosely around the knees. On "Low!" they spring back up onto their toes in a freestyle half-crouch that may be easier to control than the tiptoe position of "High" but is much more painful to maintain. The focus may be oriented in any direction, but the actor must be careful not to lead with the chest in the act of standing, instead moving the center. Nor is it merely a matter of shifting the center smoothly to a new center of gravity; keeping a strong "line" of connection between actor and point of focus is important. Whether between actor and "adversary" or actor and audience, the gaze must be concentrated and steady. Since the commands can come at any moment, the exercise demands the ability to reach a new center of gravity quickly and to hold it firmly without shake or wobble or excessive expenditure of energy. On the other hand constantly moving into the same set of positions suggests laziness – or lack of imagination – and must be avoided. As Katoh and Ingulsrud admonished trainees:

Don't just let things continue of themselves. If something isn't quite right, adjust it next time. If the body is a mirror [of your state], make sure you're looking into the mirror [for self-diagnosis]. Try to imagine what "the eye of god" or the eye of the audience is focused on, and if you don't like what you see, work to change it. The more things you are monitoring, the better your concentration. The more you're struggling to maintain control with this overload, the more interesting you are.[34]

In this improvisational discipline, too, Voice can be added in either the "High" or the "Low" position. Especially in the "High" position, unless a sense of resistance is created in the center, the Voice will come out of the chest. While novices may begin by trying to create a loud voice when asked for "strength," intensity is what is called for, and this is a product of *compression* of energy in the center, as if the voice were coming out from under a heavy stone placed in a pickle jar (*takuan ishi*). Tenacity of concentration, a sense of not letting go when another level of complexity is added, requires a strenuous mental effort – as in any language acquisition.

The Walks

As already noted, the Walks have increased in number over the years, from Brandon's Five to Gotoh's Nine and Allain's Ten. One of the ways this may have happened is through the long-term application of Brandon's fifth discipline, "Improvised walk." However, like *Shikko* ("Squat walk," Brandon's "Duck walk"), some were already separate exercises that have since been added to this "warm-up" run of different ways in which the feet can make contact with the floor.

For rehearsal training in Melbourne, "Walks" replaced "Stamp and *Shakuhachi*" as the "kickstart" to each session in the Merlyn Theatre, perhaps because the discipline is more group-oriented and less individualistic, and serves to remind the company of the "rules of the group." As Gotoh has noted, different circumstances require different starting disciplines.[35] In any case the Walks also begin with a fast stamp (*Ashibumi*).

According to need, they can be done to the relatively slower tempo of *Shinnai Nagashi* music or the faster tempo of *Voodoo Suite*. For beginners the hands are neutral, but in rehearsal training performers make individual choices which may relate to what they are doing in performance. For example, in *The Chronicle of Macbeth* the Farewell Cult entered to "Slow walks," holding a copy of *Macbeth* as their catechism; in training the way each actor found to hold the book was meant to be part of the physical exploration of an individual case history of obsession and despair. But whatever the gesture tried out, it had to be maintained through any one type of walk. This is done in sequence, in single file across the stage space, care being taken to ensure an equal distance is kept between each performer in the line (a sense of *ma* helps to develop company cohesion for more complicated performance moves). On reaching the other side of the stage, performers "peel off" and return (via the upstage walkway at Toga) to the starting point for the next type of walk.

1. *Ashibumi* (Foot stamping) – used in Noh, Kabuki, flamenco
This is equivalent to the first part of "Stamp and *Shakuhachi*" except that movement is forward in a straight line. Knees are flexed, and the knee-lift for the stamp must be maintained at the same level throughout. For this exercise in Melbourne, Katoh and Ingulsrud encouraged the group to "chase after the feeling of stability following each stamp ... even if it's only for a split second; you need to get to that point of stillness *between* moves by 'applying the brakes (*tame*).'"

2. *Uchimata* (Inward "pigeon-toed" walk)
This forward walk derives from Kabuki stylization of a court lady kicking the hem of her ceremonial kimono forward so as not to trip on it. Knees are bent and held together, and toes pointed inward in a pigeon-toed manner so that feet slide flat on the floor in an inward sweeping motion. As in all these exercises, maintaining the sense of "stop" at completion of each move is important. Each walk offers a different sort of challenge to the center and a different sensibility.

3. *Waniashi* (Bow-legged walk, literally "crocodile feet")
Knees are bent sharply out and toes curled in so the actor walks forward on the outside edge of the foot "as if pedaling a bicycle." The torso is held in the *koshi o dasu* position of Noh, the upper body tilted forward slightly and pelvis thrust out behind. The sensibility is rural and may have been inspired by Kathakali, Toga farmers, or Hijikata's Butoh.

4. *Sotomata* (Outward walk)
Knees are bent in and held together while heels are kicked out to each side in turn, striking the floor on return with the instep. Great care must be taken to hold the center still in this "throwing sideways" challenge to forward movement.

5. *Tsumasaki* (Tiptoe)
Keeping as upright as possible, performers rise on the toes to take tiny but very rapid steps forward across the floor, as if on stilts. The point is to keep the knees straight, pulling the legs out from the center of the body. A smooth, gliding motion must belie the jerkiness of the steps.

6. *Yokoaruki* No. 1 (Side-step walk) – used in Kathakali
Facing forward, actors move to the left, parallel feet sliding in little semi-circular sweeps, the leading foot starting with the trailing foot closing, as in the first two parts of *Ashi o hôru* but without taking either foot off the floor; in this sense it is like a sideways *suriashi* (see Walk 9).

7. *Yokoaruki* No. 2 (Side-step walk and Foot stamp)
Instead of the feet sliding in sideways sweeps to the left, the right foot is raised to maximum height and made to strike the floor across the left foot, slightly in front and to the left of it. The left foot is then pulled up from behind the right and stamped beyond it to the left so that the center of gravity is equidistant from each foot. This alternating sequence of "cross-legged" and "legs-apart" stamps is sometimes called "Scissor step." Another, more difficult, variant of it keeps the fast, aggressive leg lifts but takes out the stamp, thus forcing rapid alternation of aggressive and gentle elements.

8. *Ashi o hôru* (Throwing the feet)
Only steps 1 and 2 are repeated here, although the back leg is also stamped into position beside the leading one before the leading leg is again thrown out to the left and stamped. Care must be taken to ensure that the center does not rise involuntarily with either leg lift or stamp.

9. *Suriashi* (Sliding walk) – used in Noh
Actors flex knees and shuffle fast forward, being sure to maintain nearly continuous contact between the floor and the soles of the feet. An even speed is important but the shifts of center in the hips from side to side must be "blocked" so that no shake is evident in the upper body.

10. *Shikkō* (Squat walk, Brandon's "Duck walk")[36]
The walk was used for formal presentation to *daimyo*, as in Lady Kaede's formal presentation of her husband's war helmet to Lord Jiro in Kurosawa's *Ran* (*King Lear*). Actors squat on the toes, with upright back and arms raised, palms up, as if carrying a ceremonial object on a tray, and shuffle rapidly forward across the space. Great compression of energy is required to hold the center steady and turn a jerky, irregular shuffle into a smooth, fluid glide.

11. *Backward movement*
The walks can be done backward as well as forward. This idea seems to have been added sometime between 1985 and 1993 when Suzuki started putting his veteran actors into baskets and wheelchairs to create new obstacles for them to overcome. It is an advanced discipline because it works against the body's habitual physics; it also requires a high level of concentration to maintain a set distance between performers in a sequence when the person in the line "ahead" cannot be seen.

Kanjinchô

As Brandon has noted, the actions for this discipline are loosely based on the *roppô* (six directions) exit movements used by Benkei in the Kabuki play *Kanjinchô* (*The Subscription List*). It is also the name of the Kabuki music used.

Actors stand with knees out and bent in the "box" position, in a circle (the disciplines which require circling seem to be older). To the first musical section they perform *Fumikae*, kicking the right leg forward to waist height, holding, stamping down hard, and then repeating with the other foot in a continuous counterclockwise movement, stamping twenty-four times. *Fumikae* appears to have been recycled from *Kanjinchô* as a basic (*kihon*) discipline for beginners.

In the second section *Fumikae* is continued twenty-four times, but the *roppô* arm gestures are added, left arm fully extended forward with palm out and fingers splayed to suggest energy, the right arm cocked by the right ear as the right leg is lifted.

In the third section actors repeat the *Fumikae* leg positions twenty-two times but add *kitsune* (fox) gestures, closing the fists and cocking the wrists in the same positions as for *roppô*. In other words, where hands were powerfully open in (2), they are closed and bent in (3). The pose, also called *neko* (cat), can suggest a panther striking prey with its paws.

This movement was first used in performance at the close of the 1978 *The Bacchae*, when fox masks were worn by the maenads.

The fourth section is like the second in that the same leg and arm movements are used, but the center is further destabilized after each stamp by the addition of a hop forward on the stamping foot. The moves are repeated twenty-eight times to complete this musical section.

Brandon notes that this was a favorite discipline of the WLT, and it has certainly been adapted in a number of ways for expressive use in *The Trojan Women* and *The Bacchae*. In particular Togawa's maenad frenzy seems to have combined elements of *Kanjinchô* with the strenuous backbend of Brandon's "Metal ladder" discipline (see Chapter Six).

As can be seen above, Suzuki Training is a structured system which aims to build speed, strength of energy, stamina, stability, and concentration in a modular manner. It moves from the simple to the complex, and from the mechanical to the creative. Basic principles and the "rules" of each discipline are given by instructors before starting, but are endlessly repeated at later stages since individual learning takes place at varying rates. In a teaching situation explanation of technical points is usually reserved for the short break after completion of each exercise. By then the trainee has practical experience of what is being discussed. In rehearsal training it is enough for Suzuki to call out reminders to individuals as they perform. Interestingly, no Voice disciplines are undertaken independently of Movement disciplines. For Suzuki, "Speech is an act of the Body."[37]

The actor's ability to fascinate is created by the amount and quality of energy radiated by the body in all directions. This energy is built through a coherent system of restraint (*tame*). As in Noh, the actor builds presence by creating the will to move but deliberately holds back on doing so until the inner tension becomes unbearably high. Once in motion, the goal is to become conscious of the body's entire structure as a kind of moving sculpture. The influence of Kabuki principles, in which action flows from one climactic freeze-pose (*mie*) to the next, is clear here – but so are its affinities with other non-Japanese theatre forms.

Meyerhold in particular refers to the stage as "a pedestal for sculpture" and adds:

The relief stage is not an end in itself, but merely a means; the end is the dramatic action which the spectator pictures in his imagination, stimulated by the rhythmic waves of bodily movement; these waves must extend into space in order for the spectator to absorb the composition of movements, gestures, and poses.

Once the principle of bodily movement in space is accepted, the stage must be constructed so that the lines of rhythmical expression can stand out distinctly. Hence, everything which serves as a pedestal for the actor, everything on which he leans, everything he touches, must be constructed sculpturally.[38]

Meyerhold makes numerous references to Japanese theatre principles in his writings,[39] and he was practically influenced by the visits to Russia of Kawakami Otojirô (1902), Hanako (1909), and Ichikawa Sadanji's Kabuki troupe (1928). Robert Wilson is yet another major Western director who asks the actor to "[t]hink of your body as a piece of living sculpture."[40] And Anne Bogart's work is clearly situated within this tradition.

Over the years Suzuki's basic concerns have remained practically focused on developing the expressive potential of his actors in the arena of physical theatre. For him, as for the Kabuki artist, "creating theatre is a process, not of staging the dramatist's text, but of using the motivation and opportunity for expression to be found in a text to establish a space where certain directors and certain *seductive* actors can exist and, at a certain moment in time, *lure on* an audience that has come, not to see a certain drama, but to experience what it is like to be in *that* particular space with *these* people."[41] Shiraishi of course has these powers *par excellence*, but by now it should be evident that, even without Shiraishi, Suzuki's ensemble could create intense, pungent productions such as *Home Medicine* and *Dionysus*.

And it is because of the pleasure he takes in carefully configuring seductive performance environments to inspire actors and alter audience perceptions that Suzuki has so often collaborated with Isozaki Arata, a major international postmodern architect. When performing works originally staged in Toga village or at the Seibu Studio in Tokyo, Suzuki would often hear audiences who had seen the production in both venues express the opinion that he had changed his interpretation, although in fact he had altered nothing. "This kind of misapprehension . . . is caused by the particular venue and its surrounding atmosphere. Through these experiences, I realized that the receptivity of the body is more or less stimulated by the atmosphere of the place and is extremely important for theatrical performance."[42] Suzuki would consciously seek out new and stimulating performance environments to set off the performance skills of his actors: spaces such as the vast weatherworn Herod Atticus amphitheatre facing the Acropolis in Athens; the neo-classical perfection of the miniature indoor Teatro Olimpico in Vicenza with its arrays of statuary; the gloomy warmth of his *gasshôzukuri* theatres with their massive black beams framing the rhythms and patterns of his actors; and the Noh stage and Zen garden at the Asaba Hot Spring in Izu, set over a quiet pond which mirrors the action above it. The experience of a Suzuki *Dionysus*, *Elektra*, or *King Lear* in such spaces is indelible – for the actors' energies shine brightest within numinous spaces which possess a dense atmosphere rivaling their own.

However, before moving on to consider Suzuki's major productions, the last word on the training process which nourishes them must come from a highly respected Suzuki veteran, Ellen Lauren:

All of the exercises . . . are basically impossible. What Suzuki is asking you to do are movements that are not seen in daily life . . . that take the body out of a habitual way of moving. Then he asks you to maintain an equilibrium and steadiness as if you held a glass of water inside the body which you don't want to spill . . . So you willfully create a collision in the body and try to control it, keeping a very strong specific outward focus at the same time . . . Suzuki thinks the actor should be doing something extraordinary on the stage, something that not just anybody can do.[43]

Adaptation of Japanese classics: *On the Dramatic Passions II* and *John Silver*

Ian Carruthers

To illustrate the range of Suzuki's use of early modern and modern Japanese classics across three decades, this chapter will look in detail at two productions: Suzuki's first international success of 1970, *On the Dramatic Passions II*, and a production not seen abroad, a 1996 adaptation of Kara Jûrô's play *John Silver*.

Suzuki's adaptation of Japanese classics began very early in the life of his company as a matter of survival, when Betsuyaku suffered a four-year period of writer's block. In 1968 Suzuki first started to shape exercise pieces into "collage drama" with *Folkloric Analysis of The Lower Depths*.[1] The process was refined in 1969 with *On the Dramatic Passions I*, and finally the company started to draw critical notice. When Suzuki's first major success came with *On the Dramatic Passions II* in 1970, it was less chance occurrence than the result of careful and painstaking assemblage of just the right combinations: an intimate theatre space which was owned not hired, a selective and critical use of traditional performance techniques, a powerful "shamanic" actress, and a self-reflexive use of Surrealist and avant-garde dramaturgical techniques. Even the title, *On the Dramatic Passions II*, indicated Suzuki's cautious determination to proceed incrementally by building on what had been partially successful, and finetuning what was not yet effective.

As critics raved – Yagi Shûichirô calling WLT "the best avant-garde troupe in Japan" – the four-week production run was extended for another three, drawing at least 4,000 spectators to the company's tiny theatre studio in Shinjuku.[2] *Dramatic Passions II* is memorable as the only Suzuki production so far to have an entire book devoted to its production and reception.[3] It was also the first of Suzuki's productions to win acclaim abroad. A year after the show premiered in Tokyo, it was touring to Osaka and Kyoto, and in 1972 Suzuki and Shiraishi were invited by Jean-Louis Barrault to the Théâtre des Nations Festival in Paris. Shiraishi performed two scenes from the play, the first from *Onna keizu*

Figure 16 Seigen (Shiraishi Kayoko) struggles with Sota (Kanze
Hideo). Scene 8 of *On the Dramatic Passions II*. The Récamier Theatre,
Paris, 1972.

(*Woman's Pedigree*) with Saitoh Ikuko playing the daughter, the second from *Sumidagawa hana no goshozome* with Kanze Hideo as Sôta.
[Figure 16] Her sensational performance was highly acclaimed and, as
a result, the entire cast was invited by Jack Lang to perform the full play
at the 1973 Nancy Festival (April 24–May 5). From there they went on
to Jean-Louis Barrault's Récamier in Paris (May 16–27) and the Mickery
Theatre in Amsterdam (May 29–June 10).

At Nancy, Shiraishi's acting was "one of the most talked-about subjects at the festival" (*The Drama Review*, December 1973, 22). It was
"étonnant de densité et de mobilité. Elle rend le spectacle extraordi-
naire" (*Le Point* no. 34, May 14 1973). "Jamais plus on ne pourra sans
doute parler de performance d'actrice sans se souvenir du choc en plein
coeur provoqué par la jeune Kayoko Shiraishi" (*L'Express*, May 7–13
1973). Michel Cournot of *Le Monde* (May 3 1973) was even more effu-
sive, taking two paragraphs to describe her skills, and Suzuki was also
praised as "le Grotowski japonais" (*Le Point* no. 31, April 23 1973, 64).
In August of that year, Grotowski himself visited Japan to watch WLT
rehearse, and invited Suzuki to perform *Dramatic Passions II* again at the

1975 Théâtre des Nations Festival in Warsaw (June 19–21), and at his base in Wroclaw (June 24).

On the Dramatic Passions I and II were, as Suzuki has said in a preface to the performance text,[4] "an attempt to examine the roots of stage acting, the impulses which people have deep inside their minds." His announced "actor-centered" approach was buttressed in terms of Kabuki through reference to Kikugorô VI who, like Shiraishi, "could write the body of a play on the stage." Also for the first time Suzuki asserted his independence of the classics he "quotes" by pointing out that they "have all been changed during the rehearsal. The lines themselves may have the feeling of the original plays, but the situation of this play is completely different." For these reasons he believes that, like the actor-centered texts of Kabuki, his productions "have no value in printed form."

Originally the scenes, chosen by actors to meet their own subjective needs, lacked a connecting narrative logic. Yet Suzuki's decision to have the central role played by Shiraishi as a madwoman performing classic fragments to vent private frustration would enable audiences to discover in them strange echoes of Artaudian cruelty, the intense physicality of Grotowskian "poor theatre," and Beckettian values of indeterminacy. Moreover, through being put in a vacillating, fragmentary situation similar to that of the protagonist, audiences could experience the uncomfortable realization that no objective reality exists anywhere.

The performance space and the set contributed very considerably to creating an environment which would draw attention to the intensely physical and subjectively internal nature of this confined fantasy world. The space upstairs of the Mon Cheri coffee shop was tiny, accommodating an audience of little more than a hundred in cramped conditions on tatami mats. When demand was high, as it was for *Dramatic Passions II*, staff would have to ask the audience (who had no seats as such) to squash together "like human sushi," as they would have done in the early days of Kabuki.

Since this is one of Suzuki's most famous productions, I shall provide a detailed scene-by-scene analysis of the WLT performance text.

The play starts with the distant sounds of street entertainers (*Chin don ya*) and then the war song "Rabauru kouta" ("Rabaul Ballad"), revealing the setting to be post World War II. As the stage lights go up, numerous *shôji* doors are revealed, hung from the ceiling in a seemingly haphazard pattern which suggests a surrealist collage – perhaps even a cubist fragmentation of the humanist organization of experience through "character and setting." As the stage directions indicate, they "look like they're flying away into the sky," unmoored from their everyday contexts. Center stage is a small tatami half-mat, while "[t]wo dirty tatami mats lean wrong-side up against the upstage wall, one on either side of the stage."[5] In this space two men are engaged in everyday activities, one taking off his shoes, the other, with a baby strapped to his back, washing nappies. The stage directions indicate that this is meant to evoke "[a]n ordinary afternoon in an old run-down working-class tenement."

But just how "ordinary" is it? In 1969 Beckett's *Waiting for Godot* had just been translated, and Suzuki's production of the play was broadcast on NHK TV for the first time. Moreover, to see a house-husband was highly unusual, particularly in the working class. What the scene suggests is a careful mix of the everyday and the avant-garde to heighten tension through juxtaposition. The scene does not simply portray a realistic "slice of low-life" as in Gorki's *The Lower Depths*; it dramatizes the internal mindscapes of those who inhabit such a world, suggesting how the extraordinary and fantastic exist side by side with, and can grow out of, the mud of the everyday. The effect is not unlike that of Kurosawa's relocation of Gorki to a postwar slum wasteland in *Dodesukaden* (1970).

"No way to fix it," the line spoken by the man removing his shoes, identify him with Estragon ("Nothing to be done"), and indeed the first scene is loosely modeled on the opening scene of Beckett's *Godot*. But there are major differences. At the moment when Suzuki's Estragon-like character comments, "Not bad. A good view," Suzuki has him pull out a cheap camera to snap the "Vladimir" character as he sings, "I don't care; my wife left me," while scrubbing nappies in a tub. The baby cries and "Vladimir" comforts it, then starts to move off as he says, "Let's go." "No, we have to wait," "Estragon" cautions, to which "Vladimir" replies, "It's supposed to be in front of a shrub. Is there another?" "Estragon" prevaricates with, "But this is a tree [*kyoboku*] rather than a shrub [*kanboku*]," concluding helplessly "Or maybe it's a Nanboku" ["North/South"; the name of a famous Kabuki playwright]. "Nanboku? What are you saying?" quips "Vladimir," "That we've come to the wrong place [the Kabuki theatre]?" This implies a change of direction on several levels, for when "Estragon" replies, "He's supposed to be here," a shout is heard from offstage, delivered like the Kabuki playstopper *Shibaraku!* ("Hey! Wait a minute!"). As "Murasaki kouta" ("Purple Ballad") plays to a steel-guitar melody, the actress Shiraishi Kayoko appears in male kimono, bellows, "Heeere I aam!," and strides center stage to acknowledge the audience, posing in a Kabuki *mie* with her eyes crossed. "Godot" has appeared and is female.

From this point on "It's a Nanboku." More precisely, Scene 2 is the Iwabushi Hermitage scene from Tsuruya Nanboku IV's famous Kabuki melodrama *Sakurahime azuma bunshô* (*The Scarlet Princess of Edo*). The stage directions sketch the basic situation: "This scene involves a mad-woman who triumphantly plays the role of Priest Seigen, while the two men keep her company, acting as if they are enjoying watching a play . . . to kill time. The madwoman triumphantly tells the same story again and again, so the two men play jokes on her." In Nanboku's play Seigen is a corrupt priest who seduces a young boy into a love-suicide pact which the boy keeps but the priest does not. Years later, after becoming the respected head of a large monastery, Seigen meets Princess Sakura and, on the strength of an improbable coincidence, leaps to the conclusion that she must be the reincarnation of his boy-lover Shiragiku.[6] Suzuki destabilizes this wild plot further by having a woman (Shiraishi) play Priest Seigen and by having the man who plays "Vladimir" (Tsutamori Kôsuke) speak Princess Sakura's lines while he washes his baby's nappies. "Estragon" is made to estrange the situation still further by taking snapshots of the pair with a cheap camera.

The madwoman (Seigen) threatens Princess Sakura ("Vladimir") with a knife, but ends by schizophrenically playing out both roles herself, dashing from one side of the stage to the other to deliver both sets of lines, while "Vladimir" and "Estragon" applaud her death throes. At its end Shiraishi rises from her stage death and, in *roppô* fashion, arms and legs "flying in all six directions," exits down the *hanamichi* as herself. Such virtuoso displays of acting skill are not uncommon in Kabuki (witness the 1988 production in England of Kanagaki Robun's 1886 *Hamlet*, in which the Prince carried out a *hikinuki* quick-change claptrap routine which transformed him into Ophelia before the audience's eyes).

In Scene 3, after Shiraishi has gone, her onstage audience return to killing time. While waiting for the madwoman to reappear, they specu-late on whether she recognized them or whether, indeed, "she was the same person" they knew; they then decide to play out the Nanboku roles themselves. "Vladimir" begins with Sakura's lines "How could I, how could I kill you? Please forgive me dear Seigen," and "Estragon" closes by mimicking Seigen's theatrical exit down the *hanamichi*.

In Scene 4 Shiraishi's "Heeere I aam!" is repeated and the music of "Purple Ballad" restarts. But on her return Shiraishi has become a *different* Seigen, and the two men must scramble for their cues. This time she has chosen to play the Nun Seigen in the Myôki Hermitage scene from Nanboku's *Sumidagawa hana no goshozome* (*Cherry Blossoms at Sumida River*). A reminder of the theatrical nature of her transformations is the props box she carries onstage for her role. In this scene the tenement dwellers "Estragon" and "Vladimir" are required to play the role of villagers who have just saved a young Nun from jumping into the Sumida River. (Princess Hanako has become the Nun Seigen because her lover Matsuwaka is about to marry her younger sister Princess Sakura.) But before the conflict between the two sisters can begin, mediated by their wet-nurse Tsunajo (played by "Estragon"), the two men attempt to lighten the madwoman's depression by reverting to their roles of "Vladimir" and "Estragon."

From the props box "Vladimir" offers the madwoman/Seigen what he calls "a beautiful flower" (actually a magician's coiled-spring flower which opens and closes mechanically). He also offers her his child's bib as "a coat."[7] When this fails to amuse, the pair hop around in a song-and-dance routine about *al fresco* bathing in the "Snow Country" of northern Japan. These antics at last draw a laugh from the madwoman/Seigen ("That's the best medicine," notes "Estragon") and the two men play out the scenario of Vladimir and Estragon attempting to leave. The twist here is that after the initial "Let's go. Yes, let's go," they do indeed grab some of the madwoman's stage props and make an exit.

The stage now darkens and in the spotlight Shiraishi takes a mask out of her box, puts prayer beads around her neck and starts to sharpen a kitchen cleaver on a whetstone.[8] [Figure 17] The stage directions indicate that "the image of this scene is an abstract portrayal of a woman's jealousy or desire for revenge" and the sharpening of the cleaver "symbolises the heightened emotions of *On the Dramatic Passions II*." Suzuki is careful to point out that it is not an esthetic object like a samurai sword, but a tool for daily life and "could be a woman's only weapon." When "Vladimir" and "Estragon" reappear as the wet-nurse Tsunajo and Seigen's sister Princess Sakura the latter's greeting to Seigen/Hanako is tritely conventional: "You haven't changed; you look quite well." Seigen's angry reaction is to remove her mask and snap, "No, I have changed a lot I'm ashamed to say." Family relations are at the root of the problems of this play set in the attic of an old Japanese house.

Putting Nanboku's theatre into an estranged traditional domestic setting allowed Suzuki to examine the roots of an indigenous "Theatre of Cruelty" predating Artaud. At least one French theatre critic was astute enough to recognize this when reviewing *Dramatic Passions II* at the Nancy Festival in 1973: "Ce théâtre de la cruauté, de la violence, de l'incantation, avec lequel l'Occident s'empoigne, les Japonais découvrent qu'il est une partie d'eux-mêmes, peut-être la plus vraie."[9]

Figure 17 The madwoman playing Seigen (Shiraishi Kayoko) hones a kitchen knife. Scene 4 of *On the Dramatic Passions II*. Waseda Shôgekijô Studio, 1973.

This vivid experience was not only embedded in language and literature, it was also for Suzuki a living scar:

> Here's a scar from *moxa* [showing arm]. When I got into mischief, I got burned. Parents wouldn't do such things to children nowadays, but at that time it was used to teach kids a lesson . . . When students came to study *gidaiyû* (puppet-theatre chanting) with my father, I got hit with the tobacco pipe if I laughed . . . And so those lustrous black-beamed houses with their sliding doors in Toga village are definitely a good thing. But the misery on the other side of the screen is very real. For me such a place acts as the most powerful stimulus to the production of dramatic feeling today.[10]

Nanboku's and Izumi Kyôka's gothic melodramas were useful to Suzuki in exposing the dark underbelly of traditional culture; they illustrated how unbearably and "inseparably one is connected to the other members of a Japanese household" (51). Such complex feelings, clearly presented here in the struggles between Hanako and Sakura, also lay at the root of Suzuki's engagement with Greek tragedy, the subject of the next chapter. His childhood experience helped to make him resistant to the Shingeki brand of socialist realism encountered both in his university drama club and in the Shingeki establishment: "What they said was very revolutionary and what they did was very logical, which made them appear free, but I couldn't help thinking that human relationships at the bottom of the pyramid were very different from the way they operated. I rather had the feeling that it could be worse" (55). As a young director he therefore decided to explore this underworld of the young, workers, and women in all its ambiguities because he could not "believe in the value of a westernization which merely replaces Japanese traditions unexamined" (56).

Suzuki's first major success in exploring the gap between these cultural traditions was with *Dramatic Passions II*, in which he directed extracts from classic Japanese plays "in a European way so . . . the tension between Japanese and Western perspectives showed very clearly" (57). Later, with *The Trojan Women* and *The Bacchae*, he would reverse the process, starting to break down the segregation between Shingeki and traditional performance techniques by inviting eminent Noh and Shingeki actors to take part in his "alternative" productions. At the same time he would also work to refine an acting method which could employ elements of both traditions which could be used flexibly not only in Japan but internationally.

Dramatic Passions II stands at the beginning of this process, when Suzuki was feeling his way forward by trial and error. But it was also a planned process. "For me a movement is an attempt to close that gap" between theory and practice. The consistency of Suzuki's long-term concentration on this problematic can be seen very early in his career in his approach to the following extract from *Sumidagawa hana no goshozome* in which he splits identities and blurs the line between illusion and reality.

In Scene 4 the Seigen who has stripped off her mask to answer polite social inanities with "No, I have changed a lot" has indeed shifted identity from Princess Hanako to Nun Seigen. Her lover Matsuwaka has also undergone a change of name as well as a change of heart in becoming her sister's fiancé Yorikuni. For Suzuki the interest of Nanboku's play lay in the very instability of these "social role-play" positions which predated Japan's exposure to the West but which readers of Erving Goffman's *The Presentation of Self in Everyday Life* (1959) would appreciate. In this respect it should be pointed out to those with a Christian name as fixed as the "soul" it identifies that name change was not unusual in Japan before Meiji. For Japanese brought up to accept Buddhist ideas of impermanence and karmic transformation, identity was a more fluid matter, and name change often accompanied social or functional change. For instance, the great actor/playwright usually known as Zeami answered to at least four different appellations during his lifetime: Fujiwaka as a young boy, Motokiyo as a young man, Saemondayû at court, and Zeami in his artistic maturity. He is also known to have taken a Soto Zen priestly name in retirement; and, after death, would have been given yet another Buddhist name.[11]

Subjectivity is treated in a highly mannered way in both Tsuruya Nanboku and Izumi Kyôka, and the fascination for Suzuki seems to have been its fortuitous link with the indeterminate world of Beckett in which "there is no absolute standard which can objectify the self or establish one's identity."[12] Like the Noh fan, even props can take on different identities through intersubjectivity. The bib which "Vladimir" has supplied to the madwoman as "a coat" is, in this scene, identified by Princess Sakura as belonging to her fiancé Yorikuni. When questioned about it Seigen faints, and when revived pronounces, "This is Matsuwaka's coat," trumping her sister in absurdity by then claiming Sakura has poisoned the tea to remove her as a rival. The twisting plot reveals its deep embedding in the complicated intersubjectivities which Suzuki has discussed in terms of the metaphor of a traditional Japanese household (*ie*). Suzuki's critique of the lack of any substantial objective base for these interactions is signified, among other things, by the bib – which calls into question the veracity of both sisters and suggests the way we project internal realities onto external existence. Suzuki's production of a-play-created-by-a-madwoman underwrites a strategy for uncovering and "making visible" the invisible world of the subconscious by which we are all "possessed."[13]

Suzuki makes no attempt to create verisimilitude, for this would be counterproductive to his attempt to expose the gap between conscious and subconscious worlds, as well as the concomitant gap between traditional Japanese and modern Japanese – or Western – values. After ripping apart her traditional prayer beads to show what she would like to do to her sister and wet-nurse, Seigen shines an electric torch into Tsunajo's face and cries, "I'm ill with jealousy." Moreover, the fact that electric torches were foreign to Nanboku's world, but as normal a part of this woman's environment as prayer beads, serves to point up – and prevent naturalization of – the gaps Suzuki wishes us consciously to negotiate between these various worlds. As Senda Akihiko was one of the first critics to point out, Suzuki dramatically weaves found elements from Beckett, Nanboku, Kyôka, Shakespeare, Chekhov, and Euripides to create a complicated interaction in the gap between the playwright's text, the physical realities of the performers themselves, the roles they play in different styles, and the level of the director's critique presented through grotesque juxtapositions in the *mise en scène*. On one level the socially driven reactions of Sakura and Seigen, who both struggle to commit suicide with the cleaver out of shame, are as poignantly absurd in their failure to blame Yorikuni as their Victorian counterparts Betty and Mrs. Saunders are in failing to blame Clive's adultery in Churchill's *Cloud Nine* (I.v). On another level, as one audience member remarked in response to a questionnaire handed out at a Kansai performance of *Dramatic Passions II* in 1971, it is fascinating to try to discover the reality of the actress under her masks (JPAF archives).

Grafting Beckettian indeterminacy onto Nanboku's already unstable base creates a critique which aims to be as deliberately inconsistent as Brecht's tries to be consistent. Suzuki undercuts the ghostly element in Nanboku (which audiences in nineteenth-century Edo accepted as much for entertainment as for edification) by ghastly parody. When Shiraishi's "madwoman" speaks the lines of Nanboku's Seigen (who is trying to make her sister swear to give up her fiancé), she attaches a string to the writing brush she passes to Sakura – and visibly yanks it away while making conventional Kabuki ghost noises (*hyû doro doro*). The levels on which Suzuki reworks Nanboku are complex, but for our purposes it is sufficient to show how, even as Shiraishi heightens the dramatic situation and blurs the line between illusion and reality, Suzuki works to undercut it with such theatrical devices as the-writing-brush-on-a-string, and the handsaw which mad "Seigen" presents to her sister as a literalization of their grudge match (in Japan the expression "grudge saw" is used). Most astonishing of all is the toilet roll she triumphantly presents to Sakura as "our family treasure, the Miyakodori scroll" – and then tears up "to spite Matsuwaka." Her hysterical ripping of the roll gets as out of control as the action in Peter Weiss's *Marat/Sade*, and leads to a similar reassertion of straight-jacketed reality as "the man playing Tsunajo finally manages to knock Shiraishi unconscious" and fasten her wrists to three heavy chains hanging from either side of the stage. When the chained "madwoman" returns to consciousness in Scene 5, she will become Ochô in a scene from Izumi Kyôka's turn-of-the-century gothic novel *Onna keizu* (*Woman's Pedigree*).

The confusion of levels of reality is evident in this designation of Shiraishi as, rather than the "madwoman," the one "knocked unconscious." Around this action, in the pre- and post-production stages, Suzuki worked a double confusion. The actor he cast to play the role of Tsunajo was Fukao Yoshimi (later to become Shiraishi's husband in real life).[14] And it is the process by which "physicalised bodies speaking the multivocal tongues of a group" (31) came to create Scene 5 that he describes as manic:

Our practice probably looked crazy. When new ideas inspired us, we sometimes rehearsed until 3 or 4 o'clock in the morning. Actually Shiraishi's mother told us she thought Shiraishi was obsessive. When she was young, apparently she wouldn't take baths for a while at a time . . . [But that] experience worked well for her. If she said Ochô's words "*Ah-ta*" (dearie) with that smell in mind, it would have the right atmosphere, but if she said "*Anata*" (My dear) after taking a hot bath, she wouldn't have been able to create the feeling of a crazy prisoner longing for romance . . . Shiraishi's dramatic tension came out of a concentration on the surface of her skin, but it was not simply a sanitized mental concentration . . . her body became objectified . . . To me the scene . . . is a modern version of *The Story of Miss O* . . . I told the group to tie up Shiraishi and actually whip her on-stage. We made a rule that she'd speak after being hit. After a stroke, she'd utter "Mr. Hayase!", and get beaten again. Then she'd concentrate on the painful feeling and say her next line . . . We worked to the limits of our concentration. It must have been similar to Grotowski taking Ryszard Cieslak to a church to practise [*The Constant Prince*]. If you had been watching it in a non-theatrical context, it might have looked like sado-masochism . . . But Shiraishi kept reassuring us that she was alright, and that it would not be enough if she simply said "Mr. Hayase" without any physical context for it. Then later on she was able to create the feeling . . . even when she wasn't hit. That was the way we practised in 1969. We couldn't have done such things unless the feeling of the whole group was at fever pitch . . . That was how I realized the importance of having a high level of energy in the group.[15]

Furthermore, Suzuki's stage directions reinscribe the "madwoman" of Scenes 2–4 as "an old . . . unhappy woman," hidden by her family in a garret, who has nothing better to do than amuse herself with lines of a novel she knows and loves. His directions for Shiraishi indicate that she "should not be concentrating on performing Ochô," and that it would also be best "to try to create a balance between grim reality and melodramatic fiction". Like the uncertain gap between "Priest Seigen" and "Nun Seigen," the fact that Shiraishi's fundamental role was also shifting further destabilizes any notions we might have started to construct about the play's consistency. Suzuki embraces multiple perspectives through a Maeterlinckian "interchanging of the roles" in order to deny the idea of "character as an inner essence."[16]

On top of this Suzuki can select this scene as typifying *his own* experience: "My experience of being Japanese can be described like this: being tied up with a chain coiled around the body, struggling to escape, releasing urine on the tatami while being beaten, crunching pickles while sitting trapped, repeating '*Ah-ta*' (dearie). At the time, I could direct *Dramatic Passions II* with real feeling, stretched as I was between love and hate" (57).

So Scene 5 begins with Shiraishi in a spotlight, speaking Ochô's words "*Ah-ta*."[17] The stage seems to expand around her – to represent consciousness – as it is lit up, and the actress's body also seems to dilate as she takes on the role, rising from a formal-seeming bow to the half-squat *kamae* (ready position) of a Noh actor about to begin *shimai* (dance). The words she speaks are dark and mysterious, intimate and meditative at the same time, with many pauses for reflection in which thought seems to travel on under the skin: "*Ah-ta*, isn't it a beautiful moon? What a color . . . Well, I don't mind if the whole world is dark. I'm already living in darkness now . . . (*seeming to answer something we do not hear*) Yes. Be frank with me dear, we knew it from the beginning. We are man and wife but it's a secret. I enjoy this strange situation. There is no moon or snow."

Then, in reply to something else we do not hear, she stands straight up with an answering shout of "Yes!" The lights snap to blue and simultaneously the music of "Purple Ballad" returns. Shiraishi dances like a geisha in time to the music, esthetically stylizing her gestures and showing off her body and its attached chains as if the latter were a directorial comment on the former. In attempting to explain details

Figure 18 The madwoman playing Ochô (Shiraishi Kayoko) twisted up in restraining ropes. Scene 5 of *On the Dramatic Passions II*. Waseda Shôgekijô Studio, 1973.

realistically, we might think that an old gramophone record is playing somewhere in this house, but Shiraishi's acting, aided by the surreal set and the lighting change, all powerfully combine to suggest that she hears her lover and the music in her head.

At "I desperately need you," she runs stage right "as if chasing Hayase's vision," reaches the end of her chain, swivels around into a crouch, and cracks it like a whip (perhaps to emphasize her puppetlike enslavement). Then, twisting the chains tight around her body like a cocoon [Figure 18], she pleads, "Please hold me again . . . You don't know what a true geisha is. I will, I will die . . ." As the old woman goes on with her speech, "So then, you told him you were going to leave me," a young girl comes in with food on a tray and starts preparing it. The old woman pauses, and when there is no response to her line from the girl, gets up from her mat, grabs the girl's hair and shakes and hits her "for forgetting to say Hayase's line," crying out, "You stupid girl! You stupid child!"

Immediately, to underline this mood swing, the music changes to "Uramachi kouta"("Back Street Life") and the girl replies with a line which could be either Hayase's or her own response to her mother's extratextual comment on her daughter's forgetfulness: "Please forgive me. I'm sorry. I did promise you." Mother and daughter exchange several lines of dialogue between Hayase and Ochô, and at the girl's (Hayase's) line, "Well then, will you agree to separate from me?," Shiraishi petulantly grabs a large *daikon* (Japanese radish). She crunches a big piece, spits it out half chewed, then takes another bite, another chew, spitting in stylized parody of an angry child forced to finish her meal before being allowed out to play. "There, I will leave you now," says the old woman (Ochô) as she throws the largely uneaten radish away (in France it became a baguette). But with "Mother!," her daughter breaks out of role to push a spoonful of food into Shiraishi's mouth. Her mother's "Is that for consolation?," said as she knocks the spoon away, could be either Ochô to Hayase or mother to daughter.

The effect of this is to suggest that the two women operate on separate channels but occasionally converge. Shouting "Mother! If you don't eat, you'll die," the daughter twists Shiraishi's arm and forces her to eat. But the old woman sticks doggedly to her reality as "Ochô," gasping between forced mouthfuls, "Is this what the professor sent for me? I was confused and nearly wasted it." But then the pressure of reality becomes too great, and she accidentally urinates into her kimono. We realize this because of her sudden transformation: she stops talking, says, "Ah! Ahhhhh," and slowly turns out her knees, both to look between her legs and to avoid the spreading (virtual) puddle. Incontinence is obviously a common occurrence, for she quickly goes down on all fours, lifts up the back of her kimono, and gets on with her lines about buying tigerlily for Hayase while she waits for her daughter to clean her with tissue paper. When the show went to Paris, the Japanese press was somewhat apprehensive about this scene's effect on the national image. "So much action – even toilet action – on the stage: the mad actress goes to Paris," read one anxious headline in *Shûkan Myôjô* (April 23 1972).

What Suzuki dramatizes are the crossings and recrossings of different levels of consciousness. Bent over, requesting Hayase to "Please look after the lilies for me," Shiraishi pauses at "And then . . ." and seems to take off in a completely different direction with, "Well, why? Isn't that very far? So Shizuoka is further away than Hakone from here." The effect is not so much of madness as of a monomaniacal concentration on the object of her obsession in which links in the chain of thought have been suppressed from speech. Its function seems to be to remind us that the play world presents externalized "flashes" of a largely unexpressed inner world of fantasy which can be glimpsed only through the expressivity of her bodily reactions to inner sensibilities. This obsession, which "took off" in a graceful dance to the music of "Purple Ballad," was initially balanced by a measure of physical control; however, as excitement carried away control, accidental urination became the first sign of a mind/body split. The second was the completely unselfconscious legs-open squat Shiraishi took to rip out pages of her daughter's schoolbook while speaking Ochô's lines about the need to support herself by hairdressing. On seeing the wanton destruction of her textbook, the daughter's patience snaps, and she beats the old woman with her pencilcase, screaming "Die! Die! Die!" She then slams down the bare frame of a *shôji* door in front of her mother to signify her reincarceration.

The music stops here to suggest a major shift of consciousness: the mother's return, however momentary, to awareness of her daughter's presence. But, as the girl backs away, we remain unsure whether mother really is addressing daughter, or whether Ochô still speaks to her imaginary Hayase when she says, "Each of us goes a different direction . . . If I fell, would you come to me? I must choose one of two forks in the road; it's like cutting your body in two." Shiraishi's tone is plaintive but its object remains unclear, again making us self-reflexively aware of the utter subjectivity of our responses to a "reality" we sense but cannot fully comprehend.

From here (Scene 6) the play jump-cuts to a story in the novel *Bakeichô* (*Ghost Ginkoh Tree*) by Izumi Kyôka. The Artaudian doubling of two scenes from Tsuruya Nanboku's "Seigen" plays is deliberately followed by the pairing of scenes from Kyôka novels. And again the similarities serve to foreground the differences. A man (played by Suzuki Ryôzen) crawls in, carrying "a toilet bowl and . . . a big bag. He is very thin from jealousy and sickness and has a fierce expression on his face." He calls "Osada, Osada," and when Shiraishi answers "Yes?," *Bakeichô* has begun. This time it is the man who urinates as he speaks while injecting himself in the leg, vomiting into the bowl, and whining self-pityingly. In another cleaver scene, the husband plays a psychological game with his wife, taking out a knife and tying himself to the *shôji* door as he says:

You are going to leave your dying husband here and go off hand in hand to a hotspring with Shibanosuke [her lover]. I don't mind what you choose, but if the neighbours notice . . . they'll think of you as a bad woman . . . Don't be sly, just kill me. You'll be the murderer of your husband and the public will know . . . Which do you choose, to leave me or to kill me?

No music accompanies this drab, mean-spirited scene, which is focused on the man, but Suzuki resolves it with black comedy. When

Shiraishi/Osada finally settles her dilemma, jabbing him in the back with the knife, the sick man suddenly flees with the toilet bowl in one hand and the "prison door" tied to his back, screaming at the top of his lungs, "Wah! Help, help me!" Only at this point, with the start of Scene 7, does music return "at full volume" in the form of Miyako Harumi's pop song "Sarabade gozansu" ("Farewell Now").

The idea that it signifies a woman's change of consciousness seems to be supported by the stage directions, which indicate that "Shiraishi takes off the chains . . . and starts to dance to the song." The lack of any anchoring context within which to understand Suzuki's *découpage* or the old woman's shifts of imagination can finally only serve to make us more aware of how our imaginations must work to construct with even the slenderest of threads. And also aware of how easily, in so doing, we may enmesh ourselves. As Suzuki has affirmed in interview, "I think I'm close to Beckett . . . This means I believe there is no absolute standard which can objectify the self or establish identity . . . But what I'm saying is that people who live in the real world also have fantasies and illusions. And I'm saying that *these have no end and cannot be solved*"[18] (my italics).

Yet another travesty of love is played out with a cleaver in Scene 8, which reverts to a different scene from Nanboku's *Sumidagawa*. This time Nun Seigen (Shiraishi) comes face to face with the disgraced samurai Sarushima Sôta (Ono Hiroshi) who has, he claims, been sent to kill her by her sister Princess Sakura and ex-lover Matsuwaka. Sôta offers to spare her life in return for sexual favors, but the verbal argument soon turns physical, Seigen is accidentally wounded in the struggle, and Sôta is forced to finish the job he has been sent to do.

The stage directions indicate that Sôta kills Seigen with a cleaver, not a sword as in the Kabuki version. Suzuki points out that "[i]n the past audiences enjoyed the killing scene not simply as a play, but as a spectacle," but when he says, "I want this scene to be a spectacle," he presumably means a different kind of spectacle, closer to the grotesque than the esthetic. The scene pits the two most famous performers of the WLT against each other: Shiraishi Kayoko and Ono Hiroshi, who had played the lead role in Suzuki's productions of Betsuyaku's *Zô* (*The Elephant*). The two were played against social stereotypes, one being a bold, passionate woman, the other a quiet, flinching man. The critic Kan Takayuki has described Ono in performance in 1970 as "poker-faced, nonchalant, nonexpressive,"[19] while Betsuyaku has pointed out the contrast between Ono's passive mode of acting and Suzuki's "aggressiveness of animosity": "Ono's acting often seemed to scatter into space, and Suzuki repeatedly and forcibly rendered it into something more physical and concrete. Through these processes, extreme dramatic tension gradually emerged onto the surface."[20]

As the following dialogue shows, such an acting style was well suited to portrayal of Sôta:

SÔTA: You did this; how could you injure me like this!
SEIGEN: Yes, you wanted to kill me.
SÔTA: Never, never! How could I kill you? I wanted to show you I was seriously in love, but you are wounded. What a stupid thing I did to you. You should rest and try to mind the wound. I will do anything to your hateful Princess Sakura for you. Please change your mind, dear Seigen!

But when Suzuki took Scenes 6 and 8 to the Théâtre des Nations Festival in 1972 as part of a Japanese delegation research seminar on "Physical Movement," the role of Sôta was appropriated by Kanze Hideo. His acting was less "flinching" than refined, the legacy of his early training as a Kanze School Noh actor.

Another unusual feature of this scene was Suzuki's stage direction that "only this scene should faithfully follow the emotions in the original script." His strategy is not immediately apparent. Why should this scene not emphasize the gap between the old woman's play world and her reality, as the others had done? The answer, I think, lies in its placement as the last scene; it creates a stark contrast. Thus, if Shiraishi is successful, it demonstrates the power of the great actress to convince us of the truth of her presentation of "dramatic passions," even when we have repeatedly seen that they are not hers. On another level it can also be seen as the final revelation of the powerful emotions "buried deep in my heart" which have hitherto lain beneath the surface of the old woman's role-playing. As Suzuki has said in interview, perhaps echoing Chikamatsu on the fine line between the real and the unreal, "It is not realism, but it is real."[21] (It is no accident that Suzuki will be training young Moscow Art Theatre actors in his Method and directing them in *King Lear* at the MAT in 2004.) The disgraced samurai Sôta makes something like this point in a metatheatrical Kabuki statement at the beginning of the scene, retorting to Seigen, "I don't care whether you are a nun or a traveling actress. Will you be my wife?"[22]

The ghoulish, voyeuristic nature of this prolonged, sordid killing was highly applauded in Paris, as was Kanze Hisao's stylized performance of female jealousy in the Noh play *Dôjôji*. However, what made the play so sensational in Japan was its revelation of a new way forward for Japanese stage acting caught in the barbed wire of the great divide between Shingeki and traditional theatre. The new possibility opened up was one in which "the impulses which people have deep inside their minds" (director's note to text) could be revealed externally through the device of a play-within-a-play. In Japan – and France and Poland at least within Europe – it was recognized that this device paradoxically involved the use of traditional acting methods and dramatic structures to convey a modern condition, subverting Western realism from deep within the domain of traditional Japanese culture. More astonishingly, the chief exponent of this recycling was an ex-office girl with no training whatsoever in either Noh, Kabuki, or Stanislavskian realism. So famous has Shiraishi become in Japan, and indeed around the world as a "shamanic" performer in the tradition of Okuni (foundress of Kabuki), that she is one of only a handful of nontraditional performers who have since been invited to perform with traditional Noh and Kabuki actors.[23]

JOHN SILVER

John Silver and *Kachikachiyama* (*Mountain on Fire*) were performed together in July 1996 at the Toga Summer Festival as vehicles for two of the three remaining veterans of Suzuki's old guard: Takemori Yôichi and Shiohara Michitomo. Neither had played a leading role before, although both were senior actors of great experience. For Takemori's benefit, Suzuki had revived a 1995 ACM production by Hasegawa Hirohisa of Kara Jûrô's *John Silver*, in which Ômori Kikuyo had originally played the role of the transvestite Koharu. For Shiohara, Suzuki created a new adaptation of Dazai Osamu's 1945 folktale *Kachikachiyama*, which he had first directed in 1967 as *Usagi to tanuki* (*Rabbit and Raccoon*).

The double bill marked a strategic shift from the production of foreign classics (1982–95) to the production of modern Japanese classics. The new direction also marked an established artist's return from a new angle to interests he had held in the period 1967–69, immediately before *Dramatic Passions II* had catapulted him to national and international prominence. In that period he had worked closely with Betsuyaku Minoru, Satoh Makoto, and Kara Jûrô, three of the five playwrights[24] whom Tsuno Kaitarô had seen as initiating the Little Theatre movement's innovative experiments with "multidimensional expression." Suzuki had successfully produced Betsuyaku's *The Little Match Girl* between 1966 and 1968, Satoh's *My Beatles* in 1967, and Kara's *The Virgin's Mask* in 1969 (the first and third of these plays had won the Kishida Prize for Playwriting in 1968 and 1969 respectively).

Tsuno has argued that the purpose of the Little Theatre movement's break with Shingeki realism was:

to use the pre-modern popular imagination as a negating force to transcend the modern [Shingeki]. We feel that, although Shingeki's break with the classical Noh and Kabuki was both justified and inevitable, it nonetheless cut us off from the sources of our traditions and trapped us within the restrictive confines of a static, bourgeois institution. Today we are seeking to reaffirm our tradition, but not as our predecessors did in the years leading up to the war. To them, reaffirming traditional values meant an atavistic and uncritical reinstatement of a fictitious, idealized past. We, on the other hand, are attempting to reaffirm our tradition, even when we find it distasteful, in order to deal directly and critically with it. Our hope is that by harnessing the energy of the Japanese popular imagination we can at once transcend the enervating clichés of modern [realist] drama and revolutionize what it means to be Japanese.[25]

Suzuki had played an active role in the *Shôgekijô* (Little Theatre) movement which initiated this program, and was now returning to it with the hindsights of a quarter-century of theatre making. When he was interviewed in 1995, he seemed to have been stung by Matsuoka Kazuko's observation that "there are few modern plays that you have directed," replying, "Not quite. I did Betsuyaku Minoru and Kara Jûrô."[26] However, this had been in the 1960s, and seemed only to confirm a tide of opinion in 1990s Japanese theatre circles that Suzuki's work was no longer "relevant" because he "only performed Western classics." Just one year later he was adapting Kara Jûrô and Dazai Osamu.

Suzuki's choice of Dazai and Kara as vehicles for this new localization of his efforts was well considered, for both are consummate stylists. A new avenue of exploration presented itself because his previous work with foreign classics had been in translation. Despite the fact that some of his translators and literary collaborators have been outstanding (such as Matsudaira Chiaki and Ôoka Makoto), there often exists a large gap between good translation and the immediacy of great writing. Suzuki had become particularly conscious of this when, in working on *The Chronicle of Macbeth* in 1992, he had accessed the power of Shakespeare's poetry through his Australian actors. As he articulated the problem in the 1995 interview: "Honestly speaking, the most difficult thing is the text . . . Ninagawa was accepted [abroad] simply because he had the power to command the space . . . [But] if British audiences understood Japanese, they would think Shakespeare's words were dead."[27]

Of course the major compensating factor in doing foreign classics in translation was that they opened a window to an international audience who would be primarily responding to the visual appeal and musical, kinetic energies of the production. However, by 1995 the cumulative weight of Suzuki's commitments seems to have influenced his decision to concentrate on nurturing a younger generation of Japanese artists at home (in SPAC and through Theatre InterAction) rather than continuing to pursue success abroad: "These days I have been [too] busy training foreigners. So I would [now] like to concentrate on producing good productions in Japan."[28]

Kara Jûrô was a particularly wise choice. As David Goodman has put it, Kara's "vitality of language, refusal to compromise with reality, and ability to give form to the subliminal fantasies of the Japanese people have made him the most popular and marketable of Japan's playwrights young or old."[29] He was a colleague and friend and, like Suzuki, "a devotee of Surrealism," famous for his view that "reality is nothing more than an arbitrary social construction that can be challenged and altered by art."[30] Moreover, adapting a living author with such views was not likely to create difficulties, Kara goodnaturedly telling Suzuki in rehearsal that the latter's alterations and resituation of the play had been very well worked out.[31]

In a program note to the 1996 Toga production of *John Silver*, Suzuki synopsized the play in this way:

the female protagonist wishes to escape from the unhappy circumstances in which she finds herself. Her passionate desire has turned her into Koharu, wife of the burly one-legged pirate John Silver, without her realizing it. Kara Jûrô's words, which brilliantly describe a human being in trapped circumstances and the hopeful fantasy produced to counteract it, are well lifted out by Hosokawa Toshio's music in the Toga Sanbô space.

In the 1996 Saitama program, Suzuki was more revealing of his creative process: "For some time I've been thinking of creating a play using Hosokawa Toshio's violin melodies. As I listened to them, the phrases that floated up unbidden from my subconscious were those of Kara Jûrô. The mysterious meeting in myself of Hosokawa and Kara created this play."

Suzuki was squaring his desire to use live music with a wish to produce a contemporary Japanese master-stylist in his own vein. (Although the name John Silver is taken from R. L. Stevenson's *Treasure Island*, Kara's adaptation ironically borrows little more than one or two motifs.) In interpreting Kara's elusive theme as "the need of human beings to fantasize," he was drawing together a web of associations. Beckett's *Waiting for Godot*, Kobayashi Hideo's idea that "history is a problem of memory," and the fabricated "tradition" of the AUM Shinrikyô cult all presented symptoms of a twentieth-century malaise that a local audience could contemplate collectively and individually. Suzuki hoped to attract both intellectuals and a younger *manga*-reading generation through the theme he drew from Kara. The problem of "the need to fantasize" was foregrounded theatrically in two ways. First, by having a male actor cross-dress, thus keeping the question of gender identity and social construction always before the audience's eyes; and second, by maintaining their self-conscious awareness of image-projection through use of a mirror-wall set. Whereas Kara's 1965 *John Silver* was set in a public toilet in a waste lot (appropriate to recent memories of a still unreconstructed Tokyo), Suzuki's production in the affluent 1990s is set in a retro mansion.

Since Suzuki couches his theme in the form of a murder-mystery melodrama, the play begins in darkness to the powerfully nostalgic strains of Urushihara Asako's violin. As the lights come up, three nurses and a cross-dressed Barber (Takahashi Hiroko) are seen polishing the sliding glass screen-doors of the house in time to the music with big, sweeping motions which reveal their red underwear (what Kara provocatively calls "the panties of memory").

The screens are so extensive, reaching right across the stage, that they mirror everything in front of them, actors and even audience, ensuring that both they and we are self-consciously drawn into this "hall of mirrors" search for identity. The nonsensical, Absurdist action of Kara's play quickly confirms Suzuki's point in the program note that "in modern society even the identity of groups to which people belong are collapsing." And it pointed up the desperate way in which individuals and groups can create subcultures of "hope-giving illusions spun out of fabricated history, as is seen in the case of AUM Shinrikyô" (Saitama program 1998).

Even SCOT history, it seems to me, could be seen as parodied. The set (which had traveled to the RSC in 1994 for *King Lear*) is a mock-up of the Toga Sanbô – but not quite. The paper of its sliding screens (*shôji*) is replaced by glass, and its interior decoration reflects the decadence of the Bubble Economy years. Center stage is a red Japanese armchair without legs in the shape of a giant clam; directly in front of it is a smaller white seashell masking a footlight but also serving ironically to highlight the unprepossessing occupant as a grotesque Botticellian Venus. Behind stage right is a retro-prop, a black pram containing a doll in pirate uniform. Stage left stands a large polished-wood kangaroo holding a drinks tray (its pouch containing a liquor cabinet).

As the nurses and Barber polish the glass sliding screens upstage, an unattractive-looking man who calls himself Koharu (the name of a famous Chikamatsu heroine) self-consciously crosses the stage. Correcting his appearance to fit his self-image, he is made up like a Kabuki *onnagata* (female impersonator). Yet his dress is a white wedding kimono and the long black wig of a stage ghost (on entry he even poses against a fake Sanbô pillar to visually quote a famous *kata* symbolizing the unsatisfied desire of a *hannya*, a malevolent living spirit, in *Aoi no ue*). In his hand he/she carries a mysterious white violin case. Koharu wavers between her menials, who appear behind her as images of desire (young nurses in miniskirts and red panties) and derision (the Barber, played by Takahashi Hiroko as a man in fat-suit and Groucho Marx moustache).

Scene 2 begins as the latter exit and two prostitutes in black negligées and bare feet peer in through the glass at the transvestite, casing her joint. Kuboniwa Naoko and Tateno Momoyo play the Older and Younger Sisters as tough, streetwise, cheerful human rats. Without knowing it they, too, are looking for "Silver." To the one this means spoons, to the other it means the man who "went away like an express train [after] I was raped." They approach Koharu and start to nose round the gender question:

YOUNGER: Hey you! What color is the memory of a man? . . . Does your
    stomach ache from just thinking?
OLDER: What kind of smell was it? Lavender? Or the smell of mosquito coil?[32]

Each tries to "buy" Koharu's memory, and then to bully it out of her by threatening to strip-search her to her underpants. [Figure 19] Meeting with no response from Koharu, who huddles in her "shell" clutching the violin case, Older Sister pulls a knife but is wrestled to the ground by Younger Sister and persuaded by Koharu that, if they want to hear her "threadbare memory," they must stick the blade point into the floor, make the handle quiver, and listen. So they do. Older Sister asks, "What's that? Ain't 'Brmm Brmm' a man's memory?" With quite a bit of scatological play, the scene establishes Koharu's point that "Memories can't be followed"; however, the two prostitutes are tenacious and eventually latch onto the idea that her memories lie in her treasured violin case, which they offer to "suck" and "squeeze."

In Scene 3 the old Gentleman (Tsutamori) appears in a red-and-black bathrobe with a white towel over his shoulder. A civil servant working in a museum as a custodian of memory, he claims to take nocturnal swims in the ocean where he once "bumped into 74 dead bodies." As he speaks

Figure 19 The street girls (Tateno Momoyo and Kuboniwa Naoko) shout abuse at the cross-dressed "Koharu" (Takemori Yôichi). *John Silver*. Saitama, 1996.

a Boy (Katoh Masaharu) in shorts, shirt, and straw hat enters, listens, and when asked by the Barber to come in, departs without explanation.

Next, in Scene 4, the Gentleman succeeds in getting the transvestite to open her violin case. Inside is a prosthetic leg belonging to Koharu's lover (John Silver), who suddenly left his job at the Benten bath-house (Benten is the goddess of music) and disappeared in search of adventure "down the long gray platform of the Yamanote Line" (JR railway track circling Inner Tokyo). The contrast between the mundane imagery and the woman's impassioned delivery is incongruous but reinforces Suzuki's point that fantasy feeds on hope – which only death can cut off. "It was a tranquil day, but the sea was rough," as Kara's prose has it.

In Scene 5 the Boy reappears with a butterfly net and launches into the story of its loss "nine years and seven months ago." Narration carries him imaginatively into action as he catches a Black Admiral. The surprise extension of his long retractable-handled butterfly net, as physically vivid as a lizard's tongue capturing a fly, stands for the imaginative capture of reality in Katoh's hands. The Boy's happiness appears to reside in his being able to shut out everything else. He is distinctly uninterested in the Barber's identification of him as Number 73,[33] and runs off with the remark, "Hey, the bank can keep this net in their safe, can't they?"

In Scene 6 the Gentleman tells Koharu, "There's someone I should let you meet." As he sits in the barber's chair to have a haircut, the *enka* strains of "Yagiri no watashi" ("Yagiri Ferry") come in, ten un-clothed mannequin dolls descend from the flies over the set, and the lighting change reveals two John Silvers on the other side of the glass. One has one leg, uses a crutch, and is blind (Nakayama Ichirô); the other crawls on his hands because both legs have been amputated at the knee (Ôsawa Atsushi). They get the transvestite Koharu to sing "our hon-eymoon song" and then both deny being the real Silver, pointing out to her that "the one who summoned us was you." When she cries "Who were you?," they reply, "Memories of odds and ends." Again the *enka* "Yagiri Ferry" plays as two giant video screens descend just above the set (the effect is reminiscent of the surreal suspended *shôji* in *Dramatic Passions II*) and a silent video of a huge Hokusai-like breaking wave is split across both screens.[34] The effect is breathtakingly spectacular and strangely moving, but utterly unanalyzable in its subconscious impact.

In Scene 7, as this melodramatic moment of pure fantasy ends, Koharu repeats "Odds and ends of memory" and her two Silvers tell her they will soon die, "Because, Koharu, you don't exist anymore, and Silver never existed from the beginning." Ghosts multiply in the glass and vanish as the light fades.

In Scene 8 the two prostitutes reappear, a violinist in nurse's uniform looks on from the orchestra pit, the video screens are flown, and the dolls descend again, bathed in blue light. The Barber finishes the Gentleman's haircut, and together they persuade Koharu, "You aren't anything like Koharu. You're a grotesque apparition . . . A monster . . . You're Num-ber 74." The transvestite cries, "If those people were really Silvers, I'd be alright. Even if I prove to be Number 74 . . . I really want to know the truth!" But the old Gentleman's answer is ambiguous: "Only what was reflected in front of your eyes just now was the truth." The sliding screens at the back are, of course, by turns reflective, transparent, or opaque, depending on how they are lit. Often the audience can see two Koharus, one from the front, the other from behind, and sometimes the image of one actor is superimposed on another as they stand in front of and behind the glass under different lighting conditions. (The lighting designer responsible for these effects was Shiohara Michitomo.) This is the point of the Gentleman's comment, "Though you want to embrace two people with your four legs, try to reflect your shape well. For that reason, this scene is set in a barber's shop [he offers her the barber's chair]. You aren't anything like Koharu. You're a grotesque." The imagination is not simply reflective, it is capable of overlaps, fragmentations, and distortions – a transvestite in crisis at the barber's.

"The saying that people change is true," the transvestite replies as the old Gentleman takes a sake bottle from the kangaroo dumb-waiter's pouch "to celebrate the voyage of the coffin ship." But as they raise their glasses in a toast, the tapping of a crutch is heard – and the sound of a violin. The Gentleman breaks the frozen moment with a vigorous denial of the possibility of Silver's return:

GENTLEMAN: Even if that fellow were him, the only thing I'd do for him is give him the number 75.
BARBER: I tell you, he's the only one who survived.
GENTLEMAN: Even a survivor, once back, can do nothing when his number's up.

Bathetically, in Scene 9, at the moment when the transvestite expects to see the second coming of Silver, the sound of the crutch stops – and the Boy steps through the open screen doors with a crutch in his hands. In the wreck of Koharu's hopes, he describes how he found it on the beach. Then, after an absurd exchange of non sequiturs about his "identity" as Number 73, the tapping sound of a crutch is heard again, accompanied by violin. The audience laugh, and as the Gentleman and Boy leave, the nurses return to polish the "windows of the soul" with the Barber; they do this in time to the music, making large sweeping motions that expose the nurses' red panties and wobble the Barber's grotesquely padded bottom, while Koharu sits like a stone.

For the last time the two prostitutes return, popping their heads over the glass screens like Japanese ghosts as the violinist mounts the steps from the orchestra pit to take possession of the stage with her nostalgic playing. The Sisters describe this desolate space as "a museum, because there are dolls in it" (Koharu, clutching her prosthetic leg, is as motionless as the pirate doll in the pram behind her and the naked mannequin dolls suspended overhead). In this museum of memory, their nonsensical talk reveals that they have both forgotten everything. They laugh and jeer – and again Silver's crutch is heard tapping its way along the corridor behind the glass screens. But this time it is the Gentleman who appears (the museum curator). Is he to be the Sisters' next victim, Number 75 – or are they to be his?

YOUNGER: I've taken a fancy to that fellow's eyes.
OLDER: I'll take them out . . . then I'll give ya the left one.
YOUNGER: Scary!
OLDER: Are ya really scared?
YOUNGER: Just try to touch it, here. (They touch.) You too!

What this account cannot capture is the brilliance of Kara's dialogue, marvelously incarnated by Suzuki's sensuous *mise en scène*, for this evaporates before the drying agency of discursive prose. Meyerhold's is still the most discerning description of the theatrical terrain within which Suzuki is working:

> The art of the grotesque is based on the conflict between form and content. The grotesque aims to subordinate psychologism to a decorative task. That is why, in every theatre which has been dominated by the grotesque, the aspect of design in its widest sense has been so important (for example, the Japanese theatre). Not only the settings, the architecture of the stage, and the theatre itself are decorative, but also the mime, movements, gestures and poses of the actors.[35]

Suzuki's own theoretical pronouncements[36] certainly support Meyerhold's dictum, "The theatre's sole obligation is to assist the actor to reveal his soul to the audience."[37] A comparison of *Dramatic Passions II* and *John Silver* demonstrates not only the distance Suzuki's theatre has traveled from 1970 to 1996, but also the difference between a Shiraishi and a Takemori.

Suzuki's Euripides (I): *The Trojan Women*

Ian Carruthers

Toroia no onna (*The Trojan Women*) was undoubtedly the Waseda Little Theatre's most artistically successful production worldwide. Arguably it ranks alongside Brecht's *Mother Courage* and Brook's *A Midsummer Night's Dream* as one of the most innovative, spectacular, and critically acclaimed productions of the second half of the twentieth century. Between 1974, when it opened at the Iwanami Hall in Tokyo, and 1989, when it was performed for the last time in Helsinki, the show had been seen and acclaimed in thirty-four foreign cities (twice in Paris, Athens, and Chicago) and in twelve Japanese cities and towns.[1] This last statistic was especially notable at a time when major theatre companies were seldom seen outside Tokyo. Only Suzuki's adaptations of *The Bacchae* (1978–2001) rival the international success of *The Trojan Women* over as many years, having also traveled to South America, Russia, and Turkey, as well as to Europe and the United States.

Ostensibly about the fall of Troy, Euripides' play was performed in Athens in 415 BC, only a year after the Athenians had massacred the entire male population of Melos and enslaved its women and children.[2] Part of the enduring appeal of this nearly structureless play is not only its protest against the horrors of war *per se*, but the way in which it reworks a heroic mythic past in terms of contemporary realities, and places women center stage as protagonists. In these respects it was an ideal vehicle for Suzuki's artistic and cultural concerns and the talents of a great actress, Shiraishi Kayoko.

In this century, as Fiona Macintosh has observed, "playwrights and directors [have] frequently turned to Greek tragedies as a safe vehicle for exploring forbidden ideas closer to home."[3] With the rise of the suffragette movement, and as World War I threatened to engulf the United States as well as Europe and the Commonwealth, *The Trojan Women* reemerged as a text for the times. It is hardly surprising then, that in 1974, with the devastation of World War II still fresh in many minds and the possibility of nuclear holocaust ever present with the Cold War, Suzuki's production should have tapped a broad and deep vein of feeling. As he put it himself, "the fundamental drama of our time is anxiety in the face of impending disaster" (program note).

Artistically Suzuki's experience of producing *Dramatic Passions II* in Europe had sharpened his awareness of what could effectively cross national barriers. When a play's story is already well known to a foreign audience, a new physically based approach can be highly effective. Not only does it become easier to follow the plot, but the changes rung on familiar material can actually enhance enjoyment and involvement. In Peter Burian's words, "tragedy is not casually or occasionally intertextual, but always and inherently so . . . a tragic plot inheres not simply in a poetic text, but also in the dialectic between that text in performance and the responses of an informed audience to the performance as repetition and innovation."[4] Thus a production which drops the opening debate between Poseidon and Athena, cuts Helen, and frames the action in the burned-out ruins of postwar Tokyo is bound to arouse more than curiosity. The history of the adaptation and updating of Greek tragedy is a long one, going back well beyond Goethe and Racine to Roman times, and was widely practiced in Europe from the turn of the twentieth century, by both playwrights and directors.[5] While undoubtedly aware of such practices (he had already produced Sartre's *The Flies*), Suzuki's preferred term for such intertextual practice is *honkadori*, a term from classical Japanese literature meaning "allusive variation."

In a comparison of Greek and Japanese traditional theatre forms, many interesting parallel features emerge.[6] Both grew out of religious rituals performed for the gods and developed into secular entertainment with mass appeal; both make use of poetry, music, dance, and spectacle together with stylized acting which involves the use of masks; and both depend on intertextuality for their discourse. More important than these similarities, however, are the differences. Greek performance traditions are long lost, which means they are now open to investigation and experiment, whereas Japan's ancient performance traditions have been preserved, but remain in danger of becoming fossilized if not fruitfully cross-fertilized with contemporary forms. Suzuki has expanded on this topic in a 1975 panel discussion:

My choice of it [*The Trojan Women*] has something to say about the state of theatre in Japan today and about the state of culture in general . . . Theatre in Japan is somewhat different from what we find in the West . . . To put it simply, we in Japan have Noh, Kyogen, Kabuki, Shingeki, and Underground theatre. When the Royal Shakespeare Company does Shakespeare, they don't perform him the way we might see one of his Japanese contemporaries performed on the Kabuki stage. The British perform Shakespeare as modern theatre. In Japan however, the classics are not a normal part of the modern theatre repertory. Chikamatsu and Nanboku are done in Kabuki. Zeami is performed by Noh actors . . . That is why in my production of *The Trojan Women* I have wished to use techniques and ideas from Noh, Shingeki, and Kabuki in the hopes that I could bring together into one single modern drama some of the qualities of each of these independent Japanese theatres.[7]

Certainly one of the major attractions of the original Iwanami Hall production in 1974–75 was the way it featured, for the very first time, major Noh and Shingeki performers (Kanze Hisao and Ichihara Etsuko) working alongside an "Underground" actress renowned for her neo-Kabuki style (Shiraishi Kayoko).[8] Even more sensational in subsequent years, after the untimely death of Kanze Hisao and the departure of Ichihara, was the way Shiraishi went on to play the former's role of the old vagrant, the latter's Cassandra, and her original role of Hecuba in three distinct styles. Not surprisingly, Fiona Macintosh can state in *The Cambridge Companion to Greek Tragedy*, "It is undoubtedly the postwar Japanese productions [by Suzuki and Ninagawa] that celebrate this internationalism [of Greek drama] most fruitfully."[9]

The Trojan Women has been called "Euripides' *Endgame*,"[10] a view which partly elucidates Suzuki's interest, given his fascination with Beckett. Not only is Euripides' play almost plotless, but, as Suzuki points out in his 1979 Milwaukee play program, it "is set in a postwar period" in which "the women are simply waiting." Indeed a number of critics have seen something of Beckett's Winnie in the old woman of Suzuki's contemporary frame-story.[11]

In describing how he set about reworking Euripides, Suzuki also explains the function of this old woman (old man when Kanze Hisao was performing):

When I decided to stage *The Trojan Women*, my first step was to eliminate from the text all the technical terms that require special knowledge . . . [leaving] only the fragments in which the characters lay bare their feelings . . . But in order to perform them in Japan today . . . the various pieces had to be organized anew into some kind of setting according to our own contemporary sensibility . . . I took several fragments from Euripides and then asked Makoto Ôoka to write some poems . . . An old woman (the main character) thinks about the characters that appear in *The Trojan Women*. In this way, what comprises the theatrical present is not the existence of characters from Euripides but a single old woman who imagines them. This character herself is . . . clearly in . . . post-war Japan. (1979 Milwaukee program)

This was no philistine "gutting of the text," however, as Suzuki shows. He was careful to balance the beautiful classical Japanese translation of Matsudaira Chiaki with specially commissioned pieces from Ôoka, a major modern poet, and translations of these were on display in the English program. A retranslation of a Western classic into local idioms which could still remain accessible to ordinary human experience accounted for a large part of the appeal of the production, both at home and abroad.

For the theatre critic Senda Akihiko, Suzuki's use of squatting onstage constituted the most interesting aspect of his critique of the modern:

It seems to me that Suzuki's experiment has taken the stuff of Greek tragedy (which constitutes, after all, the source of all Western drama) and "reread" it altogether in terms of the Japanese national sensibility and body movements, creating in the process what is essentially a new form. Further, such a production constitutes a strong critique of the kinds of productions of Western drama presented until now in Japan, productions that privilege traditional European interpretations of the text, thereby denying any role to authentic Japanese (indeed Asian) sensibilities . . . In this context, it seems to me that there is real significance in the fact that this production is being presented at the Iwanami Hall in Tokyo, . . . that very spot that so strongly symbolises this older approach to Western culture . . . So it is, then, that we are able both to witness this tragedy of ancient Greece and to have the rare experience of a drama set in contemporary Japan.[12]

The response of foreign critics was equally positive, both toward Suzuki's reshaping of the myth in a modern context, and to the acting skills of Shiraishi in particular and the company in general. On its first tour to Europe, André Tunc, professor at the University of Paris I, referred to it as "une tragédie d'une force et d'une beauté exceptionelles, un sommet de l'art théâtral de tous les temps et de tous les lieux" (*La Croix*, June 2 1977). For Pierre Marcabru, "Tadashi Suzuki réussit le tour de force de renouveler un genre noble et ancien sans le diminuer, de l'accorder à nos sensibilités modernes sans le trahir. L'extrême rigueur du travail est hommage au passé. L'extrême tension du récit un rappel du présent" (*Figaro*, May 30 1977). And Ghigo De Chiara could describe Shiraishi's Hecuba as "stupendamente interpretato," comparing it to Hélène Weigel's Mother Courage and adding that the audience "applaudito a lungo (come raramente accade a Roma)" (*Avanti*, June 9 1977).

At the Los Angeles Olympics, Kevin Kelly of *The Boston Globe* referred to it as "[o]ne of the single greatest nights in the whole sweep of world theatre," going on to add, by way of an instructive comparison, "Strictly speaking, this is not the case with [Ariane Mnouchkine's Théâtre] du Soleil [*Richard II*] . . . four hours of foreign Shakespeare proved frustrating . . . But Suzuki has so concentrated his approach that there's truly no language barrier at all" (July 1 1984). Jonathan Saville located the production's excellence in terms similar to Marcabru's, calling it "agonizingly true to the original precisely because everything in the play has been boldly revised and recreated . . . his characters are both modern and ancient at the same time"; and Michael Lassell of *Theatre* was quoted as calling the "acting so unquestionably splendid that all future stage activity in LA should be measured against it" (*Bravo*, 4:3 Spring 1985). This last was an opinion shared by Lucia Anderson when Peter Sellars invited the production to open the American National Theatre's "Major International Companies" series in Washington the following year: "the way the cast moves is perhaps the most extraordinary part of the evening" (*Potomac News*, May 24 1985).

In London, Irving Wardle would concur, speaking of "a world theatre event in the same class as the past productions of [Tadeusz] Kantor, [Habib] Tanvir, [and Shûji] Terayama" (*The Times*, April 12 1985). For Michael Ratcliffe, "The acting of Shiraishi – voice wrenched from the belly and rising through fearful colours and strains unthinkable under Western training, face gleaming with the triumph of indestructible despair – is by any standards, astounding" (*The Observer*, April 14 1985). And John Barber would describe her voice as "the conscience of mankind in contemplating the holocaust"; it "scrapes, roars and scorches like a human blow-torch" (*The Daily Telegraph*, April 11 1985). Michael Billington, too, would laud Shiraishi's "towering performance" and Suzuki's "imagistic gifts." For him, "Suzuki's achievement is to have forged a style that unites past and present," and he qualifies this, with reference to the Melos massacre, by adding that this, "after all, is what Euripides' play is all about" (*The Guardian*, April 11 1985).

Euripides' *The Trojan Women* is ideally suited, as Joseph McLellan has noted, to Suzuki's kind of adaptation "because it is not burdened with a plot" (*Washington Post*, May 29 1985). It is an ideal vehicle for a star actor, for Hecuba is onstage throughout the entire play and her presence, more than anything, gives structure to a series of exchanges with Talthybius, the Chorus, Cassandra, Andromache, Menelaus, and Helen. By the time Suzuki was considering the play in 1973, *Dramatic Passions II* had nearly run its course, and he was looking for another vehicle to match the talents of Shiraishi. Greek drama proved an ideal choice for the repertory direction in which Suzuki was now taking a company increasingly dedicated to the nurturing of exceptional physical skills.[13]

The stage setting was another contributing factor to the production's success. Although the 1974 program summary indicates that "the action takes place in the ruins of a cemetery" this is more in the nature of a virtual marker for the imaginations of the audience than a description of anything to be seen onstage. Performed in the open air, as in Toga, nothing whatever limited imagination of place except the enveloping darkness, in which only the main action was well lit. Performed indoors, as at the Iwanami Hall in Tokyo (1974–75) and the Riverside Studios in London (1985), green mosquito netting with red borders, which to Suzuki "somehow suggested something unlucky,"[14] was hung from the ceiling and lit with hints of green, red, and blue light. For different audience members this carried different personal associations. To Dan Sullivan of the *Los Angeles Times* it was like "looking at phosphorescent sea creatures through a bathysphere window" (June 20 1984). For T. H. McCulloch the drapes looked like "cobwebs on the human soul" (*Drama-logue*, June 21–27 1984). John Barber of *The Daily Telegraph* saw them as "thunderclouds" (April 11 1985), while to others they suggested "dripping foliage or ravaged skin" (Heda Weiss, *Sun Times*, May 14 1986), or "a parachute-draped, bombed-out, post-World War II city" (Richard Christiansen, *Chicago Tribune*, May 14 1986). Interestingly, one – but only one – critic complained about this "cave of pantomime drapes which is, in fact, a cemetery" (Michael Coveney, *Financial Times*, April 12 1985).

Suzuki's Scene 1 replaces the speeches of Poseidon and Athena with a Kabuki *danmari*, a dumb-show in which the cast make characterizing entrances. As a temple bell tolls:

Jizô, the Buddhist guardian deity of children, enters, followed by three figures costumed in black (incarnations of the fear of death), the Chorus, and three warriors. An old woman (Kayoko Shiraishi) comes on, guided by the dead. During the war she has lost her husband, sons and daughters. She carries a bundle containing the remnants of her home. (Los Angeles Olympic Arts Festival program, 1984)

What at first sounds like a Buddhist temple bell tolling the futility of all human endeavor, as in *The Tale of the Heike*, turns out to be electronically synthesized modern music with "underworld" associations. This becomes apparent at the entry of the god Jizô, which takes a full four and a half minutes. He carries a long staff and proceeds upstage in a brocade saffron robe, "stiff, expressionless, and with eyes fixed in the distance."[15]

Perhaps because he is to remain immobile center stage through nearly the whole ninety minutes of playing time (he makes one gesture at the very end), his entry features two extremely athletic formal movements. These serve to underline the fact that this "act of standing still" is as highly charged with repressed energy as it is in the Noh theatre. Fueda Uichirô (Jizô from 1979 to 1989) has explained that what gives the actor stage presence when immobile is fierce mental concentration, and that for him this took the form of imagining an intensely bright pinpoint of light at a great distance. So effective was this concentrated stillness that, at one performance in the moonlit Toga amphitheatre, a spider had time to spin a web between hip and spear arm to catch the mosquitos feasting on his exposed arms.

Jizô's athletic moments are peaks in a choreographed entry as precise and abstract as anything in Beckett. Everything is timed by the "bell," which sounds irregularly to enhance our awareness of *ma* (space/time).[16] As Jizô approaches center stage after the fourth toll, he seems to peer into the future. On what sounds like a synthesized drum tap ("tok"), he raises his spear arm high over head, lowers it on the fifth, raises his right leg just before the sixth, and extends it slowly to full stretch at hip level. On another "tok" he flexes the heel, toes up, and then straightens the foot, like a ballet dancer "on pointe," before lowering it extremely slowly. These are Noh skills updated for the modern stage; while none of the movements is one of the actual Noh *kata* (forms), the principles of manipulation of time, space, and audience attention are Noh derived.

In contrast to the slow, stately, ritual procession of Jizô, the three figures in black glide quickly across the stage behind the god, taking up positions in the shadows so that only their chalk-white faces glow like death's-heads. (By 1982 these melodramatic "incarnations of the fear of death" had gone.) The entry of the Chorus is even faster. They scurry in from all directions in *shikko* to form a line of crouching figures down stage right, "symbolizing humiliation and defeat" in Gotoh's words (Suzuki thesis, 301). Irving Wardle of *The Times* described their movement as "a sitting crouch with . . . legs moving at the speed of sea-coast birds" (*The Times*, April 12 1985), and this is prescient, for Cassandra will later refer to them as a "myriad flock of marsh-birds." They are both homeless survivors of World War II and captives of Troy, unkempt in tattered kimono, and carrying their few remaining possessions in *furoshiki* (knotted scarves). [Figure 20]

By contrast, the guards of the Greek army are identified not so much by their banditlike appearance as by their swaggering walk, which Wardle

Figure 20 The Chorus bring little gifts wrapped in knotted scarves to Hecuba (Shiraishi Kayoko) for her dead grandson (foreground). *The Trojan Women*. Iwanami Hall, 1974.

wryly characterized as "outdoing the articulation of the goosestep." [Figure 21] Actually, like the synthesized temple bell, its articulation is bifocal, also suggesting the *aragoto* walk of Kabuki ruffians and even of Jizô. All of these entrance walks showcase the ability of Suzuki's physical vocabulary to express differences of character through slight changes in posture and tempo. The oppressed Chorus scuttle, Jizô's raising of the whole leg to hip height is slow, smooth, and refined, whereas the bandit-samurai execute the same movement in a quicker, jerkier, more aggressive manner. The guards enter from stage right and cross behind the Chorus and in front of Jizô to sit cross-legged upstage left. This blocking echoes the traditional hierarchy of Kabuki staging, in which the socially superior occupy positions stage left and their "inferiors" stage right.

Finally an old woman (Shiraishi Kayoko) appears in black kimono and brown-and-gold sleeveless overgarment. The program outline's description of her being "guided by the dead" seems to be suggested by a slight tilt of the head and a fixed stare into the distance – although this could just as easily be read as shellshock. The bundle she carries

Figure 21 The Greek warriors (Suzuki Kenji to the left; Tsutamori Kôsuke to the right) march past the Trojan captives. *The Trojan Women*. Toga amphitheatre, 1982.

suggests that she, too, is homeless. She sits downstage center, in front and stage left of the Chorus to suggest her superior status. As the play progresses it becomes clear that her position downstage is also intended to express the idea that everything taking place behind her is a figment of the old bag lady's imagination as she calls *The Trojan Women* to the eye of the mind.[17]

Scene 2 begins with the old woman's invocation of the dead, an inserted requiem by Ôoka Makoto in free verse. This is literature in its own right and deserves quoting at length since many of its images resonate through the play:[18]

> Oh you the dead! Come live among these arid rocks.
> Then, at the ends of deep-running roots
> If you take colour, let it be the bloom of sun at dawn,
> Shimmering pearl of overflowing tears.
>
> O you the dead! Come live together on the thousand peaks
> Of this planet which holds the two ice poles.
> If you take feet, let them be feet of hyena, of ostrich,
> The fierce wind of a striking cobra.
> Oh you the dead! Leaving no traces across the limpid paths of the sky,

Come live among gold-tinted waves.
If you take song, let it be the songs of an army marching forever, love
    songs,
Cooling songs of earthworms populating without end.

Oh you the dead! Abandon us, those who live in the dark swamp
Untouched by a single ray of the sun.
And resurrect as fruit echoing taste in the mouth.
If you take breath, expelled or held,
Let it be the sacred fire our demons blow.

Return again! Resurrect! Return
O you the dead!

In Shiraishi's recitation this starts slowly, with long, weighty pauses, and gradually gets faster and lighter in a manner which recalls the *jo-ha-kyû* pattern of traditional performing arts. The "arid rocks" of the first verse seem to suggest a desert, perhaps a wasteland of the spirit, or a fire-bombed city; and the "sun at dawn" may evoke an image of the *hinomaru*, the Japanese flag, and thus be seen by some as an invocation for Japan's war dead. The third stanza's ironic juxtaposition of "an army marching," "love songs," and "earthworms populating" seems to suggest a Hamletian morality that life will regenerate: worms singing their "love songs" as they feast on the bodies of aggressors and victims alike.

In calling for the ancestors to resurrect and return to help the living, the old woman appears to be working herself into a trance state of "dreaming back," but the resurrection of the dead taking place in her memory is not just a local one. For Suzuki it is a figural means of remembering, celebrating, and thus exorcising all those who have died violently in war, from Troy to Melos to World War II and beyond.

As Shiraishi ceases the Chorus chant another poem by Ôoka, starting with a medley of different voices, but driving forward to uniformity in the last, devastating lines:

Down the rivers of Asia
Down the lakes of Europe
Down the canals of America
Down the falls of Africa
Drift human skins
Like cucumber peelings.

The message driven home is that there can be no winners in nuclear war, the "cucumber peelings" metonymically suggesting the effects of A-bomb radiation burning. The cucumber's coolness seems to be used ironically for contrast (many died in the water at Hiroshima attempting to escape the terrible heat), as well as to suggest how easily irradiated skin comes away. The lines were sufficiently powerful to have been picked up by a number of critics after Patricia Morton's report for *The Drama Review*: "The spectator is left with a . . . vision of destruction with parallels to Japan's defeat in World War II (there is an early reference by the chorus to 'human skin peeling off like cucumbers', obviously meaning Hiroshima)."[19]

Scene 3 begins with a haunting bamboo-flute melody (the music of the "Stamp and *Shakuhachi*" discipline). With grotesque groans the three soldiers rise as if from death or sleep (Samurai 1 even going through a stylized routine of brushing his teeth and gargling before "resurrection"). As they slowly approach the old woman, their threatening, intense focus stresses her and she becomes possessed by the spirit of Hecuba: "Oh Gods, please see! I bear a grudge because you are not reliable. Nevertheless, when I face unhappiness, I can't stop calling you by name. Shall I talk of past days' happiness? If I do, present pain will shoot further through my body."[20] Since Poseidon and Athena have been banished from Suzuki's adaptation and Jizô, their Japanese replacement, never speaks, the above lines make a suitable introduction.

At the beginning of Scene 4, Talthybius' lines are divided between the three samurai. This lends greater dramatic variation and interest to their rapid-fire exchanges with Hecuba and leads to a heightening of intensity as they hem her in physically and psychologically with their tales of woe: first Cassandra given to Agamemnon, then Polyxena sacrificed at Achilles' tomb, Andromache allocated to Achilles' son, and Hecuba to the "enemy of truth," that "poisonous snake" Odysseus. Social differentiation through visual and vocal means also adds interest. The three are dressed in a shabby assortment of rags, which may suggest how long they have camped out before Troy, or their brigand status – the latter also suggested by their undisciplined, roving aggression and bare feet. Samurai 2, who speaks first, wears spectacles and carries a club and Red Cross first-aid pack. He appears to be a comic, myopic lightweight, for he speaks at a higher pitch than the others and, as in contemporary Japanese delegations, does most of the initial talking while the more important figures hang back to assess the situation. Samurai 3, who carries a drawn samurai sword and sports a pot-belly beneath a dirty white singlet and blue shorts, is the chauvinist thug. But it is Samurai 1 who finally assumes control of the situation, evading Hecuba's direct questions about the fate of Polyxena with polite circumlocutions. He carries a spear and wears a ragged red robe (aiding his later identification as Menelaus).

At this moment, as Hecuba seems to withdraw into herself, saying, "Everybody please mourn my sorrow," the Greeks are startled by "a red blaze" offstage. Hecuba ironically suggests the fire is "Cassandra running out." This defies logic, but allows Suzuki to achieve a *coup de théâtre*. As the three Greeks line up to focus audience attention offstage left in the expectation of seeing Cassandra there, Shiraishi has a vital few seconds in which to begin her character transformation before we realize that Cassandra is already "here."

Shiraishi uses a Kabuki *hikinuki* quick-change technique in throwing off Hecuba's black kimono to reveal underneath the white robes of a virgin priestess of Apollo (or of Amaterasu, the Japanese Sun Goddess). The transformation is rather like that of a cicada from its shell, Shiraishi's arms thrusting from the sleeves of her outer garment and then snaking overhead as she rises possessed. Internally, this transformation comes about, as she has said, when "I change the way I breathe."[21] In exchanging the gravitas of Hecuba's sorrows for the fiery passions of Cassandra, her breathing quickens, her voice becomes lighter, brighter, and more eager, and face and body shine with youthful idealism and concentration. [Figure 22]

Scene 5 begins as Shiraishi's old-woman-as-Hecuba transforms into a youthful Cassandra. Her speech mixes images from Euripides with the language of Ôoka. Suzuki and Ôoka have sacrificed all of Cassandra's prose exchanges with Hecuba and Talthybius (in which she prophesies the fate of Odysseus and provides an extended description of her death beside Agamemnon), and much of her long monologues. This is done in order to concentrate on incarnating the act of possession. In Euripides, Cassandra begins her longest monologue with a verbal reminder of her possession – "Possessed though I am . . .," " (Hadas and McLean, *Euripides*, 183) – before launching into a highly rational, ordered account of the emotional history of the causes of the Trojan War and its aftermath both for Odysseus and for Agamemnon. From 150 lines of Euripides' original, Suzuki and Ôoka carve out about thirty lines, mostly from the initial, ecstatic sung section, choosing to concentrate on the fine irony that her wedding to Apollo will be violated by her wedding to Agamemnon, and will lead to "the utter overthrow of Atreus' house" (Hadas and McLean, 183).

It is a wise choice theatrically, for, to go straight to the heart of the matter, they choose to privilege performance text over literary text through an act of theatrical repossession. Suzuki was also wise in enlisting an established poet to burnish the thirty translated lines stripped from Euripides so that they would provide a concentrated recreation of the power of Euripides' poetry for a Japanese audience. Part of the shock is

Figure 22 Shiraishi Kayoko transforms from Hecuba into Cassandra, rising in shamanic trance. *The Trojan Women*. Théâtre des Nations, Paris, 1977.

the recognition of the synergy between the oracular origins of ancient Greek tragedy and traditional Japanese theatre. The image of Shiraishi with her hands writhing up through her outer kimono to reveal Cassandra in white beneath the black robes of Hecuba is a highly charged iconic statement – about the manifest power of a great actress, and about the rejuvenation of an old set of shamanic traditions in a new theatrical synthesis. This primal moment of ritual theatre, of trance-possession, also asserts the emotional validity of an Artaudian double movement: the powerful Japanese experience/celebration of the roots of Western theatre through rediscovery of their own indigenous ritual tradition. The cruel joy of this discovery of doubleness can be heard in the very first words Ôoka gives to Cassandra: "Nan to iu yorokobi no hi ga megutte kitta koto ka" ("Oh what a happy day has come round!"). They echo the words of the actor playing Sanbaso in that most ancient of Japanese ritual plays, *Okina* (*The Ancient One*) just after he has donned his black mask to become the god. Ôoka's full context is this:

> Oh what a happy day has come round!
> My blood is purer than crystal,
> My arms purer than flames up to the sky where Apollo dwells.
> At last the day comes round in which I set my eyes on the wedding bed,
> Eyes still occupied with a vision of the depths of unlimited darkness.
> A smiling sky welcomes and embraces me against his big broad chest.
> O earth of Troy, O winds of Troy, ripening like figs in me,
> Please help me to accept this cruel joy!
> I see my wedding bed filled with the sound of crackling torches.
> My dear departed father and elder brother, please look on.
> I shall become bride to that brave enemy king who let the worms drink
> Your limitless pure blood, and who changed my sweet Trojan agora into a lake of tears.
> Ah, rapturous sea lifting its shining hands in front of me!
> Mother, can't you see that myriad flock of marsh-birds lifting their feet in dance
> To celebrate our marriage? That song dances in the light.
> Please flutter [your sleeves/wings]
> Please dance,
> Please match these steps of mine, mother.
> Now then, Trojan maidens, kindly dance,
> Holding up tapers to light my wedding bed!

(*To the majestic, pulsing music of Kanjinchô, a Kabuki piece, the chorus dance in a circle.*)

I have quoted this entire section to show how little it owes to Euripides' words, and yet how much to his spirit. Ôoka's poetry is positively dazzling in its recreation of the original through its firm grasp of the needs and possibilities of the Suzuki actor and a recognition of, and expansion on, the ecstatic paradoxes that Euripides' passage itself builds.

For an audience unfamiliar with the details of the matter of Troy and its aftermath in the *Oresteia*, Ôoka elaborates the implied contrast vividly and concretely. By referring to Cassandra's ecstatic welcoming of the oxymoronic "cruel joy" of a "smiling sky" which "embraces me against his big broad chest," Ôoka suggests Apollo (the Sun God) as the rightful "husband" of his vestal virgin. Thus the later reference to her real bridegroom as "that brave enemy king [Agamemnon] who let the worms drink Your limitless pure blood" clarifies the doubleness of her ironic speech. Between these two images of love and death, the line "I see my wedding bed filled with the sound of crackling torches" creates a vivid visual image of the "cruel joy" she faces: her marriage bed will become her funeral pyre.

The final image of the Chorus as "that myriad flock of marsh-birds" even creates a traditional poetic ambiguity in Cassandra's request to her mother, "Please flutter / Please dance." Like the Chorus, her mother can be seen as a captive "marsh-bird" crying by the seashore, and since she wears a long-sleeved kimono, "flutter" poetically confuses the waving of sleeves in dance with the flight and run of marsh-birds. The image has an added advantage once the dance is complete, for Cassandra's "Keep back, you hovering Greek vultures" will help to unite the two separate sections of her monologue with contrastive bird imagery.

The dance which the Chorus carry out – directed by Shiraishi's marvelously expressive "snake's head" hands and writhing fingers – is performed to the slow pulse of "*Kanjinchô*," a well-known Kabuki melody appropriated for the Suzuki Training discipline of the same name. In this trainees move counterclockwise in a circle, lifting, pausing, and then stamping their feet in time to the beat (the purpose of the exercise being to challenge their center of gravity). While the allusion to tradition is clear only if one knows the melody, appreciation of the dance's expressive meaning requires no specific cultural knowledge. The Chorus dance with the bent backs of the defeated – but this is the only essential difference from the way the Greeks made their entrance; the Trojans are defeated but not broken, there is still extraordinary energy there in the way they lift knees to chest before stamping.

As the music dies Cassandra's attention shifts from the Chorus (stage right) to the Greeks (stage left) who squat around their leader's spear, which is raised above them like a standard. She pauses, deliberates, then runs to this symbol of Greek power, grabs it, and speaks out to the audience over the heads of her captors: "Keep back, you hovering Greek vultures. I won't let you set even one finger on my body." Even here there is expressive attention to detail, for the forefinger of the hand gripping the spear-shaft is extended, pointing accusingly into the audience as if it were a Buddhist *mudra* made to ward off evil. With this change of focus from Trojans to Greeks, Cassandra's mood swings, and her darkness comes flooding back: "How miserable I am," she cries as she exhorts the gods to sink the boats whose "scuppers are awash with Trojan blood."

Talthybius' half-page exchange with Cassandra is reduced to a brief choral "Spit it out! Spit it out!," but it remains efficacious in interrupting and shifting Cassandra's focus yet again, this time to her mother: "Dear mother, please celebrate my good fortune." As if stuck in the same patterns of thought, she recapitulates her earlier ecstatic prophecy but in a darker, more mature malevolence enhanced by the way her hands extend like the talons of a striking eagle. In fact Shiraishi's acting is fascinating here precisely because it is sometimes uncertain, from the quality of her voice, whether she speaks as Cassandra or Hecuba; the daughter appears to be possessed by the spirit of her mother. We have seen the daughter emerge from the mother, and now witness the mother emerging from within the daughter. (In performance terms Shiraishi manipulates her breath patterns so as to oscillate between those used to present daughter and those used for mother.)

The sudden maturity of Cassandra-daughter-of-Hecuba is surprisingly against all logic as she pronounces, "That Troy which was destroyed/ In a tide of blood/ Is happier than Greece." This last great paradox must be fully embodied before it can become hair-raising, and requires the fullest cooperation between director, actress, playwright, and modern poet. Ôoka was not only a fine poet, sensitive to Euripides' text, he was also a long-time friend of Waseda Little Theatre, fully conversant with the company's style of theatre from attendance at training and rehearsals. It would be a mistake to think of *The Trojan Women* as nothing more than a convenient vehicle for a superb actress. Great performers burn brightest given great texts and directors, and Ôoka worked tirelessly with Suzuki between Euripides, Matsudaira, and Shiraishi to meet the demands of each. In support of this contention it is worth quoting the end of Cassandra's monologue at length:

Now as I lie on my wedding mattress
Decked with flowers, dawn slowly
Lights up.
Prone on a bed, newmade mad
Glittering with the joy of vengeance,
Lord Agamemnon
So sturdy and reliable
I am waiting for you –
For the leader of the Greek host
Splendid as sun or storm
To spawn his life seed, to harvest
Dead flowers.
Please wash my nails
And wipe away my tears.
Dear mother, if you do this
Please don't mourn at our country's sad fate
Nor grieve at my wedding.
This wedding
Offers an unlooked for opportunity.
However much I hate, there's no limit
To my hatred for the enemy.
The procession towards destruction starts
From my wedding bed.

At this point, as she calls to mind the boding tragedy of the house of Atreus, Cassandra explodes again into vision. Her clear hatred, fanned into fanaticism by countless acts of injustice, is so great that, not unlike a Palestinian suicide bomber,[22] she willingly embraces her own destruction along with that of her enemy:

See! I can see!
In front of me I can see my dead body.
I, I will be killed with Agamemnon.
The axe, ah how the axe flies.
I am going to die.
I hear an awful shout of destruction:
"Agamemnon die! Cassandra die!"

On this ecstatic peak the music stops, and Shiraishi drops exhausted to the ground. All her roles – Cassandra, Hecuba, and old woman – collapse in on her. She lies still as the Greeks laugh raucously (Cassandra's fate was to speak truth but never to be believed) and the Chorus chant the real mystery of the moment in another original poem by Ôoka:

Water flowing, Bone flowing, Boiling water flowing, Cloud flowing, Blood flow-
ing, Shadows flowing, Tears flowing, Eyes flowing, Ice flowing, Crows flowing,
Seas flowing, Cliffs flowing, Algae flowing – Mystery flowing.

Anyone who has experienced Suzuki Training – and we know that
Ôoka had – will have a vivid sense of the rightness of his poem as a
celebration of that moment of bright darkness arrived at in the discipline
known as "Stamp and *Shakuhachi*." At the end of the first part of this,
when the trainee lies utterly exhausted on the ground, hearing only the
pounding of blood rushing to oxygen-starved muscles and brain, life
pumps at its most elemental level, things lose their fixed form, and the
world seems to open up.

Scene 6 begins with the entrance of Andromache. Suzuki has the two
women face not each other, as they would in Ibsen, but, in the *shômen
engi* style of Kabuki, out into the audience. Sugiura Chizuko's running
entrance expressively establishes her Andromache as the proud, fearless wife of a great war-leader. In her arms dangles a featureless white
muslin doll with long, spindly arms and swollen, glovelike hands. This
represents her child, Astyanax.

Hecuba remains stoically seated center stage as her daughter-in-law
stops abruptly in front of the Greeks and begins a long, heated exchange
in what, to a Japanese audience, would be a Kabuki-style delivery, and,
to a Western audience familiar with Greek theatre, might be read as
an approximation of *stichomythia*. The lines are spoken very fast, each
woman cutting into the speech of the other so rapidly that at first they
do not make sense:

HECUBA: Oh what . . .
ANDROMACHE: Mother, the reason you feel so sad . . .
HECUBA: Isn't it a miserable thing . . .
ANDROMACHE: In my pain . . .
HECUBA: Oh Zeus!

Gradually these sharp fragments resolve themselves into rapid-fire one-
liners, and then into set speeches. An instructive instance of the interpre-
tative possibilities actors bring to a role can be found here. In the 1974
production the popular Shingeki actress Ichihara Etsuko had played
Andromache in her usual style of "the typical housewife next door" and,
while this had made her Andromache pathetic in relation to Shiraishi's
heroic Hecuba, heightening contrast between the representational and
presentational approaches of Shingeki and Kabuki, it had only served
to make her character seem small and timid.

By contrast, Sugiura Chizuko, a superb Suzuki actress capable of matching Shiraishi, played the role as the exceptional samurai wife of an exceptional leader, for whom she grieved as an equal. Her stern, forceful, gravelly voice cut and stabbed like a *naginata*, the long-bladed spear with which a samurai woman was trained to defend her home. The effect was one of Spartan rather than bourgeois virtue.

Shiraishi's first two sentences are slow and dark (as she thinks of her dead son), but mature strategy requires a lighter tone as she pleads with her headstrong, single-minded daughter-in-law along the following lines. If Andromache pleases Agamemnon, her son by Hector may live, and then – here Shiraishi's voice thickens – "some day descendants of his may return and settle Troy, and Troy be again a country." However, this stratagem is dashed when the Greeks close around Andromache to hint at Astyanax's fate: "Don't hold onto the boy ... Do not invite a struggle ... ; make the best of the situation, and you will not leave this boy's body unburied, and you yourself may find the Greeks kindlier to you."

Suzuki's decision to stage Andromache's rape gives these lines a bitter, ironic edge they do not possess in the original, for his soldiers are ruffians who scream *"Sate! Saateee!"* in Kabuki *aragoto* (rough) style. Samurai 3 kneels beside Andromache on one side and leers into her face, saying, "Let's go to Greece" (an interpolated line). As she runs the other way, she is blocked by Samurai 2, who snatches the child as the other two attack. Andromache tries to run, but, in a Kabukiesque moment, Samurai 3 grabs the end of her sash; it unravels as she spins and runs but holds halfway across the stage, preventing her escape. In the tug-of-war which follows, the warrior's sudden release of the sash causes Andromache to fall, and the hovering leader rushes over to drag her unceremoniously by one foot into the shadows behind Jizô; here her rape can remain unseen but heard.

While this is taking place, Samurai 2 highsteps, in mock imitation of Jizô's opening walk, over to the Chorus, who are crouched in fear, ostrichlike, and casually drops the doll-child in front of them. When one young woman (Suzuki Nobuko) seems to reach toward it, he grabs her wrist and casually shaves down her arm with his sword to the shoulder-joint, then slashes deep. The woman cries out and grabs the child instinctively with her other arm. To the sonorous, slowly building beat of a *taiko* (large war drum), she escapes with it across stage in a grotesque scuttle (*shikko*) which expressionistically seeks to convey the futility of her brave attempt to preserve the child, even at the cost of her own life. Her way is blocked in turn by the other two, who have now finished with Andromache, and they prod her back toward Samurai 2 (Suzuki Kenji). He stops her advance by holding his sword in front of her, she screams, "Help me someone!," and to the deafening beat of the drum they play a slow-motion tug-of-war for possession of the child. Samurai 2 now becomes truly demonic; eyes bulging and nostrils flared, he stabs her again and twists the knife in the wound to the accompanying laughter of his companions. [Figure 23] When she still will not give up, he cuts off the child's arm and waves it about in glee. As the woman staggers to her feet, still protecting the mutilated body, he cuts her down in a gruesome, slow-motion, Kabuki-style death scene. She staggers to Jizô in a heartrendingly lopsided motion and dies at his feet.

Samurai 2 casually walks back to the Chorus with the one-armed doll to play the same sadistic game over again. But this time, as he drops it in front of the Chorus, they all fall on their backs and lift their legs in the air, then scuttle screaming in all directions, knees knocking and hands moving rapidly in panic. The samurai fall about laughing, parodying their victims' panic by somersaulting across the stage with a menacing excess of animal energy, waving their arms wildly and whooping. It is an awesome display of stylized acting skills, and profoundly moving beyond words. By now darkness has completely closed in, and only Jizô is lit. Suddenly all action halts as the melancholy melody of "Tôryanse" begins, announcing the start of Scene 7.

According to the 1974 program, the scene is a "reversion to the immediate post-war period. The old woman and the raped girl [no longer Andromache but now another survivor of World War II] are alone listening to the 'Tôryanse,' a child's song. All others onstage have joined the world of the dead."

The god Jizô, unmoved throughout the play thus far, suddenly shifts his position to face fully front. At this the whole cast sit formally upright, and the lights brighten. The dead Chorus woman is discovered sitting in lotus position at the feet of Jizô, clothed in white (the color of death). The Chorus are also discovered in meditation in their original positions. Andromache, dressed only in a torn black slip, slowly rises from behind the soldiers and painfully hobbles off stage right in shock. In front of Jizô she passes a male vagrant dressed in boxer shorts and blue *happi* (workman's coat) – an image from "the immediate post-war period" – moving with his bundle in the opposite direction under an open umbrella. [Figure 24]

The "Tôryanse" melody, which continues into Scene 8 as background music to Hecuba's lament over her dead grandson, needs some

Figure 23 A Greek warrior (Suzuki Kenji) slices into the arm of the Chorus woman protecting the baby Astyanax. *The Trojan Women*. Toga amphitheatre, 1982.

Figure 24 Sugiura Chizuko as the raped woman in black slip (Andromache) limps past the spirit of Astyanax's nurse, Jizô, and the Chorus. *The Trojan Women*. Toga amphitheatre, 1982.

clarifying. It is familiar to most Japanese as accompanying a child's game in which two teams confront each other. Team A members stand facing each other in parallel lines, and arch hands to form a tunnel. Team B must run this gauntlet in single file. If captured they will join Team A on the next replay until none of Team B is left. The words of the song (sung by Hecuba in the 1979 New York performance at least) are these:

ALL: Let us pass through; let us pass through.
B: What narrow road is here?
A: It's the narrow road to Tenjin Shrine [built to placate the angry ghost of the wrongfully exiled Minister Sugawara Michizane].
B: Please let us pass through.
A: We won't let anyone pass who has no business [with Tenjin].
B: We go to donate *ofuda* [square plates] for this seven year-old.[23]
A: Going is easy, but returning is frightening.
B: Even so, let us pass through; let us pass through!

A variation of this sinister game seems to be what Samurai 2 plays with the Chorus, who sit in line. The game can also be taken as a concrete image of what has befallen Hecuba, her family, and all the Trojan women at the hands of the Alpha Team – an image of human life seen "from the lower depths."

In Euripides, after Astyanax is taken off, Hecuba must face Menelaus and argue for Helen's death before she knows her grandson is dead. And when his body is returned to her, cleaning it will be her last act before witnessing the firing of the city. Euripides' scene between Helen and Hecuba, which, in Philip Harsh's words "might at first glance seem impertinent to the sufferings of Hecuba and inconsistent with the tragic tone of the play,"[24] is not used by Suzuki. Instead, in Scene 8, he has Hecuba lament over the corpse of Astyanax *before* the entry of Menelaus and puts some of Helen's arguments into Hecuba's mouth for ironic effect. So the suspense is cut, the murder brought forward and its horror intensified by being staged alongside the rape of Andromache. The ordering also serves to give greater intensity to Hecuba's caustic pleading with Menelaus to kill Helen, for she and we have witnessed the cruel fates of Astyanax and his mother. These are touches worthy of Nanboku's sensational *The Scarlet Princess of Edo* or Shakespeare's *Titus Andronicus*. Nevertheless, Suzuki is careful to maintain sufficient distance. As Joseph McLellan points out, "The rape is brutally realistic in action but muted by the staging . . . The scene's impact . . . [is] finally strengthened by leaving details to the imagination," whereas "the infanticide is staged front and center and well illuminated, but it is obvious that the villain's sword is not hacking a real child, only a featureless rag doll" (*Washington Post*, May 29 1985). A Belgian critic has seen it in a slightly different theatrical vein: "il avait la volonté de redécouvrir les forces vitales du Kabuki, dont l'esthétique barbare préfigurait le théâtre de la cruauté defini par Antonin Artaud" (*La Libre Belgique*, April 24 1985).

Scene 8, then, begins with Hecuba grieving over her grandson. Her speech rings clear in the silence caused by the end of the "Tôryanse" melody: "Troy is destroyed, yet you Greeks were afraid of a child, a little child . . ."[25]

At the end of this long plaint, the soulful melody of an electronic silver flute floats in as a war drum keeps blood-pulse time. Hecuba remembers when her grandson clambered onto her bed, promising to bring crowds of grieving friends to her grave, "But it was the other way round." There is a long pause as she presses the little body to her cheek and grieves. "Now accursed Helen has . . . robbed you and destroyed your life, and ruined utterly your whole house." While the guards play cards, the Chorus express their sympathy. In front of the little lifeless body, they place Japanese folk toys – a drum, a ball of colored strings, a straw horse, a wooden doll – and recite another ode by Ôoka Makoto:

> Shame if you bear no boy after such painful labour.
> If you bear a girl, put her in a coloured pagoda
> And send her down a long river.
> But if you bear a boy, adorn him in gold clothing
> And give him away to a temple.

The Greeks break this funereal mood when their leader swaggers forward. Scene 9 begins as he proclaims himself to be Menelaus come for his adulterous wife:

O splendour of sunburst breaking forth this day, whereon I lay my hands once more on Helen my wife – I am Menelaus and I have laboured much for her, I and the Greek army – and yet it is not so much for the woman's sake I came to Troy, but against that guest proved treacherous who, like a robber, carried the woman from my house.

This extremely convoluted sentence is delivered with barbaric patriarchal pride: the woman is nothing, wounded self-esteem among male peers is everything. The rhetoric is magnificent, the syntax and delivery shooting forward in long sinewy turns like an anaconda after prey. The speaker needs good lungs, and indeed this particular passage (minus the self-referential aside) is one of those used in Suzuki Training to develop vocal strength. But Hecuba will stand her ground and expose the hollowness of the victor's rhetoric, turning defeat into a Pyrrhic victory.

Suzuki's *coup de théâtre* here is *not* to have Helen appear. Having Hecuba taunt Menelaus with all the things Helen *might* say, and then facetiously question his ability to keep his resolve in the face of her *legendary* beauty, Suzuki frees our imaginations from the naturalistic sight of a flesh-and-blood Helen. In Greek tragedy, of course, she would have been played by a man in a mask, but Suzuki decides against this. Cutting Helen is sensible in another way, too; it helps to speed the action forward, one and a half hours being the outer limit of any actor's endurance in this high-energy performance style. Besides, Shiraishi is taking on three roles, and never leaves the stage.

By cutting Helen's long, sophistical self-defence, and then having Ôoka reinsert some of Helen's arguments along with newly invented dialogue, Suzuki is able to have his cake and eat it. "You are not capable of killing this woman," says Hecuba, relishing exposure of Menelaus' weakness in front of his followers; "The woman will whimper to you during the long, long voyage . . .' 'Oh dearest Menelaus, why did you leave me alone . . . ? The prince of Troy abducted me and caused this war.'" As played by Tsutamori Kôsuke (1974–89), Menelaus' twitching face and lips are highly expressive. In his special pleading the hollowness of his resolve becomes increasingly exposed:

HECUBA: Lord Menelaus (*averting her eyes*), if Helen is honestly loyal to you in every way, then why did no Spartan hear her scream for help when my son took her away?
MENELAUS: It may be she was gagged.
HECUBA: But, with respect, after that she could have thrown herself into the sea when she was on board ship.
MENELAUS: She could have been under constant surveillance.
HECUBA: My son was an incomparably handsome man. When your wife saw him in his extravagant robes decorated with gold, she fell in love at first glance. She used to lead a simple life. She abandoned her own country after she lost her senses and came to Troy, a land filled with gold.

This much is based on Euripides (Hadas and McLean, 197), although Ôoka has reordered and retouched it (the shipboard detail is new, for instance, and he and Suzuki have cut the etymological reference to Aphrodite as meaning "lewdness"). What follows is invented.

When Menelaus responds angrily that it was Paris, not Helen, who ruined Troy, Hecuba accuses him of cowardice. This is dangerous, as Menelaus shouts, "Be quiet, slave. Nothing would be easier than to chop off your head!" His spear is at the ready, and quivers in his hands. But Hecuba does not back down; instead she exposes her back to him with the sarcastic words, "Well, thank goodness for that! Go ahead. (*pause*) What's wrong? Are you afraid of Odysseus?" Menelaus' screamed response is, "What's that?" (if he kills Hecuba, he will be answerable to her new master). He hesitates, then turns fractionally away to point out a Chorus member with his spear, barks "Die!" and Samurai 2 carries out the reprisal killing. As the screams die and the victim collapses, Menelaus exits with, "I'll go tell the commander-in-chief" (his brother), and gives a parting flurry of orders: "Pull Helen out; set fire to the castle; lay waste all of Troy!"

Scene 10 is signaled by the return of "Shakuhachi," the plaintive bamboo flute and guitar melody heard at the beginning of the play. Patricia

Figure 25 Jizô (Shin Kenjirô) acts as tour guide for battlefield tourists (Tsutamori Kôsuke, third from the right), flanked by the spirit of a giant Japanese soldier. *The Trojan Women*. Iwanami Hall, Tokyo, 1974.

Morton, an eye-witness to the conclusion of the 1974 production, describes it in this way:

The play ends on an unexpected modern note to blaring pop music, when three grinning tourists, carrying suitcases and voraciously flashing cameras, enter to inspect the ruins. The statue becomes a guide, showing them the castle, remarking on the brutality of war, but they are oblivious to his comments. They exit. The stage is empty, except for the man in black hat, who has been sitting stage left throughout the entire performance, his appearance also adding a contemporary feeling. He indolently lights a cigarette, then opens a torn umbrella. The play is over.[26] [Figure 25]

Since the tourist roles were taken by the actors who earlier played samurai, and since one of them is now dressed as a giant Japanese samurai in puttees (on stilts, as in Brecht's *Man is Man*), the suggestion is that some among the ex-veteran tourists are still closet imperialists. This scene was cut in the 1977 production taken abroad – but replaced by a naked fascist in red loincloth claiming absurdly that the Japanese come from another planet. Taken from Oka Kiyoshi's *The Soul of the Japanese*, the scene was recycled from the 1975 revision of *Dramatic Passions II* seen in

Poland. It drew attention from European critics for its obvious *reductio ad absurdum* of Japanese claims to uniqueness (*Nihonjinron*).[27] Nevertheless, it, too, was cut after the 1977 tour. In trying to be aggressively modern, both these exercises in youthful provocation part company too completely with the mood of *The Trojan Women*. By the American tour of 1979, Suzuki had resolved the matter. What follows remained in place from 1979 to 1989.

All of the cast rise and walk slowly forward into the darkness at the front of the stage (as in the second part of the "*Shakuhachi*" training exercise) leaving the old woman and Jizô lit but half-obscured behind them. The acting challenge in this walk is collectively to carry the whole experience of the play to the audience – and then distance it – without resorting to overt means. The extreme minimalism with which the cast play out their last moments onstage is haunting, the temperature dropping to somewhere between Noh and Beckett as they exit slowly, in line, into the darkness at the back of the stage.

As this human tide recedes, leaving the old woman behind like an empty shell, we notice that Jizô has raised his spear over his head in what appears to be an act of protection and turned toward the old woman slightly. Unaware, the old woman takes her bundle and hobbles to his feet, as if to some sheltering tree. In the silence she sits, and, as he lowers his spear, she opens her bundle. Unpacking her remaining possessions one by one, she examines, cleans, and lays them out lovingly. At the same time, in a manner impossible to describe, she quietly mutters Hecuba's magnificent words in a distanced, matter-of-fact manner which is positively harrowing after all the previous lava-flows of grief, rage, and sarcasm that we have witnessed. Just one word is altered in the text she speaks (my italics):[28]

O Troy, that once held your head so high among *Asians*, soon you will be robbed of your name and fame. They are burning you and leading us out of the land to slavery. Ah, you gods – yet why should I call upon the gods? In the past they did not hear when they were called. Come, let us rush to the pyre; our greatest glory will be to perish in the flames in which our country perishes.

The dramatic irony of the old woman's third and fourth sentences is almost unbearable for the god who stands over her. Further, her last sentences open wide the gap between her own reality in the ruins of postwar Japan and Hecuba's passionate, raw grief as she witnesses the torching of Troy. In Beckettian fashion Suzuki's old woman does not move. "Come, let us rush to the pyre," she says, but, in contrast to

Euripides' Hecuba, she continues to establish herself in the space, civilizing the desolation by her little everyday acts of carrying on. (We may remember her very first words in the play: "Oh you the dead! Come live among these arid rocks. / Then, at the ends of deep-running roots / If you take colour, let it be the bloom of sun at dawn, / Shimmering pearl of overflowing tears.") Hecuba's monologue may be about the insupportability of grief, but this old woman's actions speak survival. In a particularly brilliant and witty demonstration of the renewing power of theatricality, Suzuki changes Euripides' intentionality. On Hecuba's line, "Priam! Dead, unburied, unbefriended, yet you are unconscious of my doom," she pulls out a black shoe and inspects it. In the NHK TV recording of the 1982 Toga performance, the audience laugh at the absurd gap between Priam and a shoe, but it may well be a laugh of recognition. Could this be all that is left of the old woman's "Priam"? "Why may not imagination trace the noble dust of Alexander till he find it stopping a bung-hole?"[29]

As the old woman goes on matter of factly reciting Hecuba's lines – "The name of the land will pass into oblivion. One after another, everything disappears. Hapless Troy is finished" – she finds a hole in her old tin cup and tosses it away. It clanks a few times as it hits the ground, and this seems to awaken the old woman from her reverie, for she looks up, pauses, and says with momentary involvement and intensity, "Did you notice, did you hear? The crash of the falling citadel. Ruin, everywhere ruin – it will engulf the citadel." Within a few moments, however, she rests her head on her small portable stove and is asleep.

A young woman runs in carrying a bunch of red flowers. The abrupt energy of her entrance reminds us of Andromache, but Sugiura's new character is an Occupation rape victim, the modern reincarnation of Andromache. Dressed garishly like a prostitute in red blouse, tight blue pinafore shorts (carelessly unbuttoned on one side) and high-heeled boots which emphasize the clumsiness of her movements, she charges over to the exhausted old bag lady and yells into her ear, "Ma'am, wanna buy some flowers? It's cold, ain't it? Hey, my home's over there, that shack. Wanna stop by? I'm alone too."[30] Startled, the old woman mumbles, "What? What?," then brushes her away and sinks into sleep. The young girl next approaches Jizô, for flowers are usually offered to the gods and buddhas; however, when he does not respond, she impulsively hits him in the chest with her bouquet before staggering off disgustedly. (The 1974 program summary indicates that she does this "because, as the protector of children, he abandoned them during the war.") Immediately a popular Japanese rock song of the early 1970s shatters the silence:

> Oo, oo, oo, I want you love me tonight.
> [this refrain sung in pidgin English]
> The only thing a lone woman can do
> Is to cross her fingers, pray,
> And wet her cheeks with tears.
> Rejected by the man I love,
> Thrown out on a rainy street,
> And yet I cannot hate you.
> A weak woman can do nothing but serve.
> Should I go on or turn off here?
> Love, love, I ventured for you.
> Oo, oo, I want you love me tonight.

At the end of the first stanza of Ouyan Fifi's "Koi no jûjiro" ("Crossroads of Love"), the three samurai march back across the stage, tossing the doll between them. Jizô loses composure, as if bent backward by atomic wind. It seems as though he is torn between wanting to reach down and touch the head of the sleeping old woman, which he starts to do, and the equal, opposite, and ultimately stronger desire to keep his spear raised. With difficulty he regains his statuesque pose just as the music ends and lights fade.

It is a brilliant stroke to play Hecuba's final outpouring of tragic grief in a detached manner, and then end with an ironic series of dislocated question marks about the efficacy of religion and pop culture. For this allows our imaginations to work more powerfully in the interstices. Irving Wardle sums up the process very well:

This scheme [doubling past and present] . . . yields a brilliantly economical means of bringing Grecian and nuclear desolation into . . . focus. The one image I shall retain is of the old woman going through the surviving domestic items in her bundle, side by side with the saffron-robed immortal: naturalism sharing the space with ritualized formality. Suzuki is not locked into a closed equation of Troy and Hiroshima, but has extended the work to modern Japan as a cry from the destitute camping out in wastelands of degutted TV sets and quadraphonic record players.[31]

Despite the fact that there are no "degutted TV sets" on Suzuki's stage – or more precisely, because of it – Wardle illuminates the way audiences can sympathetically fill in indeterminacy (in his case, perhaps, by thinking of the destitute in Thatcher's Britain in the wake of the 1984 coalminers' strike). The strength of Suzuki's directorial solution lies not in trying to do too much in the dying moments, but in exercising restraint and being true to both the momentum of *The Trojan Women* and his initial conception of it as the dream of an old woman in a devastated present.

Suzuki's initial stimulus, like his friend Takahashi's, was overwhelmingly personal:

He remembers the planes flying low over the roof, some with red suns on their wings, some with stars . . . Seven-year-old Tadashi Suzuki was "very much afraid". Below lay the port, where the planes would dive. He remembers the shrieks of the bombs, their sizzling misses in the harbour and animal roars when scoring hits. But most of all he remembers the women trying to protect the children. The wooden houses with paper walls could ignite from a single splinter of shrapnel. The helpless anguish on his mother's face as she shielded him left a wound deeper than shrapnel could leave. It's the memories and the need to exorcise the emotional wounds of that childhood that lie at the heart of Suzuki's radical reinterpretation.[32]

Nevertheless, he "wanted to make a play on a theme that concerns everyone, beyond differences of nationality or historical time," and to do that he had to "treat it on two levels."[33] It is an ironic ending which suggests at once how close those cultural levels can be, and yet also how far apart.

Suzuki's Euripides (II): *The Bacchae*
Ian Carruthers

There are, as Fiona Macintosh has observed, numerous versions by Suzuki of Euripides' play *The Bacchae*.[1] Perhaps this is not surprising, considering Suzuki's work methods and the fact that, from 1978 to 2001, he has restaged the play some thirty-one times and in at least seventeen foreign cities. To add to the confusion, Suzuki has produced the play under two separate titles: *Bakkosu no shinnyo* (*The Bacchae*) until 1990, and *Dionysus* thereafter. However, while there have been any number of minor variations over time to suit the talents of outstanding individual performers and Suzuki's current thinking, these two are the basic repertory versions. What is clear, moreover, is Suzuki's attraction. In his own words, *"The Bacchae* is one of my favourite plays because it deals directly with such problems as religion, politics, family and gender."[2]

To Greek scholars such as J. Michael Walton, there isn't "anything revolutionary in suggesting that a search for the Greek sense of theatre may well find more points of contact in an oriental rather than an occidental tradition."[3] And, in the wake of the 1960s "youth revolution" epitomized by Richard Schechner's *Dionysus in 69*, Suzuki's choice of *The Bacchae* in 1978 was a highly appropriate one. Euripides, who "[a]s ever . . . looks for a new dimension in the story, and, with the aid of a variant version, changes the emphasis,"[4] would have appreciated Suzuki's political timing – in particular his seizing on the much-repeated line about Dionysus coming "from Asia" – in addressing issues of racism in the year that Edward Said's *Orientalism* was published.

The Bacchae, which has been called "the most representative play of all Greek tragedy,"[5] has remained a perennial favorite from classical to modern times in part because of an intense theatricality which calls for more than usual acting skills, and in part because its interpretation is so fascinatingly difficult. Plutarch's anecdote about the Parthian annihilation of Crassus' army in Asia Minor suggests how the play's metatheatrical confusions of art and life can grip enthusiastic actors and audience across the ages: "when the head of Crassus was brought to the

[Parthian] king's door . . . a tragic actor, Jason by name, of Tralles, was singing that part of *The Bacchae* of Euripides where Agave is about to appear . . . Jason handed his costume of Pentheus to one of the chorus, seized the head of Crassus, and assuming the role of the frenzied Agave, sang these verses through as if inspired."[6]

Suzuki, too, learned how effectively, in Peter Burian's words, "myth serves as a vehicle for confronting contemporary political realities and illustrating [one's] own philosophy."[7] His own theatrical agenda, which addresses the need to find ways of resisting the totalizing domination of Japanese theatre by foreign forms, led him to discover in *The Bacchae* an ideal form with which to "speak back." His 1989 program makes this clear:

> This production deals with the way society responds to the introduction of a strong, alien cultural or religious presence. There are three basic types of response which are dealt with in the production; Agave embraces and enthusiastically accepts the new religion, Pentheus furiously fights against it, and Kadmus takes the third option by forming an alliance with it.[8]

For Suzuki *The Bacchae* successfully raises issues associated with the problematic history of intercultural relations. Although it seems to strike chords wherever it has traveled in the world, the play's relevance to modern East-West relations is especially evident. Forcibly "opened" to foreign trade in 1868 under threat of such political "dismemberment" as the Western powers had already exacted in China, Japan had rapidly "caught up" with the West through a full-scale modernization program which saw her achieve grudging recognition on "the world stage" after defeat of the Russian army at Port Arthur and its Pacific and Baltic fleets in the Sea of Japan. However, Japan's emulation of the West in her expansion into Korea, Taiwan, Manchuria, and China had clashed with the colonial hegemony of Western powers: the United States in the Philippines; Britain in India, Singapore, Malaysia, Hong Kong and Australasia; France in Indo-China; Portugal in Timor and Macau; Holland in Indonesia; and most of these powers in the treaty ports of China. An opportunistic Axis alliance in World War II and surprising initial victories at Pearl Harbor and Singapore were followed by crushing defeat, culminating in the dropping of two atomic bombs which compelled unconditional surrender. However, despite a humbling Occupation by America and its allies, Japanese economic recovery had again been so rapid as to seem to threaten trade wars with the United States in the 1980s – that is, before the so-called Economic Bubble burst and the charge of the "Asian Tigers" faltered in the 1990s.

With this sort of historical see-saw affecting cultural perceptions, Dionysus could be seen to stand for the perils and profits of Westernization or Asianization, whether overrapid assimilation of Western values into Japanese theatre, or of Asian values by Western gurus such as Grotowski, Brook, or Mnouchkine (the latter justifying production of *Richard II* in a Kabukiesque style by quoting Artaud's "The Theatre is Oriental"[9]). Suzuki's use of traditional red-and-white striped festival bunting (*Kohaku maku*) for the maenads' costumes suggested, to this viewer at least, the colors of both Japanese and American flags. But this is not to limit the theme of *The Bacchae* to cultural politics. Suzuki also found scope to address the popular phenomenon of religious cults, which have been a part of popular international consciousness at least since the meeting of the Maharishi and the Beatles. These he saw as disastrously virulent in the activities of such a charismatic cult leader as the Reverend Jim Jones (the People's Temple; 978 dead in Guyana, 1978). And to such a list we might add David Kuresh (Branch Dravidians; 74 dead in Waco, 1993), Jodi Mambro (Order of the Solar Temple; 53 dead in Switzerland and Quebec, 1994), Asahara Shôkô (AUM Shinrikyô; 12 dead and 5,000 injured in Tokyo, 1995), and, most recently and shockingly, Osama bin Laden (al-Qaeda; more than 3,000 dead at New York's World Trade Center, September 11 2001).[10] In order to address such worldwide phenomena, Suzuki's setting, like Pasolini's in his *Medea* (1967) and *Edipo Re* (1970), "is shifting and cross-cultural to suggest the universality of mythic experience,"[11] although, like Pasolini, he is careful to supply a local frame.

THE 1978 KANZE HISAO–SHIRAISHI PRODUCTION

Senda Akihiko was the first major critic to flag the importance of Suzuki's *The Bacchae* in 1978. In a lengthy review he compares Suzuki's adaptation favorably with Schechner's *Dionysus in 69*, admitting to being "deeply impressed" by Suzuki's growing artistic mastery, and singling out for special praise his treatment of one of the traditional high points of the play, the confrontation between Pentheus (Shiraishi) and Dionysus (Kanze Hisao):

Seething emotions seemed to boil up from unseen depths as the two faced each other. Shiraishi's squatting down to bring her center of gravity closer to the earth, Kanze Hisao filled with a deep joy, with a look stretching to the heavens. Altogether a memorable encounter. Then too, Shiraishi revealed her always superb technique, which can permit her to move quickly back and forth

Figure 26 Male vagrants in women's underwear (Fueda Uichirô in foreground) cavort around Pentheus (Shiraishi Kayoko). *The Bacchae*. Iwanami Hall, Tokyo, 1978.

from the melancholic to the comic. As for Kanze Hisao's performance, among his roles undertaken outside the *nô* theatre, this was surely his most dazzling accomplishment.[12]

Kanze Hisao's approach took a hint from the second messenger's description of Dionysus as a disembodied "voice out of the sky" urging the death of Pentheus, and used it to confirm his own pre-acting habits as a Noh performer.[13] Besides being the greatest Noh actor of his generation, Hisao was a tireless experimenter; he had undertaken seven major roles outside a full Noh schedule between 1971 and 1978.[14]

Senda is particularly sensitive to the two timeframes of Suzuki's "overlapping conceptions" in 1978; he describes the one as taken directly from Euripides and "[t]he other, his own," as portraying a group of "vagrants" who "seek a vision" (Rimer, *Voyage*, 87). He shows how Suzuki, in seeking to anchor a 2,500-year-old play to contemporary concerns, uses his "vagrant group" frame-story to portray "Japanese intellectuals altogether fascinated by Western ideologies" (87). [Figure 26] By this I think Senda means the gender issues introduced into Japan through Little Theatre productions such as Schechner's.

Odashima Yûshi[15] was also appreciative of what he saw as the two main features of the production: "The first is that Suzuki has turned Euripides' world into a dream of marginalized people, whom he puts onstage at the side . . . The second is that Suzuki has Shiraishi Kayoko play the roles of both King Pentheus and his mother Agave." In the same team-review, however, Murai Shimako[16] describes herself as returning home "shaking with anger at the very thought Shiraishi Kayoko could be called an actress." She felt that "Suzuki showed me something like a Dali painting by force . . . I was uncertain whether Suzuki intended to make ironic reference to Beckett or Betsuyaku . . . But anyway I was a bit surprised that Kinoshita Junji and Ôe Kenzaburô both supported the program."[17] Even this negative review indirectly reveals the high level of support for his work among the Japanese avant-garde, despite the shock waves it caused.

THE 1981 SHIRAISHI–HEWITT PRODUCTION

Suzuki's logical next step in 1981 was to foster exchange between avant-garde artists from different national cultures. This was a particular goal of the First International Toga Festival in 1982.

The 1981 production was a bold bilingual experiment designed to open up the problematics of cross-cultural communication in the most powerfully confronting way possible: through language. A joint production between twelve Americans and twelve Japanese would be fraught with difficulties if there were no common language of communication. Indeed, the idea of two groups of actors trying to speak to each other in two completely different tongues threatened to leave its audiences in Japan and the United States gasping for intellectual air. However, Suzuki realized, from American interest in his acting workshops, that he had the basis for a rediscovered "common language of the theatre" in his "The Grammar of the Feet." Through conscious disruption of the mainstream verbal channel, his physical approach could more powerfully express the gender theme of *The Bacchae* as he saw it.

I shall not describe this production in great detail. For those interested, there are good accounts in Gotoh, Mori Hideo, and Marianne McDonald.[18] However, the frame-story is worth elucidating and the new dynamics of Shiraishi's interaction with Tom Hewitt, who replaced Kanze Hisao.

Where Euripides begins with Dionysus describing what he intends to do (so that everything is seen from his Olympian perspective), Suzuki doubly displaces the god's entrance until after we have seen the vagrants and heard Pentheus deliver his case against "that effeminate foreigner who plagues our women with this new disease."[19] The opening of Scene 2 discloses this "disease" as the male vagrants "start to mutter" and "take off their clothes to reveal women's underwear." After the Blind Man has recited a choral ode about the joys of resting "on wine's soft pillow of sleep," the Japanese chorus whisper a choral hymn to "sweet Desire" (Vellacott, *Euripides*, 203), which the American chorus repeats in English. "The recitation gets louder and louder . . . producing strange but fascinating polyphonic vocal effects" (Gotoh, Suzuki thesis, 310) as the Japanese group next praise "[t]he life that wins the poor man's common voice" and the American group follows suit. Only in the choral repetition can the audience understand everything said.

A number of Tokyo critics were ambivalent in their responses to this bilingual 1981 production. Okazaki Ryôko "admired . . . the mixing of English and Japanese," and Miyashita Norio was also deeply touched, "feeling that the world of theatre had really been enlarged [through its use of two languages]." The most positive benefit, Okazaki felt, was that it prevented the audience from slipping wholly into one set of cultural assumptions or another, and forced them to really pay attention to "the more direct effect" of purely physical modes of communication. She felt "very moved by this." Miyashita also agreed that most Japanese audience members could pick up on the dramatic energies and tensions transmitted by the actors, "even if they couldn't understand a word" of the English spoken, and pointed out that "the effect is remarkably like watching Noh."[20]

But they also found problems. For Okazaki the *katari* (narrated) sections were "impossible" and with this, on the evidence of video kindly supplied by Marianne McDonald, I would agree: "For example, the scene in which a herdsman describes the maenads on Mt. Cithaeron was quite long, and done only in English. This is a very beautiful scene in the original [but we couldn't follow it]. Also the report of Pentheus' death was only in Japanese, and it too was far too long" (Miyashita and Okazaki, "Theatre Criticism Page, " 108). Miyashita, critic for the *Asahi* newspaper, concurs, wondering where these experiments (with Kanze Hisao and Shiraishi; Shiraishi and Hewitt) would lead: "We are told that Shiraishi has natural talent as an actor, but . . . if Suzuki Tadashi's method is truly universal, I think he must be able to produce other Shiraishis . . . from now on is a really crucial testing time for Suzuki" (109).

Suzuki was to attempt to turn these technical negatives into theatrical positives in his next major revision of the play with Ashikawa Yôko; and with Ellen Lauren in 1990 he was finally able to claim that his method was capable of producing someone – an American no less – to match Shiraishi's prodigious skills.

THE 1989 ASHIKAWA–DE VITA PRODUCTION

With the departure of Shiraishi from SCOT in 1989, and in the light of the criticisms raised above, Suzuki contemplated a freer adaptation of *The Bacchae* better suited to its ecstatic content but also more controlled and disciplined in its theatricality. The bilingual experiment was continued, but all the *katari* scenes which had been so difficult for a mixed audience were cut, and, to enhance the visual emphasis required for touring, were replaced with a ritual killing of Pentheus onstage – not by Agave, but by Dionysus' priests. In seeing the play as "a struggle of state and religion," Suzuki preferred to think of the myth of Agave's dismemberment of her son as "a fabrication intended to cover up what amounts to an assassination of the king of Thebes by a religious group" (1989 program). The irrational nature of the original seemed to encourage a deconstruction of chronological narrative. To open up the story "as a series of illusory scenes," Suzuki now has Agave appear *out of sequence* with the head of Pentheus in Scene 4. The confrontation between Dionysus and Pentheus takes place in Scene 5, Agave argues with Kadmus over the slain Pentheus in Scene 6, and Pentheus appears in women's garb and is slaughtered in Scene 7.

Perhaps the most important change was that it was now a finely tempered, highly visual, and physically explosive performance. Eight years on, male actors approaching the caliber of Shiraishi had come to maturity, Nishikibe first taking over the role of Pentheus and Fueda of the High Priest (Dionysus disguised) in 1987. They were well supported by a group of priests (Nakajima, Sakato, Takemori, Katoh, Shiohara, and Hasegawa) and maenads (Togawa, Ishida Michiko, Aizawa Akiko, and Yanase Yûko) all of whom had played alongside Shiraishi and many of whom already had experience playing major roles. The company was a strongly knit, well-honed ensemble of strong individuals. And they had sharpened their communicative skills abroad, in Madrid (Festival de Teatro), Bilbao, Pamplona, Antwerp, and Stuttgart (Festival Theater der Welt) in 1987.

Finally the SCOT style was confidently set off against Butoh style, with the famous dancer Ashikawa Yôko playing Agave. For Ashikawa, who had already played Sonia in *Uncle Vania* at Toga in 1988, the challenge was to use her voice as an expressive tool (she was an internationally acclaimed dancer). However, Suzuki was careful not to overtax her, cutting back some of the dialogue with Kadmus to concentrate on her superbly grotesque dance in Agave's recognition scene. All of these innovations enabled Suzuki to split the form of Euripides' play wide apart in a bold attempt to better capture what he saw as its spirit, now suggestively interpreted as "the way society responds to the introduction of a strong alien cultural or religious presence."

Suzuki's program synopsis for Scene 1 states: "A Chorus of six men, the followers of Dionysus (god of wine), appear [dressed in priestly white vestments and carrying staves]. Kadmus asks them if they are the only followers among the citizens of Thebes. They bemoan the lack of believers and state their intent to spread the teachings of Dionysus."

His idea that the play veils a political assassination by a power-seeking religious cult is cleverly built on the lines he selects from Euripides:

CADMUS: Are we the only Thebans who will dance for him?
TEIRESIAS: We see things clearly, all the others are perverse . . .
    The beliefs we have inherited, as old as time,
    Cannot be overthrown by any argument . . . his claim
    To glory is universal; no one is exempt.
                                     (Vellacott, *Euripides*, 197–98)

But Suzuki sees through the comic, endearing qualities of the two old men of Euripides' original to paint a harsher picture, one of reactionary fanaticism better suited to contemporary realities. Where Dionysus' divinity would have been self-evident to a Greek audience (he was of course the patron deity of the very theatre festival they were attending), Suzuki is more skeptical about the way power structures can be misused in society.[21] His New Age cult is *not* universal. It has only a handful of converts, as Kadmus' line above suggests, and the ambitious intolerance he finds in Teiresias' lines (distributed now among the six priests) he makes foreshadow the action of a cult which gains converts through subversion, intimidation, and illegal acts when its expansion is blocked. His Dionysus, although still ambiguous, reflects growing public awareness of the disturbing features of Asahara Shôkô's AUM Supreme Truth cult. In 1989 AUM was battling Tokyo City Hall for recognition under Japan's Religious Corporation Law and was already "the target of complaints from parents who charged the cult had taken their children away."[22] These matters were kept firmly in the public eye by Maki Tarô, who also ran articles in the *Sunday Mainichi* about AUM's blood initiations and Asahara's criminal past. Moreover, in February 1990, "AUM was contesting no fewer than 25 seats in the Lower House" at national elections.[23]

In Scene 2 little needed to be changed in order to support Suzuki's reorientation of Euripides. The big change occurs in Scene 3, and it will underwrite all the other radical reorientations of scene order in what follows. Whereas in 1978 and 1981 he brings Dionysus onstage, as Euripides does, then keeps him offstage altogether from 1990 onward, Suzuki equivocates in 1989, using a voiceover in Scene 3 and "bringing on" the guru in Scene 5 as a vision in Agave's mind.

The scene begins with the powerful music of Perez Prado's "Voodoo Suite", which contributes substantially to the overall mood of the play, Suzuki insisting that his actors should make the music their mindscape liturgy. As Kadmus sits in his Greco-Roman chair slightly stage left of center, the six priests glide in to take up position around their chairs. Kadmus praises Dionysus, as if leading a formal service (the seven chairs are in a straight line across stage) and prays for more faith. Then, to the ritual strains of *Nasori*, ninth-century Bugaku music featuring the *shô* (Asian pan-pipes), the priests perform a dance in front of their chairs. They move in a hieratic way, like early Greek or Egyptian statues. Holding the left hand up in a stiff gesture of "peace" while the right holds the staff pointed forward and down, they lift first one heel off the ground, with the leg held straight out from the hip, and then the other. It is a minimalist but painfully hard set of movements which help to build up energy for the release of Artaudian cruelty to come.[24]

Suddenly the Voice of Dionysus declares that he will come to Thebes to punish unbelievers. The voiceover is in Japanese, high-pitched, rapid, and stridently amplified, like AUM's political electioneering loudspeaker-announcements. Kadmus and the six priests sit and listen to this impassively, as if receiving the word of God:

To these people who stand against my godhead . . . I must manifest my real divinity. If it goes well here, then I shall pass on to other countries to let them know my divine power. If, by some one-in-ten-thousand chance, government officers try to chase my women from their mountain by force, I will stand in their vanguard prepared to fight. For that reason I have hidden my god's form and appear here in human shape. Come my worshippers, . . . reveal my real power to Kadmus' kinfolk.[25]

It must be remembered that these stridently powerful and brilliantly articulated choral voices speak in Japanese; thus Dionysus' godhead remains veiled in mystery for a foreign audience (I describe the production seen in Melbourne) until Jim De Vita throws the verbal switch.

On "Come my worshippers," a chorus of maenads appear, led by Ishida Michiko (stage left) and Togawa Minoru (stage right). Their dance is a Suzuki "Moving statues" exercise to *Nasori* music in which, on every irregular beat of the big drum (disguised under the reedy, squealing *shô* and the regular gong), the actors suddenly assume new positions, all different, before moving on to the next Kabukiesque pose. The effect is like looking at the Elgin Marbles or the Winged Victory of Samothrace under strobe lighting, the actors' impassive presences coolly communicating a sense of life through a physically powerful, and powerfully restrained, acting technique. Also, because the costumes are voluminous and boldly striped red and white, the eye is forced to dart rapidly between six simultaneous, individual actions in a hunt for the grammar of formal relationship behind individual choreography (the actors create their own, although Suzuki composes the whole).

Togawa Minoru is superlative in communicating the fierce, panther-like energy and exultant passion of the maenads. The role was undoubtedly his greatest creation in a long career.[26] With long hair flying loose, he drags forward the train of his costume in a sensually abandoned state of possession, clawlike hands hitting at his train like an eagle striking its prey, lifting it up with a step forward, and then, with catlike speed, repeating the sequence. At the end of this dance sequence, Togawa faces his audience – surely by now rapt in his cruel display – and in a stylized move, hides his right hand behind his left sleeve (as if "sheathing claws"), squats with agonizingly slow deliberation, and stares intently into the audience like a carnivore crouched in long grass. As the maenads crouch in an asymmetrical, zigzag formation, facing the audience, Kadmus welcomes them as "Zeus no miko" (shamanesses of Zeus).

Suzuki's next scene is a wonderful *coup de théâtre*, worthy of anything in Euripides. The Scene 4 synopsis announces that "Agave, the daughter of Kadmus, who has lost her reason as a result of Dionysus' influence, appears with the head of Pentheus her son. She dances with the Maenads." The stage effect makes us feel sensationally cheated; the living heart of the play seems to have been ripped away – for we expect this to be the *last* scene. Moreover, Ashikawa Yôko, who comes on as Agave, is an apparently cowed, unprepossessing woman in middle age with untidy, loose hair. She wears a large brown priest's begging-bag over a white kimono with long sleeves, and, in her right hand, carries before her the severed head of her son. She stops center stage and begins falteringly with "Tennyo no okatagata" ("Honourable angels") rather than "Women of Asia." This is Suzuki's way of suggesting how "Agave may very well have been utilised in this plot"[27] against her son.

At the conclusion of the exchange between Agave and the Chorus of maenads, *Tenteketen* music starts.

The music is used in Suzuki Training for a variety of "Slow walks." It starts with drums and metal banging and scraping and music by Serge Aubrey, interspersed with labored, amplified horse-snorting which sounds as if a great weight were being dragged up a steep hill by spirited animals. Psychologically the music is a great help to performers and audience in supplying abstract emotional weight to physical movement. The maenads, right arms raised high above their upturned heads, rotate slowly as Agave retreats to a tatami mat beside Kadmus to watch the hieratic slow-motion entry of Dionysus to a grunting, squealing saxophone. This vision of Dionysus-in-human-form seems to be hers, and, ironically, in terms of the American/Japanese postwar "special relationship," he is American.

Scene 5 opens with "[a] confrontational dialogue . . . between Dionysus and Pentheus" (program; see Vellacott, *Euripides*, 206, 219). Jim De Vita's Dionysus wears Afro-style dreadlocks, hippy beads, and a long, loose purple-and-crimson kimono stitched with gold needlework designs. In his right hand, thrust out in front of him, he carries a long clublike staff. He is a white American with a suitable handsome but drug-ravaged face and a fastidiously clipped moustache and goatee – the image of sexy and powerful cultural appropriation. He walks slowly through his crouched maenads until challenged stage right by Pentheus (Nishikibe), who holds a samurai sword sheathed in his left hand, and wears a loose brown-and-white flecked kimono. The two circle each other counterclockwise.

Nishikibe begins (in Japanese), "Well, friend, your shape is not unhandsome – for the pursuit of women . . . Tell me who you are. What is your birth?" (206). Their *stichomythic* exchange sharpens audience focus by giving us only one half of the information provided by Euripides. On Dionysus' line "The whole East dances his mysteries," Pentheus replies, "teki no yatsura wa Girishyajin yori wa zutto chie mo taranu yue sô de" ("That's because the enemy are far below us Greeks in intelligence"). To this Dionysus instantly ripostes, "In this they are superior; but their customs differ" (207).

Dionysus infuriates and fascinates the king and awakens in him the desire to watch the mountain revels of the maenads in disguise (219–20). At this point, to Bugaku music, the priests repeat their hieratic, frontal dance while, as if on another plane, the maenads perform predatory "moving statues" across stage in front of them. These actions, both static and dynamic, seem as much at cross-purposes as the different languages and music used, and serve to reinforce the visual image of conflict between Dionysus and Pentheus, West and East, on all the sensory channels. Eventually Pentheus gives himself up to Dionysus' will and goes off to dress in women's clothes (220–22).

As he does so Dionysus and the maenads execute a victory dance, celebrating the imminent death of Pentheus: at Dionysus' ferocious cry of "Yaah!," both De Vita and Togawa react simultaneously. They have been standing close together, and, on Dionysus' cry, the former heaves his staff menacingly overhead, and Togawa slumps to the floor in a grotesque crouch. The effect is to suggest lightning splitting a tree, as well as the onset of violence. The maenads bend to the flashes of Dionysus' anger, propeled puppetlike across stage from one statuesque pose to another by the maddeningly slow, driving beat of Perez Prado's *Voodoo Suite*. Togawa, with a superhuman physical effort, staggers drunkenly up, tearing to pieces an imaginary victim, and then crouches to scrape the imagined "bits" together hastily. A puppet possessed by the will of the deity, he circles Dionysus in trance: bending backward with claws extended, lifting muscular shoulders menacingly to drag his heavy train (some 10 meters of cloth), striking forward, and slowly arching backward again a full 270 degrees to strike "upside down" *behind* him – before he recoils forward like Pentheus' pine tree propeled by divine force. All this to frenzied, dynamic music. After such a ferocious display of the physically extraordinary (based on "The Ladder" discipline), mere description of Dionysus' jail-break is utterly superfluous.

Scene 6 reveals the Chorus of priests sitting in camp chairs. Kadmus mourns the devastation brought on his house through disbelief and he instructs Agave to look calmly upon what she has done (237, 239). Agave is led to believe that she has killed her son in Dionysian ecstasy: "What is it? What am I holding in my hands?" At Kadmus' reply, "You killed him!" (238), several exchanges later, she becomes deranged and perceives the true power of Dionysus.

In front of the red-and-white striped train of the maenads, to the music of Vangelis, Ashikawa performs a Butoh dance of utter darkness, miming her horror with grotesquely expressive face. Scuttling like a crab attacked by a horde of soldier ants, she staggers, falls, picks herself up half-dazed (and half-eaten), "sees" the inner image of her child-murder, cries "Waah!," and scuttles backward from her vision in a vain attempt to scratch away the billion tiny Furies burrowing under skin and into her brain. (Ashikawa uses the Butoh exercise of imagining termites under the skin, in which ants devour termites and viruses ravage ants, in order to fuel the terrible inner drama of her physical performance.) Collapsed in despair on her mat, she gasps, "Where was it done? Here at home, or somewhere else?" Kadmus replies, "Where Actaeon was torn to pieces," and from this point she sits hunched in catatonic trance, mouth agape, eyes rolled up, until the end of the play.[28]

Scene 7 begins as Pentheus appears. Nishikibe is attired in a fan-patterned female kimono with a light brown pilgrim's begging-bag slung in front over one shoulder. A woman's head-covering of the same material gives him a "horned" look. On the line, "Why, now I seem to see two suns . . . You have become a bull now," he peers forward at Dionysus in an awed half-crouch, palm up and fingers open in surprise. However, Dionysus is not in front of him; it is the unseen-but-all-seeing god-in-the-audience for whom this tragic ritual sacrifice is enacted. And it is not Jim De Vita who speaks, aloof at the side of the stage in statuesque, dreadlocked majesty. His High Priest (Fueda) manipulates the victim with biting irony in Japanese: "Your girdle has come loose; and now your dress does not hang, as it should, in even pleats." Nishikibe's stylized responses – holding his staff parallel to the ground in both hands and deliberately peering over it at one leg and then the other – signify deep anxiety.

Pentheus' concern for his appearance is comic, but this seems only to reinforce the impending horror induced by the music. It is vigorous, driving Noh music from the climax of a ghost play – but played on tape at half speed. The Noh drummers' weird cries, the strange slap and crack of drums and piercing shriek of flute are distorted almost beyond the point of recognition; and this helps to create a sense of internal crisis somewhat akin to that of a highspeed crash perceived in all the detail of slow motion. The effect could also be likened to that of being on drugs, a preternaturally heightened awareness, and, in Pentheus' case, a loosening restraint, as Nishikibe mimes him watching the Bacchic women in his mind's eye, in different acts of sex, "all clasped close in the sweet prison of love." His voyeuristic, leering laugh, as he pruriently traces an imaginary chase across stage with his finger, is cut short in an explosive snort of breath when the High Priest stalks from behind and drives the samurai sword concealed in his staff up through the ribs and lung of his victim in the opposite direction from Pentheus' trembling finger. Each priest comes forward in turn to stab or slash the terrorstruck Pentheus in slow motion, and, as he collapses to his knees, still clinging to his staff, they circle him counterclockwise with drawn swords in a motion as disorienting as the music. The circling gradually intensifies into a dizzying billowing of white garments [Figure 27] until all at once the priests step back, pause, and lunge forward as one to dispatch the sacrificial victim.

Figure 27 The priests of Dionysus stab Pentheus (Nishikibe Takahisa) to death in a swirl of motion. *Dionysus*. Toga, 1990.

Pentheus jerks upward in reflex-response, staring wide-eyed into the audience. Nishikibe's mimed reactions are the perfect theatrical substitute for the Messenger's horrific but unstageable description in Euripides:

> Agave was foaming at the mouth; her rolling eyes
> Were wild; she was not in her right mind, but possessed
> By Bacchus, and she paid no heed to him. She grasped
> His left arm between wrist and elbow, set her foot against his ribs,
> And tore his arm off by the shoulder.
> It was no strength of hers that did it, but the god
> Filled her, and made it easy. On the other side
> Ino was at him, tearing at his flesh; and now
> Autonoë joined them, and the whole maniacal horde.
> A single and continuous yell arose – Pentheus
> Shrieking as long as life was left in him, the women
> Howling in triumph. One of them carried off an arm,
> Another a foot, the boot still laced on it. The ribs
> Were stripped, clawed clean; and women's hands, thick red with
>   blood,
> Were tossing, catching, like a plaything, Pentheus' flesh.   (232)

Suzuki has sensibly elected not to describe – or stage – the famous Greek narrative. By localizing it in a ritual sword-play which estheticizes the horror, he manages to reactivate powerfully the musical dance-drama of traditional Kabuki in the apparently alien contemporary service of ancient Greek melodrama.

In the dead silence which follows, the priests withdraw to their seats and the stricken Pentheus lifts his quivering, trembling hand toward the god at the end of the maenad's red-and-white train spread in front of him; he drags himself clumsily along it to the feet of Dionysus and clutches at his sleeve to beg for sanctuary. De Vita turns impassively, majestically raises his staff high overhead – and clubs Pentheus in slow motion, bowling him over backward with the "force" of the blow. Still on his knees, Pentheus puts his hands together in supplication but is struck again on the head. In a complicated, slow-motion ballet of thrashing limbs, he now pushes himself away along the ground "in panic" with both feet and hands.[29] The god closes in slowly, stands over his victim (thus blocking audience view and increasing imaginative response) and drives his staff down into Pentheus' stomach, snuffing out his scream as if crushing a large insect.

De Vita then turns to face the audience and raises arms and staff in a hieratic gesture of victory *more* cruelly powerful for being so facially impassive; paradoxically it carries strong overtones of the Resurrected Christ of religious iconography.[30] The maenads perform ecstatic "moving statues" to the ancient Bugaku music of the *shô*, and, while the American God stands there in beautiful/terrible glory, the amplified multiple voices of Dionysus are heard as voiceover in a stereophonic, echoing, overlapping babble of Japanese. Agave, mouth agape on her Asian mat, and Kadmus tight-lipped on his Greco-Roman chair, sit behind the exultant God like "empty shells" (program description).

Around Dionysus' still form, to the deafening repetitive pulse of Perez Prado's "Voodoo Suite," swirl the maenads in strobelike, stop/start motion. As they glide into the wings, the priests stand up from their chairs, sink into breathtakingly low squats (lower than the maenads' – and therefore more powerfully affecting audience physiology) and squirm forward with frightening concentration and cunning in a hunting-animal creep, swords concealed in staves over their shoulders like fishing poles. Their fox-paw hand gestures suggest the shape-shifting, trickster abilities of Inari Kitsune, the Japanese fox-god, avatar of the goddess of theatre, Ama no Uzume no mikoto.[31] (In 1987 fox-masks were worn, but by 1989 the power of suggestion was all Suzuki's actors needed for this creative remodeling of the *Kanjinchô* exercise.) Here, if anywhere, is the conscious realization of the heightened state in which, for Artaud, "sounds are linked to movements . . . like the natural conclusion of gestures with the same attributes . . . The mind is at last obliged to confuse them, attributing the sound qualities of the orchestra to the artist's hinged gesticulation – and vice versa."[32]

The play concludes with a long take of the devastated Agave and Kadmus as the latter delivers a choral epode in an ironically "Sophoclean" summing up:

> Oh blessed is the man
> Who escapes the winter sea
> And wins his haven
> Free above his own striving.
> Let other men in other ways
> Other men surpass in wealth or power.
> He who lives each day
> For the happiness each day offers
> Him I call blessed.[33]

This 1989 version is an ecstatic, raw, disorderly Dionysian vision of Euripides. The following 1993 version emphasizes the formal ritual in a colder manner which better conveys the possibilities of the Farewell Cult frame-story.

DIONYSUS IN 1990 AND AFTER

On March 23 1990 *The Bacchae* became *Dionysus* to mark the opening of Suzuki's new ACM Theatre in Mito City. On the Pacific coast an hour north of Tokyo by express train, Mito had been a rich feudal fief of the Tokugawa clan during the Edo Period but was now reinventing itself, with the help of Isozaki Arata's new Art Center and Suzuki's theatre company, as a lifestyle alternative to Tokyo. Agave was played by the popular commercial theatre star Natsuki Mari, for whom Suzuki created a powerful new variation. Whereas in the 1989 *The Bacchae* De Vita-as-Dionysus had given Pentheus the *coup de grâce*, in this *Dionysus* Suzuki has Agave dispatch her own son onstage. In addition, human representation of Dionysus himself is banished from the production, and while the scene order is returned to chronological sequence, several contemporary frames are added, giving a "Chinese boxes" feel.

Instead of a group of vagrants, as in the 1978 and 1981 versions, three men in wheelchairs (symbolic of their crippled hopes) open the play, singing a children's song in imbecilic fashion. They are followed in Scene 2 by the Cult Founder, also in wheelchair, but pushed by an Assistant. The Founder leads a nihilistic Beckettian chant called "Farewell to all Histories and Memories" in which each line is repeated by the crippled souls who follow their guru. After Kadmus and his priestly followers offer parallel allegiance to Dionysus in Scene 3, Scene 4 saw the return of the three wheelchair-believers of Scene 1, chanting the "Tomorrow, and tomorrow, and tomorrow" speech from *Macbeth* before the entrance of Pentheus in Scene 5. In Scene 7 they returned to chant the children's song of Scene 1; and, at the end of the play, Scenes 2 and 4 were re-peated as Scenes 10 and 11 before Kadmus' closing speech ("The gods manifest themselves in many forms") in Scene 12. Here Shinto and ancient Greek religious anthropomorphism happily coincided to justify the use of the new "extraneous" material as a further "manifestation of the gods," both in terms of the classic-play-as-understood-today, and in terms of its perceived relation to other classics across space, time, and cultures.

At the Toga Festival in July 1990, SCOT actresses took over the main roles. While Ishida Michiko played the Founder of a New Age cult, Takahashi Hiroko played Agave *and* Assistant to the Cult Leader, thus helping to blur the boundary between the Euripidean story and its popular and avant-garde frames. *Dionysus* was now conceived as the first play in a trilogy, with *Macbeth* and *Ivanov*, called *Osarabakyô* (*The Farewell Cult*), and the added scenes were intended to create the rudiments of a frame-story which could aid the cross-relation of the themes of these plays (the rise to power, the overreaching, and the decline of Western culture). The idea was basically that of the 1978 vagrants extended and updated for the 1990s. It now had little if anything to do with post-AMPO feelings of betrayal and abandonment, and much more to do with the disaffection of top-flight salarymen to religious cults such as AUM (also satirised by Itami Jûzô in his film *A Taxing Woman II*).

The Mito New Year production of 1992 created a new twist. For this Ellen Lauren played Agave and another talented American actress, Kelly Maurer, the Cult Founder; both had been part of Suzuki's JPAC International Training Program since 1983. At the Toga Festival in July that year, SCOT performed the entire trilogy of *The Rise and Fall of the Farewell Cult* (*Dionysus, Macbeth,* and *Ivanov*) alongside a larger than usual contingent of American actors. Tom Hewitt, who had played with Shiraishi, was brought back as Pentheus to compete with Ellen Lauren's Agave. Kelly Maurer was Cult Leader again, Eric Hill took on Kadmus, and three more Americans played Wheelchair Believers (Jeffrey Bihr, Scott

Rabinowitz, and Tom Nelis). By having his SCOT company play priests *and* maenads Suzuki was thus able to set up a metatheatrical commentary on the double-edged nature of intercultural exchange.

From 1994 John Nobbs, the Australian dancer who played Banquo in Suzuki's *The Chronicle of Macbeth*, featured regularly as the Cult Founder alongside the brilliant Ellen Lauren as Agave, and their combination lasted through four international tours until 1998, when Takemori first played a cross-dressed *onnagata*-style Agave.

Since these variants evoked differently shaded interpretations, I shall concentrate on the 1995 production which toured to the Herod Atticus amphitheatre in Athens (for the First International Theatre Olympics in Athens, Epidavros, and Delphi) and to the Teatro Olimpico in Vicenza. It came at a crucial point in the company's international recognition. Suzuki was about to take over a new post as general artistic director of the Shizuoka Performing Arts Center and would host the Second International Theatre Olympics in 1999. Thus, in Greece, since *Dionysus* was to open the Festival, expectations of the company were high among fellow International Theatre Olympics committee members such as Robert Wilson, Heiner Müller, Yuri Lyubimov, and Tony Harrison. While the company's experience and skill were now greater than they had ever been, the expected success seemed in jeopardy when Nishikibe suddenly fell ill and had to withdraw. This occurred only a few weeks before the company was due to fly to Greece.

The mood of depression and anxiety generated in the company was palpable. As Ellen Lauren put it bluntly that night in the refectory, "It's really the quality of the acting that makes SCOT, the text is such a patched thing."[34] But the speed with which the company was able to recover suggests the strengths of their repertory and training systems. Within three grueling hours a young actor of promise, who until then had been a novitiate Priest, was taught the requisite choreography and lines, and within a further two days was showing signs of being able to fill the role (Suzuki's laconic comment to a senior actor was "Kijima wa mâ ii" ("Kijima's OK"). At this point the veterans in major roles started to rethink their parts and make minor but crucial adjustments in order to give the new sapling space in the forest canopy.

The Suzuki actor's individuality shines *more* brightly for being readily measurable against a received collective tradition, and the qualitative experience of a group which has been together for more than ten years is quite different from one which has been together for only ten weeks or so. In SCOT, given the necessary precondition of talent, longevity is an important factor relating to quality: Shiraishi had been with the company for twenty-three years, and Togawa for nineteen. By the time of the Herod Atticus performance in 1995, Tsutamori had been a company member for thirty-four years, Fueda for eighteen years, Takemori seventeen, Katoh sixteen, Shiohara and Takahashi fourteen each, Sakato and Nishikibe thirteen – and Kijima just two. Suzuki's theatrical development cannot adequately be appreciated apart from the development of his most talented actors and the "SCOT culture" they collectively create through company *esprit de corps*. Kijima was not "carried" by the group so much as his inexperience was incorporated and foregrounded to produce a quite different reading of Pentheus.

Nevertheless, as Suzuki departed for a press conference in Tokyo to announce his winning of the Second International Theatre Olympics for Shizuoka, Ellen Lauren warned, "After *The Trojan Women*, this *Dionysus* is Suzuki's signature piece. He was pleased Kijima showed he can do it, but when he returns from the press conference, reality will hit; it's going to be hell. Nishikibe was irreplaceable." As she went on to make clear, Nishikibe's loss put even greater pressure on her: "Each time I do this play it takes years out of my life; it needs so much psychic energy." The physical pressures the Suzuki performer must bear are enormous, comparable to those of an international athlete.[35] Younger actors can feed off the very high energy which a mature Suzuki actor brings to performance, but, for principals, it is harder to sustain past a certain age. Lauren well knew, as she explained later, that it was only a matter of years before she would have to make the switch to working for Anne Bogart, whose requirements of her actor-dancers are not quite as physically demanding as Suzuki's.

This, then, was the drama unfolding behind the scenes before the Athens opening. What Suzuki wished his audience to focus on was set out in his director's notes:

Consciousness is a prison, and the walls of the prison are history. History emerges out of the relation between the spirit of exuberant communal unity [the maenads] and the spirit of isolated alienated individuality [the basket and wheelchair people]. These two modes of being form the two poles at either end of the arch of spiritual history.

His second paragraph goes on to trace how experience is processed "into stories . . . myths, legends, fairytales or histories" as a means to convey hope or as a tool of repression. The ambivalence is crucial to the dramatic success of Suzuki's production, as we shall see. "Euripides' *Bacchae*," says Suzuki, "shows the process by which individuals are 'scapegoated out' of the narrative world. Agave in her moment of realization . . . makes the trans-historic leap out of the world of classical narrative . . . and begins the journey towards the opposite pole."[36]

Suzuki represents the two "worlds" of *Dionysus* as, firstly, the world Agave leaves, a world in which classical narratives are efficacious, and in which "enthusiastically passionate devotees . . . [are] living their story with total commitment"; and, second, the world of those "who have dropped out of 'the story', wandering aimlessly in wheelchairs." For Suzuki this clarifies why he does not want Euripides' Dionysus on-stage, preferring to assign his words to a Chorus of priests. His new idea is that "a group with a communal need for unity and the will to spiritually influence the masses created a 'story' called *Dionysus*." He also emphatically states that his aim is "not to stage Euripides' play but to use Euripides' play to stage my world view." Although the events of September 11 certainly gave *Dionysus* a new and shocking currency when it was performed in the United States late in 2001, Suzuki remains deliberately ambiguous about articulating links between the two onstage "worlds," the world of the Farewell Cult and the world of Kadmus, Agave, and Pentheus. The advantage of this is theatrical, in that his *mise en scène* intersects with history and can create a spark gap to ignite audience thought between the polarities set up.[37]

The interpolated scenes of *The Farewell Cult* present without explanation the "wheelchair world" of those who reject the "meaningful" social construction and alignment of history and story. It is a grotesquely absurd world, resolutely existential in its depiction of "the struggle of the defeated" and powerfully persuasive in its incongruous juxtaposition of Beckettian with Euripidean, Shakespearean, and Chekhovian worldviews. We can see the past only from the present; thus any restaging of a classic inevitably involves a double perspective – which Suzuki seeks to keep clearly before our eyes lest we "naturalize" what he estranges. Post-Seattle and the increasingly spectacular alliance of youth groups in opposition to the globalization of the IMF and the WTO, the "clashings" in a multiframed *Dionysus* can take on new and more disturbing resonances of "civilization at the crossroads."

Another important layer in Suzuki's postmodernization of Euripides was provided by his 1995 settings: the ancient Stadium at Delphi (for *Elektra*), the Herod Atticus amphitheatre in Athens (*Dionysus*), and the Teatro Olimpico in Vicenza (*Elektra* and *Dionysus*). These theatres are not only classical but neoclassical, too (Greek, Roman, and Renaissance). [Figure 28] In them Suzuki could most clearly symbolize the "dismemberment" – savage to those interested in the Aristotelian unities rather than in Euripides' evident deconstructions – of the "classical"

Figure 28 *Dionysus* at the Herod Atticus amphitheatre, Athens. The
First International Theatre Olympics, 1995. From left to right are
Agave (Ellen Lauren), the dancing maenads, seated priests, Kadmus
(Tsutamori Kôsuke), and man in wheelchair.

rational world in favor of a *"Bacchae* of Asia" based on theatrical physicality (so undervalued by Aristotle in *Poetics*). Greece is conveniently located, both physically and symbolically, at what Patrice Pavis has called
"the crossroads of cultures," and it is the image of a crossroads which
Suzuki developed in the "traffic-light" setting for his Delphi production, at "the navel of the world." At this juncture in time and space,
the Asian economic meltdown, following a bullish "charge of the Asian
Tigers," was yet another active ingredient in the cauldron of intercultural
history.

At Athens the sight of the fox-priests of this Asian Dionysus immobile
under the massively weathered columns of the Herod Atticus amphitheatre was a strangely moving experience. Suzuki had side-lit his actors
so that the double-perspective within which we view the classics today
was presented onstage in bold *chiaroscuro*. Under the columns of the
skene, the Japanese priests sat as still as so many ancient statues. The
maenads in red-and-white robes swirled in front of them across stage
from opposite directions in a manner reminiscent of the flickering flames
projected onto Plato's cave-wall. An iconoclastic Australian Cult Leader

croaked "Farewell to History, farewell to Memory" out of the darkness of the backstage; and an American Agave downstage center stared out through the darkness at the unseen-god-in-the-audience. [Figure 28]

Ellen Lauren's Agave was a magnificently bold-spirited and heroic Amazon, presenting a sharp contrast to the indecisiveness of the three wheelchair-bound Believers/Drop-outs, played by Katoh, Hasegawa, and Nîhori.[38] Their treatment of a children's song about wild purple chrysanthemums (*nogiku*), parodied as "the nobly, pure-smelling flower ME" (satirizing the "me generation"), may not have registered for non-Japanese. However, the Believers' imbecilic tittering, and moments of catatonia followed by extremely athletic yet grotesque actions, drew immediate laughter and applause from the Athens audience. John Nobbs (the Cult Founder) delivered "Farewell to History" in a punk voice as viciously populist as the responses of his servant (Takahashi Hiroko) were obsequiously and suavely ironic. And this sense of double-perspective was maintained when the gravity of the fascist salute delivered by Fueda's High Priest to the entering Cult Founder was undercut by the sight of "The Leader" in a wheelchair.

Even the costumes contributed to the double-perspective. The resemblance of the maenads' red-and-white drapery to both the American and Japanese flags has already been noted; however, Pentheus' costume (also used for Macbeth in *The Farewell Cult* trilogy) was new, a vandalizing overwriting of the ancient with the modern. It consisted of a brown fish-net, perhaps signifying chainmail, over a beautifully embroidered silk kimono, which was spray-painted silver to give a steely "breast-plate sheen" to the muted colors and blurred patterns underneath (dark green at the collar with a red stain over the heart – a red needleworked chrysanthemum).[39]

The confrontation between Pentheus and the priests of Dionysus was interesting for the way in which Kijima's youthful struggle to match the saturnine power and restraint of the SCOT veterans seemed to suggest a generational battle. Kijima's simple *kendô*-style concentration and strength of voice were evident (to aid which a new "Swivel/Slice" discipline had been added to training), but his youthful enthusiasm could not match the commanding range and depth of an actor with twenty years' experience who had played Lear to acclaim at the RSC. Fueda's ability to carry fine shades of threat in voice, face, and actions was as unsettling as his fastidiously painted face, the chalk-powder contrasting, whenever he spoke, with the bright red lipstick applied even to the inside lining of his mouth. At the turning point of the play, when Pentheus ordered his army to put the maenads to the sword, Fueda swept back his right arm overhead, fingertips pointed at Kijima like the raised tail of a scorpion, and as if summoning demonic forces from the deepest folds of vocal chord and lung, cried "Ooo! Shibaraku omachi kudasai!" (a variant of the famous Kabuki cry, "Please wait a minute"). Then, as if working loose Kijima's deepest, most hidden desires with every microtonal variation, Fueda growled this out in one long, stinging question: "Tono wa yama ni iru onnadomo no sugata o goran ni naritaku wa arimasenuka-aah" ("Would you like to *see* their revels on the mountains?").

The moment of Pentheus' trance-possession was initially accomplished by the power and control of two great actors. Nishikibe's response to Fueda had been to hold his breath for a very long time – as if Fueda's words had physically deflated his lungs – until, sweat popping from a glistening red face, he would gasp these expletives: "BAN'kin (long pause) o tsundemo (shorter pause, and then the voice dropping an octave in a rush of air) mitai" ("I'd pay pots . . . to see . . . *that* sight"). Kijima was able to approximate the vocal range but had difficulty projecting the release of dark desires which the more mature Nishikibe could summon with leering side-cast eyes and saliva-filled, twisted mouth. Yet Kijima's youthful innocence served well enough, his energy and concentration holding under Fueda's *tour de force* barrage to maintain the sense of trance-possession needed to propel him offstage for costume change. In this version the acrid cruelty of Dionysus rather than the lecherous voyeurism of Pentheus was exposed.

In the musical interlude which followed, Suzuki created another double-vision as the three Believers of the Farewell Cult returned in their wheelchairs, shadowed by three maenads of Dionysus. They performed "Moving statues" to the Bugaku beat of *Nasori*, swiftly adopting new and individual poses on the irregular beat of the big drum. Where the movements of the women of Bacchus were powerfully confident and beautifully sculptural, those of the male Farewell Cult believers were crabbed, timorous, and grotesque. Together they created a compelling juxtaposition that was both horrific and funny. The maenads' entry behind the wheelchair men seemed to suggest the possibility of a day of reckoning when they could reassert female power over these spiritually crippled males. Just occasionally their abstract dance movements confirmed it, as when Tateno's arm at shoulder level swept over Katoh like a scythe and his head dropped onto his shoulder as if decapitated.

When Kijima-as-Pentheus was finally dispatched by all the priests at once, he did not crawl to Dionysus as Nishikibe had done in 1989. Dionysus was now nowhere and everywhere, and so Pentheus' crumpled body remained slumped center stage. However, it served as an especially effective reminder that Dionysus had uncoupled logic from feeling when Lauren entered from backstage crying, "Women of Asia . . . happy was the hunting." Even the killing is doubled, and at this moment we are made aware of the gap between the killing we have seen and the killing we now hear about. Holding the "head" of her "prey" aloft in exultation for all to see (itself a doubled image of present joy and future sorrow), she had to step over the sprawled body of Pentheus to enter. When she did so in Athens, her long trailing robes caught on the body, and for three heartbeats Lauren was stuck; then, without losing concentration or wobbling on one leg, she managed to drag herself over Kijima's body with a heroic effort of will which only a Togawa had previously been able to summon. This performance was certainly one of the high points of her career with Suzuki. As she had herself said, Suzuki Training was developed in order to match the extraordinary themes of tragedy with an extraordinary physical sensibility. If her performance on video in 1992 showed up some Kijima-like problems with concentration and expression, in Athens it was at the expressive level of a Nishikibe, a passionately heroic acting.

Tsutamori was positioned behind Lauren during their dialogue, and thus their exchange became a powerful psycho-drama in which the therapist positioned behind the patient had to winkle out the delusions of the patient. Tsutamori, who had modified some of his earlier exchanges with Pentheus in order to create a more heightened climax in the finale, provided a delicate balance of emotive support and rational challenge during Lauren's intense struggle with her inner demons. On "Omae ga . . . koroshita no jya!" ("*You* killed him!"), the same music of Vangelis which Ashikawa Yôko had used for her 1989 dance of horror came in. However, for Lauren it was used to highlight a moment of heroic action beyond despair: she arched backward on her knees as far as she could go, her arms thrust to the sky in a silent scream or curse, and then threw herself vehemently forward onto her fists before the head of her son. Her face glistening with sweat from the extraordinary effort, she twice made this gesture (as strenuous as the Suzuki "Ladder" discipline Brandon described), and both times it was fully expressive of what Suzuki calls "the struggle of the defeated."[40]

In the Herod Atticus amphitheatre, with its battered columns rusticated by war and weather over the centuries, her actions seemed grandly elemental. However, in the exquisite indoor space of the Teatro Olimpico in Vicenza, her actions seemed to challenge a past ideal of human perfection in the massed statuary overhead. A photograph of Agave's grim

Figure 29 "The body as moving sculpture." Agave (Ellen Lauren) enters with the head of Pentheus. Kadmus (Tsutamori Kôsuke, right) sits in meditation beside the body of Pentheus, lower center. *Dionysus*. Teatro Olimpico, Vicenza, 1994.

entrance down the central perspective street catches something of the wonder of this encounter between cultures across time. [Figure 29]

The Italians were both critically discerning and emotionally generous, and it is worth summing up audience response to Suzuki's achievement in the area of Greek tragedy by quoting from this Vicenza review:

The first part of "The Great Myths of Memory" project being staged at the Teatro Olimpico in Vicenza has concluded with the splendid *Bacchae* directed by Tadashi Suzuki. For an hour and a half the audience at the Olimpico were transfixed, such was the tension and magnetism of the actors, as well as the stage action, atmospherics, musical effects and lighting. The play was performed in Japanese and, in part, in English. Everything about it was superlative.

Suzuki has worked to focus on the space created by Palladio, exploiting its possibilities and clearly demonstrating that the Teatro Olimpico is capable of playing a fully supporting part in the total production. The set consisted of just six stylized chairs, the color of which matched the marble of the *frons scaenae* . . . The production lived thanks to actions and movements whose rhythms and articulations . . . affect the audience viscerally. The words of the Japanese text . . . became highly charged . . . No nonsense with subtitles or a simultaneous translation, which some might have welcomed. The message was entirely clear because emotionally clear. Wherein lies the strength of Suzuki's theatre? . . . He pushes his actors to a concentration which is totally unrelenting. Even when the actor isn't the focus of attention, he or she is still "tense", present, and dynamic in his or her immobility.

If our own actors, who claim to love the theatre, were able to subject themselves to this type of discipline, very few of them would make it to the finishing line, as they are involved in an externalized journey towards "recognition" rather than an inner journey towards knowledge. Fortunately we can say that there is a tendency among young actors to embrace this way of understanding the actor's art . . . The actors were all outstanding for their charismatic, focused energy. To mention only the entrance of Ellen Lauren's Agave, she comes down from the back of the central perspective holding Pentheus' head in her hands, still unaware that Dionysus has taken his revenge by having her kill her own son; she reaches the body of Pentheus lying at center stage and then gives vent to her wild grief with such power that the audience is left breathless for the whole of the scene.

Suzuki left his mark even on the curtain calls. The actors move, maintaining the ritual nature of their characters, and then exit, leaving alone, as if it were a character in the play, the Palladian space, including Scamozzi's scenery, lit up in all its splendor. Thank you, on behalf of us all, for this homage, for this splendid sentiment towards the Teatro Olimpico, towards Palladio, towards Vicenza.[41]

7   Suzuki's Chekhov: *The Chekhov* and *Ivanov*

Ian Carruthers

Suzuki's first production as a student was Chekhov's one-act farce *The Anniversary*, and his engagement with *Three Sisters* dates back to a 1961 staging which was controversial because he refused to make it a vehicle for the radical politics demanded by the Communist-dominated Waseda University Drama Society. Yet their view of Chekhov "as a critical realist, one who exposed the conditions for revolution in the present"[1] continued to inform his major productions of Chekhov in the 1980s and 1990s.

In 1986 Suzuki premiered *Three Sisters* alongside *The Cherry Orchard* as *The Chekhov*, the "Japlish" title functioning as a sign of radical reculturation. *Uncle Vania* was added as a middle play in 1988; then in a 1989 restaging, the sequence was changed to make *Vania* the conclusion of the trilogy. The addition of the new play, followed by the reordering, made each of these three productions seem remarkably different, forcing surprising new insights in the contextualized meanings generated between actors and audiences.[2] Then in 1992 he produced *Ivanov* as part of two different trilogies: *The Farewell Cult* (with *Dionysus* and *Macbeth*) and *Greetings from the Edge of the Earth*. Most recently, Suzuki produced *Kagami no ie* (*The House of Mirrors*), which juxtaposes scenes from *Ivanov*, *The Cherry Orchard*, *Three Sisters*, *The Seagull*, and Ibsen's *A Doll's House* (1998), and a new trilogy that recomposes *Ivanov*, *The Cherry Orchard*, and *Uncle Vania*. As a whole his approach is at once postmodern, building on both Beckett and the New York avant-garde, and classic, embodying Noh and Kabuki conventions hitherto ignored as *passé* by Shingeki (realist) companies. This combination is striking, Chekhov's themes used in consciously bizarre juxtapositions to present contemporary Japan. The nearest Western equivalent might be the Mabou Mines approach to the classics (which had been demonstrated in Japan at the Toga Festival in 1982 and 1984).

180

In *Engeki to wa nani ka* (*What is Theatre?*), Suzuki explained the basis of his approach to Chekhov, pointing out that:

even now we are not able to escape from the outlook of the human being which Realism advances. When I direct Chekhov, I feel the need to recreate this outlook with precision. In my production of *Three Sisters*, when the actors say "We must live", they curl up in chairs, and are force-fed rice. Or three old ladies sit on toilets, standing on top of them at the end to declare "We must live!" I can defend such stagings because humans, no matter how confused their inner life may be, cannot very well do without continually eating, excreting, and babbling everyday. Chekhov wanted to emphasize this common quality of mundane human existence so the audience might feel it. These sorts of characters divert the audience from their own paralysis for any number of hours. This is the Realism that I think Chekhov imagined.[3]

His final point here implicitly casts Chekhov as a forerunner of Beckett; and there were clear echoes of Beckett's plays in *The Chekhov*, particularly Suzuki's use of large wicker baskets to depersonalize characters. In addition his program notes for the trilogy, which defined his directorial aims, also suggested the way his stylistic juxtapositions brought out the deeper parallels:

A special feature of the characters in Chekhov is that they're incapable of facing reality . . . Their erasure of their humanity in the gap between dream and reality is a theme that has been treated by many modern playwrights. But what Chekhov described and tried to dramatise was not so much the character of the person with desires and illusions, but that very gap itself. I have tried to push this special quality in Chekhov's theatre as much as I could because this is where I think his true modernity lies.[4]

I dismantled the characters of Chekhov's story, selected only those words that seemed to express this sense [of gap] and tried to find visual equivalents for them.[5]

The stage set for *Three Sisters* is classically balanced and severely frontal. Before two *shôji* (sliding paper-screen doors) upstage left and right stand two large wicker baskets on small rostra. In front and between stand three tatty Western armchairs (by 1988 these had become visibly cleaner chairs with elegant backs). Directly in front of each of these lies three tatami mats. [Figure 30] The set can be seen as a visual diagram of the choices every Japanese since Meiji has had to negotiate between Western and Japanese modes of behavior, the sisters moving throughout the play between mats and chairs. A third, intermediate alternative, the squat, is not used in *Three Sisters*, but this again is

Figure 30 Olga (Ishida Michiko), Masha (Takahashi Hiroko), and
Irena (Ginpunchô) crouch on their chairs, flanked by Vershinin and
Toozenbach (Nishikibe Takahisa and Katoh Masaharu) in baskets.
Three Sisters. Toga Sanbô, 1989.

deliberate. The set change for *The Cherry Orchard*, which follows immediately afterward, involves nothing more than throwing dustcovers
over baskets, chairs, and tatami mats (Chekhov's stage directions for Act
IV in a different cultural context); hence the only remaining space for
acting is a narrow strip between chairs and mats. Here Ranyevskaia and
her family either stand or squat on their heels, facing front. [Figure 31]
The old-fashioned "Japaneseness" of this relaxed position had already
been noted by Senda Akihiko,[6] and *shômen engi* or frontal acting is a
well-recognized feature of Noh and Kabuki.

Most of the time the actors speak to the audience rather than to each
other, and in modern terms this helps to convey the sense that inner
fantasies are on display, for their projected dreams of a better future
are always "out there" in audience-space, and can blend with ours. All
realistic circumstantial detail is hollowed out, the emptiness beneath its
surface being symbolized by the use of large wicker baskets. The placement of each item on the set has the severe beauty and functional rigor
of Beckett's minimalist sets – or the props on a Noh stage. There is little
dramatic action (accentuating a tendency already present in Chekhov)

Figure 31 From the right, Ania (Takemori Yôichi), Ranyevskaia (Shiraishi Kayoko), Lopakhin (Tsutamori Kôsuke), and Gayev (Sakato Toshihiro) squat while Yasha (Yoshihama Hideo) swims drunkenly past in a basket. *The Cherry Orchard*. Seibu Studio, Tokyo, 1987.

and what movement and gesture there is becomes charged with tension and stylized, perhaps to suggest the fixed habits into which each "character" is locked.

What remains of Chekhov besides eating and sex is an even greater emphasis on endless talk. But, to reduce Chekhov's four acts to the eighty-minute timeframe of a high-energy Suzuki performance, everything in the text which does not serve the "through-line" of dislocation and self-contradiction is cut. In the Elisaveta Fen translation, *Three Sisters* is eighty-one pages long; Suzuki's adaptation, which adds virtually nothing at the level of literary text, keeps only about twenty pages of the original.[7] This condensation is further reinforced by removing all nonfamily members from the stage (Vershinin, Toozenbach, Soliony, Chebutykin, Koolyghin, Ferapont, Rodé, and Fedotik), leaving only Anfisa to scurry round like a malicious clockwork Clov, spying on the family and administering trays of food and cups of tea in the midst of desolation.

In short, no distracting Stanislavskian stage business of the sort which used to make Chekhov and Meyerhold weep is allowed. By further reducing all male characters to Man 1 and Man 2, who are confined to baskets and speak their lines quite interchangeably, the realist principle of character is subverted. In this way Suzuki can further increase the sense of social isolation in a "two-camera effect." The undifferentiated men, whose words give them only a momentary, ghostly reality, emerge from their waste baskets to speak to, but over the heads of, the sisters seated in front of them. The audience can see both sets of speakers clearly, but basketmen and sisters cannot establish eye-contact.

The other immediately arresting image of the production, besides the baskets and symmetrically placed stage-front furniture, is the use of umbrellas. The sisters carry them open all the time, even when eating a meal, and the basketmen also use them at the end of the play when they step out of their baskets and march forward to sing. The fact that Anfisa, Andrei, and Natasha never use umbrellas seems further to underline their marginal status in the collective consciousness of the three sisters, as well as to suggest they still maintain contact with the outside world. These Western-style umbrellas may well be "a sign of the modern," as Suzuki has suggested to Erika Fischer-Lichte in interview.[8] However, nothing in Suzuki's stage world is as simple as the dualistic approach Fischer-Lichte takes to it, in which what is being reified are signs of "the Western" and "the Japanese." There is too much indeterminacy, there are too many third terms. Even if, in the Frankfurt performance she saw in 1985, "the three sisters and Man 1 and 2 wore European clothes almost exclusively, [while] Andrey, Natasha and Anfisa were dressed in traditional Japanese garments,"[9] by 1989 this was no longer the case.

All three sisters carry shopping-bags, signifying their desire to leave for Moscow – or indeed any commercial center – while at least two of them wear an extraordinary combination of Western and Japanese clothing. In realism, costume and props usually help to define character, but in Suzuki's *The Chekhov* they produce a series of chimeras which can be read differently from different subject positions, and in different moments.

Irena, the youngest sister, sports a pale yellow-and-green-patterned kimono with butterfly sleeves, over which she wears a *hakama*-like black skirt tied at the waist. The style is that of a Taishô period (1912–26) *moga* (modern girl). Olga is more incongruously dressed, with clashing colors as well as styles, and (in the 1989 staging) wears a black pillbox hat with silver fringes suggesting either gray hair or eccentricity. Where Irena's umbrella is new and her bag smart, in keeping with her youth, the older sister carries a plastic-coated department-store bag and her umbrella is obviously aged, its fabric hanging down between the extended ribs like torn moss. Masha's costume is equally odd. As for the three male actors, they wear nineteenth-century-style dark Western suits, sporting sunglasses to look "Westernized."

Perhaps the best that can be said about this plethora of mixed cultural signals is that the parts were clearly differentiated *without* the possibility of that difference being reducible to certainty of characterization or even the cultural "allegiance" which Fischer-Lichte dualizes.

As the lights come up on Scene 1, the three sisters are discovered sitting on tatami mats at the front of the stage; and Irena's opening, "Tell me why is it I'm so happy today? Just as if I were sailing along in a boat with big white sails" (transposed from later in the scene [Fen, *Plays*, 252]) suggests that they could be regarding a distant prospect from an open veranda (*engawa*). By first striking this serene, happy note, Suzuki provides a more effective contrast to Olga's opening speech in Chekhov, which is far more subdued and even faintly gloomy: "It's exactly a year since father died, isn't it?" (249). It is as if Suzuki wants to contrast the forward with the backward looking.

Scene 2 continues this quiet mood as the music of Saint-Saëns's *Swan* glides in. The first surprise of the production occurs when two men pop their heads out of the wicker baskets upstage left and right to answer the sisters on the theme of work. Toozenbach's lines, and later Vershinin's, are divided between Man 1 and Man 2, the first making the Baron an introspective intellectual and the second portraying him as a passionate, headstrong extrovert, thus destabilizing any sense of "identity."

Scene 3 begins as a piano plays Badajevska's "The Virgin's Prayer" (with which Irena later suggests she is bored [326]). It seems to be Vershinin's signature tune, for it returns at his departure in Suzuki's Scene 9 (326). To the music all three sisters stand as if watching the entrance of a very handsome man through the audience. Their frontality allows the audience to read in each sister's face her response to the man we expect to see. However, Suzuki does not bring on Vershinin. It is Man 1 who says his lines, "Yes, we shall all be forgotten" (259), from a basket upstage – again as the introverted intellectual (no change is made to the style of delivery he used for Toozenbach's speeches).

To the music of Tchaikovsky's *Swan Lake*, we hear backstage the loud, crude voice of Natasha (played by Togawa, a man): "It's awful of me to leave the table like that, but I couldn't help it . . . I just couldn't" (271). Sobbing soon turns to sounds of passion as Andrei answers, and again we watch the sisters' differential reactions; this time to their brother's love-making with a local girl they dislike. The way Andrei's last lines are delivered – interjected by frantically comic groans and cries – suggests copulation. The isolation in self-gratification of Andrei and Natasha is tragic but funny, embodying an alternative realization of what realist interpretations of Chekhov suggest psychologically. For Suzuki speech is an act of the whole body.

Shortly afterward this is contrasted with Masha's terrible confession: "They married me off when I was eighteen. I was afraid of my husband because he was a schoolmaster, and I had only just left school myself. He seemed terribly learned then, very clever and important. Now it's quite different, unfortunately." Heralded by an abrupt change of mood in the music (Bartok's *Music for Celesta, Strings, and Percussion*) and by the sound of the wood-block clappers used in Kabuki to heighten audience expectation for the entrance of an important actor, the speech recovers the shock value it had in Chekhov's day.

If we are used to the pathetic delivery often preserved in historically "faithful" recreations, the actress's delivery here is surprisingly strong and harsh – that of an "affirmative action" Masha. Man 1 in his basket takes up Vershinin's lines, "We . . . are capable of such elevated thoughts – then why do we have such low ideals in practical life?" Repeating "I wonder why?," Masha starts to masturbate to the plummeting and soaring violin, as she and Man 1 repeat "Na-ze de-shyo-oh-oh!" ("I wo-onder wa-ah-iy"). When Anfisa enters on tiptoe, crablike, with a meal-tray, Masha tries to deflect attention with a comment about the weather ("What a noise the wind's making in the stove" [277]). But her rising excitement carries into her voice, adding another level of meaning, until, on Vershinin's innocuous line, "Are you superstitious?," the pressure becomes too great: Masha shrieks "Ye-es!" and thrusts her leg straight out from under her. She continues to concentrate on her orgasm as Vershinin declares his love, while her shamefaced sister Olga spoonfeeds her the rest of her meal with eyes averted.

From his original idea of having the three sisters standing on toilets and declaring "We must live!" while being "force-fed rice," Suzuki has found a more harrowingly commonplace but still confronting way of communicating the gap he finds between conventional surfaces and taboo-challenging subtexts in Chekhov's work. For a modern audience inured to old ways of doing a classic, Suzuki's interpretation is arguably justifiable, restoring the shock value of the original scene by theatrical means reminiscent of Wedekind's *Spring Awakening*.

The same pattern of contrasts and emotional juxtapositions continues throughout the performance, reaching its own climax at the end, as Badajevska's "The Virgin's Prayer" marks the imminent departure of Vershinin's regiment. At the sound of the music, the three sisters stand upright on their chairs, the Basket Men stick their heads out, open umbrellas, and for the first time walk forward to the front of the stage. Once they are out of their baskets, we can see that their black trousers are really knee-length shorts, and this gives them the appearance of adolescent schoolboys. They speak Vershinin's lines, "Everything comes to an end. Well, here we are – and now it's going to be 'goodbye'" (324). The lines which resonate most significantly in Suzuki's production are these:

What shall I philosophize about now? (*laughs*) Yes, life is difficult. It seems quite hopeless for a lot of us, just a kind of impasse . . . In the old days the human race was always making war, its entire existence was taken up with campaigns, advances, retreats, victories . . . But now all that's out of date, and in its place there's a huge vacuum, clamouring to be filled. (325)

To intensify Chekhov's irony, Suzuki introduces his greatest *coup de théâtre* here as the marching band starts up. It is a Nazi marching song, identified by Fischer-Lichte as a Hitler favorite, the "Horst Wessel."[10] The two Men, who have now occupied the front of the stage while the women balance on their chairs at the back, spring to life like mechanical wind-up dolls, lifting their umbrellas and pumping their arms like trombonists or conductors beating time. Man 2, the "passionate Vershinin," pumps his left arm to the beat as if its only joint was at the shoulder. Man 1, the "intellectual Vershinin," mimes the action of a Dr. Strangelove: his umbrella hand creeps up, as if on a string, to a fascist salute; he hastily brings it down with his other hand; then his head jerks back, his right eye twitches, and the sequence repeats. It is as if his will fights, but cannot resist, the fervent music. The spectatorial women on chairs also play their part in this struggle against the nationalistic mood created by a catchy tune with sinister associations. This is dramatized in the way they wrestle with their umbrellas, which take on ecstatic lives of their own, bobbing and weaving in front of their faces as if drawn magnetically toward the marching men. The active tableau seems to stylize the political process by which considered human choice is submerged in the mass hysteria of a Nuremberg-style Imperial Palace rally.

With the last words of the "Horst Wessel" march, the music suddenly changes to a contemporary karaoke number called "Yume oi zake" ("Dream-chasing Sake"). The audience burst into laughter at this absurd musical juxtaposition, but quickly settle to ponder what this unexpectedly provocative relationship of past and present may suggest. The sisters squat down on their chairs as history repeats itself (the first time as tragedy, the second – here – as farce). Man 1 and Man 2 alternate between miming the karaoke with an imaginary microphone and speaking Masha's and Irena's lines. The audience laugh as Man 2 says, "I'll give my life to people who need it," and laugh again at "I'll go on working and working!" (329). Karaoke, which became increasingly popular through the Bubble Economy 1980s, was solace for workaholics who wanted temporary relief from the harsh demands of a society that, ever since World War II, had demanded self-sacrifice of the individual on the altar of national prosperity.[11] While Man 1 and Man 2 chant, "How cheerfully and jauntily that karaoke is playing – really I feel as if I wanted to live," the audience laugh again in recognition. Karaoke, fueled by alcohol and lighting effects still gives millions of office workers and students light relief from their workaholic existence in temporary stardom.

In the darkness, as the song finishes, spotlights glow on the empty dinner trays downstage. The sisters come forward to retrieve these, and then, to Kabalevski's "Fool's Gallop," as the actors rush forward at the frantic pace of the music to cover tatami mats, chairs, and baskets with white sheets, *The Cherry Orchard* begins.

Suzuki's adaptation of *The Cherry Orchard* is more straightforward in its ordering (only eleven of Fen's sixty-five pages are retained) but much more radical in its Noh-like concentration on one character: Ranyevskaia. It is primarily a vehicle for a charismatic actress, in this case the internationally famous Shiraishi Kayoko. Gone from the play are Varia, Trofimov, Simeonov-Pischik, Charlotta, Dooniasha, and Yepihodov, and, apart from Ranyevskaia, the remaining characters are unnamed. Throughout the play they operate only in the narrow passage between the tatami mats and chairs. It is as if the human struggle to go on living in *Three Sisters* had been lost in the transition to *The Cherry Orchard*.

The waltz from Gounod's *Faust* announces the entrance of Ranyevskaia. In a one-two-three waltz-step designed to give her focus, Lopakhin (Tsutamori), Gayev (Sakato), and Ania (Takemori) move back rhythmically in a chorus-line half-crouch, lifting their legs like peasants in a wet paddy-field (the setting of the Toga Sanbô in August). [Figure 32]

The three actors are startlingly attired. Lopakhin (Tsutamori) wears a red hat and what look like work clothes (*samui*), of which the sleeves reach halfway down the forearm and the trousers end mid-calf. These have replaced Chekhov's "white waist-coat and brown shoes," but help to translate "you can't make a silk purse out of a sow's ear" and "I am rich" into Japanese terms. A red hat signifies Ebisu, god of commerce,[12]

Figure 32 Ranyevskaia (Shiraishi Kayoko) makes a grand entrance to the waltz from Gounod's *Faust* as Lopakhin (Tsutamori Kôsuke), Gayev (Sakato Toshihiro), and Ania (Takemori Yôichi) step back, in waltz time, in surprise and fascination. *The Cherry Orchard*. Toga Sanbô, 1986.

but the ill-fitting work clothes indicate the gap between Lophakin's lofty ideas ("We ought to be giants") and his parsimonious materialism, while their dirtiness serves to identify the "son of a serf." The costumes of the others are equally enigmatic. Gayev (Sakato) holds prayer-beads and wears a large-brimmed straw hat turned up at the front, black morning-dress coat and tails and white, loose *fundoshi* (loincloth) which reveals his bare, bowed legs. His eccentricity is marked as part Westernized intellectual and part rusticized conservative.[13] Ania (Takemori, a man) wore large opaque-rimmed glasses, a blue-and-white baseball cap reversed (with a television repair company logo printed on it), an untucked, oversize, long-sleeved white shirt, and blue stockings under white gym-shorts in 1988 (jeans in 1989).

Ranyevskaia's grand musical entrance is staged by Suzuki as a clap-trap so that Shiraishi may draw applause not only from the three men who give her focus, but also from her audience of fans. Shiraishi seems to acknowledge this in the way she beams with pleasure at being, once again, "back home onstage." The "cherry orchard" into which she gazes from the *hanamichi* ("flower road" or entry ramp) is filled with the shining faces of her fans, and it is as a Sarah Bernhardt or Matsui Sumako in decline that she plays the role. Dressed in funereal – but barely respectable – black, she is eye-catchingly eccentric, but oddly sexy at the same time. Her black pillbox hat, recycled from her use of it as Olga in *Three Sisters*, is hung not with a veil but with strips of silver tinsel which signify something between gray hair and a headdress designed to allure. (To one critic, Minamoto Gorô, the fringe effects also suggested Ranyevskaia's threadbare state.) Her theatrical entrance to signature music is made to suggest she is a female Faust whose social "damnation" is both gloriously individual and selfish.[14]

Part of the tragedy of Shiraishi's Ranyevskaia is that she is so busy playing a part to win applause that Lopakhin's comment "Time won't wait" (357) goes unnoticed. Suzuki comments about the way Chekhov's characters fail to face the gap between reality and their desires: "The result is people who are unable to make direct contact with the object of their desire . . . Finally, convincing themselves that all hope is not lost, they start to see visions which serve to compensate for their unrealized desires."[15] So, at the moment of the sale of her orchard when Chekhov's Ranyevskaia cries "Let's dance" (378), Suzuki's says "Let's sing together!" and, stepping out of role, Shiraishi belts out a popular karaoke song, "Hitori zake" ("Drinking Sake Alone"), rousing audiences to laughter and applause at her performance-within-a-performance. [Figure 31]

Elsewhere her face is a tragic, totally impassive Noh mask; and when having finally lost her home, she says "Let us go," she, like Beckett's tramps, does not move. It is as if she has become the ghost of the place.

Suzuki does not aim to achieve an atmosphere of poignant sadness through realistic ensemble playing. What he does, in a series of set-piece speeches by Lopakhin ("Deriganov was there"), Ania ("Mamma, you're crying"), and Gayev ("Everything's alright now"), is to measure the temperature of others around the catatonic Ranyevskaia so that we may ponder human failure. The effect aimed at seems to be suggested by a quotation, attributed to Chekhov, in which Suzuki questions "whether people need dreams because they are miserable, or whether they become miserable because their dreams are unfulfilled" (Toga Festival program, 1989).

Suzuki's reading of Chekhov leads him to seek images powerful enough to suggest the dehumanization that loss of energy, dignity, and death will bring. This was brought out in the 1988 production, where *Uncle Vania* preceded *The Cherry Orchard*. Like the other two plays, it closed with a pop song – "Karatachi nikki" ("Orange Tree Diary") – about unrequited love, played as Sonia fell asleep on one of the tatami mats used in *Three Sisters*. Then, when the music of "Fool's Gallop" came up to announce the start of *The Cherry Orchard*, the cast draped her as well as the furniture with white dustcovers. At the end of the trilogy, Sonia was rediscovered at the curtain-call so that the whole of *The Cherry Orchard* became her dream.

Suzuki's 1989 adaptation of *Uncle Vania* keeps only ten out of fifty-nine pages in the Fen translation. More of the original characters are included than in *Three Sisters* or *The Cherry Orchard*, but in a startlingly different way. All the characters of *Vania*, except for Sonia, are basket cases: Serebriakov, Yeliena, Mme. Voinitskaia, Vania, and Astrov all inhabit large wicker baskets. Only Telyeghin, Marina, and the Workman are omitted altogether.

The great number of basket people was a major visual advance on their more limited presence in the two previous plays. This would lead Suzuki, three years later, to develop a fully articulated rationale for his Basket World in *Ivanov*, premiered in Mito City in 1991. However, making *Uncle Vania* from Sonia's point of view – if not actually Sonia's dream – required another powerful central performer, and this Suzuki found in the person of Ashikawa Yôko, the great Butoh dancer.

The human failure to communicate, encouraged by excessive individualism, is the subject of Suzuki's increasingly iconic use of baskets in this trilogy. Chekhov's Sonia blames herself for being plain ("how dreadful it is that I'm not good looking" [213]) when Astrov has just complained that Yeliena is beautiful but "nothing else" (210). Yet Ashikawa, in reacting to the overheard comment "She's kind and generous, but . . . so plain" (213), can both show a shy girl's retreat into her shell, with eyes closed, and undercut its potential sentimentality by screwing up her face in grotesque bathroom-mirror images to reduce her audience to stitches.

The futility of the lives of the Voinitskaia family is further suggested when Vania peers out from his basket at his mother's basket to say, "We've been . . . reading pamphlets for the last fifty years. It's about time to stop." Since he wears horn-rimmed glasses and false nose, his mother's reply, "you've changed so much in the last year or so that I positively don't recognize you" (194), is greeted with hoots of laughter from the audience. However, the passionate performance of Nishikibe Takahisa as Vania combines with Suzuki's grotesque *mise en scène* to balance audience derision and sympathy.

Fueda Uichirô's acting as Serebriakov was another *tour de force*. He, too, wore horn-rims and false nose, but with the addition of a little

Figure 33 Professor Serebriakov (Fueda Uichirô) raves in morning
coat and loincloth as Sonia (Ishida Michiko) and a Basket Man (Katoh
Masaharu) listen. All except Sonia wear false noses attached to
horn-rim glasses. *Uncle Vania*. Toga Sanbô, 1988.

Hitler moustache. His fisticuffs with Vania suggested most effectively
how far he was prepared to go to sacrifice his daughter's rights, as well as
Vania's. His long speech about how to dispose of the estate also provided
a thematic link to *The Cherry Orchard*, which *Uncle Vania* followed in
1989. The style of his delivery – a cross between a pompous pedagogue,
Hitler at Nuremberg, and Charlie Chaplin in *The Great Dictator* – also
linked up with the "Horst Wessel" marching song in the opening play of
the trilogy, *Three Sisters*. The overall movement of the trilogy was now
clearly from tragedy (*Three Sisters*) to comedy (*The Cherry Orchard*), to
farce (*Uncle Vania*). [Figure 33]

Sonia kneads torn pieces of bread nervously in her palm as the family
fight between her father and uncle (both basket cases) turns from the
verbal to the physical. Serebriakov canes the side of Vania's basket,
screaming "Take the madman away!" (231). Vania retaliates by grabbing
the professor where it hurts (from the waist up the professor wears
formal Western coat and tails; below, he is naked except for a traditional
loincloth). This iconic moment is frozen and segmented as Sonia gives
a silent Edvard Munch scream with hands up to her open mouth. As
the "Pizzicato Polka" begins, her hands dance Butoh-style to the music

Figure 34 Sonia (Ashikawa Yôko) observed sleeping by the Basket Men (Katoh Masaharu, Nakajima Akihiko, Nishikibe Takahisa, and Togawa Minoru). *Uncle Vania*. Toga Sanbô, 1989.

(like time-lapse photography of tree-roots searching for water) and the basket people begin to jerk about and gyrate in robotic fashion.

In the midst of this farcical mayhem, Sonia moves to a different drummer, guided by an internal logic located in the music but unlocatable in the time it takes her to travel slow motion downstage from chair to tatami. She crouches on one of the mats and gradually keels over onto her side in suspended animation, like a praying mantis trapped in a spider's web. To the pop tune "Orange Tree Diary," the basket people gather round and repeat her lines from the beginning and end of the play [Figure 34]: "We shall go on living, Uncle Vania . . . We shall patiently suffer the trials which Fate imposes on us; we shall work for others, now and in our old age, and we shall have no rest . . . We shall hear the gods, . . . all our sufferings swept away . . . We shall rest . . . We shall rest . . . We shall rest" (244–45).

Through the long choral recital of this passage, a Japanese audience may think of the inhumanity of the "Work to rebuild the Nation" ethic. This took them from the brink of disaster in 1945 to prosperity, superpower status, and the bursting of the Economic Bubble by 1993 without giving sufficient thought to cultural needs, social facilities, and recreation. Karaoke as a phenomenon is a symptom of that denial, and Suzuki puts his finger on the Japanese malaise by retitling his Chekhov productions after the popular songs they contain:

> *"Three Sisters* – Yume oi zake" ("Dream-chasing Sake")
> *"The Cherry Orchard* – Hitori zake" ("Drinking Sake Alone")
> *"Uncle Vania* – Karatachi nikki" ("Orange Tree Diary")

Ashikawa remains like a statue on her side, her head and feet not touching the floor and her arms held up in front of her chest, defying gravity and pain. The show closes as the basket people babble the words of "Orange Tree Diary" in a confused, anarchistically individual manner which signals the other extreme of social behavior on offer from the West. Chanting it like a mantra, they circle Sonia in their baskets and disappear into the surrounding darkness. Baskets 1 and 2 have marched to war at the end of *Three Sisters*, are left behind by the departing humans at the end of *The Cherry Orchard*, but themselves leave behind "the last human" in *Uncle Vania*.

Although Suzuki's *Three Sisters* successfully toured to Frankfurt and Venice in 1985, *The Chekhov* was not intended for export. Suzuki transformed the plays so that the trilogy became a commentary on a specifically Japanese condition.

But the highly contemporary treatment of these realistic plays poses questions about the relevance of modern classics to the present, and their translations into different cultural idioms, which also applies outside Japan. In their new context lines from *Three Sisters* such as "It's strange to think ["strange" is a word which strikes with great force in this postmodern performance] that we're utterly unable to tell what will be regarded as great . . . and important and what will be thought of as just paltry" invite us – as they invited the Japanese audience – to reflect on the value of Chekhov for a contemporary audience, and of Suzuki's rendering of his work.

A SOLO *CHERRY ORCHARD*, NHK TV, 1989

To memorialize Shiraishi's departure from SCOT in 1989, Suzuki recorded a *tour de force* solo *The Cherry Orchard* for NHK TV. Chekhov's play was heavily edited and reshaped as a ghost play, a "theatre of the mind." To adapt an insight of Takahashi Yasunari's, it employed "the device of evoking verbally a certain image in the middle of an empty space" in a manner reminiscent of both Noh and Beckett.[16]

Suzuki cut his earlier adaptation by half again: removing Gayev and Ania and Basket Man 3 (Yasha) altogether, reducing Lopakhin to a voice in Ranyevskaia's head, but keeping Basket Men 1 and 2 (Feers) to comment on *her* death as much as on their own. In short, Suzuki used the technique of *honkadori* to draw a fresh *hana* (performance "flower") from the celebrated actress by changing the situation. The new *donnée* was that of an old woman, waiting in an infirmary for death, who cannot accept the reality that she has lost her home, and relives its glory before word of sale brings on heart attack and death.

The *mise en scène* is also new, and helps to take Suzuki's ideas a step further: Ranyevskaia sits alone in black in a smart old people's home. It is a traditional black-timbers-and-white-plaster design which looks like a Mondrian monochrome. Her white-metal-framed, red-canvas chair is also very chic. Attached to its right arm is a red box of pink tissues. To its left is a black wastepaper basket with a bold cherry blossom design embossed on it. Behind, on either side, stand two large wicker baskets on low rostra.

Lights come up on Ranyevskaia's chair with the waltz from Gounod's *Faust*. Her opening speech is from Act III: "Even if it's sold, or the auction didn't take place, it's time it was all over – so why didn't they let me know?" (Fen, *Plays*, 373). Feebly pulling a pink tissue from the box to her right, she blows her nose loudly and drops the used tissue into the basket to her left, staring down into it as she does so. She then repeats the action.

The fall of cherry blossom from the trees in the orchard, symbolizing the beauty of transience, has been replaced by Suzuki with the grotesque dropping of waste matter. Nor is this all. Ranyevskaia's senility is partly suggested by her transgression of a social taboo; in Japan it is not considered polite to blow your nose in public, still less to inspect the effluent. Age and sickness are also conveyed in her voice as Shiraishi mutters, "Our aunt in Yaroslavl has promised some money . . . (358), today my fate will be decided . . . I feel like doing something foolish, like screaming out loud" (375). Saying this, she stands, the lights go up, suggesting her altered reality, and, in her own mind (which is what is presented to us), she is visibly transformed into the self-confident, attractive woman she once was. The moment is similar to that in Mugen Noh, in which "everything is focused on the re-kindling of memory, on the emergence of a ghost out of the 'dark backward and abysm of time.'"[17] As Paul Claudel has said, "Dans le drâme quelque chose arrive, dans le nô quelqu'un arrive."[18]

Shiraishi's Ranyevskaia "arrives," looking round the bare space with a beatific smile. As she says "Oh my childhood, my innocent childhood!"

(347), her situation and action indicate that the vision is internal. Then she pauses in surprise as she "sees" her mother walking in the orchard. As if in her head, the disembodied Voice of Man 1 (Lopakhin) comes up, advising, "We must decide once and for all; time won't wait" (357). She laughs it off with, "Villas and summer visitors? Forgive me but it's so vulgar," and then launches into confession with, "I'm a sinful woman" (359). At the end of this long soliloquy, she is pulled up short, not so much by the sound of the broken string (365) as by what seems to be a minor stroke – and sinks into a low crouch as the lights dim and the Voice comes up again: "For once in your life you must look the truth straight in the face" (375). Ranyevskaia stumbles on with, "What truth? . . . You must say it differently" (376). The Voice accuses "that man" of robbing her (as in a Beckett short play, minimalist indeterminacy raises the prospect of different possibilities). She turns vicious, accusing Voice of being "trash" ("dekisokonê mega"). In shock, Voice threatens to disappear. Ranyevskaia laughs and calls "Wait! . . . I was joking! . . . Let's sing," and pink lights come up, creating the "Cherry Orchard" Karaoke Bar of her imaginative mindscape.

Transforming into her younger self, she sings "Drinking Sake Alone," and the rendition awakens two sleepers from her subconscious. Unseen in the two baskets, they applaud, and hold a short conversation with Voice, using the words of Feers to Yasha, "We used to have generals, barons and admirals dancing here . . . You, you're trash" (378). Ranyevskaia, who has been "singing with the sound off" during this conversation, returns to the airwaves with the last two lines of the song, full volume. Despite the applause of Voice and baskets, the music seems to have sapped her remaining strength, for she finishes with, "Thank you. I'll take a little rest. I'm tired." As if hit by a second stroke, she stutters, and, with the fading of pink lights, returns to her former state, hobbling slowly to her chair in the cold, harsh sanitarium light. Once there, she asks whether the orchard has been sold (383) and when told by Voice, "It has," blows her nose loudly and grotesquely again. Voice describes the auction, the music of the *Faust* waltz returns, the old woman bids farewell to her beloved orchard from her chair (397–8) – and suffers a fatal heart attack. The lights dim on her hunched frame and brighten into a ghostly glow on the Basket Men behind who finally put their heads out of their containers to comment, "My life's gone . . . I'm an empty shell. Oh you, you're just a used tissue" (398).

The choreography is very little changed from Suzuki's 1988 adaptation of the play, but the recontextualization creates an entirely different atmosphere, rendering this a dream play to match Strindberg's and rival the Noh play *Kinuta*.

IVANOV, MITO, 1992

Foreshadowed in 1986 but not produced until 1992, *Ivanov* built on but considerably refined Suzuki's achievements in *The Chekhov*. Shiraishi had left the company in 1989, and in the following year Suzuki established a winter base closer to Tokyo by taking up the artistic directorship of Acting Company Mito, an hour by express train from the capital in Mito City. This provided a younger generation of actors with the chance to work alongside SCOT in large productions while Suzuki began to build a regional network that would come to fruition in the setting up of Theatre InterAction.

The eclectic quotations of Egyptian, Greek, and Mannerist architecture in Isozaki Arata's postmodern Arts complex,[19] and the intimacy and flexibility of his Elizabethan-inspired performance space[20] fired Suzuki to conceive a performance program which would fully exploit the many new possibilities. For this purpose he reactivated an idea of Kara Jûrô's that "there are three periods in the history of the West, while there is only a single enormous one in the history of Japan." As Yamamoto Kiyokazu explains it, "the three periods to which Kara is referring are those that developed out of French classicism: the beginning, the middle, and the end. And to Kara it must look as if the West were now at the end trying to recall the beginning", while Japan was "in the middle," in "the inchoate dark."[21] Suzuki's aim was to stage ancient Greek, Shakespearean, and Chekhovian classics as *Osarabakyô – soshitsu no yôshiki o megutte I, II, III* (*The Farewell Cult – On the Style of Loss I, II, III*), an idea designed to introduce a creative tension between the linear logic of Western philosophical and theatrical tradition and the circular logic of Asian religious and cultural tradition. The framing device to link all three was inspired by the opening of Beckett's *Cascando* and begins with the adapted line, "History, if only it could be thrown away," a creative fusion of Beckett's "Story," Kara's "H.I.S.T.O.R.Y.," and ideas which may already have been circulating in Russian theatrical circles.[22]

Thus the first play in Suzuki's trilogy *On the Style of Loss*, performed at Mito in 1990, was *Dionysus*, which was about the birth of the Farewell Cult (starring Natsuki Mari as Agave). Then 1991 saw the opening of the second part of the trilogy, *Macbeth – the Rise of The Farewell Cult* (starring both Natsuki Mari and Yoshiyuki Kazuko). Finally, in 1992, the third part was premiered, featuring the same two stars in *Ivanov – the Sidetracking of the Farewell Cult*.

In a television interview given to mark the NHK TV broadcast of *Ivanov* in July 1993, Suzuki explains:

I thought *Ivanov* was interesting because it is an early Chekhov play which still shows the influence of the older forms of realism before his time. The story is very clear and Ivanov's psychology and emotions are carefully described. Whereas in his other works there are many main characters, in this, as the title suggests, there is only one. Because I thought Chekhov's way of observing human beings was so highly charged, I thought it would be interesting to try to express what I imagine goes on in the head of a single person onstage.[23]

The concentrated focus on one central character (in the first production, Anna; in the second, Ivanov) gave greater leeway for the construction of an Absurdist staging around that figure in order to present the stuff of his/her fantasy. Suzuki's approach was facilitated by his appreciation that *Ivanov* had been written for and first staged by Korsch's company, specialists in farce-vaudeville.[24] A way forward from *The Chekhov*'s avant-garde enlargement of proto-Beckettian elements lay open via a return to the popular vaudevillean elements in Chekhov's early work. The path had already been partially explored by Vsevolod Meyerhold in *33 Swoons* (1935), which was based on Chekhov's farces *The Bear, The Proposal*, and *The Anniversary*; in them Meyerhold had "isolated certain 'crazy features' of each character and exaggerated them to create a grotesque farce."[25] Suzuki, whose debut as a director had been with *The Anniversary* in 1959, was to go still further in creating "psychology" by external, presentational means.

Uchino Tadashi rightly points out that, in Suzuki's *Ivanov*, we are "made to notice how the popular and the avant-garde are successfully mixed together" and "perfectly catch the ambivalence of the modern situation of theatre in Japan."[26] And not only in Japan, for, as Gottlieb has shown, "Chekhov as the inheritor of a great *literary* tradition is well documented in numerous critical studies," but "was also the inheritor of a massive . . . popular theatrical tradition of comedy."[27] For both Russian playwright and Japanese director, the path of innovation lay through judicious creative play with elements of both traditions.

However, to those brought up on the realist tradition propagated by the Moscow Art Theatre, this performance description can feel like a slap in the face. From the very first moments of his *Ivanov*, Suzuki plays with our expectations, submitting the audience to a rollercoaster ride of uncertainty. Lights go up on two cluttered sets of props marooned on opposite sides of the stage. These represent Ivanov's study and Anna's parlor, where one reads and the other embroiders. But over their heads hang a well-lit collection of wicker baskets, and the eerie prolonged notes of a trumpet mourn and grumble in the surrounding darkness, creating a sense of isolation and unease. Suddenly Borkin the estate manager (Katoh Masaharu) scuttles in like a large cockroach (using *shikko* movement); he wears an old-fashioned lampshade on his head vaguely reminiscent of a coolie's hat. Under this he sports another visual gag: black horn-rimmed glasses with false nose and a bushy black beard. Even more disconcerting is the enormous wicker basket in which he is encased, except for arms and bare legs and feet. The overall effect is surreal, as if Jarry were directing Chekhov. But there is method in this apparent madness, for it is an attack, not on Chekhov, whom Suzuki adored,[28] but on Stanislavski; in other words, an attempt to rescue Chekhov from his Stanislavskian interpreters by restoring Meyerhold's sense of Chekhov's irony play through a mixed genre approach.

For me [Suzuki says] the play presents what goes on inside of us. For example, when an ambitious person trying to reform society is worn down or made a scapegoat by other people, he begins to lose confidence and feels a growing sense of isolation from his surroundings; he loses interest in others and starts to see them as aliens. As a result he either becomes autistic or easily emotional and escapes into a hobby or solitude. I wanted to describe the process by which one falls into "madness" through rupture with the external world, whether through excessive self-reflection, daydreaming or being oppressed. (NHK TV interview, July 1993)

The fact that this adaptation is to be seen from the points of view of Ivanov and Anna allows Suzuki to hold up a distorting mirror: "In *Ivanov* I used the basic framework of the story: only Ivanov and his wife Anna have real existence; the others don't look quite human when they appear onstage. From Ivanov's point of view they are grotesques who seem to come from another world" (NHK TV interview).

Although elements of farce are arguably as evident in Chekhov's play as they are in Suzuki's production,[29] Suzuki aims to draw-in an audience to serious contemplation of what a "restored Chekhov" might look like after all the accepted varnish of "Stanislavskian realism" has been removed. Suzuki's approach has precedents in Meyerhold's *33 Swoons* and that artist's credo that "the naturalistic theatre . . . knows nothing of the power of suggestion."[30]

Chekhov was evidently very concerned that his actors and audience get what he had intended. He tells us that he "cherished the audacious dream of summing up everything written thus far about whining, despondent people, and of having my *Ivanov* put a stop to this sort of writing."[31] However, as he records, fate was not kind to him at the first production. "The director sees Ivanov as a superfluous man in the Turgenev manner," his lead actress asks "why Ivanov is such a blackguard," and even his friend Suvorin thinks "the doctor is a great man." Chekhov's despairing response was to write a six-page character outline, providing a key to successful performance of the play as he saw it.[32] At stake was the sympathetic balance of the play, upon which depended his critique of contemporary society. And it is this balance which Suzuki also wishes to explore. His reduction of everyone except Anna and Ivanov to the status of "basket people" helps to keep their social paralysis unfailingly before our eyes. At the same time he cuts the play drastically (to the usual seventy minutes of SCOT playing time) and finds new roads to the play's meaning through farce, what Vakhtangov felicitously calls "broader realism."[33]

Suzuki's changes are intended to guard against the sorts of misinterpretation mentioned above, and at the same time to keep the audience pleasurably challenged and guessing. Although Anna and Ivanov are not in baskets (only they have full autonomy), even Ivanov wavers, clambering in and out of the basket next to his desk as crises loom and pass; and Anna is sick, confined to a wheelchair throughout. What is cut is largely the tedious realistic stage business of people mechanically eating, drinking, gossiping – and eating each other alive in their social frustration. Oddly, these signs of boredom are more effectively and pleasurably conveyed through the alienating exaggerations of the "basket people."

Although Suzuki trims almost two-thirds of Chekhov's text in order to focus on "what goes on inside of us," as with his *King Lear* he rearranges and changes Chekhov's words very little. Suzuki's Scene 1 cuts thirteen of eighteen pages from Chekhov's Act I (in the Fen translation). Scene 2 removes fifteen of twenty-two pages from Act II. However, Scenes 3 and 5 remove only nine of twenty-three pages from Chekhov's Act III (Scene 4 uses a Japanese popular song to create an absurd "musical ballet" – into which Sasha's defence of Ivanov is pasted from Act II). Yet Scene 6 involves radical surgery, excising fifteen of sixteen pages from Chekhov's Act IV. In brief, Suzuki concentrates on Act III and redistributes the elements of farce, into which the play spirals in Act IV, throughout the play. The net effect is that much of the expository detail about Shabyelski's, Anna's, and Ivanov's backgrounds are removed from Act I, much of the meaningless chatter and most of the guests and servants are banished from Act II (nine of nineteen characters are cut as Suzuki uses the shorthand of absurd costumes and props to suggest the futility of their goings-on); and all the conventional writing of Act IV disappears: Lvov's challenge, the general household hysteria of the wedding guests, and Ivanov's suicide. The last act particularly deserved to go, for as Chekhov acknowledged despairingly at the time, "whoever discovers new *dénouements* will have opened up a new era."[34]

Suzuki's approach delivers the play to the actors, Scene 1 bending realism in the direction of farce in order to prevent easy audience identification with anyone except Ivanov or Anna. The stylized acting of Katoh Masaharu as Borkin is delightful, but rather than identify with it, we admire the potentialities of meaning which it releases and its technical difficulty (the baskets are restrictive and highly uncomfortable, especially for a *shikko* shuffle-walk). However, narrowing the focus of the play allows for intensification, and together these produce symbolism as Ivanov and Anna come to connote "male" and "female" in a field of subhumans.

Although Suzuki's interview (taken at one moment in time) seems to imply that this is Ivanov's story, his developing scenography leaves room for the actors themselves to tip the scales. The importance of the performers in helping to determine the meaning of this play was grasped early by Chekhov also: "Ivanov, alas, is being played by Davydov, which means . . . all my niceties and nuances will be fused into one gray blot . . . I'm sorry for poor Savina; I'm sorry she's stuck with that lifeless Sasha . . . Had I known . . . that she would be playing . . . , I would have called my play *Sasha* and centered everything around her role."[35] For Suzuki this insight becomes an active, open-ended principle in his repertory planning. As Uchino Tadashi shows:

The first performance of *Ivanov* at Mito in January 1992 was presented as Anna's (Yoshiyuki Kazuko's) fantasy. But in Toga [the same year] the stage action was Ivanov's (Tsutamori's) fantasy. This was an important change. At Mito Ivanov was on one side of the stage and on the other was a lot of rubbish in which Anna was sitting. In Toga, however, the whole stage was Ivanov's space. (81)

Nor was this the end of it. NHK TV's recording of the play in Mito the following year saw equal space being given to both Ivanov and Anna. At the production's opening, in the intimate Mito "black box," the dark stage persona of Yoshiyuki Kazuko weighed the play in Anna's favor,[36] especially since Natsuki Mari's reckless sensuousness in the role of Sasha would have helped to tip the scales for many with regard to Ivanov's intentions. In this venue "everyone except for Anna and Sasha was in baskets, even Ivanov,"[37] and this enabled the audience to watch a Sasha in the process of becoming an Anna.

In the Toga amphitheatre "Ivanov entered from backstage"[38] and two SCOT actresses, Takahashi Hiroko and Aizawa Akiko, replaced Yoshiyuki and Natsuki. Where these stars of stage and screen would have wilted to inaudibility in the larger public space of the amphitheatre in Toga, the laser-beam energy of SCOT actresses could shine. The athletic severity of Aizawa's playing (aided by steel-rimmed glasses) more effectively evoked Chekhov's Sasha as a young idealist with a mission,[39] but her "Sasha was in a wheelchair, which means this stage was set as Ivanov's illusion."[40] Setting the play as Ivanov's fantasy was to be clarified by the use of fireworks in the open-air space, Suzuki taking a creative cue from a cut line in which young ladies applaud and cry out: "Fireworks, fireworks!"[41] In this environment the highly experienced Takahashi was able to make Anna's repressed bitterness and eventual torrents of resentment seem like Ivanov's paranoid view of her.

At Mito, where the performance was recorded by NHK TV the following year,[42] Sasha was freed of her wheelchair (but put into a basket) and Anna was confined to a wheelchair instead. Here Takahashi's biliousness seemed to be increased by physical confinement, although the division of the stage space into "Ivanov's study" and "Anna's room" allowed for the kind of interest Strindberg generates in *The Stronger*, wherein an articulate, physically mobile protagonist vies with a sedentary silent one for audience sympathy.

In Scene 1 Ivanov is confronted at work by two grotesque basket people: Borkin and Dr. Lvov. They introduce the stock themes of debt and duty. Katoh's Borkin is a practical joker, and this is signified in costume gags as well as Chekhov's lines. Nishikibe's Lvov is more subtly grotesque, a self-righteous plain-speaker who insists Ivanov is killing Anna with neglect. He wears a blue velvet nightcap and black horn-rims, but has no false nose, which allows him a little more credibility and attractiveness.[43] Both Basket Men are at cross-purposes with Ivanov, and thus the Chekhovian theme of miscommunication is introduced early. After begging the doctor to "crawl into your shell" (which he does by sinking into his basket), Ivanov takes refuge behind his desk with the cry, "How tired I am of all of you!" Tsutamori plays the part superbly, revealing Ivanov's weaknesses but also his humanity.[44]

The Japanese translation and Nishikibe's stentorian delivery trains on Tsutamori's Ivanov the terrible charge of "egoism" (an English loan word with strong negative connotations), and the scene graphically depicts the everyday pressures to which individuals are subjected in the name of social conformity. The image of psychic attack on an individual is visually encapsulated in the musical interludes between scenes. Roger Reynolds's minimalist music[45] suggests at times lonely whale calls and, at other times, the creaks and groans of a submarine which, to avoid attack, has dived too deep. During this musical interlude half a dozen Basket Men creep in, fantastically dressed, and shriek and hop around Ivanov until he is forced to stop reading. The visual image is as surreal as Hieronymus Bosch's painting of *The Temptation of St. Anthony*. In the silence which follows, an English voiceover by Leon Ingulsrud declares in monotone, "The scene around was desolate (pause) as far as the eye could reach." [Figure 35]

Suzuki's staging of Scene 2, in which Anna catches Sasha making love to Ivanov, is elegantly simple. Chekhov had a jealous Anna follow Ivanov to Sasha's house, hoping to catch them *in flagrante delicto*. For Suzuki, since Anna and Ivanov remain on opposite sides of the stage throughout the play, all that is required to bring Sasha "between" them is her voice. She speaks from her basket behind Ivanov's bookcase "overhead," while he looks straight into the audience. Thus Anna hears Ivanov declare his love for Sasha out loud and Ivanov merely has to turn his head to Anna's side of the stage to register surprise at "being caught." In this way Suzuki makes the invisible world visible; we see a beautiful girl, in a basket-dream, stretch out her hands in yearning toward him.

Ivanov's guilty reaction to this self-exposure is to retreat into the large wastepaper basket located beside his workdesk. Here he can continue to fantasize undisturbed. The next musical interlude exposes his dream of happiness turned sour. Six brides in white enter from upstage center in wheelchairs and, to the sound of gong, drum, and a female choir chanting "Aa" at various sustained pitches, they begin to execute a long-legged dance as disturbing as any dream. Propeling their wheelchairs downstage with their feet in a slow-motion can-can, these beautiful cripples suddenly slump forward like discarded dolls, then, just as suddenly, fall backward, their legs raised and open to reveal black tights under wedding white. Ivanov watches from over the top of his basket, his voyeurism suggested by a female dummy's high-heeled legs thrust out from another basket behind his. Again to the synthesized sound of gong, drum, and choir (the actors must count the beats for each move) the brides move off in synchronized balletic goose-step, seductive and yet threatening. As they depart, an even wilder vision follows: three Basket Men tiptoe in behind "on pointe," looking like little ballerina tanks in wheelchairs *and* baskets. All are outrageously costumed.

Figure 35 The Basket People collapse and writhe around Ivanov (Tsutamori Kōsuke) to suggest social breakdown. *Ivanov*. Mito, 1992.

Scene 3, which Ivanov watches in a waking reverie from the safety of his basket, presents the drawing-room inanities as a nightmare vision of social life – what Senelick calls "cruel Chekhov."[46] Roger Reynolds's music successfully maintains the alien atmosphere created by costumes and props, with its wailing choir of female voices. The snatches of bankrupt male conversation selected by Suzuki perfectly complement the weird costumes to increase our sense of estrangement from such "aliens," heightening the defamiliarization of the familiar. Without looking at each other, these "Zulus," as Chekhov calls them (Fen, 64), face us in baskets, in wheelchairs, drinks in hand, and manically declaim such lines as "The French know what they want. They just want to rip the guts out of the sausage-makers," and "Why fight? . . . I'd collect the dogs from all over, inject them with rabies virus, and turn them loose in enemy territory." A gigantic waiter (Ingulsrud), dressed oddly in chef's hat and giant dog-collar, mechanically dispenses drinks and pickled cucumbers. After Basket Man 7 (Avdotya Nazarovna) starts to matchmake with the Count[47] on behalf of a rich young widow (Babakina), Basket Man 8 (Babakina) enters slowly, holding "her" cheek as if suffering a toothache, to exclaim, "How boring. They all just sit there as if they had swallowed pokers." Suzuki's image of a row of men in wheelchairs held bolt upright by their baskets suggests the unnaturalness of "polite behavior." As Meyerhold did with Khlestakov's costume for Gogol's *The Government Inspector* and the see-saw in Episode 23 of *The Forest*,[48] Suzuki carefully selects and exaggerates details to suggest psychology. "Do you want to be a countess? Yes or No?," is repeated with variations ("Go away . . . No, don't go away") as Shabyelsky and Borkin trap Babakina by holding her hands. The see-saw battle of wills is suggested by their swinging forward in wheelchair as "she" swings back until agreement is reached and they all rock back and forth as one. At the climactic moment, as Babakina says, "Stop! . . . Oh, I feel dizzy! . . . A countess! . . . I'm going to faint . . . I can't stand up," the Count clasps her hand and "she" lifts her leg straight out from the hip, simulating excitement.[49]

With a disgusted cry of "*Kee-hyah!*," Ivanov gets out of his basket and goes back to his desk. The Basket Men crowd around, then one of them (Lybedev) requests a private interview, and the music stops. Sasha's father apologizes for being "a milksop" who runs his wife's errands, but then grabs the desk with both hands, bows his head deeply in Japanese fashion, and begs, "Be a friend, pay her the interest!" When Ivanov demurs, he takes another tack. Removing fake glasses/eyebrows/nose

Figure 36 A chorus of Basket People with rakes, hoes, and ladles prepare for battle with Ivanov in a comic, slow-motion parody of *Macbeth*'s witches (compare with Figure 39). *Ivanov*. Mito, 1992.

to reveal his disarmingly handsome, youthful face, the actor Nakajima looks Ivanov in the eye and asks, "Where does all the gossip come from? . . . You're a murderer, an extortioner, a robber." Putting his social disguise back on, Lybedev laughs and exits, and, as Ivanov wallows in self-pitying inertia ("At twenty we are all heroes . . . but at thirty we are exhausted and good for nothing"), Roger Reynolds's sound-scape is foregrounded: distant wolves howl on the steppe, a choir wails, and the Basket Men return in panic, pursued by some nameless fear, jostling each other in manic frenzy but bunched together like sheep. Eventually Lybedev gets separated from the crowd, gesticulates wildly at Ivanov with a gabble of nonsense syllables, and then rushes off to keep up with the departing herd. The brilliant comic acting of Nakajima manages to suggest the excruciating image of an insecure man disavowing a close friend in order to ingratiate himself with a crowd he does not like. In the silence which follows, Ivanov unburdens himself of his thoughts, which show how deeply he, too, has been infected by others: "You would have to be a miserable, worn-out drunkard like Lybedev to be able to love and respect me still. My God, how I despise myself!"

Music starts, the brides in white peer out of their baskets suspended overhead, and, as Ivanov reads a literary journal, they sing the popular *enka* song "Ukigusa gurashi" ("Floating Grass Life"):

> We don't even know about tomorrow.
> You say, find someone else you like.
> Even if happiness is impossible,
> I will follow you, darling . . .
> As long as you are near it's all right.

It is as if Ivanov fantasizes about Sasha comforting him, for the song replaces his long litany of woes in Chekhov (Fen, 88–89). These Suzuki has cut for reasons of economy, but also to heighten the moment of self-indulgence in a peculiarly Japanese way. Remarkably, the *enka* lines echo sections of a later speech of Sasha's to Ivanov which Suzuki has also cut: "I dream about how I'd cure you of your depression, how I'd follow you to the end of the world . . . it would be sheer happiness . . . to . . . watch over you all night . . . or just walk with you for miles . . ." (94–95).

At the end of the first stanza of the *enka*, troika-bells are heard, but the accompanying image is one of social breakdown: the Basket Men march on doing the "Double, double, toil and trouble" action of stirring the witches' cauldron in *Macbeth*. [Figure 36] And here, by purely kinetic means, we see the point of Suzuki's connection between *Dionysus*, *Macbeth*, and *Ivanov* as steps in the confident rise, overreaching, and disintegration of a society, culture, or cult. Whereas in *Macbeth* the witches' action is full of menace and aggression, in *Ivanov* it is pathetically comic. The actors are in baskets, of course, and fantastically dressed; moreover, they carry a motley assortment of instruments (the idea seems to be taken from the stage directions to Chekhov's *The Bear*, Scene 11). However, it is the deceleration of the song's tempo on tape which best signifies a society in decline: its batteries are running flat. As their actions "run down," the Basket Men eventually lose balance and fall, helplessly thrashing about like upturned terrapin. During the song the stage is bathed in blue light (the color of Anna's long shawl). Thus the women in white appear blue when they sing, and this helps to create a biting dramatic irony which undercuts the sentimentality of the song. Sleigh-bells announce Sasha's entry upstage center in her basket, this time with umbrella open overhead. She sternly orders the fallen Basket Men to "come out" of their "stuffy rooms," but they only laugh and jeer feebly. Her father, Lybedev, addresses her as "Grandma," comments ironically that "finding a bridegroom is a tough business," and inveighs against "the youth of today" (the middle-aged Ivanov). During this exchange daughter and father take up iconic positions in the passageway between Ivanov's and Anna's rooms, Sasha with her protective umbrella raised, Lybedev with his tiny bare-ribbed parasol pointing down. The Basket Men laugh as Lybedev accuses Ivanov of losing his mind, and compete to cap each others' slanderous anecdotes about his relationship with Anna. Sasha angrily refutes these, retorting, "Ivanov is guilty of nothing except a weak character," and counterattacks, "Just looking at you the flies drop dead . . . There's something wrong, wrong, wrong." Finally the sentimental song "Ukigusa" is replayed and the Basket Men march off.

As the music comes to an end, Ivanov starts to reread his volume of *Kaizô* (*Reconstruction*), a magazine published between 1919 and 1955 as a major forum for Marxist and socialist debate.[50] On Sasha's exit Dr. Lvov comes on, swollen with righteous indignation, to proclaim, "You're killing Anna." Anna indicates she overhears this by leaning toward the passageway. Sasha returns and Ivanov desperately implores her to leave, stroking her basket as he does so. She replies, "Are you to blame because you no longer love your wife? Perhaps, *but baskets and humans are different*. Man isn't master of his feelings."[51] Ivanov resists her approaches, but the damage has been done. Anna has overheard and now harbors the *idée fixe* that Lvov's accusations are true.

Husband and wife confront each other in what is the tragicomic climax of the play, whipping each other into ever crueller misunderstandings and indiscretion. Anna speaks for the first time in the play as she asks, "Why did that *Basket* Woman come here . . . Why was *the basket* here?" This is the third of Suzuki's minimalist interpolations. By placing it at the point where the great wall of Anna's silence breaks, Suzuki has engineered a brilliant *coup de théâtre*, dramatically enhancing the effectiveness of Chekhov's wonderful scene by cutting all of her earlier speeches and all the maudlin recriminations of Act IV. Anna's use of a relentless series of absolutes which begin with "You have never loved me . . . never!" leads eventually to Ivanov's despicable "Shut up, Jew!" And then, in response to the unbearable stereophonically amplified mockery which Suzuki lends Anna's voice (from "I won't be silent . . . go . . . deceive that *Basket* Girl"), Ivanov lets fly his final, irrevocable Parthian shot, "You may as well know, then, . . . the doctor said that you are going to die soon." Takahashi's Anna gasps, "When . . . when did he say . . . that?" (Covered in sweat, the exertions of Suzuki acting register on her as the effects of terrible pain.) Realizing what he has done, Tsutamori hangs his head and weeps "God, how guilty I am!," pounding his thigh with his fist.

In the nightmare reverberation of the sound system, the cacophonous multiple monologues of the Wheelchair Brides ironically echo the internal crises of the two protagonists in a manner reminiscent of Beckett's *Cascando*: "History . . . If only it could be thrown away . . . Then you could rest . . . Could sleep." Ivanov faces the wall of his study as they slowly goose-step past, long legs in the air, and Anna turns a half circle in her wheelchair and dies.

Scene 6 (Act IV) is very short. It begins as Ivanov dons coat and tails and squats Japanese style on his chair, defiantly half-turned to the side. His last speech is confessional, to himself as much as to an absent Sasha. The Basket Men silently fill the stage to listen. It is the day of his wedding to Sasha (a year later in Chekhov, although not in Suzuki's dream sequence) and Ivanov has pangs of conscience. Saying, "There will be no wedding," he climbs onto his desk and throws his journals at three different Basket Men. Hysterical laughter turns to grief as he sobs, "I have no right to destroy others . . . What sort of new life?" He pulls out a revolver and shoots at Borkin – but the gun does not go off. Climbing into his basket, he aims at his own head, pulls a gallery of tortured faces, squeezes the trigger, and then laughs hysterically as the gun misfires yet again. In a state of catatonia, he stares out from his basket at the audience. "The scene around was desolate" is heard again as a final whispered voiceover, and the Basket Men stir, marching their baskets into line downstage. The stereophonically amplified throat-sounds of pain return from the beginning of the play, and the Basket Men panic. Hopping, squirming, and shrieking, they flee in all directions. Then, as Ivanov looks on (the scene is in his head) they fall over, wriggle, and lie still. The stage is bathed in blue light.

Like Uncle Vania's, Ivanov's failed suicide increases his despair and can only heighten the existential awareness that living is harder than dying. In this sequence of productions, most evidently in the solo *Cherry Orchard* and *Ivanov*, Suzuki seems to develop the forward trajectory of Chekhov's own expressive experiments. At the end of his life, Chekhov had conceived an idea for another play "to deal with arctic explorers [which] was to show the ghost of the hero's beloved and a ship crushed by the polar ice onstage."[52] In Chekhov's shift toward symbolism we may find the seeds of Suzuki's ideas for a ghostly Ranyevskaia haunted by regrets, and an absurd Ivanov crushed by inertia, gossip, and self-recrimination.

8   Suzuki's Shakespeare (I): *Macbeth*

Ian Carruthers

A comment made by Suzuki Tadashi to Trevor Nunn in 1970, during the first RSC tour to Tokyo, set the tone for all his subsequent work: "Now that I have seen your *Winter's Tale*, all Shakespeare performances by our Shingeki companies seem nothing but dull and shoddy imitations of Western productions. Since such imitations can never surpass the originals, I think we have no choice but to start tackling Shakespeare with our uniquely Japanese sense of theatre."[1]

Suzuki's struggle against the homogenization of art began early in his career. As he pointed out in his first collection of theatre essays, *Naikaku no wa* (*The Sum of the Interior Angles*), "To proceed to disregard the traditional Japanese arts as feudal relics, and to insist that the Japanese government fund Shingeki [Western-style "New Drama"], as in the West, is a backward step."[2] He saw clearly that "they [Nunn and the RSC] act as if there were objective standards with universal application which could be used equally to criticise Japanese theatre, Western theatre, and even African theatre." He felt that he could not in all honesty accept this, preferring to maintain that "everything is to be appreciated in a relative way."

In 1973 Suzuki produced the radio drama *Oni nite sôrô* (*A Demon There Was*) for NHK. According to Matsuoka Seigô, this was a "test pattern" for his earliest adaptations of *Macbeth*, both *Night and the Clock* and *Night and Feast III*. The drama apparently began with a chanted passage from the Noh play *Kurozuka*, "There is nothing more sad than the destiny of the people of *wabi* . . .,"[3] and went on with Shiraishi Kayoko saying, "Ah! Still there's too much stain here. Out! out, damned spot!," lines based on Lady Macbeth's speech in the sleepwalking scene. At the center of the play were a quotation from Oka Kiyoshi's *Nihonjin no kokoro* (*The Soul of the Japanese*) and passages spoken by a man possessed by Hitler-like speeches. The action, in three scenes, was set in a mental hospital. In the first scene doctor and nurse tried to cure a female patient (Shiraishi) suffering from shellshock. In the second it was the nurse who had acquired the patient's symptoms, frantically trying to

210

"erase" the bloodstains from her hands. Finally, in the third, as the doctor speaks Shiraishi's original lines, "Still there's too much stain here. Out! out, damned spot!," we realize that everything we have experienced has been occurring in his mind.[4] Suzuki's "return to roots" is evident in this experimental localization of *Macbeth*, for the dramatic structure of his short radio play derives from that of the Kyogen farce *Fukurô yamabushi* (*The Hooting Priest*), about a mountain ascetic who, in trying to exorcize a villager's itch, contracts it himself. However, the theme's modernization is also evident in his use of Oka Kiyoshi (an ultranationalist) and Hitler to show how susceptible we still are to ideological "disease."

YORU TO TOKEI (NIGHT AND THE CLOCK), TOKYO, 1975

Since the first Japanese staging of *Macbeth* in 1905, some eighteen productions prior to Suzuki's *Night and the Clock* had been mounted, most notably by Osanai Kaoru (1927) and Fukuda Tsuneari (1958).[5] However, Suzuki's was the first acclaimed for what Senda Akihiko has called "the Japanization of Macbeth" when it won the Kinokuniya Drama Prize for 1975. At the time he began his extended engagement with *Macbeth* his WLT was already well established in the public eye with the huge success of *On the Dramatic Passions II*, and he and his company were ready for new challenges.

Tackling Shakespeare in a Japanese theatrical perspective meant for Suzuki in 1975 a radical recontextualization, not only in terms of setting (a Morita Therapy sanitarium in Tokyo in 1941) but also in its dramaturgy (as collage drama). Suzuki's production incorporates elements of the following diverse texts:

Shakespeare's *Macbeth* (mixing three translators – Tsubouchi Shôyô, Mikami Isao, and Odashima Yûshi – in Scenes 3–6, 8–9, 11, 13, and 15–17)

Two pop songs, Yoshikawa Shizuo's "Hitori sakabade" ("Alone in a Bar") (Scenes 5, 18) and Fujita Masato's "Kyô mo egao de konnichiwa" ("Hello With a Smile") (Scene 9)

"Warai no jikan" ("Laugh Time"), a laughter therapy session involving no dialogue (Scene 7)

Moroboshi Ryû's "Sanpunkan speechi" ("Three-Minute Speech") (Scene 9)

Morita Shôma's *Sekimen kyôju no naoshikata* (*How to Cure Erythrophobia*) (Scene 10)

Takeda Izumo's *Kanadehon chûshingura* (*The Treasury of Loyal Retainers*) (Scene 11)

Sugamo isho henshikaihen (Sugamo Society for Editing Prison Wills), *Seiki no isho* (*Wills of the Century*) (Scene 12)

Umezaki Haruo's *Sunadokei* (*Sand Clock*) (Scene 14)

In *Night and the Clock*, after a provocative opening with *Macbeth* Act V, it gradually becomes clear that Fukao, who gets to play all the positive characters of Doctor, Duncan, Yuranosuke, and Macduff, is director of a hospital for patients undergoing therapy. Part of this therapy involves a playing out of *Macbeth*.

Scene 10 provides the key to a specifically Japanese contribution to an understanding of the play's psychology. Where Ernest Jones applied Freud to *Hamlet*, Suzuki relates Morita Therapy to *Macbeth*.[6] Scene 10 shows this therapy in use in "hospitalized Japan," not so much to cure what Suzuki has elsewhere called Japan's "cultural schizophrenia"[7] (to Westernize, or not to Westernize), as to alleviate anxiety about the need to *make* such a choice. Morita's solution is to "allow nature to take its course."

Fukao Yoshimi's opening words define him not simply as the Macbeths' physician, but as a Morita psychotherapist. In Scene 10 his patients are Toyokawa Jun ("the one who wants to become Macbeth"), and Shin Kenjirô, the "man with a morbid fear of meeting people." Shin is first identified by his odd physical behavior in Scene 7; then, in his playing of Lady Macbeth's sleepwalking in Scene 8, he reveals the symptoms which are addressed as erythrophobia in Scene 10. (In Suzuki's opinion acting, the creation of an artificial world, starts to get interesting "when a bearded middle-aged man suddenly claims to be Ophelia.")[8]

As Takie Sugiyama Lebra explains, the *shinkeishitsu* or neurotic temperament is characterized by excessive introversion, and may be biologically determined, but Japanese culture with its sensitivity to *hitomishiri* (stranger anxiety), individual fear of inadvertent social exposure, and "loss of face," reinforces this tendency. Both "altruistic" phobia (fear of hurting or embarrassing others) and "egoistic" phobia (fear of being hurt) boil down to what Kasahara calls "the threat of public display of [one's] inadequacy and imperfection."[9] For instance, erythrophobia, the morbid fear of looking straight into another's eyes lest one be thought rude (explicitly referred to in the stage directions of Scene 7), can bring on the following: insomnia (for Toyokawa in Scene 4, and for Shin in Scene 8 – both playing *Macbeth* V.i), phobias of body odor ("all the perfumes of Arabia will not sweeten this little hand"), and anthropophobia (manifest by "Macbeth" throughout).

The main tenet of Morita Therapy, according to Lebra, is acceptance of things as they are (*arugamama*), which approximates to the Zen Buddhist philosophy of "letting nature take its course" (popularized about this time by the Beatles in the song "Let it Be"). Much of this is evident in the extract from Morita's essay on erythrophobia which is dramatized by Suzuki as a dialogue between Fukao (therapist) and Shin (patient). In Scene 10 Fukao explains, "A nervous [*shinkeishitsu*] person is one who can never give up . . . [T]he only way . . . is to try our best to accept it, but nothing else." The example Suzuki uses to illustrate this concept of "acceptance" can be read as an amusing parody of his own concern about the hegemony of Western realist theatre values over indigenous theatre forms:

FUKAO: I used to complain about wearing underpants [note that Toyokawa wears *fundoshi*, a loincloth]. Westerners put us in unnecessary discomfort. I used to question why we Japanese have to wear such unnecessary things. But other people accepted it without any complaints. Moreover, they don't think of it as discomforting. Do you think of underpants as tight and uncomfortable?

SHIN: Alright, if I think about it, maybe they *are* tight, but normally I don't feel anything. (my italics)

FUKAO: If you could accept everything as it is – underpants, a hot summer, the fear of meeting people, red mail boxes – you wouldn't feel pain. When you start to explain the reasons, your mind becomes persistent and starts to feel pain. Now, can you hear the noise of a carpenter working over there? It's quite noisy, isn't it?

SHIN: Yes.

FUKAO: That's right. But you never noticed the noise until I mentioned it, did you?

SHIN: No.[10]

Once Suzuki has raised our awareness of Morita Therapy in this way, it inevitably relativizes the way we understand Macbeth's and Lady Macbeth's obsessional lines. For instance, Lady Macbeth's "look not so pale" (V.i.59)[11] becomes "Stop pulling that face" in translation, a change which helps to strengthen the speech's referentiality to the *shinkeishitsu* symptoms of a social "disease." Anthropophobia can include, according to Lebra, a "morbid fear of one's facial expressions,"[12] and this opens up a particularly (but not exclusively) Japanese interpretation of *Macbeth*. While this may seem like a trivialization of Shakespeare's tragedy to some, I would argue that, by cleverly foregrounding particular features of the play, Suzuki is able to offer *Night and the Clock* as therapy for the nation. In Kurihara Nanako's terms, "The stages of the Little Theatre movement were . . . providing a structure in which to excavate the collective unconscious."[13] In other words, a nation obsessed with its guilt for the past and with the "face" it presents to the modern world is being put on the couch.

But a shocking reversal occurs just after Fukao (the doctor) has outlined the benefit of Morita Therapy. He addresses his Chorus of patients beginning with Macbeth's speech to the Murderers:

> Well then, now
> Have you consider'd of my speeches? – know
> That it was he in the times past which held you
> So under fortune, which you thought had been
> Our innocent self.   (III.i.73–127 are used)

Perhaps with a finger pointing toward militarism's abuse of nativist Shinto beliefs in World War II (promoted innocently at first in the 1930s by academics as a bulwark against Orientalism),[14] Suzuki makes Fukao's utterance of Macbeth's lines a warning against blind faith in leaders. A therapist may turn "witch doctor" if the ability to manipulate his "patients" suggestively leads him to contravene his own therapeutic principles of "letting be." The moment is deeply problematic.

At the start of Scene 11, with all the cast onstage in "characteristic" poses as the clock ticks noisily (Toyokawa on his three-legged "throne," Fukao staring at him through the lopsided windowframe behind, Doi munching pickles) a woman's voice, that of Shiraishi, screams Lady Macbeth's lines from offstage:

> Oh! Oh! I can't clean my hands; we should wash our hands more.
> No, no, *stop pulling that face*. They are buried already. They can't come out of the grave. (translation of V.i.58–60, my italics) [Figure 37]

This is immediately followed by "the sounds of war" (a bugle blowing a charge, an announcement in English that "Singapore has fallen, the enemy forces have landed," gunfire, shells exploding); and then a Chorus of seven "mechanized humans" hobble in on sticks, carrying implements such as saws and pincers. In Suzuki's rereading of *Macbeth*, the Witches are replaced by the Murderers – a fact noted at the time by Odashima.[15] Probably these physically fractured men were, as Takahashi Yasunari has suggested, only slightly exaggerated portraits of *shôi gunjin* (wounded ex-servicemen), who were quite visible on the streets of Tokyo. They are here presented as both victims and agents of aggression – as an ambivalent symbol of the destructive force of militarism in recent Japanese history.[16]

The scene ends with excerpts from that quintessential Kabuki tragedy *Chûshingura*, which has so deeply problematized issues of justice for

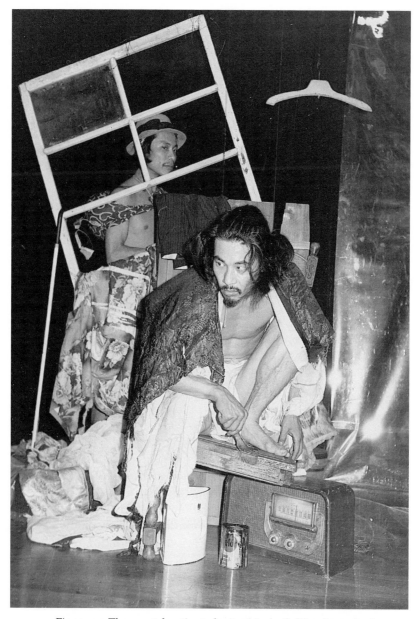

Figure 37 The mental patient playing Macbeth (Toyokawa Jun) watched by the Doctor (Fukao Yoshimi). *Yoru to tokei* (*Night and the Clock*). Waseda Shôgekijô Studio, 1975.

generations of Japanese. In it the self-righteousness of the revengers is undercut by their contempt for, and unwillingness to include, the foot-soldier Heiemon (played by Shiraishi Kayoko), who ironically saves the day when he (she) discovers and kills their enemy Lord Kira. This is fast followed in Scene 12 by another "collage shock," this time a contemporary parallel. In what is titled a "Letter Play," an old man (Doi Michitoshi) and woman (Tominaga Yumi) talk happily over a humble meal of rice and pickled radish. In another nongendered casting, Tominaga says, "I believe I am a lucky man [*otoko*] to have lived among such kind people, right?" And Doi replies, "In the last tour of duty for our Lord you were among the reliable lower ranks who risked their lives." The speech seems to refer to Heiemon in Scene 11, but Suzuki adds a turn of the screw by having Doi then recite the testament and death poem of a minor war criminal awaiting execution in Singapore. His speech is as full of ironies as Beat Takeshi's performance of the sergeant in Ôshima Nagisa's *Merry Christmas Mr. Lawrence*:

DOI: It was a short life I had, but happy and without regret. Please congratulate me. I will pray for our country to establish a society based on equality, fairness, fellowship and respect. I want to lift my voice aloud to say I am very happy to die for my country. Singapore has a fine day this morning again, and I can see the blue sky and swallows, which symbolise the peacefulness of unchanging nature, from my prison cell. Into the rising sun
TOMINAGA: To my country
BOTH: soars a swallow
   one fine May day.

Ironically, the criminal's calm of mind and acceptance of fate suggests the efficacy of a Morita cure at the very moment of death. But even more ironically it suggests that Macbeth's scapegoating of Duncan's guards and Banquo's murderers is a common practice, also found among the righteous samurai of *Chûshingura* and in the upper echelons of the Imperial Japanese army during World War II. Suzuki's inspiration for this localized rewriting are Shakespeare's "temple-haunting martlet" and the medieval European tradition referenced in Malcolm's report on the death of Cawdor:

         . . . very frankly he . . . set forth
  A deep repentance. Nothing in his life
  Became him like the leaving of it. (I.iv.5–8)

Later, in Scene 14, a section of Umezaki Haruo's novel *Sand Clock* is played out with the doctor (Fukao) taking the role of benevolent despot of "Hospital Japan." "According to the announcement of the Ministry of Public Health and Welfare, there are four reasons why the life-expectancy of the Japanese has increased," he proclaims grandly to his patients (the Chorus). Improvements in preventative medicine are cited, then the raising of the standard of living. But Fukao's long, self-congratulatory speech soon makes the inmates restive. "Are you waiting for me to die?" cuts in Toyokawa, who goes on interrupting with complaints about awful food and the director's privileged lifestyle. This culminates in geriatric revolt (which parallels the Scots' revolt against Macbeth) as Toyokawa demands, "As a human being and as a Japanese, I demand to have proper nourishment!" When Toyokawa complains about the cramped conditions, Fukao retorts, "You came to this hospital in 1941. While you were staying here, Japan lost the war. Our territory was reduced to just four islands . . . It is selfish to think that you can have space when everything else has shrunk. That kind of egoism also needs to be shrunk up!" Here a sacrosanct slogan of Japanese reconstruction, the need to sacrifice personal happiness to enable the nation to "catch up with the West," is being reduced to the point of absurdity. It was only from the late 1980s that pressure from below forced the government to pay attention to the spiritual as well as the material health and welfare of the nation.

Scene 15 continues the food image of the banquet scene with Tominaga saying to Toyokawa, "He has almost supp'd. Why have you left the chamber?" Toyokawa replies, "We will proceed no further in this business" (I.vii.29, 31–5), and then returns obsessively to the beginning of this *Macbeth* scene, with "If it were done when 'tis done . . ." (I.vii.1). The reprise of these lines, quoted earlier in Scene 13, suggests a "this worldly" interpretation of "the life to come":

TOYOKAWA: If we really do [fail], it is certain that we will have punishment *in this life*, we really will. (my italics)

Tominaga and Toyokawa, in obsessively repeating Macbeth's and Lady Macbeth's lines immediately prior to Duncan's murder, show that, as patients, they remain fixated on an event which has effectively stopped their psychic clock and thrust them deep into neurosis and phobia. The time is 1941. The year of Pearl Harbor. "We should stop doing *Macbeth*," the Doctor (Fukao) says in Scene 16, just before he is killed by his patients.

After the murder the stage directions for Scene 17 read, "The rust-eaten clock is the main character. Back to the beginning." Toyokawa returns obsessively to lines first heard in Scene 4, although repeated verbally many times since then: "One, two, three. 'Tis time. It's the start again" (translation of V.i.33–34). He pauses, and then launches into violent recital of Ross's lines:

> Alas poor country,
> Almost afraid to know itself. It cannot
> Be called our mother, but our grave;
> (IV.iii.164–73).

The poor country can only mean Japan, and as the increasingly distraught Toyokawa moves in speech from Act IV to Act V with, "I'm tired of looking at the sunlight. Destroy the world, destroy law and order!" (translation of V.v.49–50), he regresses finally to that great nihilistic speech, "Tomorrow, and tomorrow, and tomorrow . . ." (V.v.19–28).

As Scene 18 begins Toyokawa repeats the lyrics of a sentimental pop song first sung in Scene 5:

> When ev'ning comes to Tokyo, and crowds fill the city
> Lonely I sit and stare, my tears my only friend.
> Clasping a glass in my hand, what do I see?
> My lover's face is like a vision come to me.
> O night in Ginza, O beloved one that I see,
> Why won't this sake drown my soul now, and set me free?[17]

However, this time Toyokawa also tears apart a large white cloth doll. As one critic remarked ironically, "After the doll was torn open, I was moved by the beauty of the mountains of red cloth 'entrails' scattered around the stage. The ending was very colourful, reminding me of the time when I was a child, looking up at the Japanese flag."[18]

While this nihilistic action goes on, Doi, Tominaga, Fukao, and Shin carry rice tubs back onstage for another cold "banquet." As they eat, the play concludes with the following oddly irrelevant snatch of conversation:

DOI: The cherry blossoms have bloomed.
TOMINAGA: I hear the American President has declared a Recession.

Since so much of this production is culturally specific, the last word is best left with Japan's preeminent theatre critic, Senda Akihiko. In a review of the outstanding theatrical achievements of 1975, he remarks, "I think Suzuki's play is basically very trenchant criticism. There's an overall feeling that I taste – the excitement of reading a very well crafted and intellectual essay. Its power is less evident than in a Shiraishi-centered production, but it reveals more of his originality."[19]

NIGHT AND FEAST III (UTAGE NO YORU III), TOGA, 1978

Night and the Clock at the Waseda Shôgekijô Studio in Tokyo had been a remarkable first attempt to bring about a dramaturgical "Japanization" of *Macbeth*. Experimentally it went far beyond Charles Marowitz's *Hamlet* collage of 1965. Nearly half had been made up of fragments of Japanese texts, and, in acting terms, it was an ensemble piece calling for improvisation in the creation process.[20] *Night and Feast III* in 1978, by comparison, contains just one pop song and one passage of absurd modern dialogue (both found in Scene 9) and one *waka* poem from *The Tale of the Heike* (Scene 11). However, it puts back on display the acting talents of two veteran performers (Shiraishi and Tsutamori), and, as in *The Trojan Women*, brings in a star guest from the Noh theatre (Kanze Hideo) to set up a clash of performative styles, relegating inexperienced younger actors to a choral function.

Where *Night and the Clock* was dramaturgically absorbing, *Night and Feast* was theatrically powerful. Moreover, where the former was ruthlessly detailed in its reordering of scenes and lines, *Night and Feast III* follows the *Macbeth* narrative loosely: Scenes 3–6 come from Acts I–III (although not strictly in that order), Scene 7 from Act IV, and Scenes 8 and 10–13 from Act V. Only the materials for Scenes 1 and 2 are completely out of sequence; they come from Act V. But, like *Night and the Clock*, the vision of *Night and Feast III* is circular, and for this reason Scene 2 (V.ii.11–31) is repeated as Scene 13.

The scene Suzuki chooses to foreground from *Macbeth* as the key to this production is the one used to such vivid effect at the end of *Night and the Clock*, Ross's speech:

> Alas, poor country,
> Almost afraid to know itself . . . where violent sorrow seems
> A modern ecstasy . . .   (IV.iii.164–70)

The play begins as a young girl (Sugiura Chizuko) appears out of the darkness reading Tsubouchi Shôyô's translation of *Macbeth*. It is a distancing technique Suzuki will use again in his 1992 Melbourne production of *The Chronicle of Macbeth*, although quoting a different passage. Like the *shidai* of a Noh play, this poetic prologue offers a riddling key to interpretation. As Sugiura reads in a chair, a chorus of seven men peer at her over a screen. Lady Macbeth (Shiraishi Kayoko) enters along the *hanamichi* holding a paper lantern, sits on a tatami mat center stage, and, while she arranges herself, the girl exits and the men above begin a conversation which starts with Menteith's "What does the tyrant?"

(V.ii.11–31) The patriotic fervor of "Alas, poor country" concludes in its translated form thus:

MAN 1: Soon we will welcome the doctor who will cure this country's sickness. Then we'll work together with him and give our blood to cleanse the country . . .
ALL: Let's do it.[21]

The passage foregrounded here may well, at the time, have invited political reflection on the present.[22]

In Scene 3 Lady Macbeth reads her husband's letter concerning the Witches' prophecy (I.v.1–29) and, in Scene 4, Kanze Hideo (Macbeth) enters to say, "The King comes here tonight" (I.v.58–70 are used); his furtive entrance from behind reinforces the sense that his wife rules the household. To emphasize further the weakness of Kanze Hideo's Macbeth, as well as his humanity, Suzuki ironically gives him and Shiraishi the lines Banquo and Fleance exchange before their fatal ride:

MACBETH: How goes the night, boy?
LADY M: The moon is down; I have not heard the clock.
MACBETH: And she goes down at twelve.
LADY M: I tak't 'tis later, Sir.
MACBETH: Hold, take my sword – There's husbandry in heaven;
    Their candles are all out . . .
    A heavy summons lies like lead upon me,
    And yet I would not sleep. Merciful Powers!
    Restrain in me the cursed thoughts that nature
    Gives way to in repose.   (II.i.1–9)

The couple's next speech, "We fail? But screw your courage to the sticking place / And we'll not fail." (I.vii.59–73 are used), sees Shiraishi taunting Kanze Hideo by proffering the sword he has given her, only to withdraw *with it*. The scene ends at this point with the cleverly delayed reinsertion of Macbeth's "Give me my sword" (II.i.9), which now reverberates in an empty, dark room; the stage directions state, "He stands very still, looking as if he's peering into the other room." Played by the ex-Noh actor Kanze Hideo, who had also worked with the Berliner Ensemble, this *iguse*-like[23] or *gestus*-like moment of intense stasis signals a shift in the play from external to internal action.

Scene 5 (labeled "Scene of Macbeth's Unconscious Desire") is a Suzuki *coup de théâtre*. The stage directions read, "A man in the same costume as Macbeth (Tsutamori Kôsuke) appears onstage with a rabble of dirty-looking men behind him." Kanze Hideo stares in surprise at his double

Figure 38 Two Macbeths (Kanze Hideo and Tsutamori Kôsuke) face off in the banquet scene. *Utage no yoru III (Night and Feast III)*. Toga Sanbô. 1978.

and, as Shiraishi invites them to "Sit, worthy friends" (III.iv.52–57 are used), asks, "Who are you? Tell me your name!," to which Tsutamori, the man in identical costume, replies, "Macbeth!" [Figure 38]

Kanze Hideo's highly charged stillness is held for so long that it suggests the scene has shifted to his unconscious;[24] it even seems that the followers of Macbeth 2 themselves reflect on the consequences of assassination, for in Suzuki's adaptation it is they who chant Macbeth's lines, "If it were done when 'tis done, . . . But . . .This even-handed Justice/ Commends th'ingredience of our poison'd chalice/ To our own lips" (I.vii.1–12). When Macbeth 2 asks, "Was it not yesterday we spoke together?," they reply, "It was, so please you" in Yakuza dialect to emphasize their murderous intent. The extended dialogue between Macbeth 2 and the Chorus of Murderers (III.i.73–125), would seem, from the fact that Macbeth 1 is watching, to suggest that the latter is rehearsing in the court of his mind the pros and cons of action: his desire pleading for the prosecution and his conscience for the defense.

Kanze Hideo comes out of his trance state at the end of the scene when Macbeth 2 invites his rabble to join the banquet, saying "You must take on nourishment." At this point Macbeth 1 creeps up to Macbeth 2, using a *suriashi* sliding walk, draws his sword, and strikes wildly at thin air. Macbeth 2 and the Chorus of seven (guests or Murderers) scatter in flight, leaving Macbeth 1 alone. This signals the start of Scene 6, as Shiraishi's cry, "My husband!," evokes from Kanze Hideo's Macbeth a whispered, "I have done the deed," before the two plunge into II.ii.13–60. Since Macbeth 1 never leaves the stage, his "action" appears to take place in his head.

At the start of Scene 7, the Chorus, wearing long robes of black-and-white striped funereal cloth, circle the stage to chant the Witches' spell, "Thrice the brinded cat hath mew'd" (IV.i.1–21 and 37–38 are used). Then, in Scene 8, as Man 1 speaks the Doctor's lines, "You see his eyes are open," Kanze Hideo begins the sleepwalking scene in a trancelike Noh style (V.i.23–65). He speaks Lady Macbeth's lines, performing an agonizingly stylized handwashing sequence in which, "The Thane of Fife had a wife: where is she now?," is reduced to "That person had a wife . . ." Perhaps this suggests Macbeth grieving in the third person (as Macbeth 2) over his loss of Lady Macbeth's respect. It seems also to explain the jarring but appropriate insertion of a pop song about lost love called "Sadamegawa" ("Decision River") in Scene 9:

> Even if we throw everything into it,
> We still can't live by Decision River.
> For your love, even into the next world
> I want to follow you.

During the above song, the heads of three of the Chorus appear over the rafter-beam at the back of the stage, and, while "Macbeth is sewing together rags for a dust cloth" – perhaps indicative that he and his partner have swapped housekeeping roles as they have lines – they exchange incongruous back-fence gossip:

MAN 1: Lady Macbeth. Lady Macbeth forced him.
MAN 2: That old bag?
MAN 1: That's right . . .
MAN 3: What was the weapon?
MAN 1: "One strike" it seems.
MAN 2: Really? A "straight pitch"? To the King!
MAN 1: Then he took over as King.
MAN 3: He's "a pinch-hitter' isn't he? Could you do it?
MAN 1 I couldn't.
MAN 3: But you keep your eyes open even when you're asleep!

Shakespeare's three Witches have become banal gossips. However, the main point is the gender role-reversal between Macbeth and Lady Macbeth. It acquires force and conviction through Suzuki's understanding of the distinctive acting styles of Kanze Hideo and Shiraishi Kayoko: the actor coming from a Noh school renowned for its interpretation of women's roles and its "feminine" style, the actress famous for her bravura *aragoto* Kabuki-style performances. On the other hand, the Chorus's use of baseball terminology to describe the murder, and their non sequiturs, are as absurd as anything in Ionesco's *Macbett*.

Scene 10 begins with a surprising transformation as Kanze Hideo rises from his sewing, resolutely utters, "Bring me no more reports," lapses momentarily into bitterness in "my way of life/ Is fall'n into the sear" (V.iii.1–36 are used), and then defiantly chants, "blow wind, come wrack,/ At least we'll die with harness on our back" (V.v.49–50). The *jo-ha-kyû*-like arrangement of these patched passages (slow, expository introduction; emotional and narrative complication; and fast dramatic conclusion) provides a rhythmic preparation for Scene 11 which is congruent with the demands of Noh.

The stage directions in Scene 11 read, "Suddenly the sound of Noh drums and flute are heard [playing *kiri*, a fast finish] and Macbeth starts to dance." A surprise for Noh aficionados is the way the following taped dialogue (a reprise of Shiraishi's lines from Scene 8) is overlaid on top of Kanze Hideo's dance. "Wash your hands, put on your nightgown, look not so pale. – I tell you yet again . . . he cannot come out on's grave" (V.i.69–71). Stage directions indicate "The sound becomes warlike," "Macbeth stands still" to suggest the battle is in his mind, "the sound dies," and, in the stillness, Kanze Hideo "exits down the *hanamichi*, chanting":

> Like a fossil tree
> Which has borne not one blossom
> Sad has been my life
> Sadder still to end my days
> Leaving no fruit behind me.[25]

This death poem from *The Tale of the Heike* was composed by Yorimasa, a septuagenarian warrior (subject of a Noh play of the same name), who committed suicide after defeat in battle in the twelfth century. The mixing of cavalry bugles and gunfire with the poetry of *Macbeth* and *Heike monogatari* weaves a complex web of references. It may be emotionally satisfying that a Japanese Noh actor playing Macbeth in a *gasshôzukuri* farmhouse should dance *shimai* before going off to "die with harness on [his] back"; indeed, within the Noh-like context established, the action could even be seen to double as the exorcism of a disturbed spirit struggling to achieve "calm of mind, all passion spent" (a more traditional exercise than Morita Therapy). However, if the production shocked some in its absurd mixing of a contemporary pop song (Scene 9) and a medieval ballad (Scene 11) – as well as in its stabling of Shiraishi Kayoko and Kanze Hideo – we should remember, as Matsuoka Seigô does, that "Eliade's *The Sacred and the Profane* . . . was a principal theme of Suzuki Tadashi's."[26] By establishing multiple frames of reference, destabilizing self and gender, and decontextualizing time and place, Suzuki is able to produce a critique powerful enough to counter the kind of "naturalizing" view, expressed in Kurosawa's otherwise superlative *Throne of Blood*, that "Life is the same now as in ancient times."[27]

But a Noh *Macbeth* is only one half of Suzuki's dialectic. Scene 12 begins as a white-haired Shiraishi (Lady Macbeth) rises through the stage trapdoor, applying white make-up to her face like a Kabuki performer. She chants Macbeth's lines:

> I have almost forgot the taste of fears
> The time has been my senses would have cool'd
> To hear a night-shriek, and my fell of hair
> Would at a dismal treatise rouse and stir
> As life were in't. I have supped full with horrors . . .
>
> (V.v.9–13)

The scene allows her to demonstrate her histrionic skill at swift transformation. Fearless – and then tearing out her gray hairs – she asks the dread question "Is my lord dead?" (which replaces "The Queen, my lord, is dead," V.v.16) before delivering the "Tomorrow, and tomorrow, and tomorrow" speech as a lament, and lapsing into a catatonic trance "as still as a fossil." Much interest for the spectator lies in being able to compare, back to back, a distinguished ex-Noh actor exploring realism and a great Little Theatre actress recreating grand Kabuki. For both transgress the gap between the then-closed worlds of traditional and modern Japanese theatre as well as gender codes.

Finally Scene 13 signals cyclical return. *Night and Feast III* is far more subtle than Ionesco's *Macbett*, which simply grinds to a halt with Macol (Malcolm) informing his subjects that he intends to be a worse tyrant than his predecessor.[28] Suzuki has his Chorus of seven men peer over the rafter-beam at the motionless Shiraishi to exclaim, as they did in Scene 2:

MAN 1: What is that person doing?
MAN 2: Someone says *he* has become mad. (my italics)

In Suzuki's staging the object of this sentence is Lady Macbeth; her powerful onstage presence is ambiguous, but the traditional and contemporary structures Suzuki has juxtaposed create a series of "spark gaps" which test the spectators' and actors' imaginative abilities to cross. Shiraishi's new role certainly does *not* sit "like a giant's robe/ Upon a dwarfish thief" (V.ii.21–22).

The final words of the play return us to its beginning in Beckettian fashion, where it leaves us on an oracular knife-edge:

> MAN 1: Soon we will welcome the doctor who will cure this country's sickness. Then we'll work together . . . and give our blood to clean the country. We shall moisten the honourable flower's roots and eradicate the weeds . . . Let's do it! (V.ii.25–31)
>
> *Music gets louder. In the darkness, Lady Macbeth sits immobile, as if lost in thought.*

The element of fanaticism in these optimistic words is reminiscent of propagandistic speeches from World War II and, more recently, the titanic struggles of the New Left against renewal of the US-Japan Mutual Security Treaty (AMPO) in 1960. As Senda Akihiko has pointed out, "the multitude who do more than the ruler asks if told to go to war, and who also overdo beyond their leader's intention if they take part in an anti-establishment action, . . . who are always fanatically wandering around the two extremes of enthusiasm and dejection . . . is very close to the image of the chorus in Suzuki Tadashi's theatre."[29] Certainly in this decade, right up to the year of *Night and Feast III*'s performance in 1978, both the Right and the Left were sources of national embarrassment: with ex-Prime Minister Tanaka's implication in the Lockheed Scandal (1976); and Japanese Red Army attacks on Tel Aviv airport (1972), the French embassy at The Hague (1974), the American consulate in Kuala Lumpur (1975), and JAL jumbo jets at Amsterdam (1973) and Bombay (1977).[30]

It can be argued that the only way to be faithful to the spirit of a classic is to be unfaithful to its letter. Recasting it in different cultural locations and times must inevitably alter it, but in creative hands such recasting can lead to significant new cultural interventions and insights.

THE CHRONICLE OF MACBETH, AUSTRALIA, 1992

According to Suzuki in conversation, the structure of *The Chronicle of Macbeth* is much simpler than his 1991 adaptation of *Macbeth* at Mito. The *Chronicle* project was initiated by Carrillo Gantner of Playbox Theatre in Melbourne to open up Australia to the use of Asian theatre training systems such as Suzuki's. For this reason it was technically a beginners' piece for actors with only two or three months' experience of Suzuki Training. However, as Suzuki explained in interview, another important factor was that "[w]ith Shakespeare the story is generally known, so the audience are able to see what's done to that story. They can enjoy that; it's a deeper experience to compare their own perceptions of that story with the presented version onstage."[31] Unfortunately the ambiguity of the contract as to whether this was a Suzuki production with Australian actors or a Playbox production with a guest director from Japan, and union regulations which hampered selection of experienced Suzuki-trained actors from Sydney, limited his options.

The Chronicle of Macbeth is faithful to the core of Shakespeare's play (the story of the Macbeths) and respectfully preserves Shakespeare's poetry; however, as in *Night and Feast III*, it makes radical contemporary use of the Witches as Murderers ("symbols of Macbeth's passion and energy"), unmooring the "Double, double, toil and trouble" speech for choral use in Scenes 4 and 10. [Figure 39] It also transposes the action of the play to an institutional space which could be seen as the meeting hall of an infirmary (as in *Night and the Clock*), but which also extended the idea of mental sickness in a political direction. In Mito, before coming to Melbourne, Suzuki had already staged *The Bacchae, Macbeth*, and *Ivanov* as a trilogy about the rise and fall of a doomsday cult (*Osarabakyô*) in which a chant inspired by Beckett's *Cascando* was used as liturgy and framing device.

In Playbox's Merlyn Theatre a huge inverted double-cross hung over a raised central entrance, down the steps of which spilled a blood-red carpet. Asymmetrically arranged rows of white chairs glowed incandescently in the dark, as if waiting for aliens to be beamed down onto them. Like Ionesco's chairs they took on a mysterious life of their own, especially during the banquet scene in which they all – not only Banquo's seat – remained empty. This helped to suggest that the scene was taking place in the imagination of the man playing Macbeth.

Scene 1 began with Serge Aubrey's "The Burnt Garden" played at deafening volume to suggest a certain fanaticism, while figures in black kimono and nunlike wimples moved from the wings across stage, clutching copies of *Macbeth*. Reaching their chairs on the fourteenth musical beat, they turned as one, and sat. Downstage right, in front of the rest, sat an old man (who was to play the role of "Macbeth") on a golden chair. As the last bars of music ended, two cult leaders (the Reverend Father and Mother, played by Carrillo Gantner and Ellen Lauren)

Figure 39 Farewell Cult "witches" (Matthew Crosby foreground) pound their staves into the ground while chanting a fiercely energized "Double, double, toil and trouble" to intimidate "Macbeth" (compare with Figure 36). *The Chronicle of Macbeth*. Playbox Theatre, Melbourne, 1992.

appeared on a blood-red rostrum at the back of the stage to lead their followers in a solipsistic liturgical chant called "Farewell to History." It seemed to refer to their reading of *Macbeth*, for they held their closed books at chest-level while chanting, "But this one [this reading] is different from always/ Finish this one/ Then there can be rest." They then opened their books on the Reverend Mother's cue, "Today we shall do *Macbeth*. Begin reading!," and started to intone the "Tomorrow, and tomorrow, and tomorrow" speech in unison (V.v.19–28). "Out, out, brief candle!" was delivered individually in quickening succession until it became an overlapping babble of experiential difference – only to subside into the undertow of collective experience on "Life's but a walking shadow . . . full of sound and fury/ Signifying nothing." The music swelled trumpet-tongued as the words died, the cult leaders disappeared back into the darkness under their inverted double-cross, the Chorus rose slowly, turned, and exited, still mouthing the words of the text which they read as they walked. The man called "Macbeth" now rose and began, "If it were done when 'tis done, then 'twere well/ It were done quickly" (I.vii.1–2).

Complex things were going on here. Some sense of the technical difficulty – and dramatic power – of Suzuki's approach to the play is given by the director's note to Peter Curtin (Macbeth) at this point:

Peter, when you're "sitting" there as this little old man who is in trouble, as the music comes in for Scene 2, your transformation as the warrior Macbeth must take place . . . Standing up needs to be indicative of something big happening inside, not just "standing up" . . . Construct forms, sculpt movements. How many steps, how far back do you go behind your chair? (Carruthers, "Reading Suzuki," 239)

Suzuki also side-lit his actors to give them greater presence, lifting out their movements from ground and background in order to make them seem as if, in this deluded old man's fantasy, they were floating in space. The slow-motion *Tenteketen* exercise became Suzuki's basic grammar with which he "raised the stakes" of the Farewell Cult entrances and exits. Instructions for this were to maintain an even, slow-motion walk which would defy physics in its smooth tautness of line.

Curtin vividly describes the experience from the actor's point of view in the opening minutes of the play:

Imagine that you are in this position (demonstrates and holds a low knee-bend, feet wide apart). You seem to be sitting on a chair, but you're actually not; you're taking all the tension here – the *hara* – to guarantee the correct intensity for delivering your lines. So that chair can be taken away at any time and you're still "sitting" there. Imagine that you have committed yourself to this position and you're going to hold it for probably three or four minutes before your next soliloquy. Just to your left are the equivalent of about six car headlights on high-beam, and you're looking into them, and not blinking [so as to hold your focus and concentration]. Imagine that you are also listening to nine witches coming on, smashing the floor with staves. While this is happening, you count the beat so that, when they have smashed the floor thirteen times, that's when you'll give up this position, and start to make your move across the stage. When they hit the floor for the nineteenth time, you'll know there's going to be silence and you will be there with your line. (139)

Suzuki was well aware of the difficulty of what he was demanding of his actors, testing their very reason for being onstage. In interview before rehearsals started, he had insisted, "Until they've actually done *Macbeth*, they won't have a clear sense of what it is they're trying to do" (205). Hence his insistence on the importance of Suzuki Training, which was undertaken initially for two weeks in Toga in August 1991, for a further two weeks at November auditions in Melbourne, and then right throughout rehearsals in February 1992 and the entire run of the play (March–May). Early on in the rehearsal period he provided his actors with the conceptual grammar of his approach:

In Rodin's sculpture "The Thinker", the movement of thought inside is obvious. Yet no-one actually sits in this position when they want to think. Rodin has effectively lied in order to show us the truth.

Sitting in a chair is not just daily life behaviour. We can take this formalism of sitting to express something to the audience that they cannot see. What then is the man-made structure we must impose upon this action to make it clear? . . .

When working out what you're doing, there can be changes made within the structure, but these must not be improvisational changes. You must have the structure before you can really begin to rehearse. Your concentration should be on doing things as well as possible. We're all human, and we all come to rehearsal in different states each day. When we're not in tune physically it's difficult to get quickly to the required level because this kind of theatre requires great intensity. This is why I stress the idea of exercises and training before each performance. (236–33)

Along with a basic grammar of stylization, Suzuki also provided his actors with a set of hypotheses within which to understand their function within the frame-story:

1. The play is the evocation of the memories, the consciousness of the person we're going to call "Macbeth".
2. This person exists within an organisation (religious, terrorist, or otherwise) called "The Farewell Cult", and is to be destroyed somehow.

3. What we have to realise are the visual workings onstage of that person's spirit; that is, everything that takes place behind "Macbeth" onstage exists only in his fantasy.

4. Real present time begins on the two occasions when "Macbeth" sits in his chair downstage (during the "Farewell to History" chants at beginning and end of the performance).

5. The person in the cult who facilitates "Macbeth's realisation" is The Reverend Mother (who plays "Lady Macbeth" in the play-within-the-play).

6. This space is where The Reverend Father (who role-plays "The Illusion or Subconscious of Macbeth") performs psychoanalysis on the man called "Macbeth". (233–34)

The model Suzuki gave his Australian cast for the *modus vivendi* of the Farewell Cult was the mass indoctrination leading to group suicide of Jim Jones's Guyana cult. In 1992 David Kuresh's fiery shoot-out with the FBI had not yet taken place in Waco, Texas, but the "doubling" of such scenarios throughout recent history suggests the uncanny potency of Suzuki's updating of *Macbeth* for the twenty-first century.

It was the framing device's ability to turn *Macbeth* into a play-within-a-play, and the support of a coherent nonrealist acting method, which were so powerfully new to Australian audiences. In order to expand on the kind of experience the Suzuki Method was opening up for Australian actors and audiences, I shall concentrate on the two climactic scenes of Suzuki's production: Scenes 11 (V.i.1–72) and 12 (V.iii V.v.1–28, 51).

Most scenes and passages from *Macbeth* were chosen by Suzuki to show the old man drifting in and out of his "Macbeth" visions (created by unsatisfied desire). The effect of this was most fully realized in the rapid and unpredictable oscillation from one state to the other. At the end of Scene 10 (IV.i), the Witches, standing on their chairs to suggest their visionary status, show "Macbeth" a line of kings (disembodied voices projected by Chorus members from different parts of the auditorium). "Macbeth" bravely attempts to face his fears but, despite a fierce struggle, is inexorably bent by his paranoias. These culminate in a vision of "the spirit of Banquo" (played by John Nobbs) at which "Macbeth" finally quails as he realizes the futility of all his struggles. Reawakening at "Where are they? Gone!" (133), the old man returns exhausted to his chair, and immediately "sees" Scene 11 (Lady Macbeth's sleepwalking) taking place behind him – perhaps a dream-projection of his own sense of guilt? The fact that he stares glassy-eyed out into the audience while they see "Lady Macbeth" glide forward out of the darkness behind him suggests a summons from the depths of the unconscious. In a note to Curtin, Suzuki put it this way:

Each Apparition is a more difficult opponent, so you must really build. A snake, even when defeated past hope, still tries to strike. So long as we're struggling, there's something healthy about us. When the battle ceases, senility sets in. Think about the structure of this. You wring out your last energy in the struggle against the witches.

It's the death of your partner that causes you to give up . . . Make it very clear that the "brief candle" is your wife . . . This theatre is the world of your heart, which it encompasses . . . Something we weren't conscious of becomes "visible". You face your internal world. (244–45)

The emotion-charged strangeness of Scene 11 is heightened by the appearances of the Doctor and Gentlewoman who tiptoe furtively from empty chair to empty chair in a farcical ballet of fear. They are dressed absurdly: the Gentlewoman like a maid from a French farce in frilly pinafore and cap, the Doctor with Ray-Bans, stethoscope, white coat, gartered socks, and black shoes – but no trousers. Their intonations are quite unnatural, stylizing the cracked sound of their mounting fright as they approach the blood-red carpet of light down which "Lady Macbeth" (Ellen Lauren) will travel. Suzuki reinforces our sense of this as "Macbeth's vision" by setting it up as a two-camera shot. They look to the front and "see" her coming through the audience, which reverses what the audience see: Lauren entering behind them.

Although dreamlike, there is a visual logic at work, Suzuki using lateral crossing of the stage for the Farewell Cult's narrative in Scenes 1 and 13, diagonal crossing for the dynamic, violently aggressive stamping marches of the Witches in Scenes 4 and 10, and "vertical" upstage-downstage movement along the central blood-red carpet for moments of trance-possession and vision. When the little old man who sits downstage right travels into his own nightmares, he has to move laterally across to the "river of blood" and make a right-angled turn onto it "as Macbeth" in order to play out his desires: the murders of Duncan and Banquo. Up this river, beyond the dais and under the sign of a "double-cross" lies the darkened "room of power," where the murders of Duncan and Banquo take place, and from which issue the Reverend Father and Mother, whether as their Cult "selves" or as The Illusion of Macbeth and Lady Macbeth.

This carpet, then, is the runway where Suzuki's actors must "make visible the invisible." When in Scene 5 "Macbeth" emerges from the dark inner room with "I have done the deed" (II.ii.14) he must be able to convey to the audience a vivid image of precisely what has taken place there. By taking Peter Curtin physically through a range of possibilities in front of the other cast members – sitting on his chest, covering his mouth, and "slitting his throat," or plunging an imaginary dagger up through his ribcage to the heart as he tried to sit up – Suzuki encouraged him to put the precise and unmediated physical horror of the offstage moment so vividly into his body that it could be sensed onstage through the motor-memory's traumatic nervous "discharge."

The sleepwalking scene was another such moment of "traumatic discharge," this time displaced in "dreams that shake us nightly" onto "Lady Macbeth." "Out, damned spot!" was delivered in visceral anguish out of a cavernous darkness lit, apparently, by the single candle in Lauren's hand. On the line "Hell is murky," she sunk slowly into a low crouch, seeming, because of the looseness of her robes, to compact down as she moved from rostrum to the front of the stage, getting smaller and smaller in terms of height but somehow more dense in her compactness as she approached audience-space, as if about to implode under the gravity of her guilt. Physically this was real, the scene being, for the performer, a litany of screaming muscles which replaced any need for psychology. "Lady Macbeth's breakdown is terribly sad, but you can't *play* sad," was Lauren's response to my question about this in interview; "what you can play is struggle, and you don't manufacture that struggle on a presentational level; you actually put your body in the position where you're struggling" (233–34).

The parameters Suzuki gave her to work within were also clear and precise:

This sort of mad person isn't locked into a single concentration. You're doing one thing and suddenly a completely different sensibility is there. Separate movement from speech. The order of how things happened is confused, out of context. Everything happens suddenly, jerkily . . . The changes are very quick, but give them time to happen. You get smaller as you approach the front, more condensed. (241)

Lauren herself described the experience in this way:

What happened in rehearsal was that, when I began to isolate movement from voice, I got into a rhythm that drove Suzuki up the wall, a *predictable* rhythm of move, then speak, move and speak. So then I had to begin the process of "shattering time" . . . trying to jumble the timing sequence so I could keep the audience from knowing what was going to happen next. I chose to defy everything he told me about moving and then speaking. And that's how I began.

He likes it when you throw things back at him. All his tenets and rules are simply to give rise to freedom for the actor. So I began by saying "Out, damned spot!" while moving. Then I isolated it down to "Out, damned . . . spot!", in which "spot" is said in the stillness. From there I decided moment by moment how to structure my body in space . . .

But please understand, it's not simply about movement, the body is there to determine the voice. I literally counted out beats – how long in the stillness I would hold before the voice would come out of the body. You're working with your breath to create a great deal of tension and energy in the body but you've also got to be preparing to speak right away, without losing that energy. This takes enormous breath control.

Suzuki's greatest actress, Kayoko Shiraishi, was once asked how she was able to change the sensibility of the three very different characters she was playing in *The Trojan Women*. She simply answered, "I change the way I breathe". I understand now a little bit more about what she meant. Breath is a powerful force inside the body. By the audience watching you fight to control the uncontrollable, in a sense you begin to control their breathing – and indeed, when I watch SCOT performing, I find I often hold my breath for long periods of time. (222–23)

The most breathtaking moment of Scene 11 occurred in just this fashion. At "Banquo's buried. He cannot come out on's grave," the Doctor, hidden behind a chair, blurted out "Even so?," rose – and then froze in horror, hand to mouth, as "Lady Macbeth" slowly turned to look in his direction. Lauren describes the subtext of this moment:

Suzuki sets up this incredible woman going through this crisis with this French farce on the side . . . and then suddenly he slams the two worlds together. Lady Macbeth hears something and turns and looks at them. Only what you realize is that what Lady Macbeth has heard is something very different *inside* herself. It's an enormous moment. It's funny, it's horrific. I did it one day in rehearsal almost by accident. And then Suzuki said, "Really look at them", so I looked at them and turned back and he said, "No, no, no. When you look at them, hold it for a very long time, because that's the only way the audience will know you *don't* see them" . . . So now I literally count to 9 – and it's killing me (laughs) because I'm really low to the ground – and then I turn back.

Suzuki then says, "When you turn back, you've held time in a way that you've *created* something, and when you turn back the idea isn't that you've turned your body back to the audience; your center of gravity, here [in the *hara*], grabs the audience and turns *it* around so they can see with your eyes."

What I've described creates a very different physical reality in the body. Among other things, it creates a great amount of tension, and this is one of the great problems when you start working with this method. Without proper control, it creates constriction and tension and a flat-line machine-gun vocality which is probably what you hear in *The Chronicle of Macbeth* with some of the actors who've just begun this training. Like anything objective and difficult, it takes a long time to gain enough control to begin to compose inside this sensibility. It takes enormous mental as well as physical tenacity. (224–25)

As "Lady Macbeth" glides back into the darkness and the Doctor cries, "God, God forgive us all!" (crossing himself in panic with his stethoscope), Scene 12 begins with a return to reality as sudden as anything in *The Singing Detective*. Seyton-the-cook (Joel Markham), dressed in fatsuit, chef's hat, and clogs, rolls in a meal-on-wheels for "Macbeth," who returns to the state of being an institutionalized old man. Suzuki's note to Markham was that he should play Sancho Panza to this institutionalized Don Quixote. If the first transformation in Scene 2 from little old man to "Macbeth" was heroic, this reversal is tragically pathetic, and the sympathy of "Sancho Panza" helps to underline it. Everything said has a "double, double" *entendre* as Shakespeare's words peel away from Suzuki's action. "Macbeth" comes out of the trance in which he "saw" his wife's anguish, stares at his plate, up at the cook as if to say "Where am I?," gulps down his soup ("I have supp'd full with horrors" is suggested), and then returns to his fantasy with "Bring me no more . . . reports." His abuse of the maidservant, "The devil damn thee black, thou cream-fac'd loon" builds for several lines as he rises, waving fork in the air. Each line of verbal abuse seems to hammer her further into the ground, as she cowers back, fearful of being speared by flying cutlery. Our attention is divided between admiration for Katia Molino's physical virtuosity as she bends deeper and deeper backward, and concern for her safety in the face of Curtin's nursing-home tyrant. "Macbeth" disappears as, on "Take thy face hence," the fork clatters to the ground and the old man turns to his friend the cook for sympathy with, "Seyton! – I am sick at heart." He sits at "This push will cheer me ever, or disseat me now" (reinforcing the chair-of-power image) and complains feelingly, "that which should accompany old age . . . I must not look to have." Another of Shakespeare's rapid mood swings is reinterpreted at "Give me my armour!," the old man shaking his arms in a towering impotence of rage like a child "spitting the dummy." Seyton's refusal, "'Tis not needed yet," is motherly in its concern, but when the old man demands again, "Give me mine armour!," his response is to take the napkin which has covered the food and tie it round "Macbeth's" neck like a bib. The petulant demand, "Give me my staff," sees the fork returned carefully to the geriatric warrior's waving hand in such a way as to suggest that the big baby should finish his meal; and the old man's whispered, "Doctor, the Thanes fly from me," has a wonderful resonance somewhere between pleasure and despair at gaining attention but losing respect – an effect latent in *Macbeth* but released with shocking freshness in this estranging institutionalized context.

Finally, at "Wherefore was that cry? – The Queen, my lord, is dead," the old man's nightmare returns to claim him. The music of Serge Aubrey's "The Burnt Garden" returns, and Doctor, maidservant, and cook creep off.

Scenes 12 and 13 conclude the play, in circular fashion, by repeating Scene 1. On a signal from the Reverend Father, the Chorus of believers, which now includes a broken "Macbeth," rise from their chairs to chant "Double, double, toil and trouble." One significant change is that staves are no longer needed to pound the floor at this point; the same stirring motion is made, but, this time, book in hand: Shakespeare's *Macbeth* is used as the ladle with which to stir the institutional soup of history. A final surprise remains. The lights dim as the chant continues. When they come back up, and before the audience can begin clapping, the Reverend Mother announces sternly, "This concludes today's labours. Thank you. You may go home."[32]

Suzuki's contemporizing of the Witches as members of a New Age religious group may have been pinpoint accurate in the context of his 1991 Mito production of *Macbeth – The Rise of the Farewell Cult*, for shocking events involving AUM Shinrikyô's terrorism were continually bubbling up to the surface of Japanese public life between 1990 and 1996. However, for many Australians, the chief value of *The Chronicle* seemed to lie not so much in its offering of yet another interpretation of the play, although it was controversially that, but in its introduction of a new performative approach. Judging by audience responses to *The Chronicle* at the 1992 Mitsui Festival in Tokyo, seeing Australian actors working to fuse Shakespeare's original words with Suzuki's performance style was as much a point of interest in Japan as it was in Australia.[33] While almost all could appreciate the qualitative differences between the performances of Peter Curtin (Macbeth) and Ellen Lauren (Lady Macbeth), the explanation of the critic Uchino Tadashi is perhaps the most even-handed. According to Uchino, while "she obviously does not have training in Shakespearean acting, [Ellen Lauren offers] one of the best examples of how Suzuki method can be applied to Shakespearean acting." On the other hand, he thought it was interesting to see the actor playing Macbeth trying to preserve his Shakespeare training. "Obviously he is not very young and his Suzuki training is a new input. These two different kinds of physical acting are struggling within him, and never integrated – and this too is good."[34]

GREETINGS FROM THE EDGE OF THE EARTH I (SEKAI NO HATE KARA KONNICHIWA I), TOGA, 1991–2002

When comparing the ways in which Suzuki Tadashi has adapted and rewritten *Macbeth* for home and foreign consumption, it is interesting to note that he is more artistically daring when producing Shakespeare for a Japanese audience in Toga than he is when adapting the Bard for an English-speaking one in Melbourne. Raw statistics are a useful indicator of scale here. Whereas, in *The Chronicle of Macbeth*, fully 95% was Shakespeare, and only 5% inspired by Beckett, the 1975 *Night and the Clock* was 60% *Macbeth* in various translations, and 40% Japanese texts, while *Greetings* was only 25% *Macbeth* and 75% other texts.[35]

It might be suggested that what remains basic to all these Suzuki productions is what Jean-François Lyotard would call the avant-gardist concern with "investigating the assumptions implicit in modernity."[36] Suzuki has said, "I think I'm close to [Samuel] Beckett . . . This means I believe there is no absolute standard which can objectify the self or establish one's identity. But I'm different from Beckett since I emphasise the importance of fantasy in human existence . . . And I'm saying that these have no end and cannot be solved."[37] His emphasis on "the importance of fantasy" is reiterated again and again to his actors in rehearsal, both in Japan and Australia, as a process of "making the invisible visible," a preoccupation in line with Lyotard's contention that "[t]he postmodern would be that which, in the modern, puts forward the unrepresentable in presentation itself."[38]

Suzuki's updating of *Macbeth* in *Greetings from the Edge of the Earth* is much more complex and daring than his *Chronicle*, for he can confidently use it to engage a Japanese audience in a contemporary rereading of Japan. The difference between the two productions was signaled by a shift in the subject. In Australia the Witches were intended to be seen as members of a doomsday cult. In Japan, however, the Farewell Cult's use of Oka Kiyoshi's wartime speeches in Scene 3 allowed for their double-image identification as ultranationalists as well ("double, double" trouble).

Another point of difference between the productions is that, where *The Chronicle* is, for the most part, highly respectful of Shakespeare's words and structure, *Greetings* transforms *Macbeth* so much as to make the source of its inspiration almost unrecognizable, although I would argue that it is still respectful. The titles of the two plays encapsulate these differences. *The Chronicle of Macbeth* puts Macbeth into the equation, suggesting that Suzuki is using Shakespeare as Shakespeare once used

Holinshed's *Chronicles of Scotland*, as a major source. *Greetings from the Edge of the Earth* ironically emphasizes the perceptual "distance" from Shakespeare, what one might call the "flat world" view of those for whom Europe or Jerusalem stand at the center and fabled Zipangu lies at the remotest edge, the falling-off point.[39] If the tone of *The Chronicle* is somberly tragic, that of *Greetings* is lightly ironic, since this remaking of *Macbeth* is meant to challenge Japanese assumptions about center and periphery as much as Western ones. The strategy is typically postmodern, for in Charles Jencks's terms:

Post-Modernism is fundamentally the eclectic mixture of any tradition with that of the immediate past. It is both the continuation of Modernism and its transcendence. Its best works are characteristically double-coded and ironic, making a feature of the wide choice, conflict and discontinuity of traditions, because this heterogeneity most clearly captures our pluralism.[40]

In Suzuki's own terms:

The strength and greatness of Shakespeare lies in his ability to mean many things to many people. My way is to focus on one aspect as a specialist. So, to those people who expect me to deal with the complete work, I would point out that it's not something we are obliged to do in this day and age. I think it is important that people discuss Shakespeare from different points of view and deepen the possible meanings in their own ways.[41]

In his 1993 Introduction to the performance text, Suzuki explains his actor-centered approach: *"Greetings from the Edge of the Earth I* was designed around Tsutamori Kôsuke, as other productions have been around Shiraishi Kayoko."[42] In a 1995 interview he goes on to explain his distinctive angle of approach:

My stage reveals a completely new form of acting; the more you see the style, the more you see the actors themselves . . . Usually a psychotic person is my main character. And the texts of [writers like] Euripides and Shakespeare possess him or her . . . In other words, it's not a drama in which the action follows chronological time. The real drama is what transpires in the consciousness of someone who may just be sitting quietly.[43]

This personal approach, the Suzuki style, remains unaltered in both plays, but *Greetings* does have an intertextual life greater than that of *The Chronicle*. This is partly because it is fully localized, and partly because it is "a Grand Review" of three plays known collectively as *The Farewell Cult Trilogy* (*The Bacchae*, *Macbeth*, *Ivanov*). Since Tsutamori played the lead in each, he could be all three characters at once in this telescoped

Grand Review. Not surprisingly, this called for a more advanced exercise of acting skill than was evident in *The Chronicle*.

The trilogy can be seen as Suzuki's reexamination of the state of European culture from the point of view of a postmodern world in which European colonialism has ended and European culture is no longer privileged, the idea of a classical canon has disintegrated, and Shakespeare has even been banished from the syllabi of some universities. In Suzuki's words, "The idea was to depict history, almost a biography of European inner history, taking representative works from different periods . . . In other words, showing how we got from the Greeks to Beckett . . . So it's a spiritual history. And the goal is to rethink Japan's response."[44] Part of that response is to insist that since the actor is the primary vehicle for conveying stage reality, the mere imitating of Western realism would not do. Westernization should not be mistaken for modernization. To quote Suzuki again, "If a production of foreign work is to succeed [in Japan], it must somehow make reference to the specificities of Japanese society and theatrical history."[45]

What then are some of the local "specificities of Japanese society and theatrical history" which Suzuki wishes to manifest? The second paragraph of his 1993 Introduction provides clues:

How I look at Japanese inner life as it exists in the subconscious is an important aspect of my theatrical activities. In this play I have used parts of earlier works that deal with those behavioural aspects of the Japanese (who love to dream and need stimulation) which have been found to be funny . . . The story is of an old man, who could probably be called a Nationalist; at one point he passionately believes he is at one with the spirit of Japan; at another he quarrels about food; at still others he finds himself impersonating famous people. So this is a new attempt to visualise the inner world, presented with fireworks.[46]

This helps to clarify how a critique of resurgent nationalism can be filtered through Suzuki's interest in "the inner life," using humor both as a weapon and as a means of communicating more effectively with a popular audience in Toga. If the modern Japanese "love to dream and need stimulation" – and indeed a high premium is placed on entertainment in Japanese theatre – then the serious theme is best approached through comic irony and the absurd.[47] The principle of the Porter's speech is brilliantly reapplied, with a nod to Beckett's *Endgame*, in which "Nothing is funnier than unhappiness."[48]

An alternative explanation for the use of comedy in the play is its healthy centrality in a myth of the Sun Goddess Amaterasu Ômikami, which has been so important to the nation and the creation of Japanese theatre. Zeami provides the *locus classicus*. He describes in *Fûshikaden* (*Style and the Flower*) how, when Amaterasu Ômikami hid in the Rock Cave of Heaven after having been ritually polluted by her brother the Storm God, the world was plunged into darkness. The goddess Ama no Uzume solved the problem by staging an impromptu striptease dance on an upturned tub, performing so suggestively that the gods clapped their hands and roared with laughter. At this Amaterasu Ômikami became curious and put her head out of the cave, upon which light returned to the world.[49] It is a measure of Suzuki's cultural self-assurance that he can "look both ways" as skillfully as this, recognizing the equal importance of humor in Shakespeare's most intense tragedy, and of *modoki* (parody) in the religious origins of Japanese performance tradition.

I believe that one crucial factor not mentioned by Suzuki in his Introduction to *Greetings* was probably omitted because it was so much in the media at the time. This was the passing of Emperor Hirohito, who died in 1989 at the age of 87. In his lifespan Japan had risen twice on the wheel of fortune to superpower status; it had also been directly involved in the death throes of military imperialism, both European and Japanese.

The choice of *Macbeth* as a vehicle for a retrospective on the imperial theme was an apt one, given the saturation of the media with documentaries on every aspect of the Emperor's sixty-three-year reign. Because this material was so well aired publicly, both nationally and internationally, it did not need explicit reference; however, because it, like the Australian Bicentennial Celebrations of 1988, was such a potent site for mythmaking and political contestation, ironic treatment could provide intellectual distancing.

The particular spatial and temporal contexts of the production of *Greetings* are also important to note, for it took place at the Toga Festival in August, in a remote region of the Japan Alps. Its audience included local farmers from the surrounding valleys, as well as two kinds of "outsider": urban Japanese who had made the day-long journey from big cities such as Tokyo, and the handful of foreigners who had made the even costlier pilgrimage from abroad. Suzuki had moved his company out of Tokyo to Toga village in 1976 as a way of challenging received notions of center and periphery, and *Greetings* has been performed there almost every year from 1991 to 2002.

The time of year and its attendant associations were also factored into the performance. High summer is when people go on holiday, fleeing the heat of the cities for the cool of the mountains. At such a time it seems as though half of urban Japan is dreaming back to a vanishing way of life in the *furusato* (the old home village). In such a location at such a time, Suzuki could more easily get his audience to negotiate the gaps between agricultural and urban, traditional and modern, indigenous and imported values.

Summer evenings are also the time for fireworks, which feature prominently in the play. City journals regularly advertise such displays to draw tourists to local beauty spots. It is also the time for ghost plays in the Kabuki theatre (fear being a cooling experience for Kabuki theatregoers; the conventional drum sound for a ghost's entrance in Kabuki, *hyuu doro doro*, is the sound of a little gust of wind on the back of the neck). Associations such as these are given different twists in *Greetings*. Exploding fireworks in a production which aims to make "the invisible world visible" can very effectively suggest inner joy, war, Hiroshima – or a series of strokes and hemorrhages. [Figure 40] And if Lady Macbeth appears to be absent in *Greetings*, she is "an absent presence," both in the Farewell Cult's invocation of the Sun Goddess to return, and in Shiraishi Kayoko's disembodied voice on tape (whispering lines from Lady Macbeth's sleepwalking scene).

A Toga audience would know that the reputation of Shiraishi (who performed those lines in *Night and the Clock*) still haunts the company she left in 1989. It would also be aware, through Suzuki's careful collage, of the implications of Lady Macbeth's absence in a national perspective. The Iwato myth of Amaterasu Ômikami's disappearance into the heavenly Rock Cave is familiar to every child. Suzuki's firm grasp of such Japanese contextual associations inevitably made *Greetings* a richer performative experience than the Australian *The Chronicle of Macbeth* could ever hope to be.

Since few readers will have seen *Greetings* and familiarized themselves with its extraordinary layering of "found" texts, my analysis is necessarily synoptic. However, because of the play's self-conscious Surrealism, interpretation is far from easy. As Andre Breton[50] has remarked, "The strongest surrealist image is the one that . . . takes the longest to translate into practical language."[51]

The Grand Review, as *Greetings* is subtitled, begins with a wildly funny scene. As an Old Man sits center stage, priests enter in large wicker baskets (reminiscent of Nell and Nagg in their dustbins in *Endgame*), dance to the "Pizzicato Polka," and then discuss their problems with hyperdigestion. (Perhaps this absurd topic, lifted from *Night and Feast III*, Scene 3, is meant to suggest the problems Japan has had swallowing so much of Western culture so quickly). A circular discussion about Lord Buddha's diarrhea[52] gets interrupted by a sentimental pop song, "Yoru no hômonsha" ("My Night Visitor"), and, at this point (Scene 2) a Chef,

Figure 40 Fireworks explode around the Old Man who imagines himself to be "Macbeth" (Tsutamori Kôsuke). *Greetings from the Edge of the Earth I*. Toga amphitheatre, 1993.

played by a very large American (Leon Ingulsrud), enters daintily on tiptoe, pushing in a meal-on-wheels for the old man.

This is recognizably the scene from *The Chronicle of Macbeth* in which Seyton puts a bib round Macbeth's neck when he calls for his armor (V.iii). However, to designate the Old Man and his attendant as Macbeth and Seyton would be a misleading oversimplification, for at different moments in this production they also role-play Don Quixote and Sancho Panza, and Hamm and Clov. In his own imagination the Old Man also becomes Kadmus and Ivanov, Oka Kiyoshi, the director of an old people's home, and the patriarchal leader of the Farewell Cult. Image, text, and music cue these postmodern transformations.

The Old Man sings along to the pop song, then, in Scene 3, launches into a wartime propaganda speech of Oka Kiyoshi's about the creation of Japan by the gods and "[t]he pure spirited acts committed by Kusunoki Masashige...to preserve the royal line"(4).[53] A Chorus of crazily dressed men in wheelchairs enter from a darkened backstage, as if from the subconscious, chanting a kamikaze-style dedication to the Sun Goddess who has hidden "again behind the rock door of heaven." "Again" seems to suggest the disasters of World War II, for the wheelchair men invoke the popular catchphrases of Japan's economic recovery: "We have to work hard, sacrificing our lives to petition the Goddess to return." This prose chant is followed by a song which ironically echoes the logic of Japan's colonial expansionism:

> Many people but little land,
> Our Japan's woes
> Should be solved by our own hands.
> Let us forge a New World
> In the fire of our fighting spirits. (5)

The clenched-fist gestures and martial marching action suggest to me that it parodies the Witches' "Double, double, toil and trouble" litany in *The Chronicle* as well as the circularity of ultranationalist ideology. However, Suzuki was careful to provide other elements in the *mise en scène* which helped to distance his audience from what they were witnessing. Certainly they found this spectacle of *Yamato damashii* (Japanese fighting spirit) to be extremely funny,[54] executed as it was by absurdly dressed, athletic "old men" in nursing-home wheelchairs. But the Chorus's invocation of the *Lebensraum* concept ("Many people but little land") is hard to miss.

Scene 4 begins with a rapid review in dumbshow (*danmari*) of European cultural history as represented by Euripides, Chekhov, and Beckett.

"How we got from the Greeks to Beckett" and the devastation of Hiroshima provides the context for "rethinking Japan's response" to its unreflecting imitation of European colonial imperialism.

First to erupt onto the stage/into the old man's thoughts are the maenads from *The Bacchae*, announced by the threatening sounds of Perez Prado's "Voodoo Suite." They are followed by the doll-women of *Ivanov*, by a caustic Geisha (with telescope) reminiscent of Clov in *Endgame*, and, out of the present, the priests of the Farewell Cult, chanting "History/ If only it could be thrown away." As the Wheelchair Fanatics line up on stage around the Old Man, he rises to deliver a message from the Ministry of Public Health and Welfare, citing "four reasons for the increase in the average life expectancy of the Japanese"(7).[55] This self-congratulatory official monologue quickly deteriorates into a debate with the increasingly irate Wheelchair Fanatics about the relative nutritional merits of Japanese and American food: "As Japanese and human beings we demand proper food: miso soup, fish roe, and raw eggs!"(8). The audience laugh at the jokes and the idea of the aging ultranationalists of "Nursing-Home Japan" being put on a starvation diet and preserved as "mummies."[56] But behind the jokes, they know, lie serious political issues, for February 1983 had seen the complete collapse of the national system of free health care for people aged seventy or over.

From food the argument turns to living space. The Old Man as nursing-home director denies requests for better living conditions by referring to the war: "As you know, Japan lost the war and shrunk to just four little islands. When Japan shrank, naturally the space you occupied also got shrunk. Isn't that natural? Asking for the same space while others' space has been reduced is asking for too much. This kind of selfishness must be completely shrunk up!" (9). Familiar government requests for self-sacrifice, put in this paternalistically absurd way, draw yet more laughter from the audience.

In Scene 5, as the consequences of aggression sink into the consciousness of the rebellious inmates of "Shrinking Japan," a tape is heard of ex-SCOT member Shiraishi Kayoko whispering Lady Macbeth's lines from the sleepwalking scene (Scene 11 of *Night and the Clock*):

> Wash your hands very clean . . .
> Those people are all dead and buried.
> Don't you know they can't come out of the grave? (9)

As swift as thought, this is followed by sounds of war, gunfire, fireworks, a US cavalry bugle sounding the charge, and an American voiceover ironically announcing that "the enemy forces have landed." (Is this Pearl

Harbor or the Rockefeller Center "takeover" during the Bubble Economy period of Japanese corporate raids on American real estate?) The Farewell Cult members file off in their wheelchairs to do battle, singing "Many people but little land . . . let us forge a New World" only to return immediately in defeat chanting:

> After the war
> The Sun Goddess hid again behind the rock door of Heaven.
> The land of Japan is in mourning; all joy has vanished.
> We have to work hard, sacrificing our lives to petition the Goddess to
>   return. (9)

This vision of the horrors of war, estheticized in Kabuki style by the use of fireworks, gives way to sordid reality as the Japanese Old Man (Tsutamori) and his American servant/partner (Ingulsrud) revisit their love/hate "Cold War" relationship in dialogue reminiscent of *Endgame*. Since 1993, however, when Kuboniwa Naoko took over the servant role, new dialogue has been added appropriate to the gender change.

Scene 6 replays the earlier dumbshow (*danmari*) with a difference; this time the Geisha, doll-women and maenads reappear in reverse order. The aggression of "Voodoo Suite" and the maenads is now replaced by the nostalgic strains of "Karatachi nikki" ("Orange Tree Diary"), a pop love song. Thus gender politics, it appears for me, comes to the fore at the end of the play as it does in the twilight of empire. The old man is enthralled by the saccharine sentimentality of the song, even inviting the audience to join in. (This draws a huge laugh.) However, the Geisha, originally played by the saturnine Takahashi, deconstructs the love song with a raucous, goose-stepping rendition. As it ends, the Old Man announces, "Excellent! Japanese songs are truly excellent" (which draws another huge laugh from the audience). He then withdraws into fantasies of Macbeth's last moments, exclaiming, "Seyton, bring me no more reports!," and we have returned to the dialogue of *Macbeth* V.iii.

Getting the audience to laugh at the self-importance of the Old Man seems to be a way for Suzuki to lance the boil of ultranationalism through ridicule. His interpolations in Shakespeare's text also have point. "What's *America*, was it not born of woman?" gloats the old male chauvinist. And when the answer to his question "What soldiers, patch?" comes back as "The *Allied* Force, so please you," he throws down his chopsticks in a fit of anger – only to turn calmly to his American servant and say, "*Seyton, pick that up please!*" The action is certainly incongruous, but precisely why it is greeted with more gales of laughter from the audience is not clear. Perhaps its playfully symbolic relationship releases the tensions created by real-world trade disputes between Japan and America. Or perhaps it triggers group recognition of the self-indulgent behavior of tyrannical, live-in elders in Japan's "*ie* (family) State."

Yet another interpolation prepares us for the final revelation of the scene, "If thou couldst, doctor, cast the water of *Japan*, find her disease." But it can also remind an audience of Japan's industrially polluted rivers and the mercury poisoning responsible for Minamata disease. What cost catching up with the West? The final interpolation in this scene is the climactic one. At "Wherefore was that cry?," we get "*Japan*, my lord, is dead."

In Scene 7 the Old Man is left alone onstage with his grief as Serge Aubrey's "The Burnt Garden" plays. He totters to the back of the stage, which opens onto a hauntingly beautiful lake and mountain, and screams at the Sun Goddess/Lady Macbeth embodied in the landscape of Japan, "Kiero! Kiero!" ("Out, out, brief candle, life's but a walking shadow"). If we think of the Old Man as a patriarch mystically married to the land, his action here also seems to suggest *kuni-mi*. This is a ritual of gazing on the land, carried out by emperors, shoguns, and even the heads of peasant households. In Herbert Plutschow's words, "It may be performed from . . . any high vantage point which allows one a view over occupied, used or cultivated land. In the ritual category of *kuni-mi* I would also include *mi*, which involves the contrary, namely looking at something high from below."[57]

The latter category would be the most appropriate since the Old Man is looking up at the foothills of the Japan Alps. In terms which invite a feminist reading of the scene, Plutschow concludes, "The *kuni-mi* also has a political meaning. The emperor, mantled in divine power, reaffirmed human occupation of the land by his gaze."

At this point the wheelchair patriots return, chanting "History! If only it could be thrown away, we could rest, could sleep!" – suggesting the deeply ironic conclusion that there is "no end to the karmic process."

What I hope to have demonstrated here is that, even when the verbatim use of Shakespeare's text is so minimal and the modes of expression so different, Suzuki's use of *Macbeth* is a brilliant meditation on "the imperial theme" at different social levels and across a range of cultures, times, and styles. As Charles Jencks reminds us, postmodernism is "conceived as a wide language which cuts across high and low taste cultures with a double-coding that still holds the integrity of each voice."[58]

Greetings is an extreme case which will, I realize, allow many to say "This is not Shakespeare," but even then, if we truly respect cultural difference, it will have to be admitted that Suzuki has creatively adapted the Scottish play to engage contemporary Japanese sensibilities in as complex and vital a way as, say, Heiner Müller's *HamletMachine,* Robert Wilson's *Lear,* or Peter Greenaway's *Prospero's Books.* When we realize that Shakespeare is not all we need to know in order fully to appreciate the strategies of his usefulness in non-English-speaking countries, then Suzuki's *Greetings* may be seen as no longer speaking from "the edge" but from another, equally important, but not dominant, community center. To quote Sakai Naoki:

Unless the historical and cultural world is seriously challenged and influenced by another, it would never reach awareness that its own world can never be directly equated to the world at large, and would continue to fantasize about itself as being the representative and representation of the totality. Eurocentric history is one of the most typical cases of this: for it, the world does not exist.[59]

The last word on this subject properly belongs to Takahashi Yasunari, whose chapter on *King Lear* closes our Suzuki account.

Suzuki's Shakespeare (II): *King Lear*

Takahashi Yasunari

King Lear (1984–2001) was Suzuki's first work which, instead of being a collage, built itself "single-mindedly" upon a Shakespearean play. (I shall hereafter refer to this work of Suzuki's as *The Tale of Lear*, the title used for English performances). In it Suzuki has refrained from interpolating extraneous texts, although he does heavily cut the original. At the play's first performance (Toga, 1984), this caused certain negative reactions in some of Suzuki's hitherto friendly critics, one even complaining that the version was "uncharacteristic" of Suzuki because it was too "consistent" in the semantic structure of the drama as a whole.

Suzuki has framed Shakespeare's *King Lear* within the fantasy of an old man in a hospital (or nursing home). Obviously an ordinary specimen of present-day society, the Old Man must have suffered similar (although, of course, much more pedestrian) familial misfortunes in his own life. In all probability he was put into the nursing home by his daughters. Apparently he had been reading *King Lear*, and he now identifies with Shakespeare's hero. The storyline of *King Lear* was compressed into a 100-minute show rather faithfully without serious dislocation of the original play, despite an all-male cast and many cuts in the text. The concomitant implication was that the visual beauty of the dancelike movements and the costume was a little too "seamless," as if stylization had become an esthetic end in itself.[1]

Important changes, however, found their way into a new production (Toga, 1988). This version, first performed in English with an all-American cast, was later to be repeated with a mixed cast as well as an all-Japanese cast both in Japan and abroad. Contrary to the impression of "semantic consistency" referred to above, Suzuki exploited to the full that sharply distancing effect which had always characterized his works. The newest and most telling device responsible for this effect was the introduction of the Nurse (played by a male actor). At the outset of the play, she finds a book on the floor beside the chair on which the Old Man is sitting, probably dropped from his hand as he drowsed. The Nurse picks it up and, squatting by the chair, starts reading it silently

247

but avidly,[2] with a box of popcorn beside her. Handel's stately, hypnotic *Largo* announces the beginning of the Old Man's fantasized enacting of the Lear story, but the slow-moving ritualistic entrance of courtiers is disturbed (for the audience although not for the courtiers) by a raucous cackle from the Nurse.

If the play-within-a-play structure was already clear in the first production, the new version added another framework. The continual presence of the Nurse leads us to suspect that the dramatic action going on onstage is not only a figment of the Old Man's fantasy but also a representation in "real time" of what she is reading. We keep wavering between the two possible perspectives. The double framework, in other words, is far from clear-cut. From time to time the structure is turned inside out, and parallelism becomes intersection.

For instance, the Nurse, besides being a nurse and thus situating the drama in a contemporary nursing home, plays the role of the Fool in Shakespeare's text as well. In the "riddles" scene, where Lear and the Fool engage in a one-sided combat of wits about the nose standing in the middle of one's face, or the oyster and its shell (*King Lear*, I.v), the Nurse even manages to carry on a semblance of conversation with the fantasizing Old Man. What she does is to read aloud the lines of the Fool directly from the book she is reading. It may look as if she is improvising, but she is not. Hence a preposterous ambiguity: is this a case of improbable coincidence between the Old Man enacting the story and the Nurse reading it, or should we rather think that the Old Man is enacting just what the Nurse is reading?

Such confounding interactions punctuate and puncture the illusion of the audience, if not of the Old Man. The Nurse's repeated cackles, intruding on the actions taking place on stage, suggest that she probably represents a younger generation for whom Shakespeare's *King Lear*, which she apparently has now come across for the first time in her life, must read like a variety of comicstrip. Her cacophonic laughter bursts out in moments which, in usual interpretations of *King Lear*, would be most unlikely to elicit comic reactions, as, for example, when Goneril tells the blinded Gloucester to "smell his way to Dover," or when the wounded Cornwall says, "Untimely comes this hurt."

The confusion of levels which undermines the illusion is pushed to the extreme when it is seen to involve the Old Man himself. In the Dover scene the Old Man as Lear is wheeled in by the Nurse in a hospital garbage cart. Wearing a washbasin on his head instead of a wreath of flowers, he sits up in the cart and delivers the lines on "the great stage of fools," rising to evermore passionate heights of tragic eloquence as he

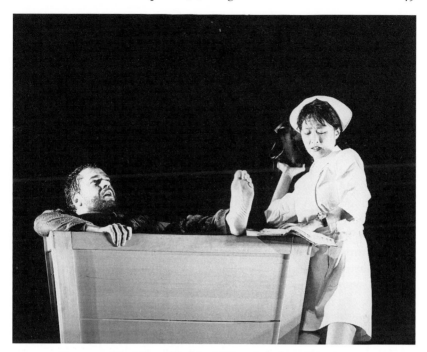

Figure 41 The Nurse (Yoshiyuki Kazuko) plays the role of Fool
during the felt-footed horses scene with King Lear (Tom Hewitt).
King Lear. Tokyo Globe, 1989.

stands precariously balanced on its edge. But something strange happens in between the savage vision of felt-footed horses and the horrendous cry for murder: suddenly noticing that the Nurse is engrossed in the book, he alters the tone of his speech for a second to say, "Will you stop reading, please?" [Figure 41] This is the only instance in the play where Suzuki has ventured to add a "fake line" to the original text. Immediately after this most radically self-destructive turn, the Old Man switches back to his Shakespearean self to cry, "Kill, kill, kill!" and then to implore, "Let me have surgeons, I am cut to the brains" (curiously resonant lines, by the way, in the hospital setting), before running fleet of foot offstage.

It is not just the Old Man who is shocked to see his tragic performance unheeded by the Nurse. We, the audience, are also taken aback: could it be that the Old Man has been aware (at least, partially aware) of reality all the time? We are faced with an enigma similar to the one we experience when reading *Don Quixote*. Ultimately such destabilizings of dramatic unity or clashings of the levels of signification force the audience to ask fundamental questions concerning dramatic experience. What is it that makes a theatrical representation feel truly "authentic"? How can a classic text generate the power to move a contemporary audience? Can it do so only if textual purity is preserved intact, or must one necessarily and consciously bring out the fissure between then and now, there and here? Can the actor relate to the classic or foreign text without articulating the gaps yawning between him and it? How is it that the audience can (if it can) be made aware of the fictitious nature of acting and yet be genuinely moved? Can tragic emotion be at the same time punctured and kept deepening?

Or it might even be arguable at this point that, for Suzuki, Shakespeare's text is merely a pretext in order to pose these questions as pithily as possible to himself, to his actors, and to the audience. But what a formidable task it is! Suzuki has to wrestle with the overwhelming richness of the original text in order to extract what is for him its essential elements through making drastic cuts and rearrangements of lines, scenes, and characters. Kent must be cut; so must the reconciliation scene between Lear and Cordelia (IV.vii) as well as their joint captivity (V.iii). These are some of the precious but ineluctable sacrifices offered on the altar of Suzuki's kind of "theatre of cruelty."

On the other hand, however, it would be rash to complain that Suzuki's vision is simply too gloomy and cruel to let him retain any episodes which might hint at hope of redemption. For instance, it is not true to say that at the end of the blinding scene Suzuki has cut, out of willful cruelty, the concluding lines spoken by Gloucester's two loyal servants: "I'll never care what wickedness I do, / If this man [Cornwall] come to good." Peter Brook, in his famous 1962 production of King Lear, also cut the same redeeming lines. Both Brook and Suzuki are justified in following the text of the First Folio rather than the 1608 Quarto. (Suzuki, admittedly, has gone a step further in making Gloucester himself give Cornwall a wound; but this, I believe, is due to the necessity of reducing the number of characters.)

Or take the final scene. Belying our expectation, the dying Edmund is allowed to say the repentant lines, "Some good I mean to do, / Despite of mine own nature." Most importantly, the entire dramatic action, from the entrance of the Old Man as Lear carrying Cordelia in his arms through to his collapse on top of her body, is enacted with full sincerity, with no tongue in cheek. [Figure 42] There seems to be nothing to undermine the belief that the emotion welling up in the audience is genuinely tragic, except for the fact that Cordelia is played by a bearded male

Figure 42 Lear (Fueda Uichirô) carrying in the dead Cordelia
(Mishima Keita). *King Lear*. Mito ACM theatre, 1993.

actor – or does the fact bother the audience? It is my impression that the
audience has long since ceased to be alienated by it. Even the Nurse,
we observe, joins the others in watching the death of the Old Man / Lear
with what looks like a serious expression.

But the point is that the play does not really end there. We see that the
death of Lear, as enacted in his fantasy, coincides with the actual death
of the Old Man himself on the stage. (The perfect doubling here reminds
me of the effect caused by Samuel Beckett's novel *Malone Dies*, in which
the hero-narrator seems to die precisely as he narrates the death of the
hero of his story.) Or, for that matter, it could be interpreted that both
deaths coincide with the Nurse coming to the last page of the book. All
the characters which have so far been real only to the Old Man, having
played out their roles for him, must now disappear. The stage is left
empty save for two presences – one the body of the Old Man on the
floor, the other the Nurse sitting with the book in the chair, which had
been occupied by her patient at the outset of the play. Then, finishing
the book with great relish, and closing it with a bang, she bursts into
another of her unstoppable laughs. This is the last of what we see and
hear as the stage dissolves into darkness.

The total impression of this ending is absurdly comic without
ceasing to be frighteningly tragic, or rather tragedy and comedy here

passionately and separately assert themselves, insensible to each other. It may be argued that Suzuki here pushes the Absurdist vision of Jan Kott wildly beyond the point that Peter Brook reached in his production. It is as if Suzuki were determined to go against Aristotle, refusing to build up tragic emotions of fear and pity, which the audience needs to taste to the full in order to be released at the end of the play. What he compels us to experience is not a tragic emotion as such but a kind of tragic emotion which simultaneously comprises critical reexamination of itself. The framing device is particularly effective for this purpose. The juxtaposition of the Nurse's comic absorption in the book of *King Lear* with her professional indifference toward her pathetic patient generates a savagely conflicting effect.

Yet it will not do either to look upon *The Tale of Lear* as a comment on the inhuman system of modern hospitals or to read it as an iconoclastic parody of the classic play. It is rather an unflinching anatomy of the human psyche by means of a dramaturgy which can both move us toward a tragic emotion and, at the same time, cast a cold eye on it.

The same goes for the question of "stylization" mentioned earlier. It would have been far too easy for Suzuki, should he have been so minded, to create a self-contained beauty of stylized acting such as we encounter in Noh, Kabuki, and Ninagawa's *Macbeth*. What he does is to keep deconstructing the stylized beauty he has just come closest to creating.

The use, for example, of Handel's *Largo* and Tchaikovsky's *La danse espagnole* might sound beautifully harmonious with the stylized motions of the actors, but we cannot readily yield to the beauty, conscious as we are of the sobering onstage figure of the Nurse. *La danse espagnole* might be arguably a pathetic evocation of the bygone splendor of Lear's royal court, but we must also admit the helpless sentimentality of nostalgia: the meaning of that splendor has obviously grown as incomprehensible to the Old Man as to the audience, as evinced by the indecipherable hieroglyphic finger-signs of the dancers. The whole point seems to me to lie in the ironical gap between the signifier and the signified. The costume of the courtiers also thrives on the ambiguity of its semantics: it looks vaguely medieval, neither Japanese nor Western, suggesting both regal splendor and beggarly tatters. The fact that it does not relate to any specific culture is stressed, paradoxically, by its flagrant contrast with the universality of the modern uniform worn by the Nurse.

The points I have made, however, may not be so obvious to some (if not all) Western spectators as they are to some (if not all) Japanese ones. It is interesting to compare differences in the reactions of American and British critics when the play toured the United States (1988) and London (1994), bearing in mind the fact that the American tour was English-speaking with an all-American cast and the London one was Japanese-speaking with an all-Japanese cast.

On the whole the Americans were more receptive of, in the words of one critic, "Shakespeare the likes of which you've never heard." Although baffled by the "cerebral, and surpassingly strange adaptation of *King Lear*," the critic of *The Washington Post* is able to see the performance as "a meeting place of ritual, reason, and madness." The Nurse's "discomfiting laughter" does not prevent him from taking it as Suzuki's device for maintaining "an ironic distance" from the text. Another critic, writing in *The New Republic*, admits that he finds some parts of the work "a bit too technical and somewhat exotic," but he is surprised to find that the Western actor is "perfectly capable of subduing ego and vanity to an Eastern discipline"; he is open-minded enough to marvel at "how much we can learn from the Orient about our own traditional masterworks." A third reviewer (*Time*) denies that this is an "auteurist direction run riot," stressing that the work "focuses its innovations more on the play's psyche than on the director's." He, too, concludes, "for the most part this work sparks the audiences to think anew about Shakespeare's original intent."[3]

By comparison, British critical reactions were strikingly hostile: "Something coals-to-Newcastle about importing foreign language productions . . . listening to the matchless poetry in an incomprehensible tongue" (*The Daily Telegraph*); "Does the world need another Japanese production set in a mental hospital?" (*The Times*). *The Guardian* critic writes, "Where Shakespeare's *Lear* offers us a fluctuating image of moral chaos, Suzuki's implies that we are all mad or spiritually crippled. It reduces the multi-dimensionality of Shakespeare."

I have, in a way, tried to refute some of these objections in advance. I hope to have shown that Suzuki's power to arouse strong antipathies both abroad and at home derives from his uncompromising questioning of theatrical art. In a Japanese context, however, it may by now be safely surmised that he has traveled so far in his quest for a new dimension of theatricality that few but the die-hard purists among critics would talk about his desecrating the holiness of traditional forms. It would no longer be possible to categorize his style as either Japanesque or Westernized.

It would, then, be a pity if, in the Occident, Suzuki's refusal to join in Bardolatry should be taken to mean disrespect. On the contrary, *The Tale of Lear* should be regarded as a unique way of paying a profound homage to a great Western dramatist who excelled supremely, among other things, in the art of making drama out of metatheatrical questioning of drama. It is, in a sense, another attempt to prove the truth of the poet Ted Hughes's definition of Shakespeare: a "quarry of raw material."[4]

POSTSCRIPT

The Vision of Lear, an operatic version of *The Tale of Lear* on which Suzuki collaborated with Japanese composer Hosokawa Toshio, had its world premier as the opening piece of the Munich Biennale Festival in April 1998. The opera is unique in that, reversing the customary order, here theatrical direction has preceded musical composition. Hosokawa has composed the music to suit the details of Suzuki's *Lear*, with the differences that the Japanese text used by Suzuki has been replaced by Shakespeare's original English, and that the roles of Lear's daughters were performed by female singers. The cast, chosen after auditions for the Munich production, comprised various nationalities: American, German, Japanese, etc. They had undergone a month of intensive workshop and rehearsal in Japan, immersed in Suzuki Training, and learning every physical movement from Suzuki's original cast on what might be called a "man-to-man (or in some cases, man-to-woman)" scheme. The impression I received from the last dress rehearsal in Japan in March 1998, was that Hosokawa's music as embodied by the singers succeeded, despite (or because of) its hypermodern ring, in producing movingly emotional effects at the same time as it made the opera look even more hypnotically ritualistic than the drama.

   As for the Nurse, Suzuki and Hosokawa agreed that she should be the only character in the opera who did not sing: she was played by the same male actor (Katoh) who had played the part in the last version of the drama. Incidentally, I should add that, already in the last dramatic version as well as in this operatic version, there appeared on stage a second Nurse (Nîhori), also played by a male actor, the first Nurse's minor double, as it were, with no lines to speak, augmenting the grotesque and the comic. The Nurse's function (I treat the two Nurses collectively as a singular presence here) remained the same as I have described above, both alienating and highlighting the poetic tragedy with her comic guffaws. The German critical responses in *Berliner Zeitung*, *Frankfurter Allgemeine*, *Süddeutsche Zeitung*, and others seem to have ranged from rave to puzzled wonder.

Notes

Chapter One. Rethinking Japanese theatre: cracking the codes

1. Robert Wilson, "Theatre That You Have to Rethink," in *SCOT: Suzuki Company of Toga*, trans. Takahashi Yasunari, Matsuoka Kazuko, Frank Hoff, Leon Ingulsrud, and Jordan Sand (Tokyo: Japan Performing Arts Center, 1991), 82. Hereafter cited as SCOT booklet.
2. *One Step on a Journey* and *The Chronicle of Macbeth*, dir. Tony Chapman and Zi-Yin Wang, SBS TV, 1992.
3. "*Reading Suzuki Tadashi's* The Chronicle of Macbeth *in Australia*," ed. Ian Carruthers (unpublished proceedings of the Melbourne Performance Research Group Conference at Melbourne University, October 3–4 1992). Hereafter cited as "Reading Suzuki in Australia."
4. See, for example, Noel Purdon in *The Adelaide Review*, March 1992, and David Gyger in *Opera Australia*, April 1992; also audience response statistics in Ian Carruthers and Patricia Mitchell, *Theatre East and West: Problems of Difference or Problems of Perception?* La Trobe University Asian Studies Papers, Research Series no. 6 (Melbourne: La Trobe University, 1995), 20–30, 40–43.
5. Wilson, "Theatre That You Have to Rethink," in SCOT booklet.
6. Suzuki Tadashi, *Engeki ronshû: ekkyô suru chikara* (*Collected Theatre Writings: Energy that Knows No Boundaries*), (Tokyo: Parco, 1984), 142; also Gotoh Yukihiro, "Suzuki Tadashi: Innovator of Contemporary Japanese Theatre," doctoral thesis, University of Hawaii, 1988, 20. Hereafter cited as Suzuki thesis.
7. The writing of Tanizaki Junichirô offers an earlier similar stance. See Masao Miyoshi, *Off Center: Power and Culture Relations between Japan and the United States* (Cambridge, Mass.: Harvard University Press, 1994), 126–48, especially 127: "[Tanizaki's] attitude towards both the 'traditional' and the 'new' Japan was from the very beginning problematic – that is, equivocal, qualified, tentative, ironic – and he seems to have been quite at ease with this ambiguity."
8. Saitoh Setsurô, ed., *Suzuki Tadashi no sekai* (*The World of Suzuki Tadashi*), (Tokyo: Shinpyôsha, 1982), 118–28. Trans. Noyuri Liddicutt and Ian Carruthers. Hereafter cited as *Suzuki Tadashi no sekai*.
9. *Suzuki Tadashi no sekai*, 124; 46–47, 49.
10. Kan Takayuki, *Sengo engeki* (*The Postwar Japanese Theatre*), (Tokyo: Asahi shinbunsha, 1981), 131; Gotoh, Suzuki thesis, 23.
11. There were 5,800,000 demonstrators a day in Tokyo alone, according to Takabatake Michitoshi, "'Shûdan gurumi undô' o kanô ni shita heiwa to

minshushugi no jikkan" ("The feeling of peace and democracy that enabled the 'Mass Movement'"), in *Asahi jânaru*, October 1 1981, 30–37; Gotoh, Suzuki thesis, 27. See also George R. Packard III, *Protest in Tokyo: The Security Treaty Crisis of 1960* (Princeton: Princeton University Press, 1966).

12. *Suzuki Tadashi no sekai*, 46, 49.

13. Ibid., 52.

14. Ibid.

15. Ibid., 60–62.

16. Ibid., 56.

17. Suzuki Tadashi, "Shojo-saku izen: Waseda Daigaku Jiyû Butai jidai" ("Before My First Professional Production: the Era of the Waseda University Free Stage"), in *Betsuyaku Minoru no sekai* (*The World of Minoru Betsuyaku*), (Tokyo: Shinpyôsha, 1982), 11–13; Gotoh, Suzuki thesis, 31.

18. *Suzuki Tadashi no sekai*, 55.

19. Takahashi Hidemoto, Matsumoto Yoshiko, and Saitoh Ikuko, eds., *Gekiteki naru mono o megutte: Suzuki Tadashi to sono sekai* (*On the Dramatic Passions: the World of Suzuki Tadashi*), (Tokyo: Kôsakusha, 1977), 41. Trans. Noyuri Liddicutt and Ian Carruthers. Hereafter cited as *Gekiteki ST*.

20. *Suzuki Tadashi no sekai*, 64.

21. Bungakuza (Literary Theatre Company), Haiyûza (Actors' Theatre Company), and Mingeiza (People's Art Company).

22. *Suzuki Tadashi no sekai*, 72. For the theatre culture of the time, see Thomas R. H. Havens, *Artist and Patron in Postwar Japan: Dance, Music, Theatre, and the Visual Arts, 1955–1980* (Princeton, N. J.: Princeton University Press, 1982), 144–80.

23. J. Thomas Rimer, trans., *The Way of Acting: the Theatre Writings of Tadashi Suzuki* (New York: Theatre Communications Group, 1986), 102, 110.

24. *Gekiteki ST*, 42.

25. Fujita Hiroshi, "Mittsu no gekidan: Kansai Geijutsuza to Sehai to Jiyû Butai" ("Three Companies: The Kansai Arts, Young Actors and Free Stage"), in *Shingeki*, June 1962, 42–44; trans. Gotoh, Suzuki thesis, 43.

26. Directed by Suzuki Tadashi for NHK TV broadcast, 1969.

27. Tsuno Kaitarô, "Preface to *The Elephant*," in *Concerned Theatre Japan*, 1.3 1970, 60–70, 60; trans. Gotoh, Suzuki thesis, 44.

28. David Goodman, *Four Japanese Plays of Hiroshima and Nagasaki* (New York: Columbia University Press, 1986), 185, 190.

29. Suzuki's program notes for his 1994 RSC Barbican production of *King Lear* and 1995 Delphi *Elektra* were still entitled "The World as a Hospital."

30. *Gekiteki ST*, 43.

31. Ibid., 46.

32. *Suzuki Tadashi no sekai*, 75.

33. Ibid., 75. Senda Koreya comments on the conservatism of mainstream audiences who "want to see famous plays with famous stars." See *Concerned Theatre Japan*, Summer 1970, 72–73; Havens, *Artist and Patron*, 156n.

34. *Suzuki Tadashi no sekai*, 78.
35. Ibid., 78–79.
36. Ibid., 79; Takubo himself puts it at 1,670,000 yen on p.190.
37. Havens, *Artist and Patron*, 159.
38. "Chû" is an alternative reading of the "Tada" in "Tadashi" and onomatopoeically suggests the "cute" sounds of a mouse or suckling child.
39. *Suzuki Tadashi no sekai*, 190.
40. *The Little Match Girl*, in Robert T. Rolf and John K. Gillespie, eds., *Alternative Japanese Drama: Ten Plays* (Honolulu: Hawaii University Press, 1992), 27–51, 36.
41. Rolf and Gillespie, *Alternative Japanese Drama*, 17.
42. Dômoto Masaki, "Kabe no naka no hanabana" ("Flowers Within Walls"), in *Shingeki*, January 1966, 90–94, 93; Gotoh, Suzuki thesis, 53.
43. Takada Ichirô, "Gendai no butai hyôgen" ("Modern Stage Expression"), in *Teatoro*, January 1968, 75–81, 78; Gotoh, Suzuki thesis, 50.
44. Suzuki Tadashi, *Engekiron: katari no chihei* (*Collected Theatre Writings: Horizons of Deception*), (Tokyo: Hakusuisha, 1980), 215–16; trans. Gotoh, Suzuki thesis, 52.
45. *Suzuki Tadashi no sekai*, 80.
46. Suzuki Tadashi, *Naikaku no wa: Suzuki Tadashi engeki ronshû* (*The Sum of the Interior Angles: Suzuki Tadashi's Collected Theatre Writings*), (Tokyo: Jiritsushôbô, 1973), 304–5. Trans. Tony McGillycuddy and Ian Carruthers. Hereafter cited as *Naikaku*.
47. Gotoh, Suzuki thesis, 71; for review, see also Kudô Takashi, "Koten engeki no jizoku to jisoku" ("Continuation and Self-Support of Classic Theatres"), in *Shingeki*, July 1968, 66.
48. *Gekiteki ST*, 57–58; Gotoh, Suzuki thesis, 76.
49. Asô Tadashi, "Iyoku-saku zoroi daga" ("Despite Many Enthusiastic Works"), in *Teatoro*, February 1969, 73, includes a review of *The Lower Depths*; Gotoh, Suzuki thesis, 74.
50. The film of *Marat/Sade* was released in 1967. Kanze Hideo, a colleague of Suzuki, certainly knew of it when he was interviewed by Albert Harris in 1971. For him the production's most interesting feature was the fact that "each actor had to express two different personalities." See Albert Harris, "This Radical Noh: a study of two productions by Kanze Hisao and Kanze Hideo," doctoral thesis, Ohio State University, 1973, 365. Kurosawa's *Dodesukaden*, a recontextualization of Gorki's play to postwar Japan, was also in development.
51. *Suzuki Tadashi no sekai*, 153
52. David Goodman, *Japanese Drama and Culture in the 1960s: the Return of the Gods* (Armonk, N.Y.: M. E. Sharpe Inc., 1988), 179–223.
53. Asô, "Iyoku-saku," 73–74; trans. Gotoh, "Suzuki thesis," 75.
54. There is a pun here. Miiko was the nickname of Takahashi Michiko, the actress who played the central role.

55. For example, in the essay "Riken no ken" in *Naikaku* (61) Suzuki discusses the contemporary relevance to the actor of Zeami's theory of self-objectification. See J. Thomas Rimer and Yamazaki Masakazu, *On the Art of the Nô Drama: the Major Treatises of Zeami* (Princeton, N.J.: Princeton University Press, 1984), 81. Suzuki argues that "[t]hese views of Zeami are demonstrated in the following excerpt from *The Relationship between Infants and Adults* by Merleau-Ponty" (61–62). Later on in *Naikaku*, in "Engeki no kotoba" ("Theatrical Language"), Suzuki states that, "collage is not a dishonourable pursuit if it is understood as a technique supported by the theory of surrealism . . . my conscious state whenever I direct is always a wish to achieve the unconscious. In fact, when I direct a piece on stage, I construct at one time and in one place a wide variety of styles that have propagated by themselves in my memory, rather than building a homogenous set of verbal raw materials. Critics may describe this as parody, but I prefer to think of it as *honkadori* ['allusive variation,' a term from medieval Japanese poetry] . . . I might describe this metaphorically as an act of breaking down one set of value perceptions, while at the same time constructing another set of value perceptions . . . So when on stage, I cause a slippage in the words I speak and the actual physical movements I make as a means of providing a glimpse of something the audience was not anticipating. This making physical perceptions themselves into words may also be an influence from Merleau-Ponty" (229–32).
56. *Naikaku*, 303–4.
57. Ibid., 292.
58. *Gekiteki ST*, 205–6.
59. *Suzuki Tadashi no sekai*, 151–52.
60. See Glenn Shaw, trans., *Tôjûrô's Love and Four Other Plays by Kikuchi Kan* (Tokyo: Hokuseido, 1925), 13.
61. *Suzuki Tadashi no sekai*, 152–53.
62. See Brian Powell, *Kabuki in Modern Japan: Mayama Seika and his Plays* (New York: St. Martin's Press, 1990).
63. *Naikaku*, 296–98.
64. J. A. Schumpeter, *The Theory of Economic Development* (Oxford: Oxford University Press, 1911, rept. 1961).
65. Rolf and Gillespie, *Alternative Japanese Drama*, 252.
66. James Brandon, "Training at the Waseda Little Theatre: the Suzuki Method," in *The Drama Review*, 22.4 1978, 29–42, 31; although Brandon describes training in 1976, Suzuki asserts "we began working out the disciplines in 1972," and a 1969 photograph of *Dramatic Passions I* suggests that at least the Kanjinchô discipline was operative by then.
67. Yagi Shûichirô in *Gekiteki ST*, 194, 197.
68. Frank Hoff, "Suzuki Tadashi: the Sum of Interior Angles," in *The Canadian Theatre Review* 20 1978, 20–27, 24.

69. Sekiguchi Ei et al., "Shui" ("Prospectus"), in *Shingeki*, February 1972, 68–69; trans. Gotoh, Suzuki thesis, 84. For similar conflicts within the Little Theatre movement in England, see Steve Gooch, *All Together Now* (London: Methuen, 1984), especially 39–40, 46–47.

70. Ôzasa Yoshio, *Dôjidai engeki to gekisakka-tachi* (*Contemporary Theatre and Playwrights*) (Tokyo: Kôsôsha, 1980), 104; Gotoh, Suzuki thesis, 84.

71. See Ayako Hotta-Lister, *The Japan-British Exhibition of 1910* (Midsomer Norton, Avon: Japan Library, Curzon Press, 1999), 221–22.

72. Jean-Louis Barrault, *Souvenirs pour demain* (Paris: Editions de Seuil, 1972), 293–94; trans. Jonathan Griffin, *Memories for Tomorrow: the Memoirs of Jean-Louis Barrault* (London: Thames and Hudson, 1974), 250. See also John K. Gillespie, "Aesthetic Impact of Noh on Modern French Theatre," doctoral thesis, Indiana University, 1979, 261.

73. *Kanze Hisao: shika no fûshi* (*Hisao Kanze: the Form of the Final Flower*), (Tokyo: Heibonsha, 1979). Photograph 2 pages before p.85.

74. Harris, "This Radical Noh," 31.

75. Barrault, *Souvenirs*, 292; trans. Griffin, *Memories*, 248.

76. Ibid., 292; trans. Griffin, *Memories*, 249

77. Rimer, *The Way of Acting*, 26

78. James Brandon, "Shakespeare in Kabuki," in Minami Ryuta, Ian Carruthers, and John Gillies, eds., *Performing Shakespeare in Japan* (Cambridge: Cambridge University Press, 2001), 49–50.

79. Donald Keene, *Nô and Bunraku* (New York: Columbia University Press, 1973), 43.

80. A dramatic dance with a special tempo performed before the masked *shite* (main actor) jumps "blind" into a falling bell (lined with lead weights) in the Noh play *Dôjôji*.

81. Harris, "This Radical Noh," 34.

82. *Oedipus* program, in ibid., 207.

83. Rimer, *The Way of Acting*, 70.

84. Ibid., 71–73.

85. *Suzuki Tadashi no sekai*, 86.

86. "Kawaraban: man'in fudadome de omemie" ("News: Sold Out Performance"), in *Shingeki*, November 1972, 25; trans. Gotoh, Suzuki thesis, 143.

87. *Gekiteki ST*, 169.

88. This was almost unheard of at the time. Havens's research shows that "[b]y one count, the average number of performances for plays put on in Tokyo by the nine top companies fell from 14.9 in 1965 to 10.5 in 1976, and it is even lower today. Houses customarily held 300 to 500 spectators and were rarely more than two-thirds full, unless the bill was Shakespeare or *Streetcar*. Only Shiki [the largest commercial company producing musicals] could count on drawing 10,000 or more to each of its five regular productions." Havens, *Artist and Patron*, 160.

89. *Suzuki Tadashi no sekai*, 192–93.
90. Shiraishi Kayoko featured in a cameo role in the first, and not at all in the second.
91. The Shizuoka Performing Arts Center publication on the 1999 Second International Theatre Olympics opens with an article by Nakamura Yûjirô and Isozaki Arata and concludes with a review by Takahashi Yasunari of the First Theatre Olympics. See *Theatre Olympics techô: bessatsu gekijô bunka* (*Theatre Olympics Notebook: Theatre Culture Supplement*) (Shizuoka: SPAC, 1999).

Chapter Two. Inaugurating an age of decentralization

1. Saitoh Setsurô, ed., *Suzuki Tadashi no sekai* (*The World of Suzuki Tadashi*), (Tokyo: Shinpyôsha, 1982), 92. Trans. Noyuri Liddicutt and Ian Carruthers. In the same volume see also the section on "The Risks of Worldly Success" in Takahashi Yasunari and Suzuki Tadashi, "Engeki o kataru: zen'ei to koten no kakawari" ("Theatrical Discussion: the Connection Between Avant-garde and Traditional Theatre"), 138.
2. *Suzuki Tadashi no sekai*, 106. The anti-Stanislavkian comment is reminiscent of Meyerhold's "the play will be read in costume and makeup." See Edward Braun, ed. and trans., *Meyerhold on Theatre* (London: Eyre Methuen, 1969), 125.
3. J. Thomas Rimer, *The Way of Acting: the Theatre Writings of Tadashi Suzuki* (New York: Theatre Communications Group, 1986), 80–1.
4. *Kôdansha Encyclopedia of Japan*, ed. Gen Itasaka (Tokyo: Kôdansha, 1983), vol. 8, 176.
5. *Suzuki Tadashi no sekai*, 100.
6. Ibid., 102.
7. Rimer, *The Way of Acting*, 81.
8. *Suzuki Tadashi no sekai*, 182.
9. According to Thomas Havens in his *Artist and Patron in Postwar Japan: Dance, Music, Threatre, and the Visual Arts, 1955–1980* (Princeton, N.J.: Princeton University Press, 1982), "production expenses tripled between 1960 and 1970, then more than doubled again during the next ten years, rising 48 percent faster than the overall cost of living in Tokyo during the same two decades. Faced with these figures, the shingeki groups began refusing to take costly chances on new or experimental plays" (162). In footnote support of this argument, Havens cites an article by Kurabayashi in which he "puts the cost of an average production at [US] $5,555 in 1960, $12,500 in 1965, $16,666 in 1970, $30,000 in 1975, and $67,500 in 1980 at prevailing rates of exchange. In current yen terms, on an index with 1960 as 100, this represents a rise to 300 in 1970 and 625 by 1980. The Tokyo consumer index rose from 100 in 1960 to 176 in 1970 and 422 in 1980." See Kurabayashi Seiichirô, "Zuisôteki ni sengo shingeki o kangaeru" ("Occasional Essays: Thoughts on Postwar Shingeki"), part 3, in *Teatoro*, May 1979, 110.

10. Rimer, *The Way of Acting*, 94.

11. *Suzuki Tadashi no sekai*, 90–96.

12. *Kôdansha Encyclopedia of Japan*, vol. 8, 176.

13. Marilyn Ivy, *Discourses of the Vanishing: Modernity, Phantasm, Japan* (Chicago: Chicago University Press, 1995), 34ff. For the "Exotic Japan" poster, see p. 52.

14. Rimer, *The Way of Acting*, 101.

15. Ibid., 102; *Suzuki Tadashi no sekai*, 194. To Suzuki's Spring and Summer Festivals, the Toga municipality would add a Buckwheat (*Soba*) Festival and a Snow Festival in February.

16. "Toga: Village for Theatre," in *Profile of a Nation: the Japanese People and their Activities, Part IV*, Kyodo TV (for the Ministry of Foreign Affairs), 1985.

17. *Suzuki Tadashi no sekai*, 94–95.

18. Ibid., 90.

19. Ibid., 105–6.

20. Ibid., 185–86.

21. Senda Akihiko, "Waseda Shôgekijô Toga Sanbô kaijô kinen kôen" ("the Waseda Little Theatre's Inaugural Performance at the Toga Mountain Hall"), in *Bijutsu techô*, November 1976, 114–15; Gotoh Yukihiro, "Suzuki Tadashi: Innovator of Contemporary Japanese Theatre," doctoral thesis, University of Hawaii, 1988, 156.

22. Mori Hideo, "*Utage no yoru* wa ame datta" ("It Rained for *Night and Feast*"), in *Shingeki*, November 1976, 22–27.

23. Inspired by Yanagita Kunio's *Legends of Tôno* (trans. Ronald A. Morse [Tokyo: the Japan Foundation, 1975]) and the writings of his disciple Origuchi Shinobu, Kanze Hisao had studied the 400-year-old tradition of folk Noh performance in Kurokawa village, Yamagata. He and Suzuki were responding individually and artistically to the "folklore boom" of the 1960s and 1970s. See Hori Ichirô, *Nihon no shâmanism* (Tokyo: Kôdansha, 1971); Yamagami Izumo, *Miko no rekishi* (Tokyo: Yûzankaku, 1971); Honda Yasuji, *Nihon no matsuri to geinô* (Tokyo: Kinshôsha, 1974); and Carmen Blacker, *The Catalpa Bow: a Study of Shamanic Practices in Japan* (London: Allen and Unwin, 1975).

24. *Suzuki Tadashi no sekai*, 98.

25. Ibid., 96–97, 143.

26. Ibid., 104.

27. Ibid., 184–85.

28. Ibid., 118.

29. Ibid., 143.

30. *Nonsensu Taizen (Summa Nonsensologica)* (Tokyo: Shobunsha, 1977) and *Doke no bungaku (The Literature of the Fool)* (Tokyo: Chûôkôronsha, 1977), on Beckett, Carroll, Shakespeare, Cervantes, and Rabelais.

31. Takahashi Yasunari, "*Kagami to kanran* or *The Looking Glass and Cabbages*," in *The Looking Glass Letter* (the Lewis Carroll Society of Japan Newsletter), no. 3, February 1995, 6.

32. Takahashi, *The Looking Glass Letter*, 6–7.
33. Suzuki Tadashi, *Katei no igaku* (*Home Medicine*), in *Shingeki*, February 1979, 176–94. Trans. Eguchi Kazuko and Ian Carruthers.
34. Senda Akihiko, "Fuhen no ashimoto" ("The Universality of Walking"), in *Shingeki*, October 1979, 26, 29.
35. Braun, *Meyerhold on Theatre*, 199.
36. *Suzuki Tadashi no sekai*, 104.
37. Rimer, *The Way of Acting*, 23.
38. Senda Akihiko, "Waseda Shôgekijô," in *Bijutsu techô*, 115; Gotoh, Suzuki thesis, 156.
39. William O. Beeman, "Tadashi Suzuki: The Word is an Act of the Body," in *Performing Arts Journal*, 5:2 1981, 89.
40. See Okuni's recycling of shamanic and Noh elements to create Kabuki in Akemi Horie-Webber, "A Study of Folk Religious Elements in the Early Kabuki Theatre," doctoral thesis, University of California at Berkeley, 1982, 22, 99.
41. J. Thomas Rimer, trans., *The Voyage of Contemporary Japanese Theatre: Senda Akihiko* (Honolulu: Hawaii University Press, 1997), 168–71.
42. Uchino Tadashi, "Images of Armageddon: Japan's 1980s Theatre Culture," in *The Drama Review*, 44:1 Spring 2000, 86.
43. *Suzuki Tadashi no sekai*, 99.
44. Readers interested may consult pages 64–65 of the SCOT booklet (*SCOT: Suzuki Company of Toga*, trans. Takahashi Yasunari, Matsuoka Kazuko, Frank Hoff, Leon Ingulsrud, and Jordan Sand [Tokyo: Performing Arts Center, 1992]) for a list of performers invited to Toga between 1982 and 1991. Saitoh Ikuko has kindly provided me with copies of all company programs.
45. Rimer, *The Way of Acting*, 95.
46. Janny Donker, *The President of Paradise: a Traveller's Account of Robert Wilson's* the "*CIVIL warS*" (Amsterdam: International Theatre Bookshop, 1985), 59.
47. Arthur Holmberg, *The Theatre of Robert Wilson* (Cambridge: Cambridge University Press, 1996), 23–24.
48. Donker, *President of Paradise*, 105–10.
49. Ibid., 59–61.
50. Ibid., 55. According to Saitoh Ikuko, Wilson also wanted the Kabuki *onnagata* Bandô Tamasaburô, but he was unavailable.
51. Donker, *President of Paradise*, 58-59.
52. In reality it was President Grant who saw Noh on a state visit to Japan in 1879. See Donald Keene, *Nôh and Bunraku* (New York: Columbia University Press, 1973), 44.
53. Donker, *President of Paradise*, 66.
54. Ibid., 65.
55. Ishii Tatsuhiko, "Higeki: Atoreusu-ke no hôkai no muzan na shippai" ("The Miserable Failure of 'Tragedy: The Tragic Fall of the House of Atreus'"), in *Asahi Journal*, January 16 1984, 99; Gotoh, Suzuki thesis, 163.

56. Suzuki Tadashi, *Engeki to wa nani ka (What is Theatre?)*, (Tokyo: Iwanami Shoten, 1988), 122. Trans. Kameron Steele and Ian Carruthers (1–114), and Kumi West and Ian Carruthers (115–71).

57. Milwaukee Repertory Theater, StageWest of Springfield, M.A., Berkeley Repertory Theatre, and Washington D.C.'s Arena Stage.

58. Arthur Holmberg, "The Liberation of Lear", in *American Theater*, July/August 1988, 12–19, 12.

59. Shiraishi would go on performing freelance, most notably as the Waki to Kanze Hideo's Shite in a performance of *Sotoba Komachi* directed by the Butoh artist Tanaka Min in August 1995 at Hakushu in Yamanashi-ken; and as Titania in Ninagawa Yukio's *A Midsummer Night's Dream*, 1994.

60. Many Butoh artists had already toured abroad, and Ashikawa, the last and most important disciple of Hijikata Tatsumi, had won acclaim at the Paris Festival d'Automne as early as 1978. See Jean Viala and Nourit Masson-Sekine, *Butoh: Shades of Darkness* (Tokyo: Shufunotomo, 1988), 98–99.

61. Ashikawa was performing Sonia in Suzuki's *Uncle Vania* in Toga in the summer of 1989. Jim De Vita had played in Suzuki's bilingual *King Lear* at the Tokyo Globe in April 1989.

62. Suzuki, *What is Theatre?*, 117.

63. See the ACM Mito homepage <http://www.co.jp/mito/Tower/ isozaki3.html> page 2. For photographs of the Mito arts complex and the ACM theatre, see K. Itoh et al., eds., S. D. Henshûbun, *Arata Isozaki, 1985– 1991, Part I* (Tokyo: Kajima shuppankai, 1993), 28–29; *Part II (1976–1984)* contains photographs of Isozaki's other constructions for Suzuki.

64. Suzuki, "Three Facets of European Drama" and "European Drama from a Director's Perspective," in *What is Theatre?*, 26–48.

65. Suzuki, *What is Theatre?*, 89.

66. In Japanese, Saratoga means "south Toga," an in-joke among SCOT actors.

67. Bogart has generously acknowledged her debt to Suzuki in *A Director Prepares* (London: Routledge, 2001); chapter 5 in particular begins with an illuminating anecdote on Suzuki's attitude toward Shiraishi's performance work, and goes on to discuss "stereotypes" positively in terms of Japanese *kata* (movement patterns).

68. See Ian Carruthers, "Deny Thy Father and Refuse Thy Name: Suzuki Tadashi's *Waiting for Romeo*," in *Asian Studies Review*, 20:3 April 1997, 26–34.

69. Warren Susman, *Culture as History: the Transformation of American Society in the Twentieth Century* (New York: Pantheon, 1984), cited in Peter Hall, *Cities in Civilization* (London: Weidenfeld and Nicolson, 1998), 977–78.

70. See *Shizuoka-ken butai geijutsu kôen – shisetsu gaiyô (Shizuoka Performing Arts Park – an Outline of the Facilities)* for photographs of Nihondaira facilities. For photographs of the theatres in Granship, see *Granship Magazine* (March 1998).

71. The Second International Theatre Olympics opened on April 16 with Robert Wilson's *Hamlet: A Monologue* and Suzuki's *Cyrano de Bergerac*, followed by

Zhang Zhong Xue's *Chuan Ji* (April 17), Mark Zakharov's production of Chekhov's *The Seagull* (April 23), and Jean-Claude Gallotta's dance piece *Almost Don Quixote* (April 30).

In May several younger groups were given a showing (thus fulfilling the letter of the Charter contract about "training and encouragement" of younger generations), Miyagi Satoshi directing Hirata Oriza's adaptation of the Kabuki classic *Chûshingura*, and Gerhard Bohner a dance piece, *In the Golden Section* (May 1). These were followed by Les Ballets Africains' dance spectacle *Heritage* (May 4), Monica Viñao directing Javier Daulte's *Geometria* (May 5), Jean-Claude Gallotta directing the SPAC dancers in *La Chamoule* (May 7), Omar Porras-Speck producing Lorca's *Blood Wedding* (May 8), Tony Harrison reading *Fire and Poetry* (May 14), Georges Lavaudant with Brecht's *A Respectable Wedding* (May 15), Suzuki directing a Roger Reynolds music-theatre collage called *At the Edge* (May 21), Daniele Desnoyers with his dance piece *Discordantia* (May 22), and Suzuki again with *King Lear* (May 26).

Nuria Espert's *La Oscura Raiz* (based on Lorca's *Blood Wedding*) and Theodoros Terzopoulos's version of Heiner Müller's *Hercules* (in a co-production by Greece and Turkey) opened on June 4. They gave way to Robert Wilson's *Madame Butterfly* (an American, Italian, and Japanese co-production) on June 5, Pawel Nowicki's *Don Juan de Molière* (June 6), Yuri Lyubimov's adaptation of Dostoyevsky's *The Brothers Karamazov* (June 10), Antunes Filho's *The Trojan Women* (June 11), and Suzuki and Hosokawa's opera *Vision of Lear* (June 12). The latter closed the festival. (Only opening dates are given above.)

72. Theatre InterAction pamphlet, 1996; trans. Eguchi Kazuko and Ian Carruthers.

73. For example, Ninagawa Yukio teaches in Tokyo at Tôhô Gakuen College, Senda Akihiko at Shizuoka University of Art and Culture, and Hirata Oriza at Obirin University.

74. Suzuki, *What is Theatre?*, 90.

75. Ibid., 130.

76. Theatre artists were known derisively as *Kawaramono kojiki*, "beggars of the dry riverbeds" (riverbeds were performance areas in summer because they were public land and required no rent). These strolling players were at the very bottom of the social scale but, perhaps because of their "untouchable" status, were believed to be endowed with "magical" powers (what Suzuki prefers to call "artistic objectification").

77. Suzuki, *What is Theatre?*, 131.

Chapter Three. Suzuki Training: the sum of the interior angles

1. James Brandon, "Training at the Waseda Little Theatre: the Suzuki Method." *The Drama Review*, 22:4 1978, 29–42. Page numbers for all subsequent references to this edition are given in parenthesis after each quotation.

2. Gotoh Yukihiro, "The Grammar of the Body," in "Suzuki Tadashi: Innovator of Contemporary Japanese Theatre," doctoral thesis, University of Hawaii, 1988, 183–237.

3. Paul Allain, "Suzuki Training," in *The Drama Review*, 42:1 1998, 66–89.

4. Kevin Saari, "Suzuki Training" and "The Relationship of Suzuki Training and Viewpoints," in "The Work of Anne Bogart and the Saratoga Theatre Institute: A New Model for Actor Training," Ph.D thesis, University of Kansas, 1999, 134–76, 177–202.

5. I gratefully acknowledge Deborah Leiser-Moore's generosity in allowing me to read her Suzuki masterclass notes from 1991.

6. J. Thomas Rimer, *The Way of Acting: the Theatre Writings of Tadashi Suzuki* (New York: Theatre Communications Group, 1986), 8.

7. Ibid., 6.

8. Julian Hilton, *Performance* (London: Macmillan, 1987), 93, 97.

9. Anne Bogart, *a director prepares* (London: Routledge, 2001), 144. See also J. Thomas Rimer and Yamazaki Masakazu, *On the Art of the Nô Drama: the Major Treatises of Zeami* (Princeton, N.J.: Princeton University Press, 1984), 76; Yoshi Oida and Lorna Marshall, *The Invisible Actor* (London: Methuen, 1997), 42; and Eugenio Barba and Nicola Savarese, *A Dictionary of Theatre Anthropology: The Secret Art of the Performer* (London: Routledge, 1991), 14, 88.

10. "Interview with Suzuki Tadashi [1995]," in Minami Ryuta, Ian Carruthers, and John Gillies, eds., *Performing Shakespeare in Japan* (Cambridge: Cambridge University Press, 2001), 204.

11. Rimer, *The Way of Acting*, 12.

12. Deborah Leiser-Moore's Toga training notes, 6.

13. Interview after *Dionysus* in the NHK TV series *Suzuki Tadashi no sekai* (*The World of Suzuki Tadashi*), 1993.

14. Saari, "The Work of Anne Bogart," 343–44.

15. Taken from my field notes for Suzuki Training in Melbourne, September 1991, 1:54. See also Suzuki's distinction between two basic types of trainee in Minami, Carruthers, and Gillies, eds., *Performing Shakespeare in Japan*, 204.

16. Ibid., 202.

17. Brandon, "Training at the Waseda Little Theatre," *The Drama Review*, 30.

18. "This point of focus is needed in order for actors to have something to relate to [outside themselves]." For Suzuki the audience replaces the priest of Dionysus in the modern theatre as the focus of attention. See Leiser-Moore, notes, 18.

19. Barba and Savarese, *Dictionary of Theatre Anthropology*, 12.

20. Ibid.

21. Rimer and Yamazaki, *On the Art of the Nô Drama*, 75.

22. Ibid., 81.

23. Bogart, *a director prepares*, 93.

24. *W. B. Yeats: The Poems*, ed. Richard J. Finneran (London: Macmillan, 1984)

25. Donald Keene, *Anthology of Japanese Literature* (New York: Grove Press, 1955; rept. 1960), 258–59.

26. Illustrations of these exercises may be found in Brandon, "Training at the Waseda Little Theatre"; Gotoh, Suzuki thesis; and Allain, "Suzuki Training".

27. *Ma* is perhaps best known in the West through Isozaki Arata's "Space-Time in Japan: *MA* Exhibition" in Paris, November 1983. See K. Itoh et al., eds., S. D. Henshûbun, *Arata Isozaki, 1976–1984* (Tokyo: Kajima shuppankai, 1984; rept. 1991), 112–13.

28. Rimer and Yamazaki, *On the Art of the Nô Drama*, 81; Barba and Savarese, *Dictionary of Theatre Anthropology*, 109.

29. Brandon, "Training at the Waseda Little Theatre," 37–39.

30. Leiser-Moore, "Shakuhachi," in training notes, 2.

31. Cicely Berry, *The Actor and his Text* (London: Harrap, 1987), 25.

32. Ibid, 24, 28, 22, 26.

33. My field notes from Melbourne training, September 1991.

34. Training notes, September 1991, I:26.

35. Gotoh, Suzuki thesis, 227.

36. Brandon's "Duck Walk" suggests instability or clumsiness. It is referred to as "Cockroach walk" by Suzuki's actors to evoke the smoothness and stability required.

37. Saari has adequately addressed Allain's objections ("Suzuki Training," 81–84) to the use of Suzuki voice in English from the SITI perspective (Saari "The Work of Anne Bogart," 194–96).

38. Edward Braun, ed. and trans., *Meyerhold on Theatre* (London: Eyre Methuen, 1969), 89, 91.

39. Ibid., 65, 86, 97–100, 112, 117, 141, 149, 258.

40. Arthur Holmberg, *The Theatre of Robert Wilson* (Cambridge: Cambridge University Press, 1996), 146.

41. Ibid., 13. My italics.

42. Suzuki Tadashi, *Engeki to wa nanika (What is Theatre?)*, (Tokyo: Iwanami shoten, 1988), 140. Trans. Kameron Steele and Ian Carruthers (1–114), and Kumi West and Ian Carruthers (115–71). Suzuki builds on Zeami's theory of performance, as can be seen in Rimer and Yamazaki, *On the Art of the Nô Drama*, 18–20.

43. Minami, Carruthers, and Gillies, eds., *Performing Shakespeare in Japan*, 123.

Chapter Four. Adaptation of Japanese classics: *On the Dramatic Passions II* and *John Silver*

1. *Gekiteki ST*, 57.

2. Gotoh Yukihiro, "Suzuki Tadashi: Innovator of Contemporary Japanese Theatre," doctoral thesis, University of Hawaii, 1988, 80; Senda Akihiko, "Jûjiro

mokuroku" ("Catalogue Crossroads"), in *Dôjidai engeki* (*Contemporary Theatre*) 3 1970, 175.

3. Takahashi Hidemoto, Matsumoto Yoshiko, and Saitoh Ikuko, eds., *Gekiteki naru mono o megutte: Suzuki Tadashi to sono sekai* (*On the Dramatic Passions: The World of Suzuki Tadashi*), (Tokyo: Kôsakusha, 1977). Trans. Noyuri Liddicutt and Ian Carruthers. Hereafter cited as *Gekiteki ST*.

4. The performance text of *Gekiteki naru mono o megutte II* (1969) has been kindly provided by Saitoh Ikuko of SCOT and is translated by Yoshida Masako and Ian Carruthers.

5. This seems to quote from Meyerhold's famous production of *A Doll's House*, in which the realist set was stacked "back to front against the stage walls, symbolising – or so Meyerhold claimed – 'the bourgeois milieu against which Nora rebels.'" See Edward Braun, ed. and trans., *Meyerhold on Theatre* (London: Eyre Methuen, 1969), 183.

6. For a translation of the play, see James Brandon, *Kabuki: Five Classic Plays* (Honolulu: Hawaii University Press, 1992).

7. Suzuki would reuse the same props twenty-two years later in two different adaptations of *Macbeth*, the bib in *The Chronicle of Macbeth* (1992) and the mechanical flower in *Greetings from the Edge of the Earth I* (1993).

8. In 1973 Shiraishi created a *hannya* style "mask of resentment" with her face. However, SCOT archives show that she also used a *ko-omote* Noh mask to create a more compelling juxtaposition between impassive "face" and resentful action.

9. François Jacquemont, "D'hier à aujourd'hui: violence explosif au théâtre japonais," in *L'Est Republicain*, April 27 1973.

10. Saitoh Setsurô, ed., *Suzuki Tadashi no sekai* (*The World of Suzuki Tadashi*), (Tokyo: Shinpyôsha, 1982). Trans. Noyuri Liddicutt and Ian Carruthers. Hereafter cited as *Suzuki Tadashi no sekai*, 124–25. Subsequent page numbers in parentheses in this chapter refer to this book.

11. J. Thomas Rimer and Yamazaki Masakazu, *On the Art of the Nô Drama: the Major Treatises of Zeami* (Princeton, N.J.: Princeton University Press, 1984), 31, 73, 243 passim.

12. Suzuki interview in Minami Ryuta, Ian Carruthers, and John Gillies, eds., *Performing Shakespeare in Japan* (Cambridge: Cambridge University Press, 2001), 201.

13. Suzuki Tadashi, *Naikaku no wa: Suzuki Tadashi engeki ronshû* (*The Sum of the Interior Angles: Suzuki Tadashi's Collected Theatre Writings*) (Tokyo: Jiritsushôbô, 1973), 54, 317–18. Trans. Tony McGillycuddy and Ian Carruthers.

14. *AERA: Asahi Shinbun Weekly*, 9: 7, 1998.

15. *Suzuki Tadashi no sekai*, 84–85.

16. Elinor Fuchs, *The Death of Character* (London: Methuen, 1996) 90, 30, 50.

17. A video recording of this scene was aired by NHK TV in the series *Suzuki Tadashi no sekai* (*The World of Suzuki Tadashi*) in July 1993.

18. In Minami, Carruthers, and Gillies, *Performing Shakespeare in Japan*, 201.

19. Kan Takayuki, "Ono Hiroshi: Sufinkusu no manazashi" ("The Gaze of the Sphinx"), in *Asahi Journal*, October 4 1970, 24–26.

20. Betsuyaku Minoru, "Ono Hiroshi o itande" ("Lamenting the Death of Ono Hiroshi"), in *Gekiteki ST*, 66; Gotoh, Suzuki thesis, 62.

21. For Chikamatsu, see Donald Keene, *Anthology of Japanese Literature* (New York: Grove Press, 1955; rept. 1960), 386–90. For the Suzuki interview, see Minami, Carruthers, and Gillies, *Performing Shakespeare in Japan*, 197.

22. In the medieval period *Bikuni* could mean either a peripatetic nun or a traveling actress who dresses as a nun and doubles as a prostitute.

23. See Chapter Two, note 59, and Chapter Five, note 8.

24. The other two playwrights were Akimoto Matsuyo (whom Tsuno had singled out for her *Kaison, Priest of Hitachi*, 1965) and Fukuda Yoshiyuki (for *Find Hakamadare*, 1964). See David Goodman, "Satoh Makoto and the Post-Shingeki Movement in Japanese Contemporary Theatre," doctoral thesis, Cornell University, 1982, 72–73.

25. Tsuno Kaitarô, "The Tradition of Modern Theatre in Japan," trans. David Goodman, in *The Canadian Theatre Review*, Fall 1978, 19. Also in Goodman, "Satoh Makoto," 68.

26. Interview in Minami, Carruthers, and Gillies, *Performing Shakespeare in Japan*, 198.

27. Ibid., 205.

28. Ibid., 206. The first part of his remark seems to refer to his JPAC (Japan Performing Arts Center) program, which disseminated Suzuki Training internationally from 1983 to 1991.

29. Goodman, "Satoh Makoto," 30.

30. Ibid., 229.

31. Reported by Saitoh Ikuko at the Saitama opening in 1996.

32. Suzuki Tadashi, *John Silver*, performance script; trans. Eguchi Kazuko and Ian Carruthers.

33. Kara's adaptation of the R. L. Stevenson *Treasure Island* refrain, "74 men on the dead man's chest/Yo ho ho and a bottle of rum/Drink and the devil had done for the rest," raises expectations of a death in the final scene.

34. Braun, *Meyerhold on Theatre*, 141.

35. Hokusai is a famous woodblock artist whose *Fugaku sanjûrokkei* (*36 Scenes of Mount Fuji*) includes a well-known print entitled *Kanagawa okinamiura* (*Mount Fuji seen from behind a huge wave in Kanagawa*). The huge wave in the foreground seems to engulf a tiny Mount Fuji in the distance.

36. For example, Suzuki has said in *Naikaku* that he regards Shiraishi as "achieving Stanislavski's release of the subconscious, as achieving a state of *I-ness*" ("Shiraishi Kayoko," 183). "Theatre skills," he believes, "can only be learnt onstage . . . So it takes from 5 to 10 years to discover in yourself what is essentially yourself, and become an actor" ("What is the Realistic Theatre Now?," 329). Elsewhere he comments, "The overriding point is that I can

only set out on a characterization if I am absolutely tied to this body I was born with, to the last degree" ("On Utaemon," 14).
37. Braun, *Meyerhold on Theatre*, 38.

Chapter Five. Suzuki's Euripides (I): *The Trojan Women*

1. Tokyo (1974–75); Paris, Rome, Bonn, Berlin, and Lisbon (1977); Milwaukee and New York (1979); within Japan in Nagoya, Toyohashi, Tsu, Sapporo, Asahikawa, and Hakodate (1979); Nagano, Kanazawa, Toyama, and Ôtsu (1980); Osaka (1981); Toga, Chicago, and St. Louis (1982); the Los Angeles Olympic Art Festival (1984); San Diego, Washington D.C., London, Copenhagen, Brussels, Athens, Delphi, Thessaloniki, Frankfurt, Udine, and Toga (1985); Geneva, Milan, Madrid, Tenerife, Las Palmas, Chicago, Athens, Seoul, and Hong Kong (1986); Paris, Grenoble, Reims, Bordeaux, Stuttgart, and Toga (1987); Sydney, Tokyo, and Toga (1988); and Lahti and Helsinki (1989).
2. Suzuki's program note for his Iwanami Hall premiere (1974) shows that he is clearly aware of this (paragraph 4).
3. Fiona Macintosh, "Tragedy in Performance: Nineteenth- and Twentieth-Century Productions," in P. E. Easterling, ed., *The Cambridge Companion to Greek Tragedy* (Cambridge: Cambridge University Press, 1997), 318.
4. Peter Burian, "Myth into *muthos*: the Shaping of Tragic Plot," in Easterling, *The Cambridge Companion to Greek Tragedy*, 179.
5. Gide, Cocteau, O'Neill, Eliot, Sartre, Brecht, Pasolini, Soyinka, Fugard, and Müller had all produced adaptations, to name but a few.
6. The most detailed study in English is by Mae Smethurst, *The Artistry of Zeami: a Comparative Study of Greek Tragedy and Nô* (Princeton, N. J.: Princeton University Press, 1989).
7. From a panel discussion on "The Potential of Modern Theatre," in *Sekai*, March 1975, 146–49; translated by Frank Hoff in the 1979 Milwaukee performance program.
8. In 1976 Shiraishi would be invited to perform alongside the Kabuki actor Nakamura Senjaku in a performance of Nanboku's *Tôkaidô Yotsuya Kaidan* (*Yotsuya Ghost Stories*).
9. Macintosh, "Tragedy in Performance," 312.
10. Adrian Poole, "Total disaster: Euripides' *The Trojan Women*," in *Arion* 3, 1967, 257.
11. Michael Billington, *The Guardian*, April 11 1985; Michael Coveney, *Financial Times*, April 12 1985.
12. Senda Akihiko, "The Crouch as a Critique of the Modern: Suzuki Tadashi's *The Trojan Women* 1974," in J. Thomas Rimer, trans., *The Voyage of Contemporary Japanese Theatre: Senda Akihiko*. (Honolulu: Hawaii University Press, 1997), 50, 52.

13. Two excellent NHK TV video recordings exist of the production. The first is a complete live recording made in 1982 in the new Toga amphitheatre to mark the opening of the First Toga International Festival. The second is an extract of Hecuba's lament over the corpse of Astyanax, recorded in the television studio to mark Shiraishi's departure from SCOT in 1989. Both were rebroadcast in July 1993 as part of the NHK TV series *Suzuki Tadashi no sekai* (*The World of Suzuki Tadashi*).

14. "Mosquito Nets," in J. Thomas Rimer, *The Way of Acting: the Theatre Writings of Tadashi Suzuki* (New York: Theatre Communications Group, 1986) 114. According to Takahashi Yasunari, these were donated by him upon the decease of his parents.

15. Gotoh Yukihiro, "Suzuki Tadashi: Innovator of Contemporary Japanese Theatre," doctoral thesis, University of Hawaii, 1988, 301.

16. It tolls twenty-eight times in this seven-and-a-half-minute *danmari* section: fourteen times during Jizô's entrance, twice for the Trojan Chorus, four for the Greek soldiers, and eight for the Old Woman. Such a taxonomy of significance would probably not have been unusual in ancient Greek drama and in Suzuki's production provides what Miner would call the "ground" for the actor's "design." See Earl Miner, *Japanese Linked Poetry* (Princeton, N.J.: Princeton University Press, 1979), 22.

17. Suzuki's friend and colleague Takahashi Yasunari recalls a similar personal experience of "the night of the ferocious fire-bombing of Tokyo [in 1945], in which perhaps 140,000 people perished, describing how he, his younger sister and their parents had spent the night walking the streets dodging burning debris, his father carrying his mother on his back in a scene reminiscent of Aeneas carrying Anchises from burning Troy, in Virgil's *Aeneid*." See John Casey's obituary "Brilliant sensei built a cultural bridge between Europe and Japan – Professor Takahashi Yasunari, academic and visionary (9.2.1932–24.6.2002)," in *The Guardian*, rept. *The Age* (Melbourne) 29.8.2002.

18. It exists in two translated versions, one by Benito Ortolani in the Brooklyn College program for May 20–21 1979, the other by Thomas Fitzsimmons in the Milwaukee program for the same year. This translation by Eguchi Kazuko and Ian Carruthers makes use of both for felicitous turns of phrase.

19. Patricia Morton, "*The Trojan Women* in Japan," in *The Drama Review*, 19:1 1975.

20. These four lines, taken out of narrative sequence, are spoken by Hecuba to the Chorus after Cassandra's exit in Euripides. See Moses Hadas and John McLean, trans., *Euripides: Ten Plays* (New York: Bantam, 1960), 185.

21. Reported by SCOT member Ellen Lauren, in a lecture to my Japanese Theatre students, La Trobe University, Melbourne, 1992.

22. I use this image because Suzuki has alluded to the Sabra and Shatila massacres in Beirut in interview with Richard Stayton of the *Los Angeles Herald Examiner* in 1984 (June 17): "The theme of *The Trojan Women* is the

unhappiness of the women whose country lost the war . . . It happens everywhere in the world, even now, as in Palestine and Lebanon."

23. *Shichi-go-san* (November 15). At *Shichi-go-san* people take their children to a local shrine to pray for their health and happiness. This is done with girls and boys of three, boys of five, and girls of seven years old.

24. Philip Harsh, *A Handbook of Classical Drama* (Stanford: Stanford University Press, 1944; rept. 1967), 211.

25. Here the action jumps from Hadas and McLean, *Euripides*, 193 to 200.

26. Morton, "*The Trojan Women* in Japan."

27. See André Tunc, *La Croix*, June 2 1977; Ghigo De Chiara, *Avanti*, June 9 1977; and Patrick de Resbo, *Quotidien Paris*, May 26 1977.

28. In keeping with a return to the devastation of post World War II Japan, the word "Asian" is substituted for "barbarian." However, the better to maintain a balance of perspectives, "Tokyo" is *not* substituted for "Troy."

29. *Hamlet*, ed. Harold Jenkins, The Arden Shakespeare (London: Methuen, 1982), V.i, 196–98.

30. Gotoh, Suzuki thesis, 308.

31. Irving Wardle, *The Times*, April 12, 1985.

32. Stayton, *Los Angeles Herald Examiner*, June 17 1984.

33. Ibid.

Chapter Six. Suzuki's Euripides (II): *The Bacchae*

1. Fiona Macintosh, "Tragedy in Performance: Nineteenth- and Twentieth-Century Productions," in P. E. Easterling, ed., *The Cambridge Companion to Greek Tragedy* (Cambridge: Cambridge University Press, 1997), 313.

2. Suzuki Tadashi in interview; recorded by NHK TV following performance of *Dionysus* at Mito in 1992, and rebroadcast as part of the series *Suzuki Tadashi no sekai* (*The World of Suzuki Tadashi*) in July 1993.

3. J. Michael Walton, *The Greek Sense of Theatre: Tragedy Revived* (London: Methuen, 1984), 39.

4. Ibid. 130.

5. Philip Harsh, *A Handbook of Classical Drama* (Stanford: Stanford University Press, 1944; rept. 1967), 236.

6. "Crassus, " in Bernadotte Perrin, trans., *Plutarch's Lives*, Loeb Classical Library Series (Cambridge, Mass.: Harvard University Press, 1916), 33; Harsh, *Classical Drama*, 237.

7. Peter Burian, "Tragedy Adapted For Stages and Screens: the Renaissance to the Present," in Easterling, *The Cambridge Companion to Greek Tragedy*, 258.

8. 1989 program translated by Eguchi Kazuko and Ian Carruthers.

9. Patrice Pavis, ed., *The Intercultural Performance Reader* (London: Routledge, 1996), 97.

10. Suzuki referred to Jim Jones in particular during rehearsals of *The Chronicle of Macbeth* in 1992. The statistics are taken from a three-part Canadian documentary, *Killer Cults*, shown on SBS TV in 1999.

11. Burian, "Tragedy Adapted," in *The Cambridge Companion to Greek Tragedy*, 279.

12. Senda Akihiko, "Seijuku no kokei" ("A Scene of Ripening"), in *Shingeki*, no. 3, 1978, 22–23; trans. J. Thomas Rimer, *The Voyage of Contemporary Japanese Theatre: Senda Akihiko* (Honolulu: Hawaii University Press, 1997), 87.

13. "Preparation for enacting a role in Nô entails much more than simply disguising oneself to give the illusion of the character to be played. The Nô performer is also responsible for keeping the audience from feeling that the events unfolding on stage are a fabrication . . . The key to evoking this effect is the development of an ability to achieve *an inner sense of flight or soaring* while acting" (my italics). Kanze Hisao, "Life with the Nô Mask," in Rebecca Teele, ed., *Nô/Kyôgen Masks and Performance*, special issue of *Mime Journal*, 1984, 69.

14. *Takahime* (a readaption back into Noh form of W. B. Yeats's *At the Hawk's Well*) and *Oedipus Rex* (with Mei no Kai) in 1971, *Agamemnon* in 1972, *Waiting for Godot* (with Mei no Kai, Hisao playing Vladimir to Hideo's Estragon) in 1973, *Sangetsuki* (in a Mei no Kai exchange with Jean-Louis Barrault at a symposium of the Franco-Japanese Theatre Association) in 1974, *The Trojan Women* (with Suzuki and Shiraishi) in January, and *Medea* (with Mei no Kai) in July 1975. See *Kanze Hisao: shika no fûshi* (*Hisao Kanze: the Form of the Final Flower*), (Tokyo: Heibonsha, 1979), 97; this contains excellent photographs.

15. Tokyo University professor of English; translator of Shakespeare's Works.

16. See Mori Hideo, Senda Akihiko, et al., eds., *Theater Japan, Second Edition*, trans. Steven Comee, et al. (Tokyo: Japan Foundation, 1993), 272.

17. Kinoshita Junji is best known for *Yûzuru* (*Twilight Crane*) and plays centering on Japanese war guilt (Mori, Senda, et al., *Theater Japan*, 248). Ôe Kenzaburô, Japan's preeminent novelist, received the Nobel Prize for Literature in 1994.

18. Gotoh Yukihiro, "Suzuki Tadashi: Innovator of Contemporary Japanese Theatre," doctoral thesis, University of Hawaii, 1988, 309–18; Mori Hideo, "Yami ni sumu kami to ô" ("Gods and Kings who Live in the Dark"), in *Shingeki*, no. 3, 1978, 20–21; Marianne McDonald, *Ancient Sun, Modern Light* (New York: Columbia University Press, 1992), 59–73.

19. Philip Vellacott, trans., *Euripides: The Bacchae and Other Plays* (Harmondsworth: Penguin, 1954; rev. 1973), 203. Page numbers for all subsequent references to this edition are given in parentheses after each quotation.

20. Miyashita Norio and Okazaki Ryôko, "Engeki jihyô" ("Theatre Criticism Page"), in *Higeki Kigeki*, no. 12, 1981, 101–9.

21. Saitoh Setsurô, ed., *Suzuki Tadashi no sekai* (*The World of Suzuki Tadashi*), (Tokyo: Shinpyôsha, 1982), 67–68.

22. David Kaplan and Andrew Marshall, *The Cult at the End of the World* (London: Arrow, 1996), 24.

23. Ibid, 47.

24. In his famous essay, "On the Balinese Theatre," Artaud had commented, "Those actors . . . look like moving hieroglyphs." See Claude Schumacher, *Artaud on Theatre* (London: Methuen, 1989), 88.

25. Suzuki Tadashi, *"Bakkosu no shinnyo" ("The Bacchae")*, in *Shingeki*, 1978; trans. Eguchi Kazuko and Ian Carruthers.

26. Togawa Minoru joined the company in 1975, leaving to become an opera director in 1994.

27. 1989 program synopsis. "Women of Asia" is the rallying cry of a leader, "Honourable angels" the honorific address of a novitiate to superiors (who may be using her).

28. The imaginative projection possible for spectators of Ashikawa's dance is suggested by Richard Moore's splicing of this scene from *The Bacchae* with images of World War II footage of kamikaze airplanes dive-bombing American warships; see his *Butoh: Piercing the Mask* (Sydney: AKA Productions, 1991).

29. Nishikibe seems to have learned from both Suzuki Kenji's acrobatic acting in *The Trojan Women* and Ashikawa's dance in *The Bacchae*. Such acting is less about *feeling* panic than knowing how to *express* it physically, as Suzuki would say.

30. Senda has noted in his *Shingeki* review the "handsome restraint" of Suzuki's "controlled theatrical form" (Rimer, *Voyage*, 85).

31. Earle Ernst, *The Kabuki Theatre* (Honolulu: Hawaii University Press, 1974), 164. Another celebrated example of the transformative power of the fox-god can be seen in Kurosawa's adaptation of *King Lear* (*Ran*) when Lady Kaede attacks with a knife, makes love to, and asserts control over her husband's killer/brother in an amazing histrionic display.

32. "On the Balinese Theatre," in Schumacher, *Artaud on Theatre*, 91.

33. The translation is taken from Volonakis, used for the bilingual productions (Gotoh, Suzuki thesis, 316); compare Vellacott, *Euripides*, 224.

34. Ian Carruthers's notebook, July 1995.

35. Lauren herself came from a military family and had been an Olympic equestrian before joining SCOT.

36. Athens program, August 21–22 1995.

37. Mori, "Gods and Kings," in *Shingeki*, no. 3, 1978, 20.

38. In having them "drop out" of mainstream culture to become fanatical followers of a fringe cult, Suzuki seemed to be ironically marking the reversibility of "center" and "periphery" as cultures and subcultures incessantly war for temporary cultural dominance and the right to rewrite history. In this way he fuels debate about who oppresses whom in the play.

39. These spray-painted kimono were bought secondhand in the Kanazawa flea-market, according to Leon Ingulsrud, but in this "rewriting" the *sign* of vandalism was intentional.

40. Suzuki Tadashi, "Empty Village," in J. Thomas Rimer, trans., *The Way of Acting: the Theatre Writings of Tadashi Suzuki* (New York: Theatre Communication Group, 1986), 107–10.

41. "Dionysio, Superbo," in *Sipario*, October 10 1994; trans. David Fairservice.

Chapter Seven. Suzuki's Chekhov: *The Chekhov* **and** *Ivanov*

1. Saitoh Setsurô, ed., *Suzuki Tadashi no sekai* (*The World of Suzuki Tadashi*), (Tokyo: Shinpyôsha, 1982), 45. Trans. Noyuri Liddicutt and Ian Carruthers. Hereafter, cited as *Suzuki Tadashi no Sekai*.

2. SCOT performance texts translated by Eguchi Kazuko and Ian Carruthers.

3. Suzuki Tadashi, *Engeki to wa nani ka* (*What is Theatre?*), (Tokyo: Iwanami shoten, 1988), 20. Trans. Kameron Steele and Ian Carruthers (1–114), and Kumi West and Ian Carruthers (115–71).

4. Suzuki Tadashi, program note for *The Chekhov*, 1986; trans. Eguchi Kazuko and Ian Carruthers.

5. Suzuki, program note for *The Chekhov*, 1989; translators as above.

6. Senda Akihiko, "The Crouch as a Critique of the Modern: Suzuki Tadashi's *The Trojan Women* 1974," in J. Thomas Rimer, trans., *The Voyage of Contemporary Japanese Theatre: Senda Akihiko* (Honolulu: Hawaii University Press, 1997), 50.

7. Elisaveta Fen, trans., *Anton Chekhov: Plays* (Harmondsworth, U.K.: Penguin, 1954; rept. 1985). The Fen *Three Sisters* total breaks down into 23, 22, 17, and 19 pages for each Act in sequence; of these Suzuki keeps 6.5, 4.5, 4.5, and 4 pages. Page numbers for all subsequent references to this edition are given in parentheses after each quotation. In what follows I am indebted to Richard Moore for generously allowing me to see his dress-rehearsal videotapes of *The Chekhov* (Toga 1988–89).

8. Erika Fischer-Lichte, "Intercultural Aspects in Post-Modern Theatre: a Japanese Version of Chekhov's *Three Sisters*," in Hanna Scolnikov and Peter Holland, eds., *The Play Out of Context: Transferring Plays From Culture to Culture* (Cambridge: Cambridge University Press, 1989), 178.

9. Ibid., 177–78.

10. Ibid., 178.

11. Domoto Masaki, "Dialogue and Monologue in Noh," in James R. Brandon, ed., *Noh and Kyogen in the Contemporary World* (Honolulu: Hawaii University Press, 1997), 152.

12. "Treated well, Ebisu bestows blessings. Slighted, he wreaks havoc in the form of storms, epidemics, droughts, and other disasters." See Jane Marie Law, *Puppets of Nostalgia: the Life, Death and Rebirth of the Japanese Awaji Ningyô Tradition* (Princeton, N. J.: Princeton University Press, 1997), 120–21. Suzuki creates a canny interpretation of Chekhov's Lopakhin, who is the bearer of potential disaster as well as blessing.

13. Contemporaries describe such provincial men of substance as "progressive conservatives" who, "cherishing the establishment, gathered together to debate the abolition of prostitution, the spirit of independence, Mt. Fuji, Lake Biwa, and patriotism." See Carol Gluck, *Japan's Modern Myths* (Princeton, N.J.: Princeton University Press, 1985), 2.

14. Sato Toshihiko's "Henrik Ibsen in Japan" (doctoral thesis, Washington University, 1966) provides ample evidence of Japanese awareness of such a protofeminist "Faust" character as Hedda Gabler. Tsubouchi Shôyô's "Yuwayuru atarashi onna" ("So-called New Women"), published in 1912, had contrasted Nora with Hedda, and Hirazuka Raichô argued the need to go beyond Hedda in her historic *Seitô* (*Blue Stocking*) magazine articles "Hedda ron" ("Discussion on Hedda," October 1911) and "Yo no fujintachi ni" ("To All Women," March 1913). Sato thesis, 153–56.

15. Suzuki, *What is Theatre?*, 28–29.

16. Takahashi Yasunari, "The Ghost Trio: Beckett, Yeats and Noh," in Ikegami Yoshihiko, ed., *The Empire of Signs: Semiotic Essays on Japanese Culture* (Amsterdam/Philadelphia: John Benjamins, 1991), 257.

17. Ibid., 261.

18. Jonathan Griffin, trans., *Jean-Louis Barrault: Memories for Tomorrow: the Memoirs of Jean-Louis Barrault* (London: Thomes and Hudson, 1974), 248.

19. For layout, see K. Itoh et al., eds., S. D. Henshûbun, *Arata Isozaki, 1985–1991* (Tokyo: Kajima shuppankai, 1993), 28–29.

20. Isozaki Arata, "Introduction to the ACM Theatre," in *Quarterly Mito Geijutsukan*, no. 3, Spring 1989, 3 (http://www.arttowermito.or.jp/Tower/isozaki3.html).

21. Kara Jûrô, "The Periods of H.I.S.T.O.R.Y.," in *Koshimaki O-sen* (Tokyo: Gendai shichôsha, 1968), 67. Trans. in Yamamoto Kiyokazu, "Kara's Vision: the World as Public Toilet," in *The Canadian Theatre Review*, Fall 1978, 31. The context for Kara's statement was the "return to roots" taking place in Western theatre and culture in the 1960s and 1970s.

22. At the Third International Chekhov Theatre Festival (1998), "Chekhov's drama was seen in the widest possible context, as if the world theatre, on the eve of the third millennium, was reviewing the principal stages of its own development: classic (antique) drama – Shakespeare – and Chekhov." See Tatiana Shakh-Azizova, "Chekhov on the Russian Stage," in Vera Gottlieb and Paul Allain, eds., *The Cambridge Companion to Chekhov* (Cambridge: Cambridge University Press, 2000), 174.

23. Suzuki Tadashi, Introduction to *Ivanov* in *Suzuki Tadashi no sekai* (*The World of Suzuki Tadashi*), NHK TV, July 1993; trans. Eguchi Kazuko and Ian Carruthers. This is extensively quoted in what follows.

24. Donald Rayfield, *Anton Chekhov: a Life* (London: Harper Collins, 1997), 158. See also Laurence Senelick, *The Chekhov Theatre: a Century of the Plays in Performance* (Cambridge: Cambridge University Press, 1997), 15: "Given [*Ivanov's*]

proximity to his early farces, it very well may be that he [Chekhov] set out to write a satire."

25. Vera Gottlieb, *Chekhov and the Vaudeville: a Study of Chekhov's One-Act Plays* (Cambridge: Cambridge University Press, 1982), 55, 91.

26. Uchino Tadashi, *Merodorama no gyakushû: "watakushi engeki" no hachijûnendai* (*Melodrama's Counterattack: "Confessional Theatre" of the 1980s*), (Tokyo: Keisôshobô, 1996), 91.

27. Gottlieb, *Chekhov and the Vaudeville*, 21.

28. Before entering university he had read much of the current literature and criticism available "and adored Chekhov as if he were a god." See *Suzuki Tadashi no sekai*, 46.

29. Gottlieb shows how Chekhov's farce techniques are redeployed in the full-length plays to create the destabilizing "sad comedy" which Stanislavski found so disconcerting. When Chekhov warned Stanislavski's wife that *The Cherry Orchard* was "[a]t places . . . even a farce; I fear I shall get it in the neck from Nemirovich-Danchenko," Stanislavski retorted, "I imagine it will be something impossible on the weirdness and vulgarity of life. I only fear that instead of a farce again we shall have a great big tragedy. Even now he thinks *Three Sisters* a very merry little piece." Quoted by Donald Rayfield in *Anton Chekhov* (580) from A. P. Chekhov, *Polnoe sobranie sochinenii i pisem*, 11, 562.

30. "The Naturalistic Theatre and the Theatre of Mood," in Edward Braun, ed. and trans., *Meyerhold on Theatre* (London: Eyre Methuen, 1969), 25–26: "In the theatre the spectator's imagination is able to supply that which is left unsaid . . . It would seem that the naturalistic theatre denies the spectator's capacity to fill in the details with his imagination in the way one does when listening to music."

31. Letter to Suvorin, January 7 1889. In Michael H. Heim and Simon Karlinsky, *Letters of Anton Chekhov* (New York: Harper and Row, 1973), 84.

32. Letter to Suvorin, December 30 1888. In ibid., 76.

33. Gottlieb, *Chekhov and the Vaudeville*, 47.

34. Ibid., 38.

35. To Suvorin January 7 1889. In Heim and Karlinsky, *Letters of Anton Chekhov*, 84.

36. Yoshiyuki also played *The Farewell Cult*'s Reverend Mother in the 1991 Mito *Macbeth* (in 1969 she had acted with Shiraishi in Kara's *The Virgin's Mask*).

37. Uchino, *Merodorama*, 88.

38. Ibid.

39. "She will revive her fallen man, set him on his feet, and give him happiness" whether he wants it or not, says Chekov. "She doesn't love Ivanov; she loves her mission." Letter to Suvorin, December 30 1888. In Heim and Karlinsky, *Letters of Anton Chekhov*, 80.

40. Uchino, *Merodrama*, 88.

41. Fen, *Anton Chekhov: Plays*, 70.

42. This is the production I describe in what follows.

43. In Chekhov's words, "Lvov is . . . stupid, but his heart is in the right place." Letter to Suvorin, December 30 1888. In Heim and Karlinsky, *Letters of Anton Chekhov*, 79.

44. From Chekhov's three-page description of Ivanov's character, I extract the following: "Ivanov . . . has been to the university and is in no way remarkable. He is easily excitable, hot-headed, . . . honest and straightforward . . . People like Ivanov don't solve problems, they fall under their burden." Ibid., 76, 78.

45. Roger Reynolds, "Electro-Acoustic Music," New World Records, 701 Seventh Avenue, New York 10036 (New World 80431–2). For the Peter Terry review, see http://www.bgsu.edu/~pterry.

46. Senelick, *The Chekhov Theatre*, 185.

47. Chekhov puts "A Count" at the top of his 1880 list of absurdities, "Things Frequently Encountered in Novels, Stories and Other Such Things." See Gottlieb, *Chekhov and the Vaudeville*, 17.

48. Braun, *Meyerhold on Theatre*, 214, 199.

49. A similar gesture may be found in Meyerhold's *The Warrant*. See the photograph in Braun, ibid., 201. Suzuki's Masha echoes this gesture at the climax in *Three Sisters*.

50. Articles by Bertrand Russell and Albert Einstein appeared in *Kaizô*, "making it a leading proponent of new trends in thought and science." See *Kôdansha Encyclopedia of Japan*, ed. Gen Itasaka (Tokyo: Kôdansha, 1983), vol. 4, 113–14.

51. After "The scene around was desolate, as far as the eye could reach," the line in italics just quoted is the second of three Suzuki additions to Chekhov's text.

52. Heim and Karlinsky, *Letters of Anton Chekhov*, 442.

Chapter Eight. Suzuki's Shakespeare (I): *Macbeth*

1. Suzuki Tadashi, "Table Talk with Trevor Nunn," in *Asahi shinbun* (January 23 1970); trans Minami Ryuta.

2. Suzuki Tadashi, *Naikaku no wa: Suzuki Tadashi engeki ronshû* (*The Sum of the Interior Angles: Suzuki Tadashi's Collected Theatre Writings*), (Tokyo: Jiritsushôbô, 1973), 85–86. Trans. Tony McGillycuddy and Ian Carruthers.

3. The *Wabi* aesthetic of austere, stark beauty may be summed up in the Zen saying "tattered robes filled with a pure breeze [spirit]." See Paul Varley and Kamakura Isao, eds., *Tea in Japan: Essays on the History of Chanoyu* (Honolulu: Hawaii University Press, 1994), 195–227.

4. Matsuoka Seigô in Saitoh Setsurô, ed., *Suzuki Tadashi no sekai* (*The World of Suzuki Tadashi*), (Tokyo: Shinpyôsha, 1982), 146. Trans. Noyuri Liddicutt and Ian Carruthers. Hereafter cited as *Suzuki Tadashi no sekai*.

5. See Minami Ryuta's "A Chronological Table of Shakespeare Productions in Japan, 1866–1994," in Sasayama Takashi, J. H. Mulryne, and Margaret

Shewring, *Shakespeare on the Japanese Stage* (Cambridge: Cambridge University Press, 1998), 257–331.

6. Dr. Morita Shôma (1874–1938) of Tokyo University Medical School was a contemporary of Freud who combined European psychotherapy with Zen Buddhist tenets. See Takie Sugiyama Lebra, *Japanese Patterns of Behavior* (Honolulu: Hawaii University Press, 1976), 215–31.

7. Gotoh Yukihiro, "Suzuki Tadashi: Innovator of Contemporary Japanese Theatre," doctoral thesis, University of Hawaii, 1988, 21.

8. Takahashi Hidemoto, Matsumoto Yoshiko, and Saitoh Ikuko, eds., *Gekiteki naru mono o megutte: Suzuki Tadashi to sono sekai* (*On the Dramatic Passions: the World of Suzuki Tadashi*), (Tokyo: Kôsakusha, 1977), 106n. Trans. Noyuri Liddicutt and Ian Carruthers.

9. Lebra, *Japanese Patterns of Behavior*, 221.

10. Suzuki Tadashi, *Yoru to tokei* (*Night and the Clock*), in *Shingeki*, no. 12, 1975, 126–48; trans. Yoshida Masako and Ian Carruthers.

11. *Macbeth*, ed. Kenneth Muir, The Arden Shakespeare (London: Methuen, 1972). Subsequent references in parentheses refer to this edition.

12. Lebra, *Japanese Patterns of Behavior*, 216.

13. Kurihara Nanako, "The Most Remote Thing in the Universe: Critical Analysis of Hijikata Tatsumi's Butoh Dance," doctoral thesis, New York University, 1996, 157.

14. Stefan Tanaka, *Japan's Orient: Rendering Pasts into History* (Berkeley: University of California Press, 1993).

15. See Senda Akihiko, Mori Hideo, and Odashima Yûshi, "Kôyô naki hôkô: 75nen no engekikai," ("Uninspired Wanderings: the Theatre World in 1975"), in *Shingeki*, no. 1, 1976, 48.

16. According to Takahashi Yasunari, a famous literary example of such a *shôi gunjin* can be found in Betsuyaku Minoru's Absurdist play *Zô* (*The Elephant*), staged by Suzuki in 1962.

17. The song touched a chord with those who left rural areas after the war to find jobs in industrial conurbations; Suzuki himself was part of this demographic shift. He recalls a night job straightening newspapers coming off a cylinder press (1959); and, while dreaming of staging plays, drinking his wages in backstreet bars where "the girls would teach you popular songs." *Suzuki Tadashi no sekai*, 88.

18. Nagao Kazuo, "Gaikaku to funshutsu", in *Shingeki*, no. 1, 1976, 25–26.

19. Senda, Mori, and Odashima, "Kôyô naki hôkô," 47.

20. Suzuki acknowledges that "this performance is my own work, but in the last analysis, it is the work of everybody who contributed to performance." Director's notes, *Night and the Clock*, 2. (The performers were Toyokawa Jun, Tominaga Yumi, Shin Kenjirô, Fukao Yoshimi, Doi Michitoshi, and, in a cameo role, Shiraishi.)

21. *Night and Feast III* performance text, trans. Eguchi Kazuko and Ian Carruthers.

22. The year 1976 was the year of the Lockheed Contract Scandal which led to the arrest of former Prime Minister Tanaka Kakuei on corruption charges.

23. In Noh *iguse* indicates that the *kuse* section of the play is not to be danced, as is usual; the actor must sit motionless onstage, dancing in mind only as the music plays.

24. This is not unusual in Noh ghost plays. Suzuki would also use the technique in *The Chronicle of Macbeth* during the sleepwalking scene.

25. Hiroshi Kitagawa and Bruce Tsuchida, trans., *The Tale of the Heike* (Tokyo: Tokyo University Press, 1975), vol. 1, Book 4, 271.

26. *Suzuki Tadashi no sekai*, 146.

27. Akira Kurosawa, *Throne of Blood*, trans. Hisae Niki, in *Seven Samurai and Other Screenplays* (London: Faber, 1992), 266.

28. Eugène Ionesco, *Macbett*, trans. Charles Marowitz (New York: Grove Press, 1973), 103–5. Ionesco's interpretation is not without warrant from Shakespeare, being based on Malcolm's speech to Macduff in IV.iii.

29. *Suzuki Tadashi no sekai*, 153–54.

30. Cf. "Red Army faction," in *Kôdansha Encyclopedia of Japan*, ed. Gen Itasaka (Tokyo: Kôdansha, 1983), vol. 6, 284–85.

31. Ian Carruthers ed., "Reading Suzuki Tadashi's *The Chronicle of Macbeth* in Australia" (unpublished proceedings of the Melbourne Performance Research Group Conference at Melbourne University, October 3–4 1992), 209. Page numbers for all subsequent references to this manuscript in "*The Chronicle of Macbeth*, Australia, 1992" section are given in parenthesis after each quotation.

32. Christopher Innes in conversation has noted the similarity to the ending of Genet's *The Balcony*.

33. For audience response in Tokyo, see the 1992 SBS video documentary *One Step on a Journey*. For the extraordinarily positive response of Australian audiences as opposed to critics, see Ian Carruthers and Patricia Mitchell, *Theatre East and West: Problems of Difference or Problems of Perception?* (La Trobe University Asian Studies Papers, Research Series no. 6 (Melbourne: La Trobe University, 1995), 20–30, 40–43.

34. Uchino Tadashi's review of *The Chronicle* provided by Peter Curtin (no publisher or date given).

35. My calculations are based on page counts of these texts.

36. Jean-François Lyotard, "Note on the meaning of 'Post-,'" in Thomas Docherty, ed., *Postmodernism: a Reader* (Cambridge University Press, Harvester, 1993), 49.

37. Minami Ryuta, Ian Carruthers, and John Gillies, eds., *Performing Shakespeare in Japan* (Cambridge: Cambridge University Press, 2001), 201, 199.

38. Lyotard, "Answering the Question: What is Postmodernism?" in Docherty, *Postmodernism: a Reader*, 46.

39. In the Japanese title of *Greetings* (*Sekai no hate kara konnichiwa*), *hate* can be read as either "edge" or "end." The alternative reading, *Greetings from the*

End of the Earth, would seem to point to doomsday cults such as AUM Shinrikyô.

40. Charles Jencks in Andreas Papadakis, ed., *Post-Modernism on Trial* (London: Academy Group, 1990), 10.

41. Interview in Minami, Carruthers, and Gillies, *Performing Shakespeare in Japan*, 201.

42. Suzuki Tadashi, *Sekai no hate kara konnichiwa I* (*Greetings from the Edge of the Earth I*), SCOT company performance text, 1. Trans. Hashimoto Kayoko and Ian Carruthers. Page numbers in parentheses after subsequent quotations from the text refer to this translation.

43. Interview in Minami, Carruthers, and Gillies, *Performing Shakespeare in Japan*, 198, 196.

44. Ibid., 213–14.

45. Suzuki, *Engeki to wa nani ka* (*What is Theatre?*), (Tokyo: Iwanami Shoten, 1988), 21. Trans. Kameron Steele and Ian Carruthers (1–114), and Kumi West and Ian Carruthers (115–71).

46. *Greetings I*, trans. Hashimoto and Carruthers, 1.

47. Saitoh Ikuko has alerted me to Suzuki's dramatic irony in this production.

48. Samuel Beckett, *Endgame* (London: Faber & Faber, 1958).

49. Rimer and Yamazaki, *On the Art of the Nôh Drama: the Major Treatises of Zeami* (Princeton, N. J.: Princeton University Press, 1984), 31. See also Donald Philippi, trans., *Kojiki* (Princeton, N. J.: Princeton University Press, 1969), 81–86.

50. For the influence of Surrealism on Suzuki's use of theatrical collage see Gotoh, Suzuki thesis, 102–37. In view of the potentially political nature of *Sekai no hate kara konnichiwa*, note that, between 1938 and 1945, when Suzuki was a preschooler, Surrealism offered one of the last modes of artistic resistance to ultranationalism. See John Clark, *Surrealism in Japan* (Melbourne: Monash Asia Institute, 1997), 14–18.

51. Carlton Lake and Robert Maillard, *A Dictionary of Modern Painting* (London: Methuen, 1956), 283. See my opening comments on *Greetings* in Chapter One.

52. In the *Mahaparinibbana Sutta* the Buddha's death is described as brought on by an indigestible meal which caused excruciating pain. See Amarnath Thakur, *Buddha and Buddhist Synods in India and Abroad* (Delhi: Abhinav Publications, 1996), 89.

53. As Japan embarked on imperial expansion in Manchuria in the 1930s, official propaganda campaigns were busy glorifying such medieval imperial loyalists as Kusunoki (*Kôdansha Encyclopedia of Japan*, vol. 4, 321a).

54. Audience laughter is clearly evident here and at a number of other points in the production I recorded from the NHK broadcast on August 10 1993.

55. This was Scene 14 of *Night and the Clock*. In December 1985 the World Health Organization released a survey showing Japan to have the highest average life expectancy in the world. Factors cited were improved diet and advances

in medical treatment and drugs (*Kôdansha Encyclopedia of Japan*, supplement, "Aging population," 1–2).

56. *Sokushimbutsu*, becoming a Buddha through self-mummification, has a long history in the harsh "Snow Country" of Japan. Through self-sacrifice the dead hope to activate their spiritual power to benefit the living. See Blacker, *The Catalpa Bow: a Study of Shamanic Practices in Japan* (London: Allen and Unwin, 1975), 87–89.

57. Herbert Plutschow, *Chaos and Cosmos – Ritual in Early and Medieval Japanese Literature* (Leiden: E. J. Brill, 1990), 107–8.

58. Jencks, in Papadakis, *Post-Modernism on Trial*, 25.

59. Sakai Naoki, "Modernity and its Critique," in H. D. Harootunian and Masao Miyoshi, eds., *Postmodernism and Japan* (Durham: Duke University Press, 1989), 107.

Chapter Nine. Suzuki's Shakespeare (II): *King Lear*

1. Watanabe Tamotsu in *SCOT: Suzuki Tadashi's World* (a brochure published to celebrate the tenth anniversary of the Toga Festival), 1992, 52–55.

2. Suzuki himself, in a television interview, says that the Nurse is reading the book aloud to the Old Man, which, however, does not accord with the details confirmed by the videotaped production.

3. These quotations from the American and British press are taken from the anniversary brochure mentioned above, 51.

4. Ted Hughes, quoted by Michael Kustow in his article in *The Independent*, November 19 1994. A lone voice among London critics, Kustow deplores the devastatingly negative reception by the British critics of the foreign productions (a German *Romeo and Juliet*, an American *The Merchant of Venice*, Suzuki's *King Lear*, etc.) presented in the "Everybody's Shakespeare" Festival at the Barbican. He wonders whether the British critics are "maidenly" in "preserving our classical heritage intact" or, rather, "skinheads warning off trespassers." He quotes Ted Hughes, who came to see Suzuki's *King Lear*: "Our resistance to foreign innovations in Shakespeare production has to do with the way we internalise the complete works as a national sacred book of rites."

Select bibliography

Too much has been written about Suzuki to include it all here; the endnotes contain full bibliographic information for all works cited.

WORKS BY, INTERVIEWS WITH, OR COLLECTIONS ON SUZUKI

Suzuki Tadashi, "Table Talk with Trevor Nunn." *Asahi shinbun* January 23 1970.
Naikaku no wa: Suzuki Tadashi engeki ronshû (*The Sum of the Interior Angles: Suzuki Tadashi's Collected Theatre Writings*). Tokyo: Jiritsushôbô, 1973.
and Nakamura Yûjirô, *Gekiteki gengo* (*On Dramatic Language*). Tokyo: Hakusuisha, 1977.
Gekiteki naru mono o megutte: Suzuki Tadashi to sono sekai (*On the Dramatic Passions: the World of Suzuki Tadashi*). Eds. Takahashi Hidemoto, Matsumoto Yoshiko, and Saitoh Ikuko. Tokyo: Kôsakusha, 1977.
Engekiron: katari no chihei (*Collected Theatre Writings: Horizons of Deception*). Tokyo: Hakusuisha, 1980.
"Shojo-saku izen: Waseda Daigaku Jiyû Butai jidai" ("Before My First Professional Production: the Era of the Waseda University Free Stage"), in *Betsuyaku Minoru no sekai* (*The World of Betsuyaku Minoru*). Tokyo: Shinpyôsha, 1982.
Bunka no genzai: engeki o tôshite (*Modern Culture Through Theatre*). Toyama-ken shokuin kenshûjo, 1982.
Suzuki Tadashi no sekai (*The World of Suzuki Tadashi*). Ed. Saitoh Setsurô. Tokyo: Shinpyôsha, 1982.
Gendai bunmei no naka de no engeki no ichi (*Theatre's Location within Modern Culture*). *Bunka, kûkan* (*Culture and Space*). Meiji daigaku kôkai bunka kôza III (Meiji University Public Seminar on Culture). Meiji daigaku jinmon kagaku kenkyushô (Meiji University Cultural Science Studies Institute), 1983, 179–204.
Engeki ronshû: ekkyô suru chikara (*Collected Theatre Writings: Energy that Knows No Boundaries*). Tokyo: Parco, 1984.
Suzuki Tadashi taidanshû (*Collected Interviews with Suzuki Tadashi*). Tokyo: Riburopôto, 1984.
Kokusaika jidai no bunka (*Culture in an Age of Internationalism*). Toyama: Shimin daigaku, 1987.
The Way of Acting: the Theatre Writings of Tadashi Suzuki. Trans. J. Thomas Rimer. New York: Theatre Communications Group, 1986.

282

Engeki to wa nani ka (What is Theatre?). Tokyo: Iwanami shoten, 1988.

SCOT: Suzuki Company of Toga. Trans. Takahashi Yasunari, Matsuoka Kazuko, Frank Hoff, Leon Ingulsrud, and Jordan Sand. Tokyo: Japan Performing Arts Center, 1992. (For sale at company performances.)

Enshutsuka no hassô (A Director's Conceptions). Tokyo: Ôta shuppan, 1994.

"Interview with Suzuki Tadashi [1992]," in "Reading Suzuki Tadashi's *The Chronicle of Macbeth* in Australia." Ed. Ian Carruthers. Unpublished proceedings of the Melbourne Performance Research Group Conference on *The Chronicle of Macbeth*, October 3–4 1992.

"Interview with Suzuki Tadashi [1995]," in *Performing Shakespeare in Japan*. Eds. Minami Ryuta, Ian Carruthers, and John Gillies. Cambridge: Cambridge University Press, 2001, 196–207.

Brandon, James, "Training at the Waseda Little Theatre: the Suzuki Method," in *The Drama Review*, 22:4 1978, 29–42.

Carruthers, Ian, "*The Chronicle of Macbeth*: Suzuki Method Acting in Australia, 1992," in *Performing Shakespeare in Japan*. Eds. Minami Ryuta, Ian Carruthers, and John Gillies. Cambridge: Cambridge University Press, 2001, 121–32.

"Suzuki Tadashi's first adaptations of Shakespeare's *Macbeth: Night and the Clock* (1975) and *Night and Feast III* (1978), in *Performing Shakespeare in Asia*. Eds. Harry Aveling and Ian Carruthers. La Trobe University Asian Studies Papers, Research Series no. 9. Melbourne: La Trobe University, 2001, 18–29.

"Suzuki Tadashi's 'The Chekhov': *Three Sisters, The Cherry Orchard*, and *Uncle Vanya*," in *Modern Drama*, XLIII: 2 2000, 288–99.

"Deny Thy Father and Refuse Thy Name: Suzuki Tadashi's *Waiting for Romeo*," in *Asian Studies Review* (Journal of the Asian Studies Association of Australia), 20:3 April 1997, 26–34.

and Patricia Mitchell, *Theatre East and West: Problems of Difference or Problems of Perception?* La Trobe University Asian Studies Papers, Research Series no. 6. Melbourne: La Trobe University, 1995.

Gotoh Yukihiro, "Suzuki Tadashi: Innovator of Contemporary Japanese Theatre," doctoral thesis, University of Hawaii, 1988.

Hoff, Frank, "Suzuki Tadashi: the Sum of the Interior Angles," in *The Canadian Theatre Review*, 20 1978, 20–27.

Holmberg, Arthur, "The Liberation of Lear," in *American Theater* July/August 1988, 12–19.

Isozaki Arata, *Arata Isozaki, 1976–1984*. Eds. K. Itoh et al., S. D. Henshûbun. Gendai no kenchikuka (Modern Architects series). Tokyo: Kajima shuppankai, 1984; rept. 1991.

Arata Isozaki, 1985–1991. Eds. K. Itoh et al., S. D. Henshûbun. Gendai no kenchikuka (Modern Architects series). Tokyo: Kajima shuppankai, 1993.

McDonald, Marianne, *Ancient Sun, Modern Light: Greek Drama on the Modern Stage*. New York: Columbia University Press, 1992 (chapters 1–3).

Senda Akihiko, *The Voyage of Contemporary Japanese Theatre: Senda Akihiko*. Trans. J. Thomas Rimer. Honolulu: Hawaii University Press, 1997.

Takahashi Yasunari, "*Kagami to kanran or The Looking Glass and Cabbages*," in *The Looking Glass Letter* (the Lewis Carroll Society of Japan Newsletter), no. 3, February 1995.

"Tragedy with Laughter: Suzuki Tadashi's *The Tale of Lear*," in *Performing Shakespeare in Japan*. Cambridge: Cambridge University Press, 2001, 112–20.

Theatre Olympics techô: bessatsu gekijô bunka (Theatre Olympics Notebook: Theatre Culture Supplement). Shizuoka Performing Arts Center, Shimizu, 1999.

Tsuno Kaitarô, "Preface to *The Elephant*," in *Concerned Theatre Japan*, 1:3 1970, 60–70.

"The Tradition of Modern Theatre in Japan." Trans. David Goodman. *The Canadian Theatre Review*, Fall 1978.

SUZUKI'S PUBLISHED PERFORMANCE TEXTS

Gekiteki naru mono o megutte II (*On the Dramatic Passions II*). *Dôjidai engeki*, no. 3, 1970, 150–70.

Yoru to tokei (*Night and the Clock*). *Shingeki*, no. 12, 1975, 126–49.

Sarome (*Salome*). *Shingeki*, no. 11, 1978, 154–71.

Bakkosu no shinnyo (*The Bacchae*). *Shingeki*, no. 2, 1978, 100–20.

Katei no igaku (*Home Medicine*). *Shingeki*, no. 2, 1979, 176–94.

Ôhi Kuraitemunestora (*Queen Clytemnestra*). *Sekai*, no. 12, 1983, 302–30. Trans. J. Thomas Rimer, *The Way of Acting*, 125–58.

FILMS AND VIDEOS

Suzuki Tadashi, The Chronicle of Macbeth. Dir. Tony Chapman and Zi-Yin Wang. SBS TV, 1992.

One Step on a Journey. Dir. Tony Chapman and Zi-Yin Wang. SBS TV, 1992. (Documentary on *The Chronicle of Macbeth*.)

"Toga: Village for Theatre." *Profile of a Nation: the Japanese People and their Activities, Part IV*. Kyodo TV (for the Ministry of Foreign Affairs), 1985.

Suzuki Tadashi no sekai (*The World of Suzuki Tadashi*). NHK TV, July 1993. Broadcast productions: *On the Dramatic Passions, Solo Cherry Orchard, The Trojan Women, King Lear, Ivanov, Greetings from the Edge of the Earth I* (*Macbeth*), *Dionysus, Sansho Daiyu*.

Butoh: Piercing the Mask. Dir. Richard Moore. AKA Productions, 1991 (contains
     Ashikawa Yôko's dance of despair as Agave in Suzuki's 1989 *The Bacchae*).

WEBSITES

ACM Mito Theatre http://www.co.jp/mito/Tower/isozaki3.html
Roger   Reynolds,   *Electro-Acoustic   Music*,   reviewed   by   Peter   Terry
     http://www.bgsu.edu/~pterry
Tadashi Suzuki http://www.spac.or.jp

Index